HIMBO HITMAN

SAXON JAMES

CONTENT WARNING

While this book is about a very terrible hitman and his failed attempt at employment, there are multiple instances of gun violence throughout. Please be aware if this is a trigger for you.

THANK YOU

I want to spare a second to thank everyone who picked up Himbo Hitman and took a chance on me writing something a little different. These characters have been bugging me for years so it's a relief to finally have their story told.

If you're someone who needs a visual for the characters, you can check out my Pinterest board here:
https://pin.it/1hfvf0JRK

If music is more your vibe, you can find the Himbo Hitman playlist here:
https://open.spotify.com/playlist/1ptiMhJYJRbQ1Scngpbse6

Now grab some snacks and your drink of choice, and get ready for Perry's shenanigans.

(While every effort has been made during the editing process, if you're someone who likes to spot and report ninja typos, you can send them to: admin@saxonjamesauthor.com)

BLURB

What do you do when you're a hit man ... who's terrible at his job?

At first, I thought it would be an easy payday. A few pew pews for bad people, a couple of suitcases of cash for me. People have done worse for an honest living. Probably.

The problem is that after a couple of jobs, I've never actually managed to unalive someone, and not for lack of trying. Apparently, a basic requirement of a hitman is being a good shot.

Despite my constant duck-ups—that my boss knows nothing about—I'm given another name, and I very nearly follow through. Only after obliterating this guy's ear and his fervent pleading to spare him, I've sent him into hiding and collected the cash anyway.

But wanted people are hard to hide, and bad guys don't like paying big money for loose ends.

Now that Van Gogh has shown his face again—sans ear—I've scammed my way into his security team, which is sort of ideal since I'm now highly wanted as well.

Unfortunately, we have some "trust issues" to "work through" from our meet-shoot, and with the gorgeous bastard's brother missing, he refuses to lay low until they're reunited.

I'm not sold on the plan, honestly, but this guy has me questioning my sexuality along with my career path, and I'm at the point where I'm determined to see a job through to the end.

Or die trying.

But hey, at least then I'd finally deliver a body.

FOREWORD

Hey. Wow. Okay. We're doing this. I'm Perry, and I figured this section was for me since I'm the one driving this thing. Totally heroic and serious star of this show. Trust me, when it comes to the guy who saved the day, that's on me, no matter what St. Clare might say.

I'm a lover of smiley faces and a maker of headaches (just ask Saxon), but considering she's only giving me the ONE book (we'll see) to tell you my story, I figured I better make the most of it and get this book as big and beefy as I can.

Besides, I'm all about literacy and furthering our minds to … okay, that's a lie. The book just makes one hell of a weapon.

CHAPTER ONE

PERRY

THERE COMES a time in every man's life when he needs to grow up and get on with things. Granted, I've always been a late bloomer, and it might have taken my apartment being broken into a third time, a disappointed big sister, dead parents, and an apparent murder car for it to happen, but it's time.

I'm here.

Ready to take charge of my life and give my sister approximately one hundred fewer things to stress about.

I tug on the elastic bracelet with plastic charms that I made with my mom when I was a kid and have never taken off since. It's a steady reminder that things aren't so bad, and I need it right now because it turns out sudden motivation isn't a magical portal to finding a job. I've applied for everything that doesn't need experience, from late-night cleaners to gas station attendants to this one suspicious listing for a "personal nursemaid, no experience, must have nice feet," and honestly, I'm not even sure I'm qualified for *that*.

Putting myself out there again and again and only hearing silence back is threatening to put a chink in my positivity and send me on a weeklong reality TV binge instead.

There's nothing Judge Judy can't fix.

I need to resist though. For my sister.

Margot has always been the responsible sibling, and after our parents died, she's jacked that need up to a thousand. I wouldn't say she's overbearing, but I would say that she could worry a little less about me and my life and the cute mice I share my apartment with.

I've been desperate for money before, but this is the desperatest I've reached yet, and I'm at the point where I need anything that will pay me money.

When I approach Lethal Poison, the bar I love to hang out in because of the interesting people there, I smirk at the *help wanted* sign in the door.

Help wanted.

Wink wink.

Sure, most people don't know what that means, but I'm an intuitive, trustworthy kind of guy. I pick up on things. I talk to people.

And Lethal Poison isn't just a bar.

It's a meeting place for the most ruthless ruffians Seattle has to offer.

From thieves to vagabonds to contract killers and everything in between. I'm not … actually sure what comes between those things, come to think of it, but I don't need to know all the details. I just know that if there's something illegal you want done, there's someone to do it, and those someones hang out at Lethal Poison.

Margot wanted me to find a job, so here I fucking go.

I push through the front door, bell tinkling, and walk into the cute little bar. For a place where dangerous people hang out, it has the decor of an old speakeasy with upbeat country music always playing, the happy *chink* of pool balls knocking together in the back room, and smells overwhelmingly like Christmas cookies.

I fucking love it here.

The owner, Luther, is behind the bar, and I can only assume his parents were obsessed with Superman. Batman. One of the hero men. He gives me an upnod as I approach and pours me out my usual glass of Coke before popping a lime wedge into it. It doesn't do anything for the taste, obviously, but while I might not be a big drinker, I like to pretend to be fancy. Plus, no one asks questions about why you're in a bar if it looks like you're here to get drunk.

Luther hands over my drink, but before he can let go, I close my hand over his and lean in.

"I saw your sign," I tell him, raising my eyebrows in a way that lets him know *I* know. "Good help is hard to find."

"Sure is." Luther tugs his hand back. "Know of anyone with a bar license?"

I squint, trying to figure out what bar license might translate to in bad-guy speak. A gun license, maybe? Do contract killers need one of those? Seems a bit discriminatory; what if a gun isn't their weapon of choice?

"It's easy enough to get." I *think.*

"Well, come see me when you have one." He walks down the bar, but I quickly follow him.

"The problem is that kind of thing costs money, and I'm a bit low on funds right now."

"Not my problem."

"If you could give me something—anything—and maybe ignore the little details of licensing until after my first job, then I can go and get anything you need."

"I'm not in a hurry to get shut down, Perry."

"With everything else you're running from here"—I send a pointed look around the bar—"I find that hard to believe."

Luther gets this hard look on his face. "What are you talking about?"

"All I'm saying is that you'd really be helping me out by letting me help you out."

"Yeah, but it's not about me ignoring the licensing; it's about the fire marshal. Do you even know how to make a dirty martini?"

Again, it takes me a second to try and figure out what that could be in bad-guy speech. A dirty … robbery? What would make it dirty though? Going Rambo and covering myself in mud first? "I'm a fast learner."

"I don't have time to teach right now."

"Then throw me into the deep end."

"I'm not risking my loyal customers going somewhere else."

I huff and plant my elbows on the bar, which gets me an unimpressed look from Luther. "I really need this. I'll do whatever"—I stress the word—"I have to in order to make them happy."

"I'm not a pimp."

"Really?" I throw a look toward a guy I'd—apparently wrongly—assumed was trading sex for money last week.

Luther scowls. "*Really*. Now, unless you know how to make a killer Bloody Mary, I'm busy."

At least the Bloody Mary reference is an easy one to translate. Kill someone. He wants to know if I can kill someone. And I'm not proud of myself for my desperation or the next words that leave my mouth.

"Oh yeah. Bloody Marys. Do those *all* the time."

Luther stares at me. "What are the ingredients?"

Seems bold talking about it here, but if that's what he wants. "Well, a gun, obviously. Bullets. Umm … should probably take a protein bar or something in case it takes a while—"

"What the fuck are you talking about?"

"A Bloody Mary!" I throw in a wink he can't miss to make sure that he knows that I know we're on the same page.

"I'm going to need you to stop talking."

A spike of excitement hits me. "I have the job?"

"No."

That chink in my positivity takes another hit. "Please. I fucking need this."

"Take your Coke and stop bothering me."

I snatch up my drink and take a sip, all that cold sugar helping flood the shitty feelings from me. It doesn't last long though. I'd left this as a backup, thinking for sure that it would be an easy win. Do I *want* to rob or kill people for money? Not specifically, but I wouldn't be the first person to do it, and I don't have the luxury of morals while needing to make rent. Besides, I'm sure there are worse ways to earn a living, even if I can't quite think of any right now.

My friends are sitting around a bar table across the room, so I take my drink and make my dejected way over there. I wonder if I just show up and start cleaning the bar, whether Luther will kick me out or feel enough pity to pay me for the work.

I'm not above pity jobs.

I'll take literally anything.

Arlie catches sight of me first. She's my shadow queen, the future love of my life, and the woman I would do anything for. Mostly because I'm too terrified to say no, but, you know, incentive.

"I heard it was Carson Alexander," Everett says, but Arlie whacks him and flicks her eyes my way.

"Hey, besties," I say, pretending like I heard nothing of their top-secret bad-guy convo. I pull up a stool between Tommy and Everett, directly across from Arlie.

She stares me down. "I thought we told you not to talk to us."

"That's a rude greeting, considering I haven't seen you all week."

"I've been away."

I do a quick check around our table to make sure no one is listening in, not that it matters in a place like this. "For work?"

"Yes." Her eyes flick from Tommy to Everett, and she sighs. "You two fools have been talking to him again, haven't you?"

Tommy, always quick to laugh or make a bet, shrugs. "We like him."

Arlie glowers at Tommy, but it doesn't deter him.

"Found a job yet?" Ever asks, ignoring them both.

I set my Coke down and rest my chin in both hands. "Nope. Not even Luther would help me out."

"I thought you already had a job?" Arlie asks.

"Nothing stable. I have the occasional contract for kids' parties and sometimes run deliveries for the Chinese restaurant in my building. A month ago, I drove up north and helped out on a farm for a few weeks. Before that, I tried Ubering until my car scared off any potential customers."

"Why does your car scare people off?" Tommy asks.

"The bumper's dicey, and I think the bloodstains on my back seat must form some kind of satanic symbol."

"Sure," Ever says. "The satanic symbol. Not the, you know, potential murder that happened there."

"You don't know it was a murder."

Tommy's usual unhinged laugh peeps out. "What other theories do you have? Let's hear them."

"Injury, obviously. Maybe the previous owner was a Good Samaritan who saw someone injured and took it upon themselves to drive them to the hospital. Maybe the last car interior detailer cut their hand during cleaning? Maybe someone gave birth there?"

"Gave birth to who? The devil?"

"I'm only saying there are a lot of options."

Arlie takes a sip of whatever she's drinking, dark, almost black eyes watching me. "And where did you get this car again?"

"Some guy downtown. He was about to set it on fire, so I got it for a steal."

She nods, probably agreeing it was a good deal. "I think you're right," she finally says. "It was definitely the birth thing."

"Thank you."

Ever sighs. "She's fucking with you. It was a murder, Perry. You're driving around in a murderer's car."

"Did you check the back seat for ghosts?" Tommy asks. "Maybe that's who was scaring off your customers."

"Either way," I say before they go off on a tangent, "no one will get in the car with someone who has a sub-two-star rating, so I'm back at square one. With nothing." I play with a water ring on the tabletop, turning it into a smiley face. "My sister is going to kill me."

"Why?"

"Because I promised her I'd find something. It's why I asked Luther about, well … *you know*."

"We know?"

"The …" Not wanting to say it out loud, I make a gun with my fingers. "The same line of work you guys are in."

I feel the way the three of them share a tense look.

"Don't panic. I know what you do, I don't care, and I thought I could get in on it and make a bunch of money."

Arlie runs a concerned look over me. "What happened to that rich people services thing you were doing?"

Yet another job I failed miserably at, though I still maintain that Margot stealing my job and getting together with Elle was the reason for that one failing. "Got booted."

"Have you ever had a job that you actually *did* hold on to?"

"Umm … maybe in high school?"

"With your track record, why did you think Luther would give you a chance?"

"Because I need *someone* to," I snap. "I'd sort of like to stop being such a failure all the time."

Tommy cuffs my shoulder. "I just don't think that's on the cards for you, mate."

"Thanks," I mutter pathetically into my Coke.

Maybe if I head home now, I can coax Sir Squeakerton out for a play. I'm sure I have some peanut butter left to interest him in giving me attention.

"How do you know what we do?" Ever asks suddenly.

I glance at him and his dark eyeliner, the bald head, long earring, and leather jacket. "First, you all dress really cool. Second, I overheard Arlie talking about how she almost missed her mark because someone tipped him off that she was coming. And third" —I send a pointed look Tommy's way—"you. Last time, you got drunk and left behind a piece of paper with a name, a title, and an address on it. When you came back for it and I asked what it was, you said *the guy I have to rob, but shhhhh, don't tell anyone.*"

Arlie face-palms as Tommy's eyes flick side to side.

"Ah … can we pretend like you didn't say that?"

"I'm good with it." Then, I'm struck by a genius idea. "If you take me with you."

"Huh?"

"Take me with you to rob someone, and we can split the money."

Tommy just stares at me. "Yeah, no."

"What? Why not? It's a great plan." Surely if he's robbing rich people for pricy things, it wouldn't make much of a difference for me to tag along with him. It'd be like an episode of *Selling Seattle* where I get to snoop through a house I could never afford, except instead of the owner selling for millions, I'm taking half of their shit.

"We need to be able to get in and out quickly and without leaving a trace of evidence. Now, I don't know you well, but something tells me you'd be a walking forensics kit."

"I'm great at following directions. Tell me what to do, and I'll do it. I can be like your companion animal."

"My what?"

"You know how in all those cartoons or spy movies they have the dog who goes on jobs with them to make the travel less lonely?"

"No. And I don't think I want to."

"Please, Tommy. I need this. Please, please, please, *please*—"

"Someone shut him up," Arlie groans.

"Seconded." Luther joins our table and slides a drink toward Arlie with a piece of paper tucked under it.

I snicker at how obvious they are before tapping my nose.

"You have no fucking clue how to be subtle," Ever mutters.

Luther shakes his head. "It's a fast one," he tells Arlie. Then he sends a look my way. "And you can take Perry with you."

CHAPTER TWO

ST. CLARE

THE FIST that flies at my head is expected, even if not appreciated. I try to duck, but Onyx is fast, and while I mostly get out of the way, their fist still clips my jaw. It's a shockingly solid hit, and I stagger back a few steps, hands raised.

"*Mercy*. Motherfucker."

Onyx smirks, and I hate that they can still manage to look so sweet with their hands wrapped and raised, ready to hit me again. "I told you to block."

"Colin," I call out to my brother, who's watching us from the side of the sparring mat. "Your turn."

"I believe we agreed to five-minute sessions."

"We did. Until Onyx tried to kill me."

They laugh, securing more of their vibrant red hair back into their hairband. "It was a love tap."

"You almost took my head off."

The look they give me is pitying at best. "I thought you wanted to be able to defend yourself?"

"Colin needs it more," I say, selflessly freeing up Onyx's time for him. I've always been so generous.

My brother takes off his glasses and sets them purposely on the ground before replacing me in front of Onyx. Then I take off like the wimp that I am and find Lars on some machine that's making his normally jacked-up arms look even jacked-ier.

"Am I bleeding? Bruised? Broken?" I ask, turning my head so he can see where Onyx got me. Like Onyx's punch, the look he gives me should be expected because they barely clipped me, and here I am, acting like I've been through attempted murder.

"Dramatic?" Lars suggests.

I huff and take the bench beside him. "It's okay for you; you're used to being punched in the head."

Lars has been my best friend for years, and when Colin and I were in the process of opening our nightclub, Saint Clare's, an older club right by us started causing issues. When the owner, Yanni, threatened us, Lars quit his security job and became our full-time protection. The three of us are all in on Saint Clare's, so we really need it to do well.

Also, Lars really needs to get his ass up and do his job because I don't think bodyguards are supposed to let people punch their clients.

Even if I willingly accepted Onyx's offer to teach us self-defense.

They're still sparring with Colin, and from what I can see, both of them are having a much better time of it than I was. Colin's actually laughing, which isn't something he does a lot. He's not someone who has a lot of friends or likes being social, and while I used to bug him about it, he's happy enough doing his own thing.

It doesn't stop me from feeling proud to see him now though. We hired Onyx a week before Saint Clare's opened, and they've been a miracle of a night manager and are one of the only people besides me and Lars who seems to "get" Colin.

Lars grins at me, shiny with sweat, neck red and thick from whatever equipment he's been using. "I'm sure I read something today about Capricorns running scared."

"Oh, fuck off." I drown out his teasing as I watch Colin and Onyx spar. Onyx isn't rough with *him*. *He* doesn't get punched in the face.

When they finally finish up, Colin walks over, bright red and sweaty, glasses slipping down his slippery nose. "Need to go home and shower," he says through labored breaths.

"We have that meeting tonight," I remind him. "With the journalist."

Colin quickly nods, and his glasses slip so much they're in danger of falling off. "Yeah, I know. I'll be there."

Considering what a stickler for being on time and fulfilling responsibilities that he is, I don't doubt it.

***

Well, fuck.

Colin's late. The party lights on the dance floor below swing wildly, temporarily lighting up my office, and I quickly look around, worry creeping down my spine like the exaggerated footsteps in a horror movie. This feeling of being watched has been intensifying lately, and I'm not sure if it's for real or if Yanni's threats have made me paranoid.

Colin is the reliable one out of the two of us. Always organized, always taking this business seriously, and it's not that I *don't* exactly, but I don't think running a successful business and having no personality are mutually exclusive.

You need a sense of humor to deal with the shit we've been through.

Sometimes *literally* thanks to Yanni trying to scare us from opening.

I check my watch again, remembering opening day a few weeks ago when Colin bought us matching ones as a *we did it* gift. Colin and I have been talking about owning a club together since we were kids, and it's wild to think we made it happen. Dreams come true and all that. He had our watches made custom, with the logo for Saint Clare's on the watch face, my band platinum and his gold. Colors as opposite as we are.

But while we're opposites and butt heads, we know each other inside and out, and I love my brother more than anyone. I also know that he is never, ever late, and it's making me worried. I don't want to worry. Worrying leads to wrinkles, and I'm already thirty. Thirty in gay years is practically ancient—I don't need to look it as well.

I slide my phone from my pocket and open my recent calls, then click on his number.

Colin has a thing where he won't answer his phone before it's rung three times, so I relax, prepared to wait ... It takes me a second or two of nothing to pull my phone away from my ear again. The call's dropped out, and I'm back on his contact page.

I hit his name again, but after a second of trying to connect, it fails.

Well, that's concerning.

I shove my phone into my pocket, glaring down at the full club. Word of mouth helped the buzz spread quickly, and we've been marketing our asses off for months. Colin did the behind-the-scenes stuff, and I brought the promotional ideas. It's why we work so well together and why this place has been at capacity every weekend.

I pace over to the large window overlooking the street below. Seattle has great nightlife, and when this building came up with awesome lease terms, we jumped at the opportunity to finally open Saint Clare's. From where I'm standing, I can make out a fraction of the red-front facade of Rev, the nightclub down the road. All the sight does is piss me off after everything they've put us through. Our liquor license was delayed, they've reported us continuously to the fire marshal, and our original shipment of lights went missing. All that, on top of sending us packages of actual shit, calling in bomb threats, and having seedy-looking guys with guns lurking out the front of our place, has been too much to handle while trying to open our first business.

It's soured me to opening another one if this one does well.

Colin's always been the entrepreneur between us. It was him who wanted to start that doll repair business when we were five, and him set up with an iced tea stand every summer, and him who was mowing lawns in the neighborhood as soon as he could push a mower, and him trying to charge kids entrance fees at the local park.

I was just *there*, in awe of his ideas, ready to back him up however I could. The doll's missing an arm? Let's give her a cyborg one instead. Iced tea? I made the sign and put together makeshift coolers so we didn't have to run back and forth to the house. I was there to clean up the mowed grass and stop the kids at the park from ratting us out.

I'm the *support* person to his brilliance.

Which is why I need his ass here now.

A whistle comes from behind me, and I drop my head back at the sound. "Already?"

The music in the club below is loud, but I catch my best friend's laugh. "You set the time."

"Yeah, well, we both know I'm an idiot."

"Brom's taking them to the suite. You better get your ass down there."

"Colin's not here yet."

"*Really?*" Lars's incredulous tone echoes my thoughts. "Huh. Well, it's not like that's the worst thing. You want these guys to give you a good write-up, and his awkward rambling is fifty-fifty between being cute and being manic."

"There's supposed to be photos."

"Again … good thing. Colin's not photogenic either."

"Yeah, but it's not like I can talk about our club without him here."

"Then he should have turned up. You can't keep them waiting either, otherwise who knows what the fuck they're gonna write. It's a feature piece about the young business owners of Saint Clare's. They sort of need the owners to know who they're writing about."

I finally turn and give Lars my full attention. All six foot seven of his cocky playboy, security guarding, horoscope-loving self. "It doesn't feel right."

"I know."

It takes me a second to realize he's not reading my mind and is still talking about the feature. "No, not the interview. The guy they're sending, I looked him up. Cute as hell, single—I think—and openly gay."

"Ahh." Lars's lips tremble. "You were going to try and sleep with him."

"Bingo. But with Colin currently misplaced, I don't think it's a good idea."

"I don't think it's a good idea for more reasons than that, but whatever you need to go with."

"Okay," I say, giving in. The unsettled feeling in my gut is urging me not to do the interview at all, but we don't need any more problems. I grab my suit jacket from where I've flung it across my desk and shrug into it. "How do I look?"

Lars eyes me. "Like a horny guy who's been denied his favorite dick treats."

"Well, that's what I want them writing about me."

"Guess it depends what you want out of the article."

"To be taken seriously as a businessman?"

Lars snorts in a way that very clearly says anyone who takes me seriously can't be trusted. "Well, that's not going to do it, then."

"No shit." I scrape both hands back through my styled hair. "What if they ask questions about the businessy side of things?"

"I know I'm only the hired muscle, but how do you expect to be taken seriously as a businessman when you call it businessy and look like you're ready to throw yourself out the window just from the threat of talking about it?"

This is why I need Colin. I can charm the pants off anyone when he's the one talking about the boring stuff, and I'm worried that without him, I'll come across as empty. Snarkily confident without any of the actual skill to back it up.

Lars walks over to give me a reassuring pat on the back. "Before you go down the spiral of whatever this is, remember that you're the one who came up with the branding. You're the one who worked to make the club look like this. You did the layout and floor plan to maximize how people would use this space, and you're the one who set up all these interviews, who got the opening week buzz alive, who found influencers and reached out for cross-promotions with the businesses in the area. You know what you're doing."

I hate to admit that those reminders help. When it comes to Colin, I've always felt second best. It's nothing that he or our parents did to enforce that, but when he's the one who was a perfect student in school, who aced everything without trying, who constantly has something on the go, it's pretty easy to look around and wonder what the fuck me and my C-grade average have going for us.

Lars never lets me sit with those feelings for long.

"Thanks. I needed that."

"Dude, I know. I can read every thought in your butthead brain."

Lars needs to get laid. "Could you read that?"

"I could. And fuck you. My sex life is my business."

For a self-proclaimed man whore, he sure does keep quiet about what he gets up to during his time off.

I can gripe at him about that later though. I can't leave these guys from MediaCorp waiting any longer than I already have, and I'm going to need a good-sounding business excuse for the delay. I don't think stressing about saying something stupid is going to cut it.

"If I say something stupid—"

Lars finishes my thought. "I set a fire and evacuate the place. Got it."

He might be a pain in the fucking ass, but he's as much of a brother to me as Colin is.

"Keep trying to call him," I tell Lars. "Late is better than never."

CHAPTER THREE

PERRY

I'M GOING to be the best damn sidekick that there ever was. I've got my leather gloves. My hoodie. A mask that covers the lower half of my face and has a cool leering skeleton mouth on it. There were a ton of them online, and Elle is the most amazing future sis-in-law ever because she overnighted it to me without the invasive questions Margot would have asked.

I have a place and a time to meet Arlie, and it's been on my mind all day. I refuse to be late. I even set about five alarms in the lead-up to leaving so that I wouldn't get distracted and forget, and since I have some time to spare, I'm going to show up with a little something for her as my thanks for doing this for me.

Unfortunately, my bank balance limits what that something could be, so I settle for two coffees. We're in for a long night, so this will keep us going.

Only when I get to the front to order and the cashier asks for my name, I hesitate. If we're doing what I think we're doing tonight, I can't leave any evidence for the police. That starts now. I need to start thinking like a calculating, cunning creature of the night.

And those calculated, cunning creatures probably don't give their real names for coffee orders.

"Jerry," I blurt, proud of myself for catching this. "And Harley."

The cashier rings me up, I stand to wait, and when they call my order, I remember to answer to the wrong name. I'm already killing this thing. Pun intended.

The street outside looks cut in half, with the bright, busy road and shopfronts, and the still black canvas above it all. I love the nighttime. It makes the traffic and the people seem more magical, and when I smile at the people I pass, most of them even smile back.

During the day, people are too busy rushing around, earbuds in, talking obnoxiously loudly.

I meet Arlie a few streets over, in a shady alleyway that we probably shouldn't be lingering in—though, I guess *we're* the reason people shouldn't hang out in these places. Boy, that is going to take some adjustment.

"Got you something," I say, holding out her coffee.

She looks at it like it's about to explode in her face. "You stopped for coffee."

"Thought we might be here a while." I turn a little so she can see my backpack. "Brought snacks and a set of cards too."

"This isn't a sleepover."

"I know."

"We're not braiding each other's fucking hair."

"That's lucky, because I don't know how to do that."

"We're killing someone, Perry."

"It's Jerry."

She blinks at me. "What?"

I hold up my coffee so she can see. "Jerry. It's my alias." Then I shake her cup at her. "And yours is Harley."

"Mine is already Arlie."

"Oh … I thought that was your real name."

"No."

"So, wait. I don't even know your real name?"

The exhale she lets out is slow and measured. "No."

"Tommy? Everett? *Luther*?"

The way she looks at me answers my question.

"Wow. Okay. Can't say the lack of trust doesn't hurt—"

"We're going to be late." She takes both coffees. "Have you drunk from this?"

"Not yet. It was a bit hot."

"Good." Then she turns and throws my very thoughtful gift into the dumpster behind her. "We don't give them DNA, we don't give them shitty aliases, and we definitely *do not* go into businesses that have CCTV footage. *Come on.*"

Damn it. I didn't think about the cameras. "Noted."

"We also won't be here for long if we're doing our job right. So no need for heavy backpacks or snacks, and dear fucking god, if you're playing cards on a hit, you're just asking to die."

"I wanted to make tonight memorable."

The look she levels me with almost makes me step back a notch. "Have you ever killed someone before?"

"Not … directly?"

"Indirectly, then?"

"Well, who can say? I littered once—what if the paper blew up onto a windshield and caused a five-car pileup?"

Arlie doesn't look convinced. "Tonight will be memorable. Trust me."

"I'm just glad we get to spend this one-on-one time together."

"Still not friends."

"We'll see."

"Up the fire escape. We're cutting it close."

I glance overhead, not thrilled about how tall the building is. "How high are we going?"

"All the way to the top."

Of course we are. My apprehension is cutting as I climb the stairs, reminding myself not to look down. I'm not scared of heights, specifically, but heights have never exactly done much for me either. The higher we go, the more I'm reminded of that.

"And the rooftop is obviously necessary," I check.

"Yep."

I'm hit by a thought that immediately spills from my mouth. "You're not planning to push me off, are you?"

"Why would I do that?"

"Because I know too much. Holy shit. Was it *my* name on the paper? Is that why Luther was suddenly okay with me coming?"

"Do us both a favor and don't think for a while."

"That wasn't a no!"

I swear Arlie laughs, which can't be right because she never laughs. It must have been someone from inside one of the apartments we pass. Someone who sounds a lot like her.

I'm out onto the rooftop first, and I consider for a whole second whether to run or stop her from coming up here or … fuck, I have no clue. But maybe doing something to protect myself wouldn't be a totally ridiculous thing? Unfortunately, I am ridiculous and apparently have no survival skills because I've barely started debating with myself when she joins me.

"Fuck it. Get it over with," I say, holding my hands out to the side. "Would it be easier if I jumped?"

"Actually, yes."

I'm about to make my pathetic way over to the edge when she continues.

"Then I wouldn't have to listen to you being all dramatic anymore." She unzips the bag at her waist and pulls out a gun. The metal gleams threateningly, and it's only just now occurring to me that I've never seen one of these in real life before. I'm suddenly not so sure I ever wanted to. "Relax, we're not here for you." The next thing she pulls out is a long metal cylinder that she attaches to the gun. She must notice me watching curiously. "It's a suppressor. This one is a single shot. Bullet cases will land right here, and we'll walk a few blocks before we ditch them in the trash."

"Won't they be found?"

She shrugs. "Doesn't matter if they are. It's a ghost gun. No serial number, and the kits were bought from all over. It's untraceable, and I'm gone before anyone knows what happened."

"How long have you been doing this for?"

Arlie shrugs. "A couple of years."

"And you haven't been caught?"

"It would be more of a surprise if I had."

I'm not sure what her logic is behind that. The confusion on my face must show.

"The stats are something like only two percent of crime ends in a conviction. And it's around ten percent where there's actually an arrest made. Those people are usually amateurs."

I watch in morbid curiosity as she slides a bullet cartridge into the gun. "There's no way that can be true."

"Look it up."

"I think I will."

"Fine." She snaps back the thingy on top with a metal *clink.* "Either way, I like my chances."

"If that *is* true though … pretty much anyone could kill anyone."

"Pretty much."

"Even me."

She eyes me, her hood pulled up, covering her dark hair. "I think you'd be in the two percent."

"Ouch." I clutch my chest. "You're throwing out some hard truths tonight."

"You bought coffee."

"Would it have made a difference if it was brought from home?"

"No. The less you have on you, the better." Her eyes fall closed for a second as she groans. "You brought your wallet, didn't you?"

"Of course."

"With your ID?"

It clicks where she's going with this, and I don't want to confirm her suspicion. "No?"

I get the look again. "Still think you're not in the two percent?"

"It's possible I see your point."

"Right. Can we get on with this now?"

This being kill someone. I purposely haven't asked any questions about the mark or thought too deeply about them and having a family. In fact, the coffee and the cards and the snacks were all because I've been actively *not* thinking about it. But I need a job, and this is all that's paying right now, so I'm going to have to suck it up.

I nod and follow Arlie to the edge of the rooftop. "You're pulling the trigger, right?"

"Right. And you're not actually getting paid for tonight. This is purely to see if you can handle it."

"Okay."

"And, Perry?"

I pull my attention from the street below to where she's watching me. "If you rat any of us out, if you get cold feet and want to tell someone, if you betray me or any of the people I care about … they will kill you. Immediately. Luther's just the messenger, and the real people behind this operation are very well protected. Guys like Carson Alexander, you'd be an easy target for them."

I manage a half smile. "There you go with the trust again."

"I want to make it clear."

"Message received. Besides, like I said, I'm desperate for the—"

Before I can finish my sentence, Arlie tugs up her black mask, takes aim, and shoots.

The *chick-et, chick-et* sounds like a really loud, well, *stapler.* Then, she lowers the gun.

"It's done. Let's go."

It's … done? Just like that? A cut-off thought, a millisecond of concentration, and someone's life switches from on to off as easily as me tossing breadcrumbs to Sir Squeakerton.

I stupidly turn to the street below, and it takes me a moment of searching through the lack of panic to realize that she wasn't aiming for the street. She was aiming for the apartment across and down three flights from us. With an open window. And a dead guy sprawled out on the floor.

His tattooed arms are splayed out over his long hair, shirt pulled up to reveal a sliver of vulnerable skin, and he's not moving. I'm assuming because of the bullet holes through his neck and head.

I'm hit with too many feelings to know what I'm feeling as I stare at the suddenly dead body across from here.

"Huh," I manage weakly. "Good shot."

"Thanks. Time to go." Arlie grabs my arm and drags me away from the building and back over to the fire escape. "Pull your mask up."

I do what she says on autopilot.

"What the fuck is that?" she demands.

"My mask."

"Why is it smiling at me?"

"Thought it gave it a little something something."

I swear she fucking growls. "You don't want something something. You don't want spice or pizzazz. You want total anonymity." Arlie's eyes go big, and somehow, she mimics the exact same look as Margot. The look of complete disbelief in me. "You can't do this."

I quickly grab her arm before she can walk away. "I can. I promise."

"You'll get yourself killed, and then that's on me."

"Come on, Arlie-even-though-that's-not-your-real-name." I press my hands together in front of my chest. "Help me. I'm a pathetic no-hoper. I *get* it. But without this, I literally have *nothing*. I need you."

"You want to kill people that badly, huh?"

My whole face screws up. "I don't want to kill people at all. I just don't have a choice."

She sighs, tugging me back toward the fire escape. "We all have a choice. But fine. I'll text you an address. Meet me there tomorrow, and I'll teach you how to hold a gun. Then the rest is on you."

CHAPTER FOUR

ST. CLARE

I SHOOT up in bed with a gasp, panting through the rapidly disappearing images of my dream. It was something to do with Colin. I don't remember what or how, but that feeling of fucking dread is deepening in my gut.

Because waking up hasn't helped anything.

It's been a whole week since I've seen him.

My brother is not the kind of person who disappears.

Being unable to fix a problem is the worst kind of helplessness, and as I turn and kick my legs out of bed, the shadows press in. Deeper. Darker. This screeching urge filling my ears, telling me I need to be out walking the streets or stalking his accounts or … or …

The laugh that falls from my lips is hollow.

I'm not a criminal mastermind. I'm not law enforcement. How the hell am I supposed to find a pinprick of a person in a city this size? A wave of panic passes through me as a question flits through my mind.

Is he in the city at all?

It's one more question to join all the others I have no answers to. I reach for my phone, mostly by muscle memory at this point, and pull up his number. Still doesn't ring. I open his social media pages and hope that maybe this time there will be something. A picture of him, literally anywhere, just enjoying himself, but it's radio silent there too.

I've gnawed on my lip so many times over the last few days that it's raw and shredded. My lack of sleep is normally great for when I'm working through the night, but with my naps constantly interrupted, I'm getting low on patience.

If something's happened to Colin, I … okay, I don't know what. Still not a criminal mastermind, but with my frustrations bubbling around a hundred, I'm interested to find out.

Fighting for sleep is useless at this point, so I head out to the kitchen and turn the coffee machine on. The view here isn't as great as the one at work since we funneled all our money into the business, and I didn't save a cent for this place. Lars and I took out the rent together so we could afford something slightly larger than a shoe box and not shared with who knows what kind of vermin.

The current takings at Saint Clare's are looking promising, but we're stuck here for a while.

The creak of a door behind me makes me jump out of my skin.

Lars's chuckle fills the still apartment as he joins me in the kitchen. "What the hell are you doing?"

I wait for my suddenly racing heart to stop being so damn dramatic before I answer him. "Couldn't sleep."

"Colin?"

"Yep."

Lars's mouth flattens. "The whole thing is weird."

"You're telling me," I mutter, grabbing the sugar. "I can't shake the feeling something bad has happened."

"I'm a big believer in listening to our instincts."

"You also cleanse the apartment every other month and have a concerning addiction to horoscopes. My instincts tell me those things are bullshit. Who do we believe?"

Lars throws me an unimpressed look before taking over making the coffee. He's only in his briefs, and it really highlights why he's the muscle and I'm the … *ideas* guy.

When I'd hired him, it had been more about having a barrier between me and any drug-crazed partygoers or wannabe gangsters lurking outside. I'd never imagined for a second that I would need actual protection, but since Colin disappeared without a trace, who the fuck knows what's going on?

The police have taken it as a missing person's case and said they'll look into Rev and any potential motivation. They said a lot, actually, and it was all the right things, but no one has reached out since, and I have the feeling that Colin has been forgotten about amidst all the other missing people being reported daily.

"Let's see ..." Lars pours himself a coffee with one hand and thumbs through his phone with the other. "Here we go. Capricorn." He hums as he reads. "Interesting ..."

"What's interesting?"

"Never mind. You don't believe in it."

"I don't."

"So then you don't need to know what's interesting."

That asshole. He grins at me because we both know what he's doing. Joke's on him, though, because I can go and Google that shit myself. Except I might not get the same thing he has since I know he subscribes to certain horoscopy places.

"I know you want to tell me," I say, taking the mug he offers. "Just get on with it."

"I'm good. Oh, look. Taurus will need to run errands, and traffic might be an issue. There you go. If I'm not around, that's where I'll be."

"Bad traffic in Seattle? Wow. I'm sure glad you had your horoscopes to give you the heads-up."

"Yours was better."

"I'm sure it was."

He's bouncing on his toes, and I know it's killing him. I don't believe in horoscopes. I know they're wild guesswork and vague enough that you can interpret them to any aspect of your life. The errands and traffic thing was specific, but those aren't a huge reach. All it takes is Lars remembering he needs to do something, and suddenly, he remembers his horoscope and dubs it right. Self-fulfilling prophecy and all that.

Even with all that rationalizing, it doesn't dim my curiosity.

Lars is downing his coffee like the faster he drinks it, the easier it will be to keep his mouth shut.

I sigh and turn to lean against the counter. "Tell me."

"Fine. Apparently, you're going to get into an altercation with a business or romantic partner, and you'll need to try and see things from their point of view before turning it into a bigger deal than it is."

Okay, that was almost as specific as his was. "I don't have a romantic partner …"

"Could be a good sign that Colin will show back up though."

I'm not going to put all my hope about that into a horoscope. "Sure. Some random person on the internet said it, so it must be true."

"We'll see, I guess."

Considering I'm missing my brother, need to look at hiring someone to balance our books while he's MIA, and have a club to run and a potential rival to keep on top of, his horoscope is low on my list of concerns. I'd gladly welcome a fight with my brother because then he'd fucking be here. In fact, the second he shows back up, I'll hug him, then chew him out for ditching without notice.

There has to be a simple explanation for where he's gone. Thinking about missing people and crime and his life being at risk is too much for my feeble brain to wrap around, and the only way to keep my cool is to remind myself of how unlikely it is.

We're two unknown brothers who opened a business. We don't have a lot of money, we're not important, we don't get involved with bad people.

Colin has just forgotten to check in. And charge his phone. And return to his place. They're all totally normal things that can be explained away.

Without a word, Lars puts down his mug, then steps closer and pulls me into a hug. "He's okay."

"He fucking better be." I refuse to think of the alternative.

***

Come the fuck on, Colin, we have a horoscopic altercation to get to. Another night, another full club, another day of looking over my shoulder, sure I can feel eyes on me.

I'm frustrated, worried, and so damn horny with no desire to get that energy out.

I fucking hate it here.

Lars has been gone longer than he said he'd be, and I wouldn't be surprised if he's getting some distance from me moping over my brother.

I scrub my hands down my face, frustration getting the better of me. Where the *fuck* is Colin? All this worry can't be good for me —doesn't he care about my health? It's almost like he's forgotten that he's supposed to be the considerate one. He's left me to flail. I don't like flailing. Especially in a club we've put our whole souls into that has only just opened. This is a flail-free zone.

"Brothers are the fucking worst." I stalk back to the desk, glimpsing the irritating feature about Saint Clare's still open on my computer screen.

It only pisses me off more.

The guy did his job. The write-up is a glowing review of the club and everything *I've* accomplished. It doesn't matter how many times I mentioned Colin in that fucking interview, he was only given one small line at the bottom. Every time I reread what's on the screen, my anger creeps higher, and I'm fully expecting to rage email that journalist at some point.

The following feature can be all about how fucking unhinged I've gotten.

I pinch the headache growing between my eyes and consider, again, whether I need to reach out to this guy and—instead of biting his head off—ask if he can get the word out about Colin. The police are doing sweet fuck all, so that might help?

The most frustrating part is that I've given the police their answer. It's no coincidence that we got threats not to open the club, opened, and then Colin went missing. It has to have been those assholes at Rev. There's no other answer. No one else has an issue with us. As much as I'd like to hope that Colin took himself on a vacation, I know him. He wouldn't leave like this. Which means that he was forced to.

And there's only one answer to who would force my brother to disappear.

A small part of me wants to be offended that they only went after him, but I can't blame them. It's barely been two weeks, and I'm already in way over my head—they don't need to get rid of me when I can't even run this place properly. They just have to wait out my complete incompetence.

While I wait to discover what the hell happened to my brother.

I'm not good with waiting. Or curiosity.

I chew my thumbnail, staring at the screen, trying to figure out what the hell I can do to stop being so gut-wrenchingly helpless, and all I can think of is that if the police won't do their jobs, I'll fucking do it for them.

I'm clearly not also a target, or I would have gone missing by now too. I'm not smart or sneaky and don't know how to cover my tracks. So if they're not after me, there's no reason why I can't pay them a little visit and start getting some of the answers I need.

Lars is still doing whatever the fuck he's doing, so I grab my jacket and make for the door. I'm not going to be gone long, in a place as public as Rev, I'm not worried about anything happening there. Afterward, well, who the fuck knows what they'll do. I'm not even sure I care at this point.

The not knowing is causing a brain itch, and if this is what I need to do, fuck it.

I take the stairs down from my office into the employees-only section of the club. There's a door at the end of the hallway that leads to our back courtyard and parking spaces, which has a gate into the small through street behind us.

Almost as soon as I step outside, that creepy crawling feeling hits me again. It's been hanging around all week, setting in randomly and suddenly, and I can't help but do my usual look around at what the fuck could be making my skin prickle like this.

As usual, there's no one here.

Colin going missing has me paranoid.

Ignoring my car, I cross the courtyard, where two of our bar staff are sharing a vape, and let myself out into the street behind our building.

Rev is only a few blocks away, and where they have specifically targeted a demographic who listen to rage music, doesn't mind fighting, and the drug trade in there is high, we went in the complete other direction. Latest hits, drug checks at the door, and a zero tolerance for violence. We've started out strong on both the drugs and the fighting and already given out bans so people know we're serious.

Saint Clare's and Rev couldn't be any more different, and there are more than enough customers to go around.

Their issues with us can't be that we're competition.

I leave the through road and walk along the busy street, that feeling of being watched even heavier out here. Every few steps, I can't stop from looking around, but the restaurants and theaters in this part of town make it hard to spot anything out of the usual, as *everything* is wild and strange and fun.

It's one of the reasons we were so set on opening in this part of town. The lease wasn't cheap, but Colin knew it was worth it.

A passing woman shrieks, making me jump, but the friends with her break into answering laughter. Fuck me, I'm on edge. This isn't normal.

When I get to Rev, as usual, the line is stretched out down the street, and the surly bouncer at the door is giving people the stink eye. We have Onyx on door duty, and they're the most bubbly, flamboyant ex-MMA fighter I've ever met. Colin and I loved them instantly.

Our brand is welcoming. Rev's is intimidation.

So. Fucking. Different.

Would they really take my brother over a little territory dispute when they're not suffering?

Really?

Instead of heading to the front door to make a scene, I duck down the alley to the left. Like our place, this one leads around the back to the employee entrance. I can ask one of their staff to let Yanni know that I'm looking for him then we can have this out without strangers witnessing our business.

But before I can get there, I slow my footsteps, and the doubt comes back to me. What if it wasn't them?

Big bad nightclub bosses making people go missing feels like a reach. Sure, I don't have any other suspects in mind, but this isn't a little *close or else* empty threat. This is a big fucking deal. A big fucking deal where I'm very possibly going to piss them off more or hand them the knowledge that I'm splashing around solo right now with no clue which way is up.

And I have no interest in making them feel that happy tonight.

I turn and sink back against the wall. It's filthy down here. Graffiti and litter everywhere. Food and who knows what bodily fluids trampled into the dirty concrete. A dumpster that smells like rotten fruit down the other end, the smell so strong it's making my eyes water.

All that just goes to show how completely fucking mindless I'm being here. The least I could have done was bring Lars. Maybe reached out to the police asking for more information. Hell, maybe they already questioned Yanni and didn't think to let me know.

Are police supposed to give the heads-up about stuff like that? I don't fucking know.

I tip my head back, looking toward the sky that's nothing more than deep black, melting into the shadows of the alley. The street-lamp here is blown. The noise from outside muffled. The stench of decay enough to keep any sane person from coming down here.

Something in my chest twinges, and it takes me a second to place the feeling.

I miss Colin.

My annoying, overachieving, always right older brother.

He'd give me the most enjoyable lecture about self-preservation if he could see me now. I can picture the exact way his neck would go an angry red, and concern would pinch the skin between his eyebrows.

Logically, I know I need to head back to Saint Clare's. Being here is a reach, and if they really did have something to do with Colin after all, I'm asking for trouble by being here.

Not-so-logically, my feet refuse to move, and this nagging instinct holds strong, telling me to get answers. Making decisions when I'm frustrated is futile, but at least I'm being consistent.

That prickly feeling kicks back up, stronger this time, and I know it's time to move.

But as I have that thought, a shadowed figure steps into the alleyway with me.

CHAPTER FIVE

PERRY

THE FACT I've already been set free to fly solo feels like some kind of work insurance breach, but here I am, name in my pocket, research done, with a whole few hours of training from Arlie under my belt.

When Luther handed the name over today, just like the other two times, it was with a muttered "quick and easy one for you." If all my hits are quick and easy, I might have this thing made.

I bet if contract killers had a union, there's no way I'd be let loose already. Good for me though, I guess. Arlie said I'm a good shot; she's given me a laundry list of tips that I've remembered at least three of, and tucked into the back of my jeans, under my fake leather jacket—I really, *really* need to do something nice for Elle after all these supplies—is a ghost gun similar to Arlie's.

No fingerprints, no serial numbers, no worries.

I pull out my bright pink flip phone, whack it twice with the heel of my palm to get the display to work, and check the time. I'm lurking in the shadows outside of this nightclub, and I won't be able to hang around too much longer before I'm spotted.

With any luck, this won't take more than one bullet, considering how impressed Arlie was by my aim. The first few shots went fucking haywire, but once I got used to the weight and the movement, there wasn't a single thing I couldn't hit.

I'm killer with a pew pew.

There's one problem though.

The last two jobs I went on, I ended up with cold feet. Worse, even. *Frozen* feet. I'd lifted the gun, looked my mark in the eyes, and all the fear and panic that flashed through them hit me right in the chest like they'd fired their own weapon.

I couldn't do it.

So with an apology and a pinky swear, I sent them both into hiding.

It felt like a win-win-win. They get to live, I get paid, and Luther trusts I'm a capable hitman and gives me more jobs.

Unfortunately, there are only so many times I can get away with that, and tonight, I've made myself the promise that I'll do it. I'll fire my gun for the first time. And I'll kill a guy.

I'll kill St. Clare.

He owns a hotshot nightclub—the same nightclub I'm watching—in downtown Seattle, and lucky for me, he's recently had a feature written up on him, so I know exactly who I'm after. Conventionally good-looking with that blond hair, smoldering eyes combo, and then add to that, he's probably rolling in money. It's ninety-nine percent likely that he trades drugs and kicks puppies and cheats on his wife.

And yes, my statistics come from mafia movies, but the whole art imitating life must have started somewhere, and I swear when I tilt my head just right, the photos of him have red eyes. Which means he's evil. I don't make the rules, but if he's evil and I kill him, I'm arguably a hero.

Now, *that* would have to make Margot proud of me.

And if I can't kill him, then I'm out. No more wasting my time or dishing out pinky swears. I'll be paid for the first two jobs any day now, and then I'll be paid *a lot* for this one, and that should be enough to get me by for a bit. No one can maintain a hit-a-night average anyway, and having three hundred and sixty-five deaths on my conscience wasn't one of my resolutions this year.

Though neither was being poor as fuck, so here we are.

The back gate into Saint Clare's courtyard suddenly opens, and

I jolt to life. I'd been expecting to wait out here for hours, but when St. Clare himself steps out into the street and closes the gate behind him, I straighten.

This is too easy. There's no fucking way I'm being *handed* my mark.

I know I'm not going to get a better chance than this, but I don't reach for my gun because, as weird as it sounds, I almost feel like I'm looking at a celebrity. Not, like, the famous kind. But the kind where you see them on TV or social media enough, and then you see them in real life, and it takes you a second to adjust. Plus, he's taller than I thought he'd be. Maybe my height, and I don't know why that catches my interest, but it does.

He walks off, and it suddenly occurs to me that memorizing details is pointless when those details won't exist soon enough. The bastard doesn't turn around, just heads for the road, and as much as I want to get it over with, I can't shoot the guy in the back. There has to be some kind of code about that, right?

Backstabbing totally fine.

Back banging is a no-no.

Ah, unless we're talking sex. Then the rules are completely different.

I pick up my pace, but he exits the quiet street before I can catch him. I'm not about to shoot him in the middle of all these people either, so I keep following, hoping I get the chance again. It needs to be exactly right.

Where it's quiet.

Not in the back.

But also not close enough to make out his expression.

Gah. My hands are getting sweaty, and this hoodie is feeling way too hot. It doesn't help that I have my mask and hood up either, but there are for sure cameras out here, and I'm not going to give them anything. Despite Arlie's advice, I kept my leering skeleton. I'm not sure why. But this guy was with me for that first hit, and I was okay there, so now it feels sort of like betrayal to ditch it.

We reach another nightclub, and I eye the long line. If St. Clare goes in here, there's no way I'll be able to talk my way past the bouncer. Saying "Oh, yeah, hi, I won't stay long. Only need to put a bullet in the head of the guy you just let in" would sound like I'm making shit up.

Before I can settle in for a long wait, St. Clare turns and walks into the alleyway beside it instead.

Well, fuck.

Again, this is *kinda* perfect for me. A quick look after him shows it's deserted and so dark I can barely make him out down there, but that's part of the problem.

Either he knows I'm following him, and this could be a trap, or he's looking to get killed, and that raises concerns about his mental health.

There's no guidebook for this, but surely you can't kill people with mental health issues either. It has to be some kind of unspoken rule. Maybe I should check him in to therapy first and come back later?

I really should have asked Luther more questions about this guy. Lethal Poison isn't that far away—I could pop in there and circle back in two to five business days?

Instead of going in through the back of the club, the barely visible form stops. I creep closer to the alleyway entrance and squint into the dark. It looks like he's leaning against the wall and … looking at the sky.

Jesus. This guy has less self-preservation than I do. At least I have being desperate and pathetic as my excuse. What's this guy's deal?

He's almost *begging* me to shoot him in the head with no witnesses.

Fuck. Okay. I just need to do it.

The drugs and cheating spouse and puppy thing. Yes. Bad. Very bad. I trust Luther, and Luther gave me his name, and really, this is nothing personal. I have no actual beef with this St. Clare guy; I just need to, you know, eat. Make rent. Stop having my sister worry so fucking much.

Okay, new plan. I will kill him, *then* walk away.

I'll be at the top of my game. Ending on a high. One person debrained and one more hitman off the streets. That's a fair trade. His life for the lives of all the others I could potentially end. St. Clare is doing Seattle a favor when you think about it.

I try to work myself through some of those child-birthing breathing exercises I've seen on TV, but if anything, it only makes my heart race faster.

For the love of Judge Judy, I can do this. She doesn't take stupidity from anyone, and hesitating here, with my hand tucked under my jacket and gripping my gun, is pretty fucking stupid.

I can do it. For her.

I give myself a mental butt slap and walk into the alley. It takes a minute for St. Clare to spot me. Something about his shadowy posture goes stiff as I close the distance between us. Close enough to face him but not close enough to know the exact moment he panics.

I can do this.

"Who are you?" he asks in a deep voice that plucks up the hairs on my arms.

I can do this.

"What do you want?"

I can do this. I can do this.

My grip on the gun is too tight, but I cock it, then lift it into my line of sight. This is totally fine. I've played *Call of Duty. Fortnite.* I'll shoot him, and he'll go all holographically translucent, and then I'll skip away and get the 11:47 p.m. bus home.

St. Clare's hands inch into the air. "I don't have any money on me."

Lies. He's probably got money and guns and a pocketful of party favors. He probably lures women into his club before having his frisky way with them.

"Put the gun—"

I pulse the trigger, first one going wide, but the second hits, and St. Clare drops to the ground.

The *chick-et* is quieter than I was expecting, and it takes me a second to realize it's because my sharp cry drowned it out.

"Well, *fuck*."

I should probably keep my voice down, but *fuck*. I did it. I actually fucking shot someone. This is the point where I pick up my shells, turn around, and walk the fuck away. It's done now. No regrets. No worries.

Akuna Ma-ta-tas. Still weirds me out that Disney was singing about titties, but the message applies.

I turn for the street, half expecting a row of police officers with their guns out, and I'm shocked that no one heard that or reacted or seems to even care.

Shit. I think I just got away with murder.

I'm about to put the safety on the gun and tuck it back away into my pants before I make my getaway when a long, painful groan comes from behind me.

My heart sinks.

He's still alive.

Because *of course* he is.

I turn my back on the street and head back in that depressing direction.

St. Clare rolls over as I reach him, bleeding heavily from the ear, hand pressed to it to stem the flow, breathing harder and faster than I was when I was following him. He might not be dead, but hey, I got close. A couple of inches to the left and he'd be trying to catch brain right now.

"Sorry," I explain, torn between helping him with the bleeding or shooting him again. "I was aiming for your head. I'm not a very good shot."

"Fuck you!"

"Wow, talk about a hostile work environment," I mutter. "Look, if you hold still, this will be over quickly. It's a minor setback. We can do it." My eyes catch the blood staining the cement behind him. "Though I do wish you didn't bleed all over the street. That's going to be a bitch to clean up."

His breathing has turned to a heavy pant. Probably from the pain, I guess. "An inconvenience? You're trying to kill me."

"Shh ..." I glance down the end of the alleyway. "Keep your

voice down. I can't afford to be caught. My sister says I wouldn't do well in jail."

"You can't … What the fuck is happening …"

Considering he was close to losing his head, I can understand his confusion. "Look, I should probably get this over with. I hear it won't hurt if I shoot you straight in the head. Or was it the chest? Shit, I'm only new at this." I raise the gun, alternating between which area to shoot as I rack my brain to remember. Given I tried the head last time and it's hurting a hell of a lot, maybe the chest?

"Wait! Don't I get last words?"

Shit. He's right. "How rude of me. Of course. Right. How do we do this? Ah … God?" I give the bleeding man an uneasy smile. "It's been a while," I explain. "St. Clare needs, umm … safe passage to … heaven? That doesn't sound right—"

"What are you doing?"

"I know I'm not a priest, but I'm doing the best I can here."

"I said last *words*, not last *rites*."

"Oh …" It dawns on me that he wants to be the one to say something. "Go on, then."

"You know what? Just kill me."

I perk up. "Can I?"

"No!" he snarls. "Jesus, what is wrong with you?"

"Hey, you're the one with a gunshot wound, so should you really be asking that question?"

Pain spasms across his face, and when he pulls his hand away, the blood staining it is bright red. It's still bleeding. A lot. If I was lucky, the wound would finish the job for me, but I'm not lucky, and as each second ticks by, I'm becoming increasingly worried that I won't finish things either.

I let out a frustrated growl, rubbing the heels of my hands into my eye sockets, careful not to poke myself in the eye with the gun. "Why can't you be dead already?"

He makes a choking nose. "Am I supposed to apologize for that?"

"It would make me feel at least a little better, if I'm honest."

"You shot me in the fucking ear!"

"And *I* already apologized for that." I pace a few steps away and back again, trying to find that same pump-up speech about puppies and … and …

Shit, now he's sweating. And looking pale.

I could end all this by ending him.

I could do it.

Except I really, really can't.

I'm so fucking angry with myself when I duck down, yank his jacket from his shoulders, and turn to his shirt instead.

"The fuck—" St. Clare tries to slap my hands away. "—you doing?"

"I need your shirt."

"Fuck off."

I go for his buttons again, and again, he slaps my hands away. I hit his back, and he *shoves* me, and before I know it, we're fucking wrestling against the pavement as I try to get his shirt off and he tries to stop me.

"I'm trying to …" I pant, holding off a hit to the head. "Help you."

"You shot me!"

I belt his shoulder. "Why are you *so* hung up on that?"

"Hung up? It happened a few minutes ago." He sends a strong kick to my thigh, but I grab his leg with the hand holding my gun and manage to pin both his wrists to his chest with the other. We're both panting, both glaring at each other, and he's looking *really* worse for wear now.

"I need your shirt so I can tie it around your head. To stop the bleeding. They do it in movies all the time."

He's still glaring, slightly shaking, breathing an uneven mess as he slowly nods. I'm half expecting him to attack when I slowly release my hold on him, but he doesn't, and I take it as a good sign.

I set the safety and tuck my gun back into my pants before going for his buttons again. He lets me this time. He doesn't say anything, and the lack of conversation is starting to make things really, really awkward. I've never undressed a man before, and sure this might be a life-or-death situation, but I'm not sure that makes it any easier.

"Why are you sneaking around a dark alley anyway?" I ask him, tugging the shirt from his shoulders. "I couldn't *not* take a shot when you went to the trouble of setting it all up for me."

He doesn't answer, and I try not to hold it against him.

"You really made this more difficult than it had to be, you know? If you'd just let me kill you ..."

If anything, his glare gets glarier.

At least he lowers his hand when I lift the shirt, and his cringe of pain as I set it in place gives me a quick break from his death stare.

I should probably tell him I have no clue what I'm doing, but it doesn't seem right to freak him out anymore. So I do what I can, hope it's enough, and once I've got the thing tied tight to his head ... I make the mistake of looking down at him.

His blond hair is in bloody tufts near his ear and chaotically spiked where I've tied the shirt. His eyes are confused and wary and scared and full of hatred all at once. But the photos and article didn't do him justice. There's a *something* around him that he doesn't need a leering skeleton mask to produce.

"You can go now," he grits out.

I'm about to do exactly that before I remember that I can't let him waltz off into the night. "Actually, there's one more thing."

He looks ready to hit me again.

"Have you ever heard of a pinky swear?"

CHAPTER SIX

ST. CLARE

I RUN. Hard. Ignoring that I'm shirtless and bleeding. Ignoring the way people stop and stare and one woman calls out *Are you okay?* as I bolt past her. My heart is hammering so fast I feel like I'm about to vomit it up, and I'm pretty fucking sure that's not a good thing when you're trying to *stop* the rapid bleeding.

I need to get to Saint Clare's. To Lars. Until then, I can't stop in case this is some sick game. Nearly kill me, set me free, then hunt me down like prey.

My ear is fucking *burning,* and I don't know if the bleeding has stopped, but I'm woozy from the adrenaline flooding through me. The through road behind my building comes into view, but I don't feel any better running down it. It's as empty as the alleyway was, and every second that passes, I expect to be shot in the back.

I can barely process what happened; my brain is too full of *run, run faster*, and that's what I do.

The courtyard gives me an illusion of safety, and I think I take my first breath once I get back inside. I don't stop running though, just fly along the hall, then sling myself up the stairs two at a time.

Even my office door can't bring me relief, and my hand is trembling and sticky with blood as I try to get the door unlocked. It finally clicks open, and I stumble inside, then slam it, lock it, and the relief hits all at once. I stagger toward my desk, and the last of my energy leaves me as I sag to the floor, leaning back against the wall.

What. The fuck. Just happened?

I pull out my phone and quickly text Lars to get his ass here now. He's going to be pissed I went alone, but I doubt it will come close to how pissed I am about being shot.

And then … everything that happened afterward.

I close my eyes, and the masked man flashes in front of my face. He was … that was … I don't even know what to make of it.

Watching him gesture like a madman with that gun in his hand was fucking terrifying, but …

Well, it's the "but" that has me thrown. Because I'm sure he helped me at the end there. I reach up to touch the shirt he's tied tightly around my head, remembering the concentration on his face. Those huge brown eyes that looked better suited to a dog than a person.

I open the messages to Lars and quickly add:

Bring painkillers.

Now that the rush is slowing down, the pain is coming in hot. It's less like a burning sensation and more like a whole head explosion with the way the migraine is building. He said he only hit my ear, but did he? Am I actually dying and don't fucking know it?

I could grab my phone and check, but I'm sort of terrified by what I'll find.

The office door flies open, and Lars rushes in. His eyes cast over me before scanning the room, hand on his gun.

"What the fuck happened?"

"Not sure, actually."

"Were you attacked? Are they still here?"

I give him a bemused smile. "Went for a little walk. Got a little shot. Do you have the painkillers?"

He releases his gun to pull them from his pocket, eyes still wild with concern. "Reilly, I—"

"Let me take these. Then we can talk. Drugs first." I throw two pills into my mouth and swallow them dry. The discomfort ranks low on my list for tonight, and I know Lars is dying for information, but I need a second. Need some of the pain to go away so I can fucking think right.

"First," I mutter, reaching to untie my makeshift bandage, "I need you to take a look. He said he got my ear, but with how much it hurts, I wouldn't be surprised to find there's a giant hole in my head." I grit my teeth as I remove the shirt. Peeling it away from my ear feels like a thousand tiny tears, and I'm hoping since it's so stuck to the site that the bleeding has stopped, but I have no clue what's happening up there.

"Shit ..." Lars mutters. "What happened?"

"Just tell me if I'm going to die or not."

"Ah ... no. No dying."

"Right. Then how bad is it? On a scale of *You're being a Dramatic Asshole* to *Probably Need a Hospital*?"

"That depends."

"On?"

"You had an ear at one point, right?"

My eyes screw closed because that's definitely *not* what I wanted to hear. "It's gone?"

"Maybe, like, fifty percent? Hard to tell."

"Shit."

"You definitely need a hospital."

I push to my feet and make my way over to the wet bar, where I pour myself out a glass of scotch. I'm itching to take a sip, but trying to drink anything right now makes my stomach turn. Everything feels so unsettled. I'm torn between whether to pace or drop to the floor. To punch something or curl up into the fetal position.

All I know is that I can't go to a hospital. First, there's no way my insurance will cover a bullet hole. Second, the police will definitely be called, which folds into third, the masked man.

His *pinky* swear.

"All I need," he said, expressive eyes pinning my gaze, "is for you to promise you'll go away. If you disappear, no one will know that I didn't

follow through, and then if they think you're dead, no one else will come for you. Get it?"

"You want me to fake my own death."

That threw him for a second. "Not in the leave blood trails or a suicide note way or whatever. But leave the city. Disappear. Take your family or whoever with you, and try not to kick any puppies on the way."

"What do you get out of it?"

"A payday I really fucking need." He held up his little finger between us. "Do we have a deal?"

I'm still not sure I believe him. *"Fine," I'd snapped. "But I'm not doing ... that."*

He bounced his gloved pinky between us. "I'm sorry, but I can't let you go unless you seal the contract."

So I did it. Wrapped my little finger around his and watched the way those curious eyes crinkled at the corners, over the top of his unhinged mask. Under his hood, I'm sure I made out dark hair, but who knows if it was real or a wig or a trick of the shadows around us.

"Reilly?" Lars pulls me from my head as he takes my arm and turns me to face him. "I'm serious. We need to get that looked at."

"Do we have a first aid kit here?"

"Dude, no. Come on. You were *shot*. We need the hospital, and we need to go to the police. Maybe if they see all this, they'll start to take things with Colin seriously."

And maybe they'll catch the ridiculous man with the gun and terrible aim, or maybe they won't. One of those things is more likely, and when they don't catch him, he'll come back to finish the job.

"No."

"What do you mean *no*?"

"No, we can't go to the hospital. Or the police."

"That's going to get infected."

"Then you better clean it really fucking well." It's risk infection or a redo of tonight, and I know which one I'd prefer.

He's silent as he studies my face. "What the fuck happened?"

Now that the pain has started to trickle away, I take a sip of my drink and walk over to collapse in one of the chairs by my desk. I kick out the other one, and Lars takes it.

"Is this the kind of story you're going to tell me and I'm going to wish you didn't?"

"Probably."

He takes a long breath. "Okay. I'm ready."

I fill him in on everything. Starting with the anger that drove me to Rev in the first place and ending with my very close brush with death and an elementary school promise.

"So he *tried* to kill you?" Lars asks, looking as confused as I am.

"Obviously."

"And then he helped you and promised to let you go if you keep quiet?"

"Exactly."

Lars huffs, leaning back in his chair and extending his long legs out in front of himself. "You're a fucking idiot for going there alone."

"You weren't here."

"I was … fuck. I was stuck in traffic." He's barely holding his frustration together. "You should have called me. You almost fucking *died*."

"But I didn't."

"But you might have."

"And yet, here I am."

Lars crosses his arms. "This sounds fishy."

"Wouldn't know. I'm deaf now."

He rolls his eyes and for the first time almost looks amused. I'm not totally joking, though, because there's a soft ringing when things are silent. "It's a cosmetic … setback. You can still fucking hear."

"Maybe, but not with all this blood in my ear." I tilt my head to the side like I'm trying to clear out the block.

"I'll get the first aid kit and try to …" He gestures at my ear. "I think you might need more scotch."

"Noted."

"And …" Lars studies my face again. "You're going to do it? Hide out?"

"I don't think I have a choice."

"But you also don't have the luxury of disappearing. Colin beat you to it."

That makes me straighten, hit with an idea. "Wait. Do you think this guy got to Colin first?"

"You think he's the reason Colin's missing?"

My heart is beating a little faster. "It's not exactly a stretch? He showed up to kill me and told me to disappear. If someone put a hit out on me, wouldn't they have done the same to my brother? And if it was the same guy …"

"Colin could be dead, or he could have been issued the same ultimatum you were."

He's right. "Schrödinger's Colin."

"I don't think you're supposed to joke about your missing brother after being shot."

"How many people do you know with a missing brother who've been shot to fact-check that?"

He thinks for a moment. "Just you."

"Cool. Then it's allowed."

"What are you thinking?"

"I'm thinking we need to find this fucking guy and hope he gave Colin the second option."

Lars's knees bounce beneath where his elbows are resting on them. "That doesn't sound like you're planning to disappear."

"Nope." Maybe I'm just asking for the guy to show up and kill me, but getting him alone again is sort of what I need. Besides, it's not like I'm going to dance down the fucking street and advertise that I evaded a hitman, now am I? I can keep a low profile while I look out for this guy. It's no issue.

"Fine," Lars says. "But from now on, you don't go anywhere without me. Got it?"

He really thinks he needs to threaten me? I point to my ear. "There is no fucking way I'm letting you leave my side."

CHAPTER SEVEN

PERRY

UNLIKE THE FIRST two times I've done this, something isn't sitting right. Don't ask me why—the super-secret pinky oath is sacred, so I shouldn't have any worries there—but I'm not so sure that *St. Clare* knows that.

I dunno. There was something in his cunning eyes.

Something calling me stupid and a terrible shot.

If you ask me, being a terrible shot has worked in his favor, so I'm not sure the taunting was warranted.

Hurt my feelings a little bit, if I'm honest.

The truth is, though, I'm not cut out for this line of work. It's a fact I probably should have cottoned onto after that first time out with Arlie, but sometimes I need the point hammered home with me.

And it has been hammered.

Multiple times.

With every missed shot.

Turns out that hitting a target that's sitting there waiting for it is easy. Hitting a human target isn't.

Probably because they, you know, move.

Luther is behind the bar, and I walk right up to him, oozing confidence and giving him absolutely no reason to doubt my story. I knock on the bar top and flash him a smile.

"Just wrapped up a job," I tell him, which is code for *I killed a guy*, not that I want to think about that.

Luther eyes me for a second before pouring me a Coke and dropping a wedge of lime into it. "I'll add it to your account," he says, code for *great job, Perry, you're the best, I'll send that payment through. The payment you're getting for killing a guy*, not that I think about that either.

"Thanks." I take my drink and go to turn away when he speaks again.

"You've got a real taste for it."

It takes me a moment to realize he's not talking about the drink. "Oh, uh, yeah. It's … delicious?" I'm not sure I'm speaking bad guy right, but he gets it.

"Need another?"

Uh-oh. Considering I'd begged him for the three jobs this week, I didn't think this was an allocation type of arrangement. More of a request when I can fit it into my schedule deal.

"Ah. Damn. I just signed on for a kid's birthday party this weekend," I tell him, pulling the lie out of my ass. "And there's distance growing between Sir Squeakerton and me, so I really need to get in some quality time with him because he's, quite frankly, an asshole when he's neglected. Chews through all my clothes. And then I need to house-sit for my sister's girlfriend in … umm, December? Which will bring me *back* to the issues with Sir Squeakerton and spending time with him. But, hey. I'll come talk to you in February. I should have a gap in my schedule then." That gives me a good six months to find something permanent to use as an excuse.

Luther looks me over. "One Coke won't keep you hydrated for long."

"I know how to make things last."

I swear I feel Luther watching me the whole time I walk away.

Not that it matters. If this guy stays hidden—and he will if he doesn't want a repeat visit—then no one will ever figure out what I know. It's the perfect crime.

Besides, once I have the money, what's Luther going to do? Go to the police? I can picture how that conversation will go down.

"Where's Everett and Arlie?" I ask, reaching where Tommy is sitting at the usual table.

"Dunno. Working, probably."

I slide onto the stool across from him. "Just finished a job myself."

He looks me over, clearly surprised. "Really? And how are you finding it?"

Terrifying? Horrible? Something in need of trauma pay? "Interesting?"

The way my voice goes up at the end makes him laugh. "Yeah. It sure is."

"I don't think it's for me though. I've got a really busy schedule coming up, and trying to fit it all in … you know how it is."

He grins as he lifts his glass to his mouth. "Couldn't pull the trigger, huh?"

"Actually, I pulled it a lot of times." Too many times. Many triggers have now been pulled, with a zero percent hit rate.

Tommy's eyebrows jump up, and he sets his glass back on the table. "Shit. Wouldn't have picked that."

"Why?"

"Because you're … *you*."

"Devastatingly charming and resourceful?"

"I was thinking more of a wishy-washy good guy."

"*Good* guy?"

He shrugs. "Don't take it so hard. Most people see that as a positive thing."

"I'm a total badass, what are you even talking about?"

"Right, yeah, my mistake." He can't keep the humor off his face. "Don't kill me in my sleep."

He's mocking me, but calling him on it might get us deeper into the conversation where I insist that I could do it and he asks me how and I have nothing, and then suddenly, he knows I'm full of shit.

Thankfully, my banking notification lights up on my phone,

distracting me, and when I glimpse the amount listed, I almost fall off my seat. "Sh-sh-shit."

Tommy outright cackles.

"There are four zeros here."

"Yup."

"I'm fucking rich."

His cackle becomes a sudden frown. "Calm down, it's ten Gs."

"Is this for *all* three jobs?"

"My guess it's for one. And they've probably underpaid you because you're so green."

"Under … paid?" My jaw drops, and I stare at the screen again, waiting for a little minus sign to appear before the numbers, which would make a whole lot more sense. "Fuck."

"I suggest you turn those notifications off. You don't want anyone seeing a large deposit out of the blue and then have them start asking questions. That's your business."

"Right. My business." I stand suddenly, half-drunk Coke forgotten about. "I have to see Elle."

"Who?"

"My sponsor."

"Like AA?"

"No, like, a crime sponsor."

Tommy tilts his head, and I'm surprised the momentum doesn't throw him sideways off his stool. "I don't want to know, do I?"

"She's taken anyway." I shove my phone back in my pocket. "Talk later!"

It really is incredible how quickly all my problems have suddenly disappeared. No more jobs, a fat-as-fuck bank account, and a little breathing room to figure out what the hell is next. And if Tommy is right and I have two more payments coming my way … fuck. My head feels all spinny just thinking about it.

First though, take Margot and Elle out for dinner.

Second, well, whatever the hell I want.

***

I wish someone, at some point in my life, had sat me down and said, "Perry, being a barista is your calling."

Turns out, much like with shooting a gun, I'm a natural at putting together all the wild coffee orders people come in with.

Unlike with a gun, these shots aren't going to kill anyone.

I'd applied for this job during my pitiful resume blast and assumed, since I didn't hear back, that they weren't interested. Then, the day after botching the St. Clare job, they called me for an interview, and I went straight into training. It's like it was supposed to be.

Sure, I'm only a street away from the Saint Clare nightclub, so in hindsight, it's lucky I sent the guy into hiding.

Now, I get to spend my day surrounded by the smell of caffeine, the buzz of customers, and get a real boost from all the talking I'm literally paid to do.

These guys are *paying* me. To *talk* to people.

Plus, I get all the free coffee I want. I think. No one has told me otherwise, and I've downed at least three of these babies this morning.

"Welcome to Toasty Roast," I say, turning to the next in line. "What can I get—"

My throat swallows the words as St. Clare gives me an impersonal smile. A stiff, impersonal smile. The kind of smile that says, *sorry I broke our pinky swear, but I've found you, and now I'll be the one to shoot you in the head, thanks.*

But the word he says doesn't match the ones in my head. "Cappuccino."

I blink at him for a second. "W-what?"

Concern crosses his face. "I'll have a cappuccino, thank you."

"Like … the coffee?" I clarify, trying to decipher whether this is code for something I don't know. Like … shit. Umm. Maybe I'm gonna cap-a-ccin-hole in your head? I shake the thought away because that's a reach even for me.

He glances over at where a huge guy is sitting at a table behind the big coffee machine, then back at me. One corner of his lips trembles upward. "That is what you sell here, correct?"

"But what about—" Thankfully, I cut off before the words *pinky swear* can leave me. My brain is still chugging along at a sluggish pace, but somehow, I fill in the blank. "Sugar?"

St. Clare shakes his head, and I clock the small bandage over his ear. "No, thank you."

I'm waiting for any sign of recognition but it doesn't come.

"Right. Ah." I'm numb as I ring him up and stutter out the price. He hands over cash and I take it and he pays and I give him change and then we're looking at each other and I'm lost as to what happens next.

"Is there a problem?" he asks, gaze flicking down to where I'm still holding on to the five-dollar bill.

I wrench my hand away. "I'll call when it's done."

I serve the next person, then get to work on the two orders. Part of me wants to duck down and army crawl my ass out of here. Sure, no one will be there to stop the cafe being ransacked, but the alternative is handing over a drink to the guy I almost killed and wishing him a good day.

Any day he's not up for murder probably is a good day, to be fair, but it's not like I can say that either. In fact, it's better that I don't say anything. Just hand over the drink with a grunt and go back to the next order.

I can do that.

I mean, I don't have to talk to *everyone*.

My palms are clammy as I finish up his coffee and walk it to the pickup counter. "St. Clare?" I call, and it's only once the words are out of my mouth that I realize I didn't ask him for his name.

Fuck. Like, I'm sure he didn't recognize me—thank you, skeleton mask—but do I want to give him any more fucking clues so he can put it together?

I really can't be blamed for being so unsettled though. I've got the caffeine jitters, I'm on a high from making so many people happy this morning, and then his shockingly propor-tionate face shows up out of the blue, barely a foot away, when that shockingly proportionate face is *supposed to be* staying hidden.

I keep my gaze pinned to the coffee, knowing it'll be easier to just shove it at him and run away.

He gets to the counter, and my pulse is out of fucking control. "Thanks."

"No good—*all* good." Shit, I'm fucking sweating. "Have a dood gay."

The mortification of those words makes me look up on instinct, wanting to know if he caught the fumble, and judging by the huge smirk on his face, he definitely, definitely did.

His blue eyes are waiting for mine to catch them, and the heat rushing my neck is filling me with the urge to say more that's so overwhelmingly powerful it's a struggle to keep shutting up.

"A dood gay?" He leans his hip against the counter. "What would that be, exactly?"

"It was supposed to be *good.*"

"A *good* gay?" His grin stretches wider, and my embarrassment claws deeper. "How did you know that's my type?"

By this point, my head is threatening to go supernova, and it takes me a second to realize what he's saying and … wait. Is he … *wait.*

St. Clare blatantly checks me out.

He's fucking hitting on me.

He's hitting on the guy who almost killed him.

The urge to laugh rolls over me, and the only thing that stops it in its place is the worry I'll come across as wildly homophobic. Which I'm not. Guys have hit on me before. It's fine. It's cool. Gives me a little zip of confidence even.

And, like now, even sometimes manages to scrub the ever-present words from my brain.

"Uhhhhmm …"

He reaches over and drags a long finger along my plastic charm bracelet. "This is cute."

"Th-thanks. It's my happy charm."

"Happy charm?"

I try to gather up my confidence that's currently shredded on the floor. "When I'm down or whatever, all it takes is one look at it to make myself feel better."

He eyes me curiously. "I like the idea of a happy charm. Maybe I should get one."

"You should."

"I should." St. Clare takes a long sip from his drink. "Damn, that's good." He nods my way. "Have a dood gay ..." His eyes flick toward my name tag. "Perry."

CHAPTER EIGHT

ST. CLARE

"THAT'S YOUR THIRD COFFEE TODAY," Lars mutters as I lift it for a sip.

"Are you caffeine shaming me?" I ask, squinting at my computer and trying to make heads or tails of these fucking spreadsheets. "After the ordeal I just went through?"

Lars chuckles, lounging in the chair across from me, occasionally clicking or typing loudly on his laptop in a way that's so sporadic it's making my eye twitch. "Sure. The ordeal. That's what's caused this sudden addiction. Not the new barista you're thirsty for."

I'm not surprised that Lars has picked up on it when I've done nothing to hide my interest. Not from him or me … or Perry. Fuck. He's so hot. A sweet, rambly mess with shoulders that look too broad for him to know what to do with. Then there's the way his smile lights up his whole face like it's the easiest thing in the world. Watching him move around that tiny cafe counter is like watching an overexcited Doberman in a china shop.

Truthfully, Perry isn't the kind of guy I normally go for, but something in his voice gave me this instant hit of familiarity, and the more I see of him, the more interested I become.

"Good thing they serve drinks there, then."

"Something tells me the tall glass of water you want isn't actually on the menu."

I finally let my attention free of the spreadsheets. "Why?"

"He hasn't asked for your number yet. Any queer dude would have gotten your message by now."

"Maybe he's closeted?"

"Maybe. Which is another reason why you should let it go."

Lars is right, and normally it would be easy to leave it alone, but I swear, every time I go in there, it's like he wants to say something to me but holds back. That, combined with the flustering and rambling, are all giving me good signs. I shrug. "He's cute."

"We get plenty of *cute* guys in here every night, and from what Onyx says, a lot of them are on the lookout for you."

That's not good when I'm supposed to be disappeared right now. "What's Onyx been telling people?"

"You're on a business trip."

"Good."

"Might want to stop visiting the cafe next door if you want people to believe it though."

Back to this again. I could stop visiting and consuming enough caffeine to wreak havoc on my blood pressure, but then how will I ever have a chance with this guy? Maybe Lars is right and I don't have a shot in hell anyway, but Perry can be the one to tell me that.

At this point, we haven't done anything more than make small talk while he gets my drink ready, but when I went in today, I got his *real* smile. Then he called me his favorite customer. And drew a smiley face on the lid of my cup that I glimpse every time I take a sip.

I'm starting to understand what he means about a happy charm.

Lars straightens suddenly. "Oh, hey, I got it."

"It?"

"Surveillance from the night you were hit. I told the restaurant across the road that my boss got mugged and asked if they could send through the footage. I wasn't sure they would."

A chill creeps along my spine. "What are you hoping to find?"

"Don't know. Where he came from? Some detail that might give us a starting point to finding him? All you picked up was the hoodie and skeleton mask, but what if there was something else?"

"I doubt a paid assassin would leave clues behind."

"Yeah, but paid assassins don't tend to patch you up and send you on your way either."

I swallow around the lump in my throat. If he'd taken a shot and I'd gotten away and that was the extent of my interaction with him, it would be easy to let my anger and fear take over.

But the man took my fear and twisted it into confusion, and now, that night is a melted lump of indecision in my mind.

"Is there anything there?" I ask, wanting to distract him.

Lars clicks loudly again and falls silent, watching the screen. "You wanna look?"

"Not in the slightest." All I need is to see my would-be murderer saving a granny from being hit by a car, or rescuing a kitten up a tree, or ... or ... whatever. He's already trying to replace the monster image with a good-guy one, and I don't want any part of it. Because of him, I'm missing a chunk of my fucking ear. Sure, I could have been missing a whole lot more, but I don't think that earns him brownie points.

He wanted me dead, and if his shot had been a fraction closer to my skull, I would be.

So fuck him and his fake concern.

"Not a great angle," Lars says, suddenly clicking again. "But this could be him."

"Great."

"Do you want to check?"

"Nope."

"But—"

"Unless he's getting out of a car with a clear license plate showing or holding a sign with his address up to the camera, I'm not sure it's going to tell us much."

"I'm sort of hoping that we see him meeting with the owners of Rev. *That's* something we can go to the cops with."

I don't bother pointing out *again* that we won't be going to them with anything.

Lars watches for a bit longer. "Shit. There you are."

"Right."

"Damn it. The video ends before I can see whether he follows you out."

Lars stands up and stretches his arms over his head. "I'm going to head down there and ask for more."

"You're pushing your luck."

"Nah." He flashes his smug look. "The manager took a liking to me."

"Of course she did."

As fast as his teasing appeared, it vanishes, and he pins me with his serious face. "Stay here. I mean it. No coffee, no need for fresh air. Nothing. I'll be back soon."

Like I'm going to argue with him. I'm more than happy to hole up in my office or my apartment if it means not risking my life again. As much as it would be easier for me to have the guy find *us*, there's no guarantee he would let me talk before firing, and there's no point ignoring his warning if it's not going to lead me to Colin.

"I'm as protected here as anywhere," I remind him.

"I'll be fast."

Lars leaves, and I take it as a sign for a break. Numbers are hurting my head, and my posture isn't winning any awards either. I stand, stretching my arms over my head like he did and daydreaming about how Saint Clare's was *supposed* to go.

Me and Colin, stressing over entry numbers and staffing and keeping enough stock on hand. Bickering over who to invite to our VIP areas and how much to pay ourselves out of the takings.

I was never, ever supposed to be dealing with a missing brother and a fucking murder plot.

Screw it. The bookkeeper I hired will have to swamp through the numbers and talk to me about it later since she understands this shit better than I do.

All the coffee I've drunk today is making me need to piss, so I duck into my private bathroom across from my office, empty my bladder of what's probably ninety percent coffee, and then avoid my reflection as I wash my hands.

I don't need the reminder that I look tired as shit and have a mangled ear.

Maybe while Lars is gone, I can let myself nap. Just a teeny bit. This week has thrown enough shit at me to fill a year, and I didn't sign on for any of it.

I like anonymity, and I may have some regrets about my name being in neon letters above the door.

And the feature article.

And all the social media posts I've been tagged in.

The thing is, our nightclub needed a face, and Colin flat out refused to do it, so it's not like I had a lot of choice. It was supposed to be temporary. Something we did early to get people engaged—the person-to-person attachment always works better with selling a brand—and then the focus on me was supposed to stop as soon as we were doing well.

If only I'd known someone was seeing my face out there and plotting out the best way to destroy it.

I return to my office, locking it behind me so that Lars doesn't have a fucking meltdown, and decide I might as well try to fill in this spreadsheet one more time.

The prospect of more hours in front of the screen makes me want to rip my eyes out though, so when a throat clears behind me, I'm almost relieved.

Until my brain catches up with me.

"Your ear doesn't look too bad."

My back locks up, and I hate that I've relived that night so many times that my brain recognizes his voice as familiar. "Why don't I cut off half of your ear and see how you like it?"

When he doesn't reply, I get the courage to slowly turn and face him.

He's half sitting on my wet bar, skeleton mouth mask in place, hood up, one elbow propped on his knee, while the other hand holds his gun loosely between his legs.

"You pinky swore," he says, which catches me off guard.

"Yeah, well, lucky for me, we're not in kindergarten, and that means shit all."

His heavy eyebrows pull tight. "It means something to me."

"If I can get over the ear thing, you can get over that," I throw back dryly. The fact he's trying to make out like this is a totally normal conversation and that his gun isn't here to make me feel threatened pisses me off enough to keep the fear away.

"You forgive me?" he asks.

If I didn't know better, I'd say he lights up, but it's hard to tell anything when half of his face is covered. "No. This isn't the type of thing you get to be forgiven for."

"But technically, it was an accident."

He's got to be kidding me. "It was only an accident because you missed my fucking head."

"A *happy* accident." He groans and rubs his head through his hood. "I was hoping we could move on from all that."

"Move *on*? Is there something wrong with you?"

"My sister would tell you there's plenty."

I latch onto that detail. "You have a sister."

He twitches, realizing he's said more than he should have. "Uh, no?"

"You *just* said."

"Well, maybe I was throwing you off." His hand twitches tighter on the gun. "It doesn't matter anyway."

"Why not?"

"Because you broke our promise. Which means that I *have* to kill you."

My fear kicks up a notch. "You don't have to do anything."

"But you're making me."

"I'm not," I hurry to say. "Look, I needed to ask you a question. That's it. All I've done since that night is come here or stay home. Only one person has seen me in that time."

"Plus everyone in the cafe."

My eyes narrow a little. "You've been following me."

"Umm, yes. Obviously. What else would I have been doing?"

"That's fucking creepy."

"You didn't keep your word!"

The slight whine in his tone makes me laugh. "Now who's hung up on small details?"

He looks at me expectantly, and it takes a second to figure out why he's waiting. "You want me to apologize for that?"

"I thought we had an understanding."

"You. Shot. Me."

He has the fucking audacity to roll his eyes, and like his voice, I've clearly been thinking about him too much because they seem familiar too. "And now you're making me do it again."

I throw my hands up. "Can you wait a second? My brother's missing," I explain, and I don't know why, but I actually have hope that I can win him over. "How would you feel if your sister went missing?"

Those eyes of his give away too much, but it's clear he doesn't like that.

"Yeah, it sucks. And I thought, well, if you had orders to kill me and instead told me to disappear, that *maybe* you did the same for Colin."

It's a long shot, but I'm desperate, and I hold my breath while I wait for him to answer me.

"I haven't seen a Colin," he says, and my hopes crash. "I didn't even know you had a brother."

I slump back against my desk, fear forgotten as hopelessness tries to take over instead.

The masked man stands and moves closer. "Wish I could help."

"You're sure?"

He shrugs. "Positive. My list of names isn't long. I'm new."

Finally, my laugh breaks free, and I swear his eyes crease up too. "Yeah. I could have guessed that."

"*Damn.* Right where it hurts."

"I'm sorry, are you telling me that I *hurt your feelings*?"

"And not for the first time."

"You are really bad at this, aren't you?"

With the hand not holding his gun, he pinches his fingers an inch apart. "I'm calling it a learning curve."

Then the familiarity vanishes, and he lifts his gun my way.

All of the relaxed air sucks from the room as I stare at that barrel again.

"You don't have to do this," I whisper.

"Yeah, I do. You broke our trust."

"To be fair, you probably shouldn't be trusting complete strangers at all. Consider this a life lesson."

"Sorry that I like to see the best in people."

"Is that before or after you blow open their skulls?" The bottom of his eyes twitch, like he's cringing at that imagery. "Is that what you want?" I push. "To take me away from my friends and family? To splatter my blood over my desk? Will that make you feel good?"

"I get the feeling it'll come down to being you or me, and I sort of like where my blood is right now."

"Funny. I could have said the same. But if you can do it, then do it." I'm totally fucking bluffing here because if he *does it*, I die. Not a fan of that outcome, so I hurry to continue. "I'm sure you don't think about all those other people you've killed when you're trying to go to sleep. Your sister must be so proud to have a murderer in the family."

Again, the grip on his gun tightens when I mention her. It draws my attention past the barrel. Past his hand wrapped tightly around the metal.

To his wrist.

And the bright red plastic strawberry peeking out from under his sleeve.

A happy charm.

My thoughts screech to a sudden halt.

Fuck.

There's no fucking way.

I'm about to say his name when he drops his gun hand suddenly.

"Last chance," he says, like he's trying to sound intimidating, but it comes out all wrong.

All I can picture is the slightly dopey sweetheart bumbling around behind the counter at the cafe. "Last ... chance?"

"You need to leave. Disappear. I mean it this time."

"Right."

He rubs his head again, and this time, I'm *sure* I get a glimpse of dark hair. I'm overlaying my memory of Perry with this guy in front of me and coming up with match after match. "Close your eyes while I leave."

Stupidly, I do exactly that.

I don't question whether I'm making myself an easier target, and when I hear the soft creak of my office door pulling open, I'm not at all surprised.

A second later, I look.

He's gone.

And now I need to figure out what the hell I'm going to do with this information.

He hasn't seen Colin. He's useless to me. One call to the police will remove him from my life, and then I won't need to worry about disappearing.

Except.

If he is working for someone like he claims he is, there's nothing to stop them from sending someone else. That someone else might not be so easy to scare off.

It's like playing Russian roulette with serial killers.

Who do I want to off me first?

CHAPTER NINE

PERRY

"YOU'RE IN A FOUL MOOD," Elle says, leaning across the counter at work while Margot ignores us both in favor of her coffee.

"Me? Mood? Nope. I'm totally and completely fine."

"You've spilled two coffees since we've been standing here, love."

I'm not sure how that's proof of anything, but now she mentions it, I am feeling … jittery? Annoyed? Expectant?

Definitely not foul.

But there is something off that's making it impossible to be happy in the moment and give my customers all the love and attentiveness they deserve to start their day with. I might have the teeny, tiniest idea of what's gotten me so shamoozeled in the first place too.

St. Clare.

I don't hate him, and I couldn't kill him, so I'm screwed if he doesn't listen to my very empty threats this time. Maybe *I* could contract a contract killer and pay them a chunk of what I was paid. Like a pyramid scheme of premeditated murder. That would free up all of my everything, and I'd be able to go back to coffees and Sir Squeakerton and the daily scramble of bill balancing. I haven't killed anyone, but if I stick it out in this life, it's only a matter of time, and I'm not interested in that for me, if I'm honest.

No judgment to Luther and Arlie—I'm sure they're the bestest lil killers—but I'll sit this one out.

So long as St. Clare does.

My deal with him wasn't difficult either. The other two people I was supposed to kill managed to do it just fine, so as far as I'm concerned, St. Clare is trying to be difficult. It wouldn't be my fault if I shot him, really, because he's been given lots and lots and *lots* of warning.

"Perry?"

"Huh?" I glance up at Elle, and this time, even Margot is watching me. "What?"

"I asked if there's anything we should know?"

That makes me pause because I can only imagine their reaction to finding out about my almost job pursuit and how close I'd come to being successful at it. Instead, I grab the can of whipped cream and shoot it at her nose.

Elle jolts back with a screech before bursting into way-too-loud laughter. Then she turns to my sister. "Be a dear and lick it off my face."

"We're in public," Margot answers, completely deadpan, and I'm about to tell her not to be such a killjoy when Elle steps closer and rubs their noses together. Whipped cream smears between them both, and it makes me all schmoopy to see someone who constantly challenges Margot and pulls her out of her shell.

Then Elle licks the whipped cream off Margot's nose before my sister can dodge her for the napkins.

They're so sweet. I've loved Elle from as soon as I met her because I've never seen Margot so ridiculous for anyone, and also, we match. Both a little lost and a lot carefree, only Elle has the money behind her to be so irresponsible. Me, not so much.

Margot finally wrangles her and wipes the mess gently from Elle's face. The softness in Margot's expression clears out the restlessness I've been feeling because this is all I ever wanted. Everyone in my life to be happy.

"We'll see you tonight?" Margot asks, dot of cream missed near her jaw.

"Sure will." I reach over to clean it off for her. "My turn to bring dinner."

Even the suspicion she eyes me with doesn't clear out my good mood.

Instead, it's two words that reach me as they're leaving.

"Good morning."

I swing around to find St. Clare at the register. Tussled blond hair a little damp from the rain we had this morning, and blue eyes sharply watching me. My brain nearly explodes, and I'm so, so close to asking him what the hell he thinks he's doing, but then that would sort of give me away, so I swallow back all the frustrations instead.

"St. Clare." I pull up at the register, heart beating as erratically as that first day he popped up out of nowhere. "Surprised to see you here."

His eyes narrow a smidge. "Why? I'm here every morning."

Shit. Yes. That. "Cappuccino?" I squeak, trying to say as little as possible. I doubt he'd spontaneously make the link between me and his would-be killer, but who the fuck knows what could give me away.

The problem is that the back-and-forth banter we've perfected over the last week gives me a buzz, and the need to feel that is wrestling with my annoyance. Which is making me even more annoyed.

And St. Clare's unwavering stare isn't doing much to help the jitters. Maybe I shouldn't have had that second coffee already.

I'm so nervous I feel like I need to shake out every limb, but I keep it contained as he nods.

"Please."

I ring up the total, and he pays with cash like usual, only instead of like usual, I throw his change back as fast as humanly possible. It's past our morning rush, and unfortunately, I have no other customers waiting, which means when St. Clare moves around to the pickup counter, he's the sole focus of my attention.

When all he does is watch me, I can't hold it in anymore.

"So … fun morning? Good morning? Everything is good?"

"Everything. What about you?"

"Just have a, umm, problem. Nothing major." I glare at him, but apparently, the glare has no effect because he goes on looking at me.

"A problem?"

"A …" I squeeze the handle of the milk jug tighter. "Coffee-related problem. It's fine though. I'll deal with it."

"Right."

He's not his usual friendly self, and that isn't making it any easier to shake the anxiety or behave like a normal human.

"You don't seem like yourself," he says.

"Yeah, well, you don't seem like yourself either," I throw back. Well done, Perry, ten points. Totally taken the heat off yourself.

Only St. Clare's gaze gets gazier, and my jitters get jitterier.

I almost drop my third coffee of the day and manage to get my shit together as I pour his milk in, shake some chocolate over the top, and slam the lid on with a triumphant "Ha!"

"Ha?" he echoes.

"I'm done."

"Right." He reaches for the cup I place on the bench between us. "No smiley face today?"

He's taunting me. At least, I'm ninety percent sure he's taunting, and I'm not at all in a taunting mood. Sure, most of the time, I find it fun, but on days like today, where my actual bones want to be anywhere other than restricted to my body, I'm like a powder keg under a hot flame. "Smiley faces are a privilege, not a right." I'm hoping that will send him on his way, but he doesn't look in a hurry to leave.

"Did I do something wrong?" His eyes hold mine, and my guts are a mess of indecision.

Succeeds in a high-pressure environment? Normally that would be a big fat tick on my resume since I'm a hard guy to rattle, but knowing how to act in front of the guy who's *supposed* to be in hiding because he's *supposed* to be dead is a new one, even for me. It's going to take me some time to adjust.

"Nothing. Nope. Not one thing." I grin wide, hoping it comes across as genuine. And failing, apparently, because he doesn't return it.

"You know, Perry, you have very pretty eyes."

I almost swallow my tongue. "Ah, w-what?"

"They're trusting. Sweet." There's a small pause I'm compelled to fill in but have no clue where to start. *"Memorable."*

"Memorable?"

He keeps on staring. "Not eyes I'd forget in a hurry."

"Are—are you … *hitting on me?*" His tone doesn't feel right, but the words have me thrown. Do guys usually compliment other guys' eyes? I do a quick mental search to try and figure out if I ever have before, and nothing specific comes back to me, but it does seem like something I'd do. Not sure I'd use the word *pretty*. Maybe cool. Interesting. The way he said memorable doesn't feel like a good thing though.

St. Clare tilts his head, the only change to his expression the way his tongue flicks out for barely a peek as he wets his bottom lip. It's gone too fast, but the tiny pink glimpse keeps playing in my mind. The way it makes my throat dry feels like a warning.

"Just stating facts."

"Ah. Yes. Th-thank you. You have a, umm, very pretty …. ah, mouth?"

His lips twitch involuntarily, finally giving me a quick break through the intensity. "My mouth?"

"Sure."

"Are *you* hitting on *me*?"

My eyes shoot wide. "Just stating facts. I'm straight. Very straight. Very, very straight."

"Straight." He picks up his cup and takes a slow sip.

The fact he's still standing there and not at all running and hiding like we *goddamn agreed* has the pulse in my throat throbbing.

"Pity," St. Clare says. "My pretty mouth can do a lot of very pretty things."

The blood drains from my head. I might be shit at speaking bad guy, but I can speak innuendo, and the suggestion of having that mouth wrapped around my ... around ... *that* ... has the blood relocating to a very specific part of my anatomy instead.

I swallow roughly. "That's ... that's good to, umm, know." I plant both hands firmly on the counter to stop from adjusting myself into a more comfortable position.

St. Clare's gaze finally breaks from mine and drops to them instead. Then, he reaches across the distance between us and grabs my little strawberry charm, giving it a tug. The bird, smiley face, and flower charms all shake with the movement.

"You know, Perry," he says, leaning in, and when he looks back up at me, his gaze is cold. "I could have sworn I've seen this somewhere before."

"Impossible. My mom made it for me."

"So it's one of a kind."

"Yep."

"And no other person in the world has it?"

I have no idea where he's going with this. I stiffly shake my head.

"And you haven't lent it to anyone?"

"Why would I do that?"

St. Clare's smile is smug. "You wanna know where I've seen it?"

Suddenly, I'm not so sure I do. Actually, I'm very, very sure that I don't want to know where he's seen it because wherever that was has pissed St. Clare off, and it's giving me a bad feeling.

A bad, sickly, sinking feeling that maybe Arlie was right.

"It's actually, uh, time for my break. Must be going. Good talk. See you later." Before he can answer me, I yank my hand away, the bracelet snapping back against my wrist as I leave the counter empty and scramble toward the back.

Casey should be almost done with her break, and while mine isn't for another half an hour, they're going to have to deal with me taking it early because I can't exactly give them the reason why.

Just a feeling, but I doubt there's a *the guy I was supposed to kill is onto me, and I'm having an itty-bitty freak-out* leave option.

This barista job was supposed to be a "no kill, new me" lifeline, and already it feels like I can't escape my past. My past of literally a week ago, but it still counts. I'm a good guy, dammit. I made the ill-advised choice to dip my toes into the world of cloaks and daggers before backing the hell out again. Surely that gains me brownie points? I didn't *actually* kill anyone. I don't know of any other jobs with this kind of disastrous trial period.

The baddie bunch *really* need to get onto starting that union.

I shoulder my way out the back door into the alleyway behind the cafe.

"There he is!"

I jump around toward the voice, door slipping from my grip, and try to place where it came from. There's a familiar *chick-et* right as the cafe door reopens, and a bullet sails past my head.

"Fuck," I shout, diving toward where St. Clare is standing in the doorway. I shove him ahead of me, and another shot goes off as I barrel back inside. The restlessness bursts out of me, and I can't hear, can't think, can't see.

Just scream, "Run!" even though he's already running, and try to keep pace behind him.

We tear past the stockroom, down the hall, and back through the swinging door into the cafe. Casey is behind the counter in front of a small line of customers, and she looks over in shock, but her "Perry, what are—" is drowned out as we shove our way through the seating area, and I haul St. Clare aside to scope out the street first.

I'm expecting another gunshot, more shouts, something or anything, but when it doesn't happen, I grab St. Clare's arm and urge him ahead. "Go!"

He runs, and I run after him. I haven't stopped to think about where we're going or who shot at us or why we're a target; I just have a feeling in my veins that it's for St. Clare, and as convenient as it would be if someone else took him out, I'm suddenly very, very not okay with that option.

I'm running off adrenaline and feelings, and I'm sure if I'd had a second to stop and think, I definitely would have left him to fend for himself.

"Down here," St. Clare yells back at me, and I'm nowhere near fit enough for this. My lungs are burning, and I'm wearing jeans, for fuck's sake. Being alive to aid him long enough for my jeans to chafe is pure luck, but I'd really like a bit more luck to be able to get out of these damn things and catch my breath.

St. Clare leads me into the bar of his nightclub and shouts at some random guy vaping to get security on the door. I don't wait long enough to see if he does, but we follow the route I took to his office last night, down the hall to the stairs and up them. My thighs protest the climb, and my speed slows down significantly. If anyone ever *did* want to kill me, all they'd need to do is chase me up some stairs.

We reach St. Clare's office, and I hesitate about entering, finally some self-preservation kicking in now that we're out of immediate danger.

Maybe this is a trap. Maybe he's leading me here on purpose. Maybe—

This time, he grabs *my* arms and hauls me through the doorway after him, so hard that I knock into him and we both almost go over.

"Watch yourself," he pants, shoving me away as he slams and locks the door behind us.

I hunch over, hands on my knees, trying to get oxygen to my—well, everywhere—and what happened finally sinks in.

"Shit. I think I almost died."

St. Clare shoots me a glare. "Join the club."

Then a third voice answers us. "And while you're doing that, why don't you fill me in on where the fuck you've been?"

CHAPTER TEN

ST. CLARE

LARS IS GOING to kill me. Which means I'm now in a room with two people who want me dead, so that's fun for me.

I didn't stop and think that through when Perry was shot at. Instead, the need to get him out of danger kicked in, and then we were running and …

"I dropped my coffee," I realize too late.

"It's okay," Perry gets out between wheezing breaths. "I made that one shit anyway."

"You owe me a refund."

He scoffs. "Think saving your life covers it."

It takes me a second to follow what he's implying. "Wait. You think they were after me?"

"Duh." He finally straightens and paces to one side of my office and back, hands planted on his hips. He's still wearing his Toasty Roast apron and a shirt that's ratty, thin, and a touch too tight. Then Perry reaches between his legs and tugs at the crotch of his jeans. "Got myself chafed, thanks to you."

"Thanks to *me*? Would you have preferred that I left you there to get your head blown off?"

"Not my head they were aiming for."

"It's exactly your head that they were aiming for."

"How do you work that out?"

I glare at him. "Maybe because they yelled out *that's him* and shot at you."

"They were shooting at you."

"Then why were you the one almost hit? Also, hate to break it to you, but I wasn't even outside when it all went down. I *only* came out to help you."

"Bullshit. I was helping you."

"No."

"You stepped outside. Then they yelled out. Then they shot at you."

"That's not what happened."

Perry finally loses some of his bluster, and he sinks into the chair beside my desk. "Are you sure?"

"Very. Unfortunately, I have experience in these situations." I'm not sure whether to say more or not, but fuck it. "Thanks to you."

"*Him*?" Lars demands.

"Perry's the one who tried to kill me."

Before Perry can react, Lars storms toward him, wraps his hand around Perry's throat, and lifts him partially out of the chair. "Who are you working for?" He squeezes so tight that Perry lets out a gargle. "Where's Colin?"

"He doesn't know where Colin is."

Lars glances over at me. "How do you know?"

"He told me last night."

"Last ..." Anger flares behind Lars's eyes. This probably shouldn't be the first he's hearing about it, but if I'd told him, there's no way he would have let me out of his sight this morning. And I needed to see Perry to confirm that I saw what I thought I saw.

Lars releases him, and Perry drops back into the chair with a gasp.

"How about we all just ..." Perry starts. "Take a second. It's been a big morning, we're tired—"

"Shut up," Lars demands before turning his attention on me. "You want to fill me in?"

It's inconvenient to go back over everything when we're potentially still being hunted, so I try to condense it as much as I can. "The masked man paid me a warning visit last night. I spotted him wearing Perry's bracelet, so I went to the cafe this morning to make sure, and then Perry ran off, was shot at in the alley behind the cafe, and we bolted for here. You're all caught up."

His shoulders stiffen. "Were you followed?"

"No clue."

Lars takes a determined step toward the door before pausing. Then, changing his mind, he walks back over to Perry and pulls a set of handcuffs from his belt. "Hands behind you."

"That isn't a smart choice for me."

"It's not a choice. Hands. Behind your back. Now."

"What if whoever's coming for us gets through you and finds us here, and then I'm handcuffed to a chair like sitting prey?"

"If they get through me, I'm dead, so I don't think I'll really care what happens to you."

Perry puffs out a huge exhale. "Fair point." Then he wraps both hands behind him.

Lars handcuffs him, checks the tightness, and leaves.

It's so quiet between me and Perry that it's clear neither of us knows what to say.

He stretches his long legs out in front of himself with a groan. "Fuck, this hurts."

"Imagine losing your ear."

"Almost did." He tries to shrug, but it doesn't really work with his arms pulled tight. "At least if they come for you, you can get away."

"They were aiming for *you*."

"Debatable. See, I don't have anyone who wants me killed, but we have proof you do."

That's the faultiest logic I've ever heard. "We also didn't have proof anyone wanted me dead until you shot at me. Welcome to the world of being wanted."

My tone is as dry as fucking possible, but when Perry turns those big brown eyes on me, I'm not prepared to feel ... sorry for him. Jesus. This whole thing is a headfuck of epic proportions.

His big white sneaker taps nervously against the floor.

"So, uh, how about those alien sightings?"

And like that, pity's gone. "Alien sightings?"

"Yeah, there's been an increase in UFOs entering our airspace." His tone perks right up. "Do you know that there's almost one hundred sightings a month on average? And it's up from that. Plus, about a quarter of people have spotted one that it can't be—"

"Wait, wait, wait. You believe in aliens?"

He blinks at me, stunned. "That makes them sound like they're not real."

I almost choke. "Because they're not."

"Sheesh," he mutters. "No wonder someone wanted you dead."

"Excuse me?"

His goofy, lopsided smile comes out. "Too soon to joke about that?"

"It will always be too soon. But I have a good idea of who wants to kill me and why. The question is, who the hell is after you?"

No offense to Perry, but being a barista and newly disastrous hitman doesn't exactly scream primary target to me.

"Ah." He shifts in the chair, shoulders obviously getting uncomfortable. "I have a sneaky widdle feeling that it might be the same people."

My face falls into a frown. "I'd say no offense, but your feelings aren't high on the list of things I care about, so why the hell would some drug lord nightclub owners give a shit about you?"

If I didn't know any better, instead of looking offended, he seems amused. "It's only a hunch, but I don't think they liked paying me for a job I didn't do."

"A job … me?"

"Yup."

"They *paid* you?"

"What?" he asks, this time sounding offended. "You were supposed to be dead. We pinky swore."

"Who's stupid enough to take some crime lord's money?"

"In my defense, I didn't know they were a crime lord."

The fact he thinks that's a defense at all proves that *he's* stupid enough. "They organized a hit on someone. That didn't raise red flags with you?"

He tries for another shrug. "Hey, man, we're all just trying to get by out here. What's one person's red flag is another's ideal quality."

"Again: organized hit. Crime lord. Those are not ideal qualities."

"Yeah, but don't we all wish we could find someone who would kill for us?"

"I've literally never wanted that a day in my life."

"Ah. Well. I am a romantic at heart, so …"

I raise my hands, giving my head a little shake. "How did we get here?"

"Well, your name came up for a job—"

"I mean this conversation."

"That's anyone's guess, but I'm enjoying myself."

He's … enjoying himself. We have him handcuffed to a chair because he tried to kill me, fucked up, and is now the one people are after, and he's *enjoying* himself. I'm struggling to work out if Perry is the most laid-back person on Earth or is completely oblivious to the danger.

He makes a smacking sound with his lips. "Any chance of some water? I'm parched."

"You're handcuffed."

"Sippy cup, maybe?"

Not for the first time in the last few weeks, I'm struggling to believe this is real and not an elaborate dream. And considering it's a choice between talking to him some more or getting him the water to make him shut up, I go for the second option.

Without a word, I cross to my wet bar, fill a cup with water and ice, and then after a second add a straw.

Then I carry it back to him.

I'm about to hand it over when I realize that without hands, there's only one option. I heave a sigh and lift the glass until the straw is right by his lips. "Drink."

I try to sound snappish and fucking fail because at that moment, Perry wraps his lips around the straw. He's so close, so suddenly, and his presence overrides every other thought in my head. His face is dusted with stubble, his large eyes are framed by dark lashes, and the thick black hair that flops over his head looks like it would be soft to touch.

Being attracted to the guy who tried to kill me feels like one more fuck you from the universe, so instead, I try to focus on his flaws.

Like the messy eyebrows. His too-big nose. The way he apparently fumbles through life, which is not at all endearing and would get annoying after a while. That he wears a child's bracelet …

Shit. I can't make myself hate any of those things.

Perry's eyes flick up to meet mine, and between that and the way he's sucking on the straw, a burning starts deep in my gut. All I can picture is those lips stretching wider as they sucked on something else.

"That's enough."

I yank the drink away and set it back on the table. If Colin could see me lusting after this guy, he'd force me to get a full medical checkup and take a week's break. Lack of sleep really does lead to shitty choices.

"Thanks," he says like none of this is anything out of the ordinary.

I don't answer him.

"No chance you have snacks up here? Only, it's supposed to be my break time—"

"No snacks."

"I'll take a chocolate bar. Salted nuts …"

"I said there's no snacks."

He puffs his cheeks up with air and lets it all out again. "Bummer."

"Bummer?" I lean against my desk, still looking down at him, less shocked at how his brain works and more curious. "Maybe it's me, but you don't appear worried at all."

"Why would I be worried?"

"Because someone wants you dead."

"We don't know for sure it was me they were after."

"We *do* know it's you they were after."

"Potato, pot-ah-to."

"That doesn't apply here when you were the only one there and you were the one the bullet almost hit."

To my surprise, Perry's lips twitch higher, and he lets out a soft laugh. "Can't say that's not comforting."

"Not the word I'd use."

He tries to move his arm, and when that doesn't work, he shakes his head instead. "Comforting that they missed. It's good to know I'm not the only one who does that."

"Th-that's what you're thinking about right now?"

"Well, I'm handcuffed to a chair. I've gotta find my silver linings somewhere."

"Most people would be worried."

He thinks that over for a second. "Yeah, sure, I can see it. But really, what does being worried accomplish? As of right now, we're safe. It's all good. Whatever comes next will happen whether we worry about it or not."

"There's no *we*," I point out on reflex, but I'm struggling to hold on to being annoyed with him. Which is ridiculous because if you can't be annoyed with the guy who tried to kill you, who can you be annoyed with? When Colin kissed my ex-girlfriend behind my back in high school, I held on to my grudge longer than that. I mean, we broke up because I'm gay, but still. Not cool.

On a scale of least to most fucked-up in life, shooting off my ear should definitely rank higher than that.

Perry gives me a sympathetic smile. "You're still thinking about it, aren't you?"

"About what?"

"You know the ..." He tugs his arm again, like he's somehow forgotten *again* that he's handcuffed. "*Pew pew.*"

"Pew pew?"

"Don't make me say it."

"Oh. So *that's* your line, is it? Not doing it, but saying it."

"It's possible I may have some regrets."

Instead of the anger I'm expecting at that, a secret little part of me is relieved. "Some, huh?"

"Well, let's face it. If my aim had been a smidge to the left, none of this would be happening right now."

My eyes almost fall out of my skull. "Wait." I have to remind myself not to laugh because this whole fucking thing is so absurd I think my brain is done. "Your regret is that you *didn't* kill me? Not that you tried to?"

"It's a natural feeling. Nothing personal, of course."

"Right. Because how could I possibly take that personally?"

"Not *you* taking it personally. It wasn't personal, *to me*. I have nothing against you. When I said you were my favorite customer, I wasn't lying. You're a, umm, cool guy."

Something about the way he fumbles over that gets my attention. Am I pissed? I should be. He *just said* he wishes I was dead right now, but apparently, I'm dumber than he is because the feeling is nowhere to be found. Instead, a smirk crosses my face. "A cool guy with a pretty mouth?"

"I-I panicked."

"Like you did with dood gay?"

The way he squirms in his seat shouldn't be so appealing. "I get flustered easily," he says, voice squeaking that bit higher than usual.

"Flustered?"

"My mouth is stupid. A big idiot. Don't trust a word that comes out of it."

"Like our pinky swear?"

He hurries to shake his head. "No, no, that was sacred."

"But I *don't* have a pretty mouth?"

For the first time since he got here, Perry looks torn and uncertain. If I'd known it was this easy to knock him out of that chill persona, I probably would have teased him sooner. "I dunno, man. They're … very … umm … pink."

"Pink?"

"And I didn't know that little bow thing was a real thing you could have without makeup."

"Bow?"

"So, sure. Some people might, like, think that's pretty. Handsome? Sexy? I don't know, but I can see the appeal is all I'm saying."

Sexy?

I'm about to cross all fuck it lines and ask him if he's ever been with a man before, but my door opens suddenly before I get the chance.

Lars slams it behind him, and he looks pissed.

It takes me a second to remember why.

Right.

Potential murder.

Guys with guns.

Perry being a dangerous assassin and not at all the adorable puppy my libido is trying to turn him into.

I clear my throat and quickly straighten, subtly putting more distance between us.

"All clear," Lars tells me. "Now, what the fuck do we do about this guy?"

Before I can answer, Perry speaks up, back to sounding like he's a guest and not our captive. "I have an idea."

CHAPTER ELEVEN

PERRY

"SHUT UP," the big guy snaps. He's almost a whole head taller than St. Clare, and judging by the size of his biceps, there's a very real possibility I'm seeing roid rage in action.

"Ah, where are my manners? I'm Perry. Who are you?"

Rager glares at me, and when he does it, it doesn't have the same reluctance as St. Clare. No, it looks like he straight up hates me, and really, is that fair when we don't even know each other? I understand we're off to a rocky start here, but what happened to second chances?

"Just say the word and I'll get rid of him," Rager says.

"Whoa, whoa, whoa," I protest. "Let's not get ahead of ourselves."

St. Clare looks like he's trying not to laugh. "Shockingly, I'm with him." He points my way. "Get rid of him? Lars, come on."

"He tried to kill you."

Those blue eyes cut to me. "But you're not going to again, are you?"

I confirm it like a good little prisoner. "No. I didn't even want to the first time, but now that we've met and spoken, that would be pretty much impossible."

"You believe that shit?" Ragey Lars snaps, throwing his arm out my way.

The indecision on St. Clare's face makes it clear he really doesn't, so I offer up my most innocent smile. The one that always derails Margot's steam when she's grumpy with me.

Instead of the explosion of trust I'm expecting, St. Clare's eyes narrow.

"We're not some shady underworld thugs," St. Clare says eventually. "We can't just get rid of people."

"So we let him kill you instead?"

"I didn't say that either."

"I said I have an idea," I remind them.

They both ignore me.

While St. Clare and Lars bicker between themselves, I shift position, trying to reduce the pain I'm in. My thighs still have that raw burn, and my shoulders are sending an ache up my neck. The least they could do while they debate my fate is help me get a little more comfortable. I wouldn't be opposed to having my hands cuffed in front of me. Or having my ankles zip-tied to the chair legs. They need to get a little creative, is all.

That cup of ice-cold water is taunting me too, and if this is torture, they're doing it right.

"Could have led someone here—" Lars is saying.

St. Clare talks over him. "I'm the one who brought him here, and like you said, we weren't followed. So what's the issue?"

Lars reaches up to tug on St. Clare's good earlobe. "Have you really already forgotten?"

"Of course I fucking haven't." He bats Lars's hand away. "All I'm saying is that he's not a threat."

"I'm really not," I back him up.

Again, with the glares. Sheesh, a man can't even protest his own innocence around here.

"Look, Lars," I try again. "I know why you don't trust me, but if you try to get to know me, it'll change all that. I'm a good friend, if I say so myself. Besides, as much as I love this cute little meeting, I can't stay long. A few hours, tops. Sir Squeakerton gets mad if I miss bonding time, and I'm meeting my sister and her girlfriend for dinner. It's my turn to buy." At least the glares are gone, but they're both staring at me now. "It might help if I give you my idea and we go from there?"

"We don't want to hear your idea."

St. Clare clears his throat. "*I'd* like to hear his idea."

"Hey, there we go! Now, that's working together."

Lars tips his head back, pinching his nose, and waves the other hand my way. "Whatever. Go."

"You're apparently highly wanted. And I'm now allegedly highly wanted—"

"*Actually* highly wanted."

"Semantics." It's a situation of he said, I said at this point, and who can tell which of us is right? "My point is that the same people are *apparently* after us both, and what's better than one? Two."

"Debatable," Lars mutters.

"So why don't I hide out here with you guys until I can get hold of Luther and find out who hired me? I can even be your bodyguard—today was our trial run. We'll team up to take down the bad guys!"

"You *are* the bad guy," Lars points out.

I let out a long sigh. "Not you too."

"Me too, what?"

"Hung up on the whole …" I drop my voice out of respect for St. Clare's ear. "Attempted murder thing."

His eyes go round.

"I've already apologized though. What more does a guy have to do?"

"This isn't really the kind of situation where a quick sorry will clear things up."

I try to work through that one myself, but I'm not getting anywhere fast. "Why not?"

"Are you seriously asking why an apology doesn't clear up you mangling his fucking ear?"

"I can't win with you people. First, I *don't* kill him. Then I patch him up, say I'm sorry, make him some awesome coffees—"

Lars turns to St. Clare. "Is this guy serious?"

"I'm afraid he is."

"I wouldn't joke about something like this," I assure him. "Does it help to know that my apology was sincere?"

Lars crosses those Christmas ham arms and leans against the desk next to St. Clare. They both stare down at me, and it's like one of those dreams where you're naked and the bullies loom over you and laugh, pointing at your *thing*. "Would you both be more comfortable seated?" I suggest.

"I'm good where I am," Lars says.

"Are you really good, or are you only good because I'm the one who suggested sitting, and now you want to be stubborn and disagree? Because I promise I won't think less of you."

They exchange a look again.

"Listen, I have no clue what those looks mean, so you're going to have to use words around me."

"They mean we think you have issues."

"They *mean* we don't know what the hell to think of you," St. Clare corrects.

I'd throw my hands up if they weren't cuffed behind my back. "See, even you two don't know what they mean. That's going to lead to some serious miscommunication issues."

"He was trying to be nice," Lars tells me, leveling a look St. Clare's way. "Because apparently, my best friend has issues as well."

"Best friend?" I look between them. "Sorry, I thought you were …"

"Thought we were what?"

"Well, I sort of got the impression St. Clare's … and then you're all protective of him …"

St. Clare's jaw drops. "You thought we were together?"

"Little bit."

"Lars is straight." Then he runs those striking blue eyes over me. "And I'm single."

Well. Okay. That's now information that I know. And definitely don't need. "Right. Very good. Thank you."

He quirks an eyebrow my way, and I almost swallow my

tongue. They're both still standing over me, and I'm not hating it as much anymore.

"Uh, should we circle back to my plan?"

"Your plan."

"To join forces."

Lars snorts. "Why does it sound like you're calling yourself a superhero?"

"Well, I *did*—"

"No." St. Clare's grinning. "We're not going over all that again. Stay focused. You want us to trust you to team up and figure out who's after us, but how the hell do we take you at your word that you won't kill us in our sleep?"

"I'm a trustworthy guy."

"You just told me your mouth lies."

"Only when it comes to compliments!"

Lars squints one eye up as he rubs at his short beard. "So you think the same people are after you both?"

"Yep. I maybe sorta claimed that St. Clare was dead and took the payday, and since *someone* broke our pact, they've obviously discovered that he's very much alive and I'm very much a liar."

"And there you bring us back to the not-trusting-you thing," St. Clare says.

Okay so I can maybe see why he doesn't believe me.

"It sounds to me," Lars cuts in before I can exclaim my innocence again, "that you owe them a fuckload of money, so you're probably the most wanted guy in the room right now."

"Allegedly."

"*Actually.*" St. Clare's whole expression is teasing.

Lars shrugs. "In that case, if you want to help me protect St. Clare, I'm sold ..."

"Really?"

"*Really?*" St. Clare sounds even more surprised than I am.

Lars laughs at us both. "Really, really."

I perk up because if Lars is on board, then St. Clare must be as well. Surprisingly, he's watching Lars, and I'm sure they're doing that silent communication thing again, but considering how off base they were last time, I'm not sure why they bother.

"Does that mean you'll let me out of these handcuffs, then?"

"Nope."

I slump. "How am I supposed to be his bodyguard if I can't even use my hands?"

"First, he has a bodyguard." Lars points to himself.

"You? I thought you were his best friend."

"Best friend *and* bodyguard."

"But not boyfriend?" I reclarify.

He pins me with a stare. "You're making me regret my decision."

"Sorry. Continue."

"*Second*, you're way more dangerous with your hands free."

I puff my chest out a little. "You think I'm dangerous?"

"Unintentionally."

Urg. Way to build me up only to break me down again. "How am I supposed to prove to you both that I'm trustworthy when you have me strapped to a chair? And, more importantly, how am I supposed to trust either of you when you've put me in a compromising position? I can't work under these conditions."

"You don't happen to have a gag on you, do you?" Lars asks St. Clare.

"Sorry, fresh out."

"And now you want to gag me." Again, I'd throw up my arms, exasperated with them both, if they weren't out of action. "I've gotta say this team isn't off to a good start. It's really starting to feel like the two of you against me."

"Starting to?" Lars is at least dropping the growly, angry man act, and even when he's fighting back amusement, he's like a giant teddy bear.

St. Clare rests his hands back on the desk and leans into them. "I'm a fan of a man in a compromising position, myself."

"Does that mean I'm your favorite?" The thought brings a smile to my face. "You and me against old Lars-y boy."

Lars runs a hand over his face. "Maybe I'll pick up a gag when I'm out next."

"I'm beginning to get the feeling you still don't like me."

"You think?"

"Come on … I thought I was winning you over."

"When it happens, I'll let you know."

"Ah-ha. You said when."

Lars catches his sigh. "Think I can talk to you outside for a second?"

"Sure, but you'll have to undo these cuffs first."

"Not you." He jabs a thumb at St. Clare. "*Him.*"

"There's that divide again," I mutter. "Do what you need to, but hurry back, okay?"

Lars doesn't even bother to answer me as he stands and heads for the door. St. Clare takes a little bit longer, attention still on me. "I don't know what to make of you."

"I have that thought about myself at least three times a day." I shift again, trying to find a more comfortable position. "I think my butt is numb."

"I'll sort out your butt once I'm back."

The words are heavy with innuendo that make my ears perk up. St. Clare was flirting with me. I'm sure he was. I've thought it before when I was just Perry, and that sort of made sense since I'm not terrible to look at and I'm pretty sure he's gay, but now that he knows who I really am and has had to evade death twice, thanks to me, I would have thought that would dull the shine. Dim the attraction. Wrangle the peen. Whatever. The point is that who the fuck is self-destructive enough to flirt with a guy who could kill them?

As he walks out, my eyes stay pinned to his broad back, and then, very slowly, they dip toward his ass.

I mean … I don't hate it?

Fuck.

What I should be asking is who the fuck is self-destructive enough to flirt with the guy he was supposed to kill?

Me, apparently.

Maybe I really do need that gag.

CHAPTER TWELVE

ST. CLARE

TODAY HAS TAKEN a wild goddamn turn, and I'm still not sure how I feel about it. Could it actually be possible that Perry wants to team up? He was fast to suggest it, which makes me think it could be a plan of his to get close to me and finish the job, but if that was the case … why didn't he finish it last night?

Apparently, it's not hard to get access to me, so would an elaborate plan be necessary?

It's a stretch.

"What do you think?" Lars asks the second we're in the hall alone.

"Does it matter? You've basically already agreed."

"I think it could work."

"Why?" Out of the two of us, I thought he'd be the one who needed the most convincing. "You were ready to kill the guy a few moments ago, and now you want to team up with him?"

"Because if they really are after him, we can use that."

"How?"

"By offering him in a trade. Perry in exchange for information on your brother."

Well, that's an angle I hadn't thought of. "And how do I make this trade when they also want me dead?"

"That's the part we need to figure out. Did the people after him see you?"

I think back to the alleyway. The door was mostly between me and the direction the shots came from, but I don't think it would have blocked enough of me from their sight. "Probably."

"Damn."

"So, how do we do this? Call Yanni and tell him we've got his man, and if he wants him, he owes us Colin and needs to promise to leave me alone?"

Lars runs both hands back through his tight curls. "When you put it like that ..." He glances at my office door. "They'll never go for it."

"Why?"

"You really think he's worth all that?"

"Depends how much they paid him for me."

Lars's expression tightens as he thinks, and I give him space to do it. He's a smart guy, and I've always appreciated his opinion on things, but trading Perry? Just handing him over to someone who wants him killed?

"It also might not be Yanni ..." Lars mutters. "God, there are so many fucking variables."

"Unfortunately for us, we need to figure it out because there's only so long we can keep him handcuffed to that chair."

"You're right." I'm almost shocked that he agrees. "We'll move him to your desk next."

That checks out. "I mean that we can't leave him handcuffed at all."

"You want to let a murderer free?"

"I doubt he's ever murdered anyone."

Lars's eyes bug out. "How the hell can you know that?"

"He told me."

"We believe him now?"

"I'm sorry, did that guy in there scream criminal genius to you?"

That derails some of Lars's confidence. "Maybe not, but he's proved he's capable of anything."

He has, which is why I'm so fucking at war with myself. The obvious answer to all of this is to get rid of him before he gets a chance to kill us first, but it feels like the equivalent of offing a helpless animal. A *baby* animal, which makes it even worse.

"Fucking hell, Reilly." Lars laughs. "You still want to sleep with him, don't you?"

I shrug. "Silver linings and all that?"

"So, what? He fucks you, then kills you?"

I frown, disturbed by that image. "Come on. That man is clearly a bottom."

"My mistake. You fuck him, then he kills you."

"Give and take is important in a relationship."

Lars groans, then turns around and face-plants into the wall. "Was I getting too good at my job? Is that why you're testing me?"

"We could argue that both times, I've needed saving, I've had to do it myself, which would tell me that you're actually the opposite to being good at your job."

"Fuck you."

"It's so hard to find good help these days." I lean back against the wall beside him and cross my arms. The music downstairs is low, making it quieter up here than I'm used to.

"We have to use him," Lars pushes. "If there's even the slightest chance that he could figure out what happened to Colin, we need to take it. I don't think it's a coincidence at all that you were with him when he was attacked. He was supposed to be here."

So that we could use him as bait, apparently.

Don't get me wrong, I'm team get my brother back through any means necessary, but is Perry really the answer? From the little I know about him, he's just as likely to screw that up as anything else in his life, and trading people doesn't really feel like the kind of deal you'd want to be sloppy on.

"This is feeling kind of trafficky to me."

Lars is silent for a while. "Yeah, I get that."

Every day that passes with no answer is another day without Colin. At this point, I'm struggling to hold on to hope that he's not dead. Worry is a heavy rock in my gut, constantly reminding me that I'm missing a part of my life.

But Lars is right. What if it isn't Yanni?

Seems unlikely, considering what an asshole he's been and that he's made vague threats about the fact we won't like what comes next. I can now confirm he's right about that. I don't like this one bit.

"I think … our first step needs to be figuring out who wants me dead."

"Okay."

"When we know that, we can work out how to handle them. As soon as those people are off my case, I can get back to looking for Colin."

"That makes sense. Let me guess: we need Perry to work out who hired him?"

"Correct."

Lars doesn't look any happier about that than I am, but not for the same reasons. "How the fuck do we put up with … all that?"

"He's an acquired taste."

"If you say so. What do we do with him?"

"At this rate …" I'm not even sure myself. "I think we have to trust him."

"Awesome. I've always wanted to be shot in my sleep."

"Does he even have his gun?"

That shuts Lars up. "I'll check him when we go back in."

"All right. Well, if he doesn't have it on him, I'd say we're okay to remove the cuffs?"

"I … guess."

I grab Lars's arm and give it a supportive squeeze. "Seriously, thank you. I'd be a scared ball in the corner if I didn't have you."

He manages a half smile. "I'm worried."

"I know …" I'm trying to figure out how to make him feel better when an idea hits me. "Read me our horoscopes for today."

"Really?"

"Yeah, go for it."

Lars lets out a heavy sigh and pulls his phone from his pocket before opening his go-to app. "Hmm ..."

"What does it say?"

"Apparently, you can't try to control everything today, or it will blow up in your face." His jaw tightens. "You need to go with the flow and try not to take things too seriously."

I have no fucking clue what to say to that. "Eerily on the nose."

"What happened to not believing in them?"

"It's hard to argue the point when I want to know what the hell I do about the handcuffed assassin, and the Capricorn daily horoscope is to go with the flow and see what happens. What's yours?"

Lars groans and clicks over. "I already read it."

"And?"

"And I don't think I want you to know."

"Why?"

He lifts his phone so I can read.

Way to go, Taurus. Today is all about meeting new friends and being open to new experiences. There's a lot of uncertainty in your life at the moment, but if you let your kind spirit guide you and follow through on your promises, you can't go wrong!

My eyebrows must meet my hairline. "New friends?"

"Shut up."

It's hard not to laugh in total disbelief. "I wonder what Perry's is."

"We're not going there."

"Why not?"

"Because I don't want to know."

I bite my lip against the most not-me thought I've ever had. "Let's make a deal. If his is as on the nose as both of ours, we'll let him hide out with us. If it's something random like traffic or money or family or whatever, we send him on his way. Deal?"

"*You*, Reilly St. Clare, are going to trust our fate to the stars?"

I wrinkle my nose. "Don't ever say it like that again."

"Sorry, but this moment is feeling like a win for me."

"It isn't."

"Maybe this is what my horoscope meant about uncertainty. It's like I don't even know you anymore."

"Got a better idea?" I throw back.

"Nope."

"Then let's do it."

Lars pulls me back so that he can go in first. Perry is still in the chair, only he's propped his feet up on the side of my desk and is rocking back and forth on the chair's back legs.

"Having fun?" I ask.

"I was starting to think you weren't coming back and was working on a plan B. I think better when I pace, but this will have to do."

"What star sign are you?" Lars asks.

"Aries, why?"

He huffs in a way that tells me he should have guessed that. For … reasons, I guess? I have no idea what an Aries is supposed to be like, but I'm guessing it's Perry.

"For fuck's sake," Lars mutters before handing over his phone.

Your luck is here, Aries! You've had a rocky few days, and you're in for a close call or two, but you're finally on the right path. Today is your day to ask for what you want, knowing it will be a yes. It's time to take those yeses and spin them into gold, the way only you can do!

Close call or two? Ask for what you want?

Well, if that's not specific enough for us, nothing is.

Lars is watching me, and I shrug. "We *did* say if it was relevant …"

"Well, fuck me." Lars pulls a small set of keys out of his pocket and walks over to Perry. Before he unlocks the handcuffs, he spends a moment patting down his jeans—I'm assuming to make sure he doesn't have a weapon on him.

"What is it?" Perry asks. "What did it say?"

"Today's your lucky day."

His whole face lights up. "I knew it. I had a feeling about today."

Lars gives a wild look to the back of Perry's head as he moves around to unlock the cuffs. "You had a feeling you were going to be shot at?"

"Of course not. I just woke up knowing I was going to like today."

"You *like* being shot at and handcuffed to a chair?"

Perry, rubbing his suddenly free wrists, scowls. "You know, it's like you're deliberately misunderstanding me."

"Why would I do that?" Lars flicks a look my way. "We're *friends* now."

"Really?"

I swear it's killing Lars not to say no. "Well, we'll see."

Perry stands, hands stretching high overhead, wrists red raw. Then he reaches for the cup of water and takes a long sip. "Okay, so first, I need to be fed and to get out of these pants. After that, we work out what to do next."

CHAPTER THIRTEEN

PERRY

LARS, being the great guy that he is, heads down to the cafe to pick up my backpack. His plan is to tell whoever's working that I'm sick and not to expect me for a few days, but I don't see how we're going to unravel a whole-ass wannabe murder plot in that time.

Which means there is a very high likelihood that I'm going to lose my favorite job ever.

Maybe this is the universe's way of getting even with me.

I chew on the granola bar St. Clare pulled from his desk drawer and look out over the nightclub. It's a great view. Still daytime, so the club isn't exactly thriving. There are a few people at the bar, drinks in front of them, working their way through ribs or wings or whatever, but otherwise, it's mostly staff going about their day and getting ready for tonight.

Maybe working in a bar could be fun? Less personal, probably, but more staff to shoot the shit with.

"What are you thinking about?"

I glance over at St. Clare's voice. "What it would be like to work here."

"You really think I'd hire you?"

"Why not?" It's hard to keep the offense out of my voice. "I'm an excellent employee."

"You literally just told me you made me shitty coffee this morning. On purpose."

There my mouth goes getting ahead of myself again. "Maybe this would be a good time to take a vow of silence."

"Is that something you're capable of?" St. Clare's eyes twinkle when I catch them.

"Probably."

That twinkle passes to his mouth as it curls into a grin. "You couldn't last five minutes."

"Not true. I've gone whole days without talking to anyone."

"You?"

"Yes."

"*Days?*"

So maybe days is a stretch. Margot checks in with me too often for that.

"*Shit.* Margy."

St. Clare blinks at me. "What?"

"I'm supposed to be grabbing Margot and Elle dinner tonight."

"Why?"

"Because I finally have money, and so now I'm trying to make up for everything they've done for me."

"And you really think you should be spending any of that money?"

He has a good point. Unfortunately, it's way too late for that. I haven't gone wild, but between rent, overdue bills, and paying Elle back for the laptop, I've spent a tidy chunk of it. If you ask me, I'm putting the money to better use than the original owner did anyway.

Why would you pay to have someone offed when there are plenty of people struggling who you can give the money to? Rich people make me sad. Sure, I'm looked down on for not having a whole hell of a lot, but I'm happy, so shouldn't that be the most important thing? When did it become some huge competition over who can be the most miserable and earn the most money?

"Perry?" he prompts.

"Yeah, I've already spent a bunch, so I don't think it makes a difference how much more I spend."

"How much do you have left?"

"Most of it." Which is better than none of it. "Maybe if I go to Luther, own up to what I did, and then pay the money back, it'll all go away."

"You said you didn't have all the money to pay back."

"Well, no, not right now. But I'm sure they could offer me a payment plan."

St. Clare stares at me for a long time. "Who do you think we're dealing with here? Dr. Evil?"

"Who?"

He ignores the question. "My point is that if these people are willing to kill you over money and me over a nightclub, you really think they're going to forgive your lie and put you on a payment plan?"

"Worth a shot."

"Sure. You let me know how that works out for you."

"I do see an issue with that plan though."

"Only one?"

"If I admit to not killing you, they'll have it confirmed that someone else needs to kill you. So then we're back to square one of you being hunted, and I'm starting to think I like you better alive than dead."

"Oh yeah? Why?"

Why? That's a fair question, so it probably shouldn't be this much of an issue to answer it. I think back on the little happy bubbles I'd get whenever he walked into the cafe and we started our back-and-forth. He's a fun guy. Friendly. Very chatty. And let's face it, lips that rare really shouldn't be wasted and left to rot. "Well, you're funny," I tell him.

"You like me better alive because I'm funny?"

"It's a good quality to have."

St. Clare turns his back on the large window in front of us and tucks his hands into his pockets. "What else?"

"What are other good qualities?"

"That I have, yes."

I swallow, worried I'm going to say the wrong thing because everything sounds like the wrong thing. "You have a brother."

"Not a quality. Try again."

"Ah … and a Lars."

His lips twitch and he shakes his head. "Qualities are like … the way you seem too big for a room. Your enthusiasm and broad shoulders and easy smile."

The smile comes alive before I can stop it. "Your confidence," I find myself saying.

"Confidence?" St. Clare sounds surprised. "My brother has always been the confident one. Nothing gets to him."

"Shit. If that's the case, I'm scared to meet him."

Some of the light leaves his face. "*If* you meet him."

"Are you embarrassed by me?"

"No. I'm beginning to think he's dead."

My heart hurts at that. If there's one way to kill a conversation —pun intended—that's it. I have no idea how I'm supposed to reply to that, except it feels like he needs some comfort and hope, and those are two things I'm pretty fucking good at.

I reach over and give his shoulder a squeeze. It's bigger than I expected, and it's sort of weird to be touching him. Sure, I did that night I patched him up, but it wasn't like this. There were too many competing emotions, and he was rudely bleeding every-where to pay attention to anything else.

"We'll find him," I say, squeezing a bit tighter.

He snorts. "I thought you were going to work on a payment plan?"

"Yeah, but that doesn't mean I have to stop helping you." I'm struck with an idea. "Maybe Luther will give me a name."

"A name?"

"Sure." I'm already getting excited over the idea. "If he tells me who organized the job, we can go straight to the source and find out what's up."

"You really think this Luther guy is your friend?"

"Oh yeah. I've known him for years. We have our own inside jokes and everything."

"Right ..."

It's clear he doesn't believe me, but that's not the worst thing. It means he cares. Which is a bit cute of him, considering we've only just met. "I mean it. I'm going to help you find your brother, umm ..."

"Colin."

"Yes. Colin. Colin will be found."

He watches me, studying my face for a moment. "Why do you care?"

"Why wouldn't I?"

"Because he's not your brother."

I finally pull my hand back. "Well, no, but I feel partially responsible for this mess."

"Only partially."

I crumple the granola bar wrapper in my fist and frown at him. "You're never going to cut me a break, are you?"

"Sorry, it might take a little bit longer than my ear takes to heal."

I eye the bandage on it, curious over how much damage I did to spurn a grudge so large. "Can I see it?"

"See ... what, you want to admire your handiwork?"

"Sure." I shrug. "I'm assuming it's horrifically mangled, judging by the way you keep bringing it up."

"Is there some kind of etiquette for getting over gunshot wounds I don't know about?"

"I'd say a week tops for minor injuries."

"Minor? You think this is minor?"

"Well, I don't think much of anything because I haven't seen it."

St. Clare looks torn on whether he wants to play into this game or not, but now that I've asked, I do really want to see it. Like this itch of expectation and curiosity I'm not going to be rid of until I get a peek.

Finally, he makes up his mind and reaches for his ear. The

dressing is taped down, and when St. Clare removes it, it takes all of my effort not to recoil.

Okay.

That looks nasty.

"What do you think?" He doesn't even try to hold back the challenge in his voice.

"It's … umm … cute."

"Cute."

"You look like an elf."

He buries his face into his free hand. "It should be a whole lot harder not to like you than it is."

"I can see that."

"So why can't I hate you and be done with it?"

It's a good question. Realistically, it would make sense if he hated me. Would be totally justified too. As much as I'd like us all to move on from this moment, I can reluctantly agree that it's a pretty big moment to move on from.

I eye the wound again. It's been stitched up, the top outside section of his ear is missing, and what's left is healing but still doesn't look great. "Have you been disinfecting that?"

St. Clare's hand drops. "Ah, mostly. Lars has been looking after it for me."

"What did the doctor say?"

"Doctor?" he asks in complete disbelief. "I haven't seen one."

"That doesn't seem smart."

"Yeah, well, someone told me to go into hiding, so my decision-making skills were questionable at best that night."

I take St. Clare gently by the shoulders and steer him toward the sofa up against the wall. "Sit."

"Why?"

It's a struggle to keep my patience. "Just do it."

His knees fold underneath him, and he lands on one side of the couch, still eyeing me curiously. "And?"

"Where are the supplies?"

He points toward the cabinet right next to the wet bar, and I open it to find a little of everything. If I had my phone, I could google this shit, but until Lars is back, I'm flying solo, and I really want to get St. Clare all bandaged up quickly. I get the feeling Lars won't be impressed with me wanting a quick glimpse.

Gauze is a given. Antiseptic wipes. Then, a small bandage with one of those little butterfly clips to hold it closed.

I half juggle, half carry it all over to the couch, then climb onto the cushion next to him. "Hold still. I have no idea what I'm doing."

"Comforting."

"A plus for effort though, right?"

"I think a more likely outcome is that I'll end up missing the other half of my ear." Then, St. Clare gives me a soft, secret smile, and something goes off-kilter in my head. "Why don't we wait until you're done before we start giving out ratings?"

All I can do is nod and try not to swallow my tongue. These reactions to him somehow catch me by surprise every time, and it's an effort to avoid the flustering my brain tries to make take over.

His ear.

I'm focused on his ear.

His gross, ruined ear.

With an exhale as loud as a dump truck, I get to work cleaning up the area. I'm slow and careful not to hurt him, picturing his ear as delicate as a butterfly wing. Or Judge Judy's patience.

St. Clare releases a breathy laugh. "Your tongue is poking out."

"Huh?"

"Do you always do that when you're concentrating?"

His question throws me because I wasn't even aware I was doing it this time, so how am I supposed to be aware of it any other time? "No clue."

"It's cute."

There're those squirmies in my gut again. I almost drop the wipe but catch myself just in time, refocusing on his ear and only his ear. Definitely not on him calling me cute.

"Sorry," he whispers.

"For what?"

"If I … if I made you uncomfortable."

Him apologizing to me is just about the funniest thing I've ever heard. He makes me the complete opposite of uncomfortable, but I can't explain that to him when I'm so fucking confused by it myself. "Why would you make me uncomfortable?"

"Most straight guys don't appreciate being called cute."

"But I am cute."

He watches me from the corner of his eyes. "You are."

"I am."

"So we agree?"

"Guess so."

He goes on watching.

I finish cleaning and move on to the bandage. This time, I notice when my tongue slips out, and I quickly tuck it back in again.

His amusement lights up his face, and when he speaks next, his voice has taken on a slight rasp. "And I'm cute too, right?"

The words slide through me like warm coffee on a cold morning. "Cute" isn't the word I would have used. St. Clare is … intimidating. Interesting. Striking.

I've let go of his ear, and he turns his head slightly so that his eyes can snag mine. "Perry?"

"Yeah," comes out before I can stop it. "Yeah, you are."

"Am what?" He's studying my face, the familiar taunting expression filling his. "Say it."

My throat is hard to get words past. "You're very cute."

St. Clare tilts his head in interest. "I didn't say *very*."

"No." Ignoring my nerves, I direct his head back around so I can keep working. "But I did."

CHAPTER FOURTEEN

ST. CLARE

SO HE'S STRAIGHT.

But he thinks I'm very cute.

And I thought this week couldn't get any more confusing.

Perry finishes bandaging my ear, and I'm a good patient, sitting there without teasing him again.

It's hard though. His big hands are so gentle. His tongue is poking out again, and the concentration lines on his forehead, mixed with his scent—lightly sweaty from our run, slightly caffeine-y from work—is making it really fucking hard to keep my mouth closed.

He agreed easily to being called cute, but I don't think he realizes he's sex on legs.

Really long fucking legs.

"Okay," he says, standing and dumping the garbage into the trash. "Next stop, Margy's place."

"No."

"But I have to."

"No, you have to do exactly what you wanted me to do and stay hidden."

He thinks that over for a moment. "I see your point—"

"Good—"

"But no one saw us come here, so they also won't see us leave, and if I really am now being targeted like you say I am, I should probably give my sister the heads-up."

"Use the phone."

When it comes down to it, we still know a whole lot of nothing, and the best thing we can do with today is make a plan and then get straight into it. Visiting sisters doesn't make the list.

"I … well, we don't really know how long this is going to take, and I have a lot of unfinished business …" Perry starts. "It's not like I can totally disappear on my job, and I need to get home to Sir Squeakerton—"

"*Who* is Sir Squeakerton?" I ask.

"A mouse."

"You have a pet mouse?"

"Well, no." He scratches his head. "There are a bunch of mice that live in the wall of my apartment. I'm friends with one of them."

"Friends. With your rodent infestation?"

"They prefer to be called little squeakers."

"I don't care what they prefer," I say, trying to imagine mice in *my* apartment. "They're wild animals. They'll be fine."

It's almost endearing the way he looks so torn until I remember that we're talking about disease-carrying mice.

"Okay, let's make a deal."

I give him a pointed look. "Because those have always gone so well for us before."

"We're working together now though. Our powers combined and whatever."

"Sure. You know Captain Planet and not Austin Powers."

"Who?"

I give up. At the risk of taking another verbal detour, I get us back on track. "What's this deal?"

"We go and deliver Margot and Elle dinner, but we won't stay. I'll tell them that I'm going out of town for a few days and that maybe they should also have a super-romantic lovers' week in Elle's apartment and not leave it for anything."

Right, because that won't make them suspicious. "You think your sister could be a target?"

Perry shrugs. "I'm still not convinced I'm a target, but that doesn't mean I'm going to take any risks with her."

"You guys are super close?"

"She is literally all I have left." The vulnerability in his tone is something I latch onto. Like his human side makes it easier to forgive myself for not being able to hate him.

If our roles were reversed and Colin could potentially be in danger because of me, I'd want to warn him too. It doesn't feel smart, but when it comes to protecting people you care about, emotion is what leads the way.

At least that's something we have in common.

"Fine," I relent. "We'll pick them up dinner—*I'm* paying—tell them whatever you want, and then we'll go back to my apartment."

"Should I grab clothes from mine first?"

"There's a good chance they could be waiting for you there."

Perry scrunches up his face. "Well, wouldn't you also think they'd be waiting for *you* at yours?"

That's also a good point.

"Fuck. Okay. Maybe Colin's?"

"That still feels risky."

Thankfully, Lars takes that moment to get back. He closes the door and locks it behind him, then tosses Perry his backpack.

I watch as Perry sinks to sit on the floor and tugs the zipper open before rifling through whatever the hell he has in there.

"We were just talking about where we should go next," I tell Lars. "Both of our apartments probably aren't safe, and I thought maybe Colin's, but what if they're watching that too?"

He rubs his short beard, thinking. "We can't stay here?"

"And what? Sleep on the floor? Besides, you'd think if someone was looking for me, this would be one of the first places they'd go."

Not for the first time, an unsettling feeling slides down my spine. Being watched, hunted, whatever, it's not a great way to exist. I'm refusing to give in to the fear, and do well ignoring it most of the time, but there are moments, like this one, where it sneaks in and throws me for a second. It's sort of hard to let things roll off you when you realize you have literally nowhere to go.

The seconds stretch on without any of us speaking.

Then Perry's voice cuts through the room.

"Hello, favoritest sister of mine."

I glance up and am shocked to see him on the fucking phone.

His upbeat tone dims a little. "Why do you always think I'm up to something?"

That pulls a smile from me. I'm with Perry's sister. If he called up and immediately gave me a compliment, I'd be suspicious of him too.

"I'm still coming tonight," he assures. "But I kinda sorta need a favor. Not, like, a big favor. More of a medium-big favor."

I have no idea what she's saying, but Perry pulls the phone away from his ear and covers the speaker. "Sorry," he tells us. "She does this. Needs to get the ranty out, then we'll move on to fixing the problem."

"*Ranty?*" explodes from the phone.

Perry cringes, and Lars lets out a full-blown laugh.

"Ah … I love you very much, and I'll see you soon," he says quickly before hanging up. "Phew. By the time I get there, she should have worked off some of her irritation."

"Or built it up ready to unleash on you."

That makes him pause. "Well. Guess we're about to find out."

Lars is shaking his head. "If you want something from someone, you probably shouldn't insult them before they've agreed."

"I wasn't insulting her!" Perry's mouth drops in offense. "It's not an insult if it's true."

"Well, that's definitely incorrect," I point out.

Perry shoves his phone deep into his bag. "We should probably go."

"Wait." Lars looks between us. "As much as I'd love to see your sister go off on you, you're not going anywhere."

"Of course I am." Perry picks himself up off the ground and

pulls his backpack on. Then he throws me under the bus by waving his finger between us. "We have a deal."

"A deal that we haven't finished working out the details on."

"What *deal*?" Lars asks, sounding very much like a dad dealing with toddlers. I'd resent the tone, but in this instance, it's probably fair.

I jump in to explain before Perry … can be Perry. "We're taking his sister dinner, telling her he'll be gone for a few days and that she should probably lie low too, then we're supposed to be going somewhere safe to work out what the hell we do next, but we haven't figured out where."

"And that's why we need to get moving," Perry says. "We'll feed them up, make them happy, and then Elle will have the solution for us. She's very smart and very rich. I've never cared much about the rich thing myself because she's not one of those asshole rich people, but it makes things easier in a pinch. And if you ask me, we're in a bit *more* than a pinch."

I look at Lars because it's not like we have a whole lot of options here. Perry's right. This is definitely more than a pinch.

"Maybe you should call her back," Lars says.

Perry looks at Lars like he's lost his mind, and seeing him give anyone that look is … a choice. "This isn't the kind of conversation you have over the phone. Over the phone is for things like *what did you want me to grab for dinner* or *hey, your parents have died in a car crash*. It's not for warning your sister you're potentially highly wanted and need a safe house."

There's so much there that I really don't know what the fuck to tackle first. Lars apparently doesn't share my confusion.

"You can't tell her you're wanted or that you need a safe house."

"Well, not in those specific words—"

"Not in any words." Lars rubs at his curls in frustration. "Look, none of us know anything yet, other than you were set up to kill St. Clare. That still has you as enemy number one in my books, so it's going to take me some time to come around to this idea that you're suddenly on our side."

"Do I look like a killer?" Perry asks.

"No, and St. Clare is determined to trust you, so I have to as well. All I'm saying is that I'm keeping an eye on you, and until we know more, I don't want to go anywhere or tell anyone anything. How do we know that the safe house your sister comes up with isn't some kind of trap?"

"You don't."

"Exactly." Lars reaches into the back of his pants and pulls out a gun that he drops on my desk. "I also found this in your bag. Who the fuck takes a gun to work in a cafe?"

"Well, it's not like I could leave it lying around at home."

"Why the fuck not? You don't carry it with you unless you're expecting to use it."

Perry sighs, tugging his backpack higher. "It's not loaded."

Lars hesitates before checking.

"I don't leave it at home because my place is notorious for being robbed."

Mice and being robbed? Where the fuck does this guy live?

"We can't stay here," I remind Lars. Even if I didn't think it was being watched, there are no beds, for one thing, and there's only so long that we can survive off granola bars.

"What about your parents?" Lars asks.

"I don't think we can go anywhere near family at the moment."

I can tell he's torn. It's not an easy choice, and when he signed up for this job, neither of us thought it would be actual life and death. We're way out of our comfort zone, and figuring out what to do isn't easy. It probably also doesn't help that I'm running off gut feeling than any kind of actual logic.

"Fine. We'll visit the sister." He turns to Perry. "But if you fuck us over, I won't hesitate to make her pay for your mistake."

Perry looks like he's wet his pants. "I have no plans for that to happen. Intentionally."

Unfortunately, his mistakes by this point are legendary, so that really doesn't give me much hope.

CHAPTER FIFTEEN

PERRY

IT FEELS strange that I only saw Margot this morning, and for some reason, when I get to Elle's place and spot her front door, I have the strongest urge to cry.

Over a door.

Someone help me.

The sushi I picked up is heavier than usual, and I'm relieved St. Clare got the bill for this one because apparently Lars eats a fuckload more than any normal human should. I tried to convince the two of them to wait in the car, but they're both standing behind me when I knock like some kind of bodyguard. Technically, I said I'd help Lars out with protecting St. Clare, but that was a total lie. If he's right that I'm the one in danger, I need Lars's protection just as much as St. Clare does.

That man is going to have his work cut out for him.

The door opens, and it's Elle's smiling face I'm greeted by. With her blond pixie cut, septum piercing, and sweet face, she reminds me of a fairy. A very mouthy, fun-loving fairy.

"Food!" she all but screams in my face before pulling me into a hug. Then she freezes, and when she slowly eases away from me, her gaze is skipping between St. Clare and Lars.

"Ahh, these are my friends."

"You have friends?"

"I have lots of friends, actually."

Elle eyes me suspiciously. "Are these friends in the room with us?"

Is she going blind? I hook my thumb back over my shoulder. "Well, yes. They're literally right there."

She looks them over, and her gaze settles on Lars. "You guys don't look like friends?"

"We're … in our trial period," he answers.

Because of course he does. "You should've asked the other one," I point out.

Elle turns to St. Clare instead. "Same question."

"Same answer." It's like I can hear his smirk as he says it.

"Where's Margot?" I step around Elle. "I'm feeling very outnumbered right now."

"Given she's been cursing your name since you got off the phone, I don't think she's going to help you."

Okay, so I really, really shouldn't have called her ranty. Though on the flip side, you could argue that if she *wasn't* ranty, I never would have called her that. This is on her. Which are words I will never utter aloud.

"Sushi's here," I call, hoping to distract her with food, but she mustn't be hangry because when I join her in the living room, which has been painted to look like a rainbow threw up in here, she's straight up glaring at me.

"Ah … food?" I hold up the bags, and Margot scoffs.

"Stop trying to distract me."

"I'm not. I'm …" I reach into the bag and pull out the spicy tuna rolls. "Bringing a peace offering." I shake the container her way.

"I'm not hangry, asshole."

"Spicy, spicy tuna …"

"*Perry.*"

I slump and slide the container onto the coffee table instead. "I'm sorry, Margy."

"Don't 'Margy' me. What trouble are you in this time?"

Elle, St. Clare, and Lars choose that moment to enter. "Ah, this time?" I try to play off her words. "I don't know what you're talking about."

"You know exactly what I'm talking about. There's *always* something."

I'm trying very, very hard not to get offended, and it might be harder to do if she wasn't, well, right. But I don't need my new friends to know that my sister thinks I'm a complete fuckup, thanks. I've put in the hard work to get St. Clare to like me, and I sort of want to keep it that way.

"So, these are my friends ..." I mutter.

She barely even looks at them. "Come on. What are we bailing you out of this time?"

An acidic taste fills my mouth, and I try to swallow it all back. I love Margot, and I hate the thought of disappointing her, but I never seem to be able to stop. "N-nothing," I say. "No favor. Just dinner."

Her expression softens from a replica of Mom's disappointment to Dad's worry. "Are you okay?"

"Always."

Margot and Elle exchange a look.

"Anyway, I have to ... to drop this off. We're, umm, headed out of town for a few days. Maybe longer—"

"What about your job?"

"I cleared it with them." It hurts to lie, knowing that I probably won't have a job next week.

"You just started. They can't be happy about that."

"I am allowed days off."

Before Margot can get cranky with me again, St. Clare takes over. "It's my fault. I have a family emergency, and Perry offered to give me a ride out of town."

Margot glares at him. "Who are you?"

"His ... friend."

"On a trial period, apparently," Elle adds.

"Well, sorry, friend," Margot says, crossing her arms. "But Perry needs his job. He can't afford to take time off."

"Maybe you two need to have this conversation literally anywhere else," Elle says. "*Away* from people."

Margot turns on her heel and storms off toward the bedroom, and I hurry after her. There's only a short, bright purple hall from the living area into the sunshine-yellow bedroom, but when I get there, she's standing by the bed, hands buried in her thick, black hair.

I close the door softly behind me, and she glances up.

"Why are you doing this?" she whispers.

"I … family emergency."

Margot rolls her eyes so hard I'm surprised they stay in her skull. "You always do this. You get a decent job, start making money, look like you might be able to support yourself, and then *something* comes up. Every time. I can't keep going through this with you."

It's hard not to cry at that. Gotta say, knowing that I keep letting her down hits me hard, but this isn't my fault. Mostly. Sort of. *She* wanted me to get a job!

Before I can start my feeble defense, she sits on the side of the bed and pats the place beside her.

I sit and immediately wrap my arm around her. "I'm an idiot. I'm sorry."

"You're not an idiot. That's the frustrating part."

"I make terrible choices, then."

That gets a tiny laugh from her. "You *really* do."

"You can tell me to fuck off, you know? Make me deal with these issues alone."

"I don't want you to do it alone. It's just … and I …"

"What?"

Her big eyes are sad all the way through when she looks at me. "I wish that *I* could help you instead of it being Elle all the time. And even more than that, I wish you'd help your damn self."

"I'm trying."

"You say that, but I'm yet to see it."

Unfortunately, that's fair.

She sighs. "Okay, out with it. What is this not-very-big but medium-big-sized favor?"

"Well … you know how Elle's brother has that apartment he doesn't use?"

Margot's mouth flattens, which isn't a good sign, but that doesn't stop me.

"Any chance we could use it for a couple of days? A week, tops. Probably. And we'll keep it super clean and look after his stuff and—"

"I thought you were going away. Family emergency?"

Dammit, St. Clare. "Look, this doesn't work very well if you keep asking me questions because I'm not smart enough to answer them all."

"Are you in some kind of trouble? Because if those men are bad news, all you have to do is give me a sign. We can protect you."

I know she thinks that, but nothing on fucking Earth will make me put her at risk. I force what's supposed to be an easy smile. "I'm fine. Nothing to worry about. I promise."

She doesn't believe me. "If something happens to you—"

"It won't. I just … we really need somewhere to go. Just for a little bit."

She eyes me. "Your apartment finally getting fumigated?"

"Something like that." There's extermination going on, but it has nothing to do with bugs.

I can tell it's completely against everything she wants to say when she gets out, "I'll see what I can do."

"You're the best." I watch her expectantly.

"Right." She doesn't make an attempt to move.

"We're sort of on a time crunch."

She gets up to leave, but before she can reach the door, I can't help but add, "Oh, and if you and Elle could call off work for a few days, maybe lie low, spend some time really reconnecting or whatever, that would be a huge help."

Margot's frozen, hand on the doorknob, shoulders pulled up near her ears. "Got it," she finally says before leaving.

I'm never going to live this one down.

CHAPTER SIXTEEN

ST. CLARE

WHEN WE STEP into the apartment, my jaw just about hits the floor. *This* is our super-secret hideout? Completely modern penthouse with new-looking furniture, a shitload of space, and parquetry floors so fucking polished I can make out my reflection in them?

It almost makes up for being shot at.

"Holy fuck," Lars lets out, striding ahead and pulling back the curtains in the living area. He reveals a deep red sunset, bathing Seattle in shadows, no neighboring building impeding the view.

So this is how the other half lives.

"Three bedrooms," Lars calls out. "One each."

"Convenient."

"I'll take the one closest to the front door. St. Clare can have the main; pest, you can have the other."

"Pest?" Perry echoes, dropping his backpack off onto the enormous couch.

"Well, you're not exactly welcome."

"I happen to think I'm an excellent asset to the team."

Lars raises his eyebrows my way. "He would."

"I dunno ..." I watch the way Perry tests out the bouncability of the couch before moving on to inspecting the random knickknacks through the space and landing in the kitchen, where he pulls open every drawer and cupboard in front of him. "He's less of a pest and more like … our mascot." *Cute* and *entertaining* being the first two words I think of when it comes to him. That, and his puppy dog eyes. "Like a pet."

Perry checks the date on a box of mac and cheese. "I could be a pet."

Of course he could.

"As long as I'm not expected to wear a tail or anything like that. I'm game to try it if that's what you really want, but I have a hunch it's not for me."

"I don't think the tail is necessary."

He drops the box onto the counter and rubs his lower stomach. The apron is gone, but his thin shirt tugs up a little, showing off the skin above his jeans. "No, but food is. If we don't get something soon, I'm gonna have to tear into two-months-expired pasta."

"We just ate," I remind him.

"I'm a growing boy."

"You're actually not."

He huffs and rips into the box.

"Stop." Lars's face is pulled up in disgust. "I'll duck down to the convenience store we passed on the way here for food and maybe some clothes if they have them. Both of you stay here. Maybe take a shower."

"Together?"

I choke on fucking air at Perry's question. "Was that an invitation?"

"Wh-what? No. I …" He thrusts his finger Lars's way. "He wasn't clear!"

Lars looks worried for him again. "I didn't think that was something that needed clarifying."

Perry's head hangs back, and I'm not sure whether he's talking to us or the ceiling. "I should have let them shoot me."

Lars's head tilts to the side. "Was *that* an invitation?"

"Just go and get food."

He's laughing as he leaves, and it's not until the front door bangs closed behind him that Perry risks a look around again.

"He's gone," I confirm.

"He called me a pest."

I'm about to point out that he is a fucking pest and that Lars still isn't over the fact Perry almost killed me, but the guy has had a hard enough night. Visiting his sister really opened up a side of him I wasn't expecting—mostly because I assumed that everyone who meets Perry falls into his spell. It happened with me, I can see it happening with Lars, and all the people at the cafe who ever said so much as a word to him brightened instantly.

His sister was fucking ruthless.

I probably shouldn't say anything, but it's not like uncomfortable conversations are anything new for us, and we don't have a lot else to talk about.

"Is she always that hard on you?"

"Who?" He turns to another cupboard and starts pulling out packaged food at random.

"Your sister."

For some reason, he looks surprised. "She's not hard on me. She's tired."

"She was really worked up." I'm not sure whether to say more, but I sort of want to make him feel better. The downtrodden look he wore should never, ever be on his face. "I didn't like it."

"Me either, but probably not for the same reasons." Perry checks the date on a box of cereal, and it must pass because he pops it open and tears into the bag. Then he heads over to sit on the enormous couch. He takes the end closest to the large windows, and with night well and truly kicking in, the city is alive with lights.

The lights in here aren't on, and I don't bother to change that as I join him. "Want to talk about it?"

"About my sister?" He turns a fruit loop over between his fingers. "I hate making her like that."

"You didn't make her like anything. She overreacted."

His sad smile doesn't do much to make me feel better about the whole thing. "If this was the only time, I'd agree with you. Margot has been there for me my entire life. Through everything. All the good and the bad, and I never doubted I'd have her support. Unfortunately, what you saw was years and years' worth of this same thing building up on her. She worries a lot, even more since our parents died, and I wish she didn't, but I can't seem to find that balance between what I want for my life and what she wants."

"What does she want?"

"I dunno …" He throws the fruit loop into his mouth and talks around it. "A good job, nice place, probably a wife and kids."

I bristle at that. "Specifically a wife?"

"Well …" His gaze flicks to me and away again, stirring that something in my gut. "No. I don't think she's ever said that. Actually, I don't think being married and having kids are requirements on her list. When it comes down to it, Margot wants me to be happy and stop stressing her out so much."

"And that's different from your list, how?"

"It's not." He sounds surprised. "When you really get down to it. I think I've reached a point where I'm so used to fucking up I expect it. Hell, I think I even welcome the challenge. The change. It keeps things interesting."

"You like fucking up?"

He's clearly at war with himself. "No. Yes? I mean, I must since I keep doing it. Some days, I think everyone is making life so much harder than it needs to be and that if we'd all calm down and see what happens, we'd be a lot happier. Not everyone needs a twelve-point plan with goals and spreadsheets. Some people have to make a whole heap of mistakes until they get it right."

I'm starting to maybe understand where Margot is coming from. Because maybe Colin is a little bit the same, and one of our last conversations comes back to me. "And some people need those goals and spreadsheets because they can't afford to make mistakes."

"What do you mean?"

I shift a cushion closer to him and turn to the side so I can see him properly. Perry mirrors me, half lying against the couch as he eats his way through a box of dry cereal. "I think we're probably more similar than I'd like."

"Why?"

"Because I'm the brother who gets to make all the mistakes and have all the fun, while Colin is always having to think three steps ahead. I don't have a fucking clue how much pressure it must be to always be thinking of everything all the time, and I guess you don't either."

"You're saying that I use up her share of mistakes?"

"Every relationship needs a stable one."

Perry crunches softly, and I reach over to steal one as well. We've already had dinner, so I might as well follow it up with dessert. "You seem pretty stable to me," he says.

"The night we met, I was planning to confront a potential crime lord solo."

His eyes crinkle. "You're good at hiding it, then."

"Before Colin went missing, I was planning to sleep with the guy writing a feature article on us."

Perry's chuckle is a warm rumble in his chest. "That could have gotten messy."

"Very. Just like this. Now. Choosing to trust the guy who tried to shoot me."

"Counterargument." He brushes off his hands and sets the cereal down, then moves closer. His knee is right by my knee. "I tried to shoot you *one* time. I've tried to help you *twice* now. One count not-murder. Two counts savior. Two is better than one."

"You've said."

"And it still stands. Plus, if we add the countless coffees I've made you, it really tips the scales in my favor."

"I can get behind that theory."

He leans in a little closer, shit-eating grin in place. "*And* you think I'm cute. That's about a thousand points on its own."

My face inches closer to his as well. "Oh yeah? Then how many points is *very* cute?"

"A thousand more than that."

My gaze darts to his lips before meeting his eyes again. I'm so fucking sure I see interest there, but with Perry, it's sort of hard to tell. He looks enthusiastic about almost everything, and I'd hate to misread him. "How many points would it be if I thought you were the sexiest guy I've ever met?"

His eyes widen like fucking Bambi, and it's like I've stolen his tongue. "I-I don't think there's a point system for that," he whispers.

"Shame. I think that would be the thing to tip the scales."

"There you go, then." He swallows roughly. "I'm not a bad choice at all. You could almost say you'd be ridiculous not to trust me. I'm a sure thing. A guarantee."

"You also have no idea what words are coming out of your mouth and how they sound right now."

"I possibly lost consciousness around the word *sexy*."

"Technically, it was *sexiest*."

"Sure, say it again. That makes everything better when you do."

It's almost impossible not to laugh. We're so close I could count every one of those long, thick eyelashes, could pluck each shade of brown from his eyes, and finally read the interest staring back at me.

"Perry …" My voice is hard to recognize. "Are you sure you're straight?"

His lips part, and I wait for the immediate confirmation. It doesn't come.

"I'm not sure of anything anymore."

CHAPTER SEVENTEEN

PERRY

ST. Clare leaves to shower, and the place where he was sitting haunts me like I could still reach out and touch him. Sitting so close should have been a lesson in hygiene, given we're both covered in dry sweat, but I only wanted to lean in more.

There's something going on in my head, and after learning about how Elle always thought she was straight until she met Margot, I have a guess at what it is. And it's not the first time.

Some men are intimidating. I look up to them. Am drawn to them. Maybe sometimes that respect turns to interest, and that interest becomes something that gets my cock going.

I've never acted on it. Never had it come on so strongly that I *wanted* to act on it, but with St. Clare, knowing that he's available and would potentially want that is giving me thoughts I've never thought before.

The last time I had this reaction to someone, it was one of the dads at a kid's birthday party I was working. He snuck away for a joint, and when I stumbled upon him, we shared that joint between us, him holding it to his lips and then to mine, progressively standing closer and closer before he cuffed me on the shoulder of my Trolls costume and disappeared back into the house.

He gave off asshole vibes. We didn't speak a word. I was able to shake off the burning lust easily and get on with my day like nothing had happened.

But I don't even smoke weed—my mom would have killed me —just like I don't usually get all tongue-tied around men and draw smiley faces on their cups.

I'd thought St. Clare was going to kiss me and *moved closer*.

I'd thought he was going to kiss me, and now I'm *disappointed* that he didn't.

Huh.

Maybe this whole thing is supposed to be my journey of self-discovery. Forget the madmen with guns—myself included—all these events were purely meant to bring me and St. Clare together. The universe is a wild and wonderful thing.

At this point, I need a silver lining, and I'm clinging to it.

The sound of the shower reaches me from down the hall, and I'm struck by a sudden thought.

St. Clare is naked.

Totally naked.

Not very far away.

He fills out those suits, and his shoulder felt nice under my hand earlier, so I can't stop my thoughts from straying to how muscular he is. I'm a big guy, mostly due to my natural state of desperate survival and fast metabolism, but his muscles are different. Gym built, I'd say. Nothing like Lars, but as I sit there, filling in the blanks and trying to remember what his body looked like the night we met, my cock gives a little tug of impatience.

I've been hard since he was sitting next to me, and I wonder if he was the same. I wonder if he's in the shower right now, water streaming over his front, hand wrapped around his dick.

I groan and press down on my groin. No matter how flirty and good-looking he is, I can resist this. It's not hard. I do it a lot.

Margot came out when she first started high school, so it's not like I'm ashamed of these feelings. It's more complicated than that. I'm one part convinced it's all in my head and doesn't count if I've never been with a man, and the other part doesn't want to … like

… encroach on Margot's space. I take so much from her that if *I'm* queer too, it's another thing she has to share with her ridiculous little brother. She had a hard time being herself in high school, but she did it anyway, whereas I was too focused on keeping my position on the football team to let myself think of anything else.

Margot had to do the hard yards.

I got to hide.

Suddenly deciding that I want to kiss a guy and then just doing it feels like a slap to the face of all of that.

Or maybe I'm confused.

It's not a stretch for me. I'm confused about ninety percent of my life that being confused about this, too, checks out. If I'm still making this many excuses to ignore my attraction, then I'm probably not ready for it, am I?

Before I can get answers to any of my questions, the front door clicks open and Lars walks in, those melon-smuggling arms full of bags.

That are probably full of food.

I perk up. "What did you end up getting? You left too fast for me to put an order in."

"I'll add that to my list of life regrets."

"I appreciate it."

Lars almost smiles as he dumps the bags onto the kitchen counter. "Got this for you."

I watch as he reaches into one of the bags and pulls out a T-shirt that he throws at my chest. I catch it and then hold it out to see the front. It's a puppy with floppy ears, big eyes, and a goofy expression. Underneath the image are the words "Friends fur-ever!"

It's the greatest thing I've ever seen. "You do love me!"

"Don't get excited. It was that or a Seattle tourist shirt, and that was the only one with an animal on it."

"Friends fur-ever …" I drag the word out and give Lars my puppy dog eyes. "You're a big softie under all that Johnny Bravo swagger, aren't you?"

"I don't swagger."

"But you are a softie."

He still doesn't acknowledge me.

"So what's St. Clare's deal?"

"What do you mean?"

"Like … why would someone want to kill him anyway? Is Saint Clare's a front for something?"

"It's a nightclub."

"Yeah, but you know most nightclubs are a front for drugs … or, umm …"

"Umm?"

"Well, *nefarious* deeds."

"Nefarious deeds, huh? You watch too many movies."

"It wouldn't be so common in movies if it wasn't true."

Lars pulls out some crackers and cheese slices and throws them both at me. "If you're eating, you're not talking."

"Not true. I'm talented enough to do both. At the same time."

"No one wants to see that."

"I'm just saying that if you think this will shut me up, it won't."

He hums and starts unpacking the bags. "I'll remember fudge next time."

"I'm up for the challenge."

I don't notice the sound of the shower has stopped before St. Clare joins us, clutching a towel around his waist, wet hair slicked back and dripping onto his neck.

"Did you find clothes?" he asks Lars, and it's lucky no one expects me to talk because shirtless is a good look for him.

He's not as big as I'd originally imagined, and I adjust that image to mesh with the real deal. Soft lines and round pecs and broad shoulders at odds with his trim waist. The towel is slung seductively low, and neither of them pays it any attention as Lars hands over some clothes and St. Clare turns to get changed in another room. As he walks away, I clock a drip of water slipping down the groove of his spine, and I follow its path all the way to the swell of his ass, barely covered by the fluffy material.

A loaf of bread hits my face, and Lars's laugh follows it.

"What was that for?"

"Looked like you needed to come back to Earth."

St. Clare is gone—pity—so I turn my attention to Lars instead. "How do you *know* you're straight?"

He moves into the kitchen and starts putting everything away. Maybe I should help him, but this is an important discussion, and concentrating on more than one thing at a time isn't my strong suit.

"I have a best friend who's gay, have never been all that concerned about labels, but when it comes to attraction, all I've ever been interested in is women."

"Right. That's … conclusive. But tell me: what if it's only ever women, and then, occasionally, you'll see a guy who gives big Dom vibes, and that sort of does it for you?"

He stares at me. "Wait. Wait, wait. Tell me … tell me you're not talking about—"

"*Shhh!*" I throw a look back down the hall. "Maybe not professional will-spank-you Dom … just … would respectfully tell me what to do and be super confident and good in bed type of …" The words I'm saying suddenly catch up to me. "You know what? Forget I said anything."

"Wish I could."

"This never happened."

"Wish it didn't."

"Pass me that bottle of Coke, please? I'd like to start attempting to drown myself."

He hands over the bottle, then crosses his arms on the counter. "Take it easy. We still need you."

"For what? Sexual harassment? I can tell you that you have a great ass, too, before I off myself if you'd like?"

"I'd prefer you didn't. What I *do* need from you is to find out this name for us. You said you could."

"Sure. Luther will be able to tell me."

"You sound confident about that."

"No reason not to be."

Lars runs his eyes over me, but not in the sexy way St. Clare does. More in the can't believe I'm real way. I'm taking it as a compliment. "No reason other than the fact the guy takes money to facilitate crime."

"Yeah, but he owns a labradoodle."

"And?"

Now, I'm struggling to believe Lars is for real. And it's *not* a compliment. I explain slowly. "He owns a labradoodle. One of the purest pooches on earth. *No one* who owns a labradoodle is a bad person. It's, like, the law."

"The law."

"Never happened."

"And you've seen to this personally, have you?"

"Don't believe me. You'll see."

"Well, considering you're doing it tomorrow, at least if you die, it means I won't have a chance to get attached."

If I die.

Well, that's one way to smack me in the face with it, I guess.

Full confidence in Luther, obviously, but also … what if I'm wrong? Could I actually fucking die? What if St. Clare is right and they really were targeting me?

That means I actually *almost* died today, and I have to say, being on the other side of things isn't a great feeling. What would Margot think if I suddenly died? Just … never came back to her? Would she be searching for me the way St. Clare has been searching for his brother?

Would she finally get a moment to relax then?

It would be easy enough to be like, "nah, not gonna do it," but we don't have any other options. Either try to get Luther to spill the info or play hopscotch between housing until these guys finally catch up with us.

All I can do is hope that Luther is the doodle-daddy I think he is.

Being reminded that the big D could be coming your way helps put things into perspective though. Does it matter if I'm attracted to St. Clare? Or other guys? If something happens to me tomorrow, no one will know much of anything about that.

At least then I won't need answers to the millions of incessant questions I have.

I force a grin Lars's way. "Guess I better not die, then," I tell him. "I can't let you get out of liking me that easily."

CHAPTER EIGHTEEN
ST. CLARE

I'M WELL and truly ready to sleep and finally rid my mind of the image of Perry sitting on the couch in his underwear, legs propped up on the coffee table as he rubbed cream between his thighs. The hitched breaths and moans were torture and becoming impossible to shake from my memories.

I already jerked off in the shower. I'd say it was a weak moment, but it's been building inside me all day, and the relief that flowed through my limbs as I touched myself thinking of him was too much to resist.

And now, thanks to that pornographic display of first aid, I'm going to have to do it again.

Perry is fucking with my head. He's not sure of *anything* anymore? Fuck me. He's either one of those straight guys who get off on a gay man's attention, or he's not so straight, and knowing that's a possibility is breathing new life into my attraction.

I tuck my hands behind my head, staring up at the dark ceiling. There are so many more important things I should be thinking about—Colin, who wants me dead, whether I'm still going to be alive in a week—that it takes real power on Perry's end to be the one coming out on top.

He has that vibe about him that makes everyone want to pay attention.

And when they don't, he unintentionally does something stupid that gets their attention anyway.

My lips tug up in a smile over that.

Do I really think Perry is an idiot? Not at all. Under the negative self-talk and his external optimism over just about everything else is a smart man who loves his sister and is struggling to find his way out of a bad situation.

A situation he put himself in, sure, but he figured it out soon enough.

I'm sure there are plenty more people out there who would have kept going until their bullet hit. And even more people who would have killed me as soon as their own life was on the line.

But instead of that option, he wants to team up and get to the bottom of this.

Because above everything, Perry is a good person.

I'd said we're more alike than I thought, but deep down, I'm not so sure I *am* a good person. Friendly and generally kind to people fits, but where Perry is putting what's right first, I don't think I'd be able to make that call. I'm too selfish.

Which isn't a fun realization to have.

Maybe I'm better off smothering myself with a pillow—at least then I'll do Perry a favor by finishing the job for him—and then Lars won't need to worry about being dragged into this mess that has literally nothing to do with him.

Maybe I should check my horoscope for tomorrow and see if offing myself is in my future.

There's a soft knock at the door, derailing those thoughts.

"Yeah?" I call out, not bothering to get up. Lars probably wants to complain about Perry some more—or do a sweep of the room to make sure he hasn't snuck in here to kill me in my sleep—and I really don't need to be standing for either of those things.

Instead of Lars though, I glance over to see Perry slipping through the small opening and quickly closing the door behind himself. His appearance makes me sit up immediately, but he doesn't have his gun.

In fact, as he leans back against the door, I realize he doesn't have much of anything. Just the too-small novelty shirt, which, by the way it clings to his muscles, was more of a gift for me than him, and his navy boxer briefs. Those are at least the right size for him, but as my gaze lingers on his crotch, I can make out just as much as through his T-shirt.

I suck a quick breath in through my nose. "What are you doing?"

"Ah …" His hands are tucked behind him, and he taps his fingers against the door. "Wanted to … say hey."

"Hey," I respond dryly, eyeing the nervous body language and the way that, even though he's in my room, he looks like he's trying to put as much distance between us as possible. "Was that all?"

"Yes." He jerks to the side, like he's going to walk out again, but stops. His chest rises on a deep breath. "No."

"No?"

"Lars thinks I'm going to die," rushes from him.

"He what?"

Some of Perry's awkwardness fades as he paces to the center of the room. "With Luther. Thinks that I'm probably going to be killed tomorrow, and I know it's probably not fair complaining about this to you, but I don't actually want to die. Even if it might seem like an easy way to avoid Margot's disappointment, I can't fix any of it if I'm dead. And I want to fix things. A lot of things. Too many things to die."

I pat the bed beside me, and Perry doesn't hesitate to take up the spot. "You said you trust Luther."

"I do! Did. I mean, I don't think he'll hurt me or anything, but then Lars put the what-if in my head, and now I'm having a case of the doubts."

"I think that's normal."

His breathing is loud, like he's working himself up. "There's so much I haven't done yet."

I tilt my head, curious. "Like what?"

"Like … I can't solve a Rubik's cube. Or play an instrument. And I've never skipped a rock, like, ever."

"You don't want to die because you've never skipped a rock?"

"Don't sound so shocked." His voice takes on that sweetly indignant higher pitch. "We didn't go to the water much as a kid. I can barely swim."

I wouldn't have guessed that. Actually, I wouldn't have guessed any of his list because when I think about why *I* don't want to die, it's as simple as I want to keep going with my life. Not that I have this list of random things I've never done. "Well, why don't you get through tomorrow, and then we'll *both* go to the beach and learn how to skip rocks together?"

"You don't know how to either?"

"Nope. I didn't realize that was a huge failure on my part."

His dark eyes meet mine, gaze flicking from one eye to the other. "What's one thing you've always wished you could do?"

"I have spent exactly zero percent of my time thinking of the answer to that question."

His lips twitch, and he nudges me. "Think now."

What do I always wish I'd done? There're plenty of things that look fun. Skydiving, riding a Jet Ski, running a train on someone, but while they sound great in theory, I'm not so sure I'd ever actually *want* to experience them. I'm an okay cook, and I have no interest in being more than that. I don't want a garden or to learn an instrument or to raise a herd of wild mountain goats ... Finally, after dismissing what feels like every hobby on Earth, I land on something super simple. Something that looks easy, that my cousins used to do all the time, and that I never mastered.

"It would be cool to roller-skate."

"Oooh, that's a good one."

Of course that's his response. "I don't actually want to go roller-skating or anything; I just want to do it. Once. So I know that I can."

Perry holds out his hand. "When we've both got the all clear, and Colin's found, and Margot's no longer pissed with me, we'll learn those things."

Considering his list of tasks to do first feels impossible, there's no risk when I reach out and shake his hand. "Deal."

"We have a lot of deals."

"We do. And I can't help but notice you're the one who comes up with them all."

He taps his temple with his free hand. "I'm the brains behind this operation."

"And what am I? Because we both know it isn't the brawn."

Perry's gaze immediately drops to my bare chest. It lingers there for long enough to make my skin prickle, and his thumb slides across the back of my hand he's still holding.

Perry swallows. Loudly.

"So there's, umm …" he whispers. "There's one thing that I … that if I die, I'd sort of like to do first."

Fuck. Just his voice and stare is enough for my nipples to harden. I really, really need Perry to stop looking at me like that, and then I need him to get the hell out of my room so I can jerk off again.

Big, sweet, and beautifully dopey. I have no idea why my body has decided it's suddenly obsessed with him, but I guess this is the torture I'm dealing with until further notice.

"St. Clare?"

Was he talking? "Yeah?"

"Do … do you want to know what that is?"

I have to kick-start my brain to remember what he said. "The thing you want to do before you die?" I internally cringe at the way I word that, but fuck it. My brain is at half capacity, and I'm glad I have the sheets pulled up over my waist because the tent I'm pitching would be enough to poke out his eye.

"Yeah."

"What is it?"

His hand tightens around mine, and he looks half-terrified, half-hopeful as he says, "I've never kissed a man before."

"Oh." The confession steals all the breath from my lungs.

"And I'd really like to kiss you."

CHAPTER NINETEEN

PERRY

MY GUT IS CHURNING with the seas of a thousand nerves. I've never felt like I could simultaneously cry and throw up, but as I send myself light-headed waiting for his response, I'm dangerously close to either one of those things.

St. Clare's pretty bowed lips have parted enough to see where his bottom lip is shiny with spit. I want to lean in and taste it. To run my tongue over that lip before pushing into his mouth. I've been in this position before—this consuming, lustful state—but never with another guy, and finally being on the edge of the experience is a relief as much as it is terrifying.

All it took was my potential murder to get me here.

I'm half-hard and hopeful. Sort of want to beg, but I won't because that would be weird. Probably. But as St. Clare goes on for longer and longer without an answer, the urge gets stronger. I'm just one man, dammit.

"You want to kiss me?" he finally asks.

"Ah, yeah. I think so."

"It's more of a yes or no answer, Perry." His voice has deepened and sounds raw, as raw as I feel.

"Y-yes." I can't stop the way my voice shakes. I really, really do want this, but admitting I want it is hard. The familiar instinct to suppress is strong, and I'm fighting that as much as I'm fighting the urge to get on my knees, ready to see his dick one time.

It's hard to know if I'm even ready for that when my heart is beating so hard in my throat that I'm close to coughing it out.

"You're breathing really fast," he says, and it feels like he's closer, but that also could be my, you know, complete and utter panic fucking with my perception. Good panic though. Definitely good. The bubbly high filling my head, the clammy hands, the urge to stand up and shake out my whole body, it's so, so good. The little jolt that spears through my gut every time we inch closer. Good.

It's all so fucking good.

"You want to kiss me because you think you're going to die?"

"Actually, I want to kiss you because you have a very pretty mouth, and that gets my dick hard."

His lips kick up with an unintentional "Heh."

"I want to do it *now* because it's a teeny tiny bit possible I could die tomorrow." I'm still holding on to my stubborn denial that it won't happen, obviously, or there's no way I'd be able to go through with it, but at least if we do this, it's one thing crossed off my list. One curiosity answered.

Will I like it?

St. Clare reaches up, fingers sliding over my jaw in a way that makes me forget which way I'm breathing. His palm finds my cheek, and oxygen eventually finds my lungs, and I'm breathing through my mouth in an intense state of expectation.

"Perry?"

"Y-yeah?"

"Kiss me."

Hearing those words makes me surge forward. My eyes squeeze closed, I grip his face between my hands, and I smoosh our lips together so hard I swear I nearly break his nose. My heartbeat is so fucking loud it takes a moment to pick up that St. Clare's grunt was *not* a good one.

He jerks back from my hold. "Well, that was aggressive."

"Thanks?"

"Not in a good way." He wipes his mouth on the back of his hand.

Wow. Right. That doesn't hurt. "It was my first time," I try to defend.

"First time what? Being *around* another human?"

"Kissing a man."

"What if I told you it's not all that different to kissing a woman?"

"I'd ask you if you've ever kissed a woman before because that was nowhere even close to being the same."

"Good. It's a relief that you don't go around attempting to pull the head off *everyone* you hook up with."

"I didn't try to pull off your head!" I'm so loud I'm surprised Lars doesn't burst in here. "I was nervous, okay? That's a perfectly normal, totally fine thing to be, and I don't think that a little, well, *passion* is such a bad thing, actually."

"I agree. It's not."

I grunt and fold my arms over my chest. "You're complaining about it pretty loudly right now."

"No, I'm complaining about your attempt to eat my face. That was completely absent of passion."

"And now you're insulting my kissing skills."

"I would be … if that was kissing."

I finally look over at him again. "Then what the hell do you call it?"

"A personal attack on attraction everywhere?"

I *humpf* and turn away again. "Well, if that's how you feel, I'll just take my attraction somewhere it's appreciated."

"I don't think that place exists, Perry."

I'm about to get up and storm out of the room when St. Clare pulls me back onto the bed almost as fast as I stand. Then he throws one leg over my waist, straddling my thighs, and like that, I've forgotten everything I was supposed to be doing.

My hands are up in front of me like a busted perp, and my jaw is down somewhere around my aching balls.

He smirks, a light breaking through the deep offense I'm

riddled with, and when he takes my hands and sets them on his hips, I finally remember how to swallow.

"You are way too high-strung," he murmurs, gaze settled back on my mouth. "And you have an abnormally large Adam's apple."

"Are you insulting me again?"

"No. It just means you can't swallow around me, ever, because it's a kink I wasn't aware I had before, and every time you do it, it makes me want to lick your throat."

I'm still in complete shock when I do it again.

St. Clare groans. "Don't test me."

This time, I do it on purpose.

He jerks my head upward before his wet tongue finds my collarbone and slides tortuously up my neck. When his lips dip back by my ear, his voice is huskier than before. "I could lick every single inch of you, and it wouldn't be enough."

Mentally, I'm imagining him doing just that. A roadmap of his mouth's expedition as it passes over the most sensitive areas.

My grip on his hips tightens as St. Clare kisses his way along my jaw. He's getting closer to my mouth, teasing the thing I want most, and when he's a whisper away, I turn my head so his mouth lands on mine.

Sweet relief fills everything from my ears to my toes, and St. Clare groans at the contact. The sound is so deep in his chest it rumbles against mine, and I want to steal that sound from him and play it on repeat forever.

Unlike our first kiss—which was totally a kiss—the pressure of controlling it is taken away from me, and I'm able to enjoy it for what it is. The press of lips on lips. Soft and slow. Hard and fast. Slow and hard. Fast and soft. It's an alternating explosion of sensations that hasn't done anything to fill my curiosity and instead has exploded that curiosity into a million more tiny pieces. My brain isn't big enough to hold all those pieces though. I barely have time to catch my thoughts as they bubble away into blissful nothingness. Nothing but his mouth and his hands on my shoulders, one of them scraping up the back of my neck to tangle in my hair and the other dipping lower, resting over my chest, thumb gently flicking over my nipple in a way that tugs an embarrassing *nrgh* from my throat.

He chuckles, lips smiling against mine before his tongue dips out to slide over my bottom lip. Without thinking, I suck it into my mouth.

St. Clare freezes, and then, with a bone-melting moan, his mouth crashes against mine. Deep and consuming, his kiss makes my toes curl over and my thumbs find that soft skin beside his hip bones as my grip on him anchors me to Earth. He holds me tighter, kisses me so deep that breathing becomes more of an optional thing. An optional thing that comes second to falling into the kiss and letting it destroy me.

My neck and cheeks are burning up, St. Clare's grip on my hair tightening, reeling us closer like a fish caught helpless on a line, and when his cock nudges mine, my eyes roll back into my skull.

I've never been so willingly trapped before, and when St. Clare goes to back off, I grunt and pull him closer.

Through our underwear, our cocks line up. Dueling hardness seeking relief, which only gets worse as he ruts against me. His bare chest is hot through my shirt, and I wish that we were wearing one hundred percent fewer clothes, but the time it would take to remove them would be wasted. I don't need to be naked to enjoy this, not when I already feel like I'm about to shoot off fucking fireworks.

I'm so blindingly out of control, and it's almost an out-of-body experience. I urge him faster as he rocks against me, balls so damn tight I need relief, nipples driving me out of my mind every time my shirt rubs against them. Our kiss has turned sloppy, driven by pure need, and if this is the passion St. Clare was talking about, I'm happy to declare him fucking correct because our first kiss had none of this. Even though it was definitely, totally a kiss.

Finally, I get the courage to free my hands from where they've been planted and move them to skin. All that skin. Bare and smooth, a light dusting of blond hair over his chest and body burning up as much as I am. My hands rub up his back before dropping again, sensory overload, holding him tight and making sure there isn't a crack of distance between our bodies.

St. Clare's teeth bury into my bottom lip, hard enough to bring out a choked-back cry but not hard enough to want him to stop. The light pain ripples through me and when he finally lets go, my head drops back, barely able to take any more.

His mouth moves to my neck instead. Prickling up every nerve in my body as he kisses and licks what feels like a live wire delivering impulses straight to my cock.

It's not enough. It's too much.

Each thought flitters through my empty brain, gone as fast as it hits, scrambled into more nonsense than has ever existed, and really, at this point, I'm not even completely sure *I* exist.

We've gone from kissing to sex in less time than I've had to think it through, and I'm glad for it. My brain gets in the way sometimes, making me do stupid shit that's the complete opposite of what I want, and without it, this is so much easier. Because I'm letting myself have this moment without anything else trying to get in the way.

This. This is what I want.

St. Clare. On top of me. Sinful hips grinding confidently against mine, pulling so much precum from me that the material separating us is sticky.

"Ah, fuck," I grunt into the dark room, and St. Clare answers me with a groan of his own.

My hands drop to his mouthwatering ass, and I thrust up against him.

What the fuck are even clothes at this point? All that exists is his mouth on my skin and his cock rubbing delicious friction right where I need it.

I stop holding back, stop trying to draw it out, just give in to the moment and let it take over. His panting, his tongue, the sweat building between our chests. The tight grip on my hair, making my eyes sting, as my fingers dig into his ass.

St. Clare thrusts against me, and I thrust against him, and my brain is like water down a drain, swirling faster and faster, building to that final release.

A pleasant zapping fills the base of my spine, and I tremble against him.

"Close," I pant. "Gonna ... I'm gonna ..."

"Me too, Perry." His rasp is right by my ear.

The sound of my name in that deep, rough tone sets me off. The high hits, a stupidly brief moment of the greatest pleasure I've ever had, and almost as fast as it fills me, it disappears again.

St. Clare shudders against me, and it's the weirdest fucking feeling, the way his cock throbs against mine. When it's over, I want to ask him to do it again. And again.

But I can barely breathe, and as soon as he untangles his fingers from my hair, I drop back against the bed, arms splayed out like a snow angel, and let the first real inhale hit my lungs.

"I think I'm dying," I groan.

St. Clare climbs off me. My eyes follow him, every movement, and then he looks down at his underwear. "Well, that was probably a dumb choice."

"Umm ... is insults after sex a guy thing or a you thing? Because it's hard to bask when you're called a dumb choice."

Amusement sparks on his face. "Not you." He waves a hand down the front of him. "Coming in our fucking pants when we're sort of low on clothing."

"Ohh ..." That's better. And a fair point. "I can't remember the last time I popped one off in my underwear."

"Can't say it's common for me either." His gaze travels steadily over me. "Damn, it's hot though."

His words hover between us. Because fuck. It really was.

"Did that help your *before I die* bucket list?"

I'm still too lost in orgasm land to really follow the conversation. "It sure helped something. Not sure of specifics. Need hydrating. And feeding."

"Do you ever stop eating?"

I rub at the ache in my lower stomach, feeling far from satisfied. "Yes? No? I think when I came, a little bit of brain shot out too."

Laughter bursts from him, and he reaches a hand down to pull me to my feet. "Go eat."

"Food. Yes."

"Wait. No. Clean yourself up first, and then eat."

That sounds like the smarter option. "Will do."

I lean in to taste his mouth one more time, and damn, even with the edge off, he kisses as good as I remember.

"Perry …" He pulls back a little. "We're going to end up back on the bed again."

I groan and physically have to pull myself away. "I'm going. Yes." Except then I make the mistake of running my gaze over him again. From his messy hair to his puffy lips to that mouthwatering body and then, finally, to the wet stain on the front of his underwear.

I have to cover my fucking eyes. "Point me in the direction of the door. I'll find it."

"Sort of worried about touching you again though."

"Fine." I take a few steps forward. "Am I close?"

"Ah, yeah. Forward some more."

I go forward some more, and when he doesn't say stop, I keep going. And keep going. And keep—

I plow headfirst into the wall.

"*Fuck.*"

St. Clare is *wheezing* he's laughing so hard, and I turn my glare on him.

"And you wonder why we have trust issues."

"All that and I'm *still* somehow attracted to you." He lifts his eyes skyward like he's in pain when *I'm* the one who ran into the wall.

That pain disappears quickly though.

Because he's *still* attracted to me.

Even after the sex.

Kinda smug about being that good.

CHAPTER TWENTY

ST. CLARE

IT'S hard to get out of bed. It's hard to do much of anything except lie here, naked, with a huge fucking smile on my face, remembering last night.

Perry was as enthusiastic under me as he is with everything else he does.

I have absolutely no clue what his reaction is going to be this morning. Given that he wasn't in a huge hurry to leave after he got off gives me hope he's not one of those guys who wants to use me for a quick come before going back to his normal life. That's not something I'm interested in entertaining, and it's happened more times than I want to admit.

The problem boils down to the fact that Perry insisted, barely days ago, that he's straight, and I know last night only happened because he started worrying he might die today. And yeah, that doesn't feel the best.

Sex, great.

Being a bucket list item, almost insulting.

I'm sure Perry didn't mean for it to come across that way because he isn't the kind of person to intentionally hurt someone —gunshot aside—but he's one hundred percent the type of person to unintentionally hurt someone. It's one of the reasons I can't bring myself to get out of bed.

The other reasons are that I'm enjoying reliving the sex, I can smell him on my sheets, and I'm also low-key worried about what he's walking into today.

Plus, my underwear is hanging over the arm of a chair, still drying from last night.

Lars took the clothes I was wearing yesterday and said he was putting them in for a wash with his, so I really hope he managed to do it because otherwise, I'm going to be disgusting.

An email beeps on my phone, and I reach over, unplug it from where it's charging, and open my inbox, expecting to find spam.

It's an email from Livy Sullivan, the bookkeeper I hired for Saint Clare's, who's been a fucking godsend so far.

Hey Reilly,

When you have a chance, I've attached a list of transactions I wasn't sure about that need allocating. If you can let me know what they're for, I'll make sure they're coded right for tax purposes.

I skim the rest of the email, which goes into more detail than my brain can probably handle, and then click on the link. There are about two pages of transactions dating back to when Saint Clare's was opened. It doesn't look too difficult, so I figure I can knock it out over coffee, and then hopefully, that will mean that we're all caught up.

It hurts that Colin isn't the one here doing it, and every day without him is another day of fear for where he is and relief that his body hasn't been pulled from the Sound.

Yet.

I scroll down to his number and click on it, mostly habit, only a little bit hoping, and get the deadline straight away. There are so many things we need to talk about and didn't get the time to. I'm almost *mad* at the way he's abandoned me. Almost, but not actually, because I know something's happened.

I've moved past hoping that he'll show up after some extended vacation, and I know Dad and my stepmom are worried as well. All I can do is keep taking it one day at a time and maybe stop getting so fucking distracted by sweet eyes and what felt like a magnificent cock. I have to believe that somehow he'll get us a name today and that the name is Yanni's.

Then … well, fuck. I don't know.

Lars made a great point that we could go to Yanni to trade him for Colin, but what then? And how do we trust that he'd keep his word anyway? I'm not exactly his favorite person.

The other alternative is to go to the police. Tell them about Perry. Tell them about Yanni hiring him, and then they can be the ones who get Colin back.

Both options throw Perry under the bus though, and I think, maybe, that Perry trusts me. He shouldn't. He has to know that finding my brother comes first, but maybe that's the reason he slept with me to begin with.

Maybe he's trying to get under my skin. Trying to make me forget.

If he was even the slightest bit more calculating than he is, I might believe it.

I sigh and grab my mostly dry underwear, pull on my *Seattle* tourist T-shirt, and then finally leave my room. Voices are coming from down the hall, and when I get to the kitchen, Perry and Lars have beaten me. Perry's sitting on a stool with an overfull bowl of overnight oats in front of him and my suit pants hung over the stool to his left.

"Morning," I say, trying to ignore the way I want to look at him, to drink in every stretch of muscle under that too-small T-shirt.

Lars answers me first. "Morning. I called Brom and told him you're working from home."

Well, that's one less thing for me to worry about. "Thanks."

"I also think we should talk about what's going to happen today."

"What do you mean?"

"Well, we need some kind of plan."

Perry stops shoveling food into his face. "A plan?"

"Yeah, you can't exactly walk in there and ask for names."

"Why not?"

Lars stares at him. "Wait. You were planning to just walk in there and ask him?"

"Well, yeah. No point in overcomplicating things."

"Except if you fuck this up, you might end up with a bullet in your head, and then we're back to square one."

Perry slowly sets down his spoon. "And you'll miss me too. Right?"

"Yes, that whole one day since you've been in my life has made you irreplaceable."

And while I appreciate Lars's sarcasm, I sort of think I would miss Perry. He's ridiculous, but he's the kind of guy you want around. "I'd miss you," I assure him, and I'm unprepared for the way he lights up.

"Good thing you don't have anything to worry about. Luther's a good guy—"

"Because he has a labradoodle," Lars adds, and I have no idea where he's getting that reasoning from.

"Exactly." Perry shoves another spoonful of overnight oats into his mouth, then talks around it. "The less we stress about it, the easier it will be. I'll head in there, have a drink or two with the gang, explain to Luther that his little side hustle has potentially put my life at risk and I need to know by who, and then I'll be right back."

"The … gang?"

"Yeah, my baddie bunch. They're total badasses—Arlie's the one who trained me, actually—and I've known them for years. We're tight."

"Thank fuck for Arlie being a terrible trainer," I mutter.

Lars is shaking his head at Perry. "Isn't the first rule of fight club that you don't talk about fight club?"

Perry stares at him for a second. "Who's in fight club?"

"I *mean* that I'm pretty confident you're not supposed to give us the names of your accomplices."

"Oohhh … no, it's fine. Arlie is an alias."

"And I'm almost *totally* confident you're not supposed to tell us that either!"

Perry throws up his hands. "Why are you so stressed about this? It's not like they can hear us."

"No, but you're about to walk into a bar where there are people who are after my best friend when you know his exact location and everything we know so far."

"Which isn't much," I add.

"But that's still information. They don't need to know how much or little we know. And, no offense, Perry, but you're exactly the type of guy who'd squeal under torture."

I can confirm that, considering the torture I put him through last night.

"Hell, they could probably skip the torture, considering how easily you gave all that up on them," Lars continues, like he's determined to drive the point home.

"You think I'm going to give you guys up?" he asks, sounding hurt.

"Probably not on purpose, but yes."

His frown deepens, and he goes back to eating.

Lars and I share a look. As offended as Perry is, Lars has a point. We can't risk Perry accidentally letting slip where we're staying and having more contract killers at the door. Even though I know that, it doesn't stop me from wanting to make him feel better.

"Lars is only saying that we need you to be careful."

Lars grunts.

"*Very* careful," I add. "We're trusting you."

His sunshiny smile comes out. "I told you: I've got this!"

It takes everything in me to almost believe him. "Yeah. So. Good luck."

"Don't need it." Perry gets up to rinse out his bowl before he stacks it in the dishwasher. "By tonight, we'll know where to start. I hope you guys are ready to be blown away by my skill."

Hell, if he wants to be this confident, who am I to bring him down?

Even if I know it will never, ever happen.

CHAPTER TWENTY-ONE

PERRY

THERE'S one thing that can be said about potentially walking into danger and your impending doom: I'm not thinking about St. Clare anymore.

Not him or his kisses or his dick.

When I woke up, it was all I could concentrate on, but sometime during my breakfast and talk of planning, that memory dripped away and was replaced by the reminder that today might not be a very good day.

I've had a lot of not-good days, and I'd like to have a whole lot less going forward. This new-perspective version of me probably shouldn't be playing with fire, but what other choice do I have?

It's fairly important that I know if I need to look over my shoulder from here on out, and the name of who's behind these nefarious deeds would really help in that department. Thankfully, Luther is a good guy. I ran a few jobs for him, they didn't work out, he'll understand. Underperforming staff is a problem in every industry.

I'm really better suited to the cafe and should be left to my own devices over there. It's the best outcome for all of us.

And paying the money back. I guess.

That part isn't the best outcome *for me*, but in a choice between a padded bank account and my organs all where they belong, it's a mostly easy choice.

I catch another whiff of myself as I huddle into my dirty hoodie.

Fuck, I wish Lars had washed my clothes with theirs. It's too cold to wear my puppy shirt, so I'm back in my hoodie, hoping that the deodorant I coated myself with will cover the stench of yesterday's dry sweat.

I mean, if I can't reason with Luther, maybe I can gas him instead?

I stuff my hands into the front pocket, sort of wishing I'd thought to bring my gun. Even if I never plan to shoot it, the weapon is enough to intimidate someone until I can get away. Or at least it is in movies.

I dispel a massive huff of air and remind myself that I've got this. I wasn't worried at all about going to Lethal Poison before Lars and St. Clare got in my head. Maybe this is part of their plan? Make me trust them, twist my thoughts, cut me off from my friends and family ... WWJJD?

Judge Judy sure as fuck would not stand for that bullshit.

It's a trying time, and I need to lean on my friends more than ever. Even if those friends like to pretend we're not friends, I know them better than that.

If we're getting down to the bare bones of it all, I could argue that Luther owes me damages for my mental well-being of the last twenty-four hours. When I went to work yesterday morning, I wasn't at all prepared to be shot at, on the run, and coming my brains out with a man on top of me.

It's hard not to think of yesterday as a glitch in the matrix, but my lack of underwear right now is proof that it happened.

Today has to go well because I'm not so sure I want to die while I'm going commando. That's the kind of thing that might become the punchline of a joke. Like when people die on the toilet. I'm much more sophisticated than that, even if the chafing on my inner thighs is trying to tell me differently.

I pause at the side of Lethal Poison and tug down the crotch of my jeans again. All this talk of planning has gotten into my head when what I really need to do is what I do best: wing it. My whole life is run off vibes, and I've done okay so far.

I scrub my ratty hair back from my face, pull up my hood, and duck my head as I push my way into the bar. Like always, I get that happy warmth of a home as soon as I step inside. Even on the morning side of noon, there are a few people here, catching up or trading stories on whoever they killed/robbed/kidnapped last night.

Surprisingly, all three of my baddies are here, so I throw them a wave before I head toward the bar.

None of them wave back. We're still playing the pretending not to be friends game, I see.

There's a woman behind the bar who I haven't seen before, and I turn my most charming smile on her. She's pretty. A dainty little face, wavy hair framing either side, and eyes that shine, and I have to remind myself that I'm not here to hit on her. I'm here for super-serious business.

"Hey, is Luther around?" I ask, trying and failing to sound professional despite the way my voice squeaks. I really need to get Lars out of my brain.

Bar girl gives me a flirty smile. "Who's asking?"

"His best friend, Perry."

Her smile dims. "Oh. He's, uh, in his office."

"Thanks. Can I bother you for a Coke before I go?"

She pours one, smile completely gone, and then adds a wedge of lime to it. Looks like Luther has briefed her on what I like, and I'm not surprised—he's a labradoodle dad. It's just how they are.

"I'll head on back."

She nods, and I make a mental note to give Luther the heads-up that she might need more customer service training. I send my friends another wave as I head for the hallway that leads to the bathrooms and Luther's office. Unlike Saint Clare's, his office is small and windowless, like a storage closet, saving the larger back room for his staff. It's a selfless choice that most employers wouldn't make.

I'm halfway toward his office when I'm yanked backward, almost off my feet. I barely get a second to be surprised before I'm slammed into the wall beside me.

"What the hell are you doing?" a voice hisses by my ear. It takes me a moment to pick that it's Arlie.

"Need a quick word with Luther."

"Do you want to get killed?" She turns me roughly so I can see her, and the worry in her dark eyes throws me for a second. "What the fuck are you doing here?"

"I need—"

She slams me back against the wall so hard my head bounces off it.

"Okay, I *need* you to stop manhandling me for a start. Damn, woman." I rub at the sore spot. "I've had a rough day, and I'd really like to head home for a nap, but I need to talk to Luther first."

"No. You really, really don't."

I finally pick up on her tone. "Why?"

Everett barrels into the hall. "What in the ever-loving hell are you doing here?"

"Like I *just* said—"

"You need to go. Now."

"Wow. And here I was, thinking my friends would be happy to see me."

Everett pulls Arlie off me. "Your name came up, and you think it's smart to walk into a bar of *people like us* and give them an easy payday?"

"My name came up?" I let that sink in. "Like someone wants me *dead*?"

"Not *someone*." Arlie's gaze flicks toward Luther's office. "Run. Go. Now."

"B-but … he's a doodle dad …"

She turns a disgusted scowl on Everett. "What the fuck does that mean?"

"Nothing that will probably make sense to us," he replies.

"She's right, Perry. You've got to get out of here before he sees you. Go through the back. We'll distract him."

"But—"

"Now, dimwit!" Arlie snaps.

I'm about to tell her that you catch more honey with bees than flies—or flies and honey? I don't know—when their intensity sinks in. My vibes are gone. They're acting like St. Clare and Lars were, and now I'm starting to feel a bit, well, stupid. Am I too trusting? Do I need to reassess my whole dog theory?

"He's still not moving," Everett says.

Arlie grabs the front of my hoodie and pushes me so hard I almost go ass over.

"Easy!"

With a growl, she pulls out a gun and points it straight at me.

My hands fly up. My heart takes off thrumming, and I glance between her and Everett in complete fucking betrayal. "W-what are you doing?"

"Don't tempt me. It'd be the easiest shot I ever took."

"But we're friends," I whisper.

"We are." Everett pushes her gun away from me. "Which is why you need to get the fuck out of here. I won't tell you again. I'm going to count to three, and if you're still in view, I'm going to let her shoot you."

"Ev—"

"One … two …"

I get the fucking message. I stumble backward over my feet but am still in clear view as he's about to say three.

But a door opens just down from us before he can.

And a voice I very much don't want to hear cuts in.

"I heard you wanted to see me, Perry."

CHAPTER TWENTY-TWO

ST. CLARE

"HE SHOULD BE BACK BY NOW," I mutter, refreshing my social media feed for the third time in the last minute. I have no idea what's actually on my screen when I'm so in my head, but every minute that ticks by is another minute of nervousness I need to sit with. "Maybe we should have gone with him?"

"Why? So we could hand whoever is after you an easy kill?"

When he puts it like that … "Isn't that what we did with Perry?"

Lars pauses whatever he's doing on his laptop. He can say he hates Perry for trying to kill me all he likes, but we both know that Lars is a good guy, and when it comes down to it, he doesn't want *anyone* to get hurt. Plus, Perry is growing on him. I know he is.

"You need to keep some distance from him," Lars warns. "At least until this is over."

"Why?"

He throws me an unimpressed look. "You know why."

Because we're planning to trade him off for my brother, and there's still a slight chance that he might want to kill me when I'm already missing half of my ear, thanks to him? "Small details."

"You're worried about him. That's not a small detail."

"That's only because we need to know who's after me."

"There's only one person who's *likely* to be after you. If he comes back with any name other than Yanni's, I'm going to be shocked."

"You never know."

"True. *I* currently have the urge to kill you right now."

I set down my phone. "What did I do?"

Lars almost looks like he wants to laugh. "Like, position? Because I wasn't in the room, so I can't say, but whatever it was, it sounded like Perry was enjoying it."

"Shit."

Now he laughs. "Yeah, shit."

"You heard that."

"You were very loud." Lars drops his laptop onto the cushion beside himself and leans forward. His elbows meet his knees, and he picks up a coaster that he starts absently tapping against the coffee table. "What were you thinking?"

"He's really hot."

"*Other* than that."

"Is there anything else?"

The tapping pauses. "Well, if you're going to be alone with some guy who tried to kill you, it would be a relief to know it wasn't just about getting off."

I can't answer that. Was that all last night was? Absolutely. I have no regrets over what happened. Perry is fucking gorgeous, and there's something about him that I like. Something that's beyond surface attraction. Like all that unrestrained sweetness and enthusiasm is mine to harness, and I can't deny that it was a big part of the turn-on.

Lars's amusement drains away. "I can't protect you, I can't do my job, if you're making stupid choices like that."

"You really think Perry's a killer?"

"It's not about what I think. It's not about him as a person at all. It's about the facts. And the facts are that he tried once. He can say he'd never do it again all he likes, but if he did it once, he can do it again."

I can see his point, but I dunno. I think now that I've had my tongue down Perry's throat, I've gotten to know him a whole lot better. "Listen, I can completely understand your concerns but I stupidly trust him. Yes. I can hear myself. Yes, I know it's misguided. You don't need to point any of that out. But I can't *stop* from trusting him anyway."

The tapping starts up again. "Okay. You're a big boy, and I really hope your trust doesn't get you killed."

"You know what? Me too."

He laughs. "How did we get into this mess again?"

"I'm still asking myself the same question. It's pretty fucking extreme just because Yanni didn't want a bit of competition."

"Cute that you think you're competition for them."

"*I* don't. They clearly do."

Lars chews on his bottom lip. "I know you trust Perry, but do you think we should head somewhere else for a few hours? Just in case?"

"You think he's going to rat us out?"

"Unfortunately, I get where you're coming from. Perry doesn't *seem* like the kind of guy who'd throw us under the bus, but I also get the feeling that Perry doesn't have to make our lives harder on purpose. He's perfectly capable of doing it accidentally."

I had the same thought. I hate that I had the same thought because I don't want to underestimate Perry or make him feel bad, but the confidence I have in him thinking things through isn't high. And hey, I wouldn't be so damn attracted to his spontaneity if he was the kind of guy who assesses risks.

Unfortunately, that's great for sex, bad for survival.

"You might be right," I allow. "But where the hell do we go? We're only here because we ran out of options."

Lars tosses the coaster back onto the table. "My parents' place, probably."

"You really want them to be caught up in this mess?"

"I don't think I have a choice."

I shake my head because the fewer people we involve, the better. Lars's parents are the kind of people you'd expect to be smiling from the front of a muffin box. Or as the American ambassadors to *The Great British Baking Show*. Even mentioning contract killers around them would be enough to make their sweet brains short-circuit.

"We'd be going to my parents' place before yours," I point out.

"Except there's a chance they're being watched."

That reminder sits heavy on my chest. I'm trying not to reach the point of everything feeling helpless, but I'm already so on edge with radio silence from Colin and now Perry that I'm not sure how much longer I can spend sitting around doing nothing.

A pounding on the front door makes me jump, and Lars immediately stands and pulls out his gun.

"Perry, you think?"

"He's got a key." Lars points to the bedrooms. "Go."

But even as he says that, a key turns in the lock, sending him on high alert. Lars shoves me off the couch and dives toward the doorway that opens onto the hall. The front door opens, and I hold my breath, waiting for shouts or a gunshot or anything that will make all hell break loose.

Instead, a sort of familiar voice shouts, "Perry, where the fuck are you?"

"Margot?" I look out from behind the couch to see her and Elle walking along the hall. I'm up on my feet before Lars throws his arms up.

"Do you want to be fucking killed?" he asks.

"But … it's only them."

"And *them* could be here to kill you."

Margot comes to a fast stop. "Kill him?" Her eyes fly to Lars's gun. "What the hell is going on here?"

"Yeah …" Elle steps around her girlfriend and takes in the room. "I don't think my brother will be too impressed if his chari-table act ends up with bullet holes in his walls."

Lars subtly lowers his gun but doesn't put it away. "Why are you here?"

Margot scowls his way, and I don't blame her. We're the ones borrowing this place. "Because my brother sent me a concerning fucking message this morning, and now he's not answering my calls. Where is he?"

Well, *I'm* not going to be the one to answer that. "He's having issues with his phone." Given how old it is, she'd have to believe that.

She glares at me instead. "That didn't answer my question."

"He went out for groceries."

"Then we'll wait until he gets back." Margot crosses her arms and throws herself back on the couch, challenging stare never leaving mine. It's so weird that she and Perry are related when they couldn't be more opposite, at least in personality. Their thick black hair, dark eyes, and angular faces give them away as siblings.

"Anyone want tea?" Elle asks, hovering, like she's torn between taking Margot's side or making sure everyone is comfortable.

"I'm good," I assure her, and Lars *finally* tucks his gun away.

"I'd like a tea. I'll help you."

The two of them disappear into the kitchen, and I'm terrifyingly left alone with Margot. She's still watching me, and I'm doing everything I can to cement the view of Seattle to memory so we don't have to address the way she's doing the same with my face.

"If anything has happened to him," she whispers, "it'll kill me."

Maybe not as literally as it will kill him, but I have the good sense to keep that to myself. "What did his text say?"

"That he wanted to let me know he's sorry and he loves me."

Fuck. "Well, that sounds ominous."

"You think?"

This is probably the part where I'm supposed to reassure her, but I'm feeling pretty fucking unassured myself. Perry was confident going into this thing, which made *me* confident as well. If he was secretly texting Margot messages like that though, I have to question if he knew more than he let on.

"Maybe we should all go back to your place," I suggest weakly.

"No. We're all staying right here until Perry gets back. From grocery shopping. For the first time in his life."

"Everyone has to eat."

Her glare deepens.

"What do you want me to say?"

"I want the truth. Why are you here? Who even are you? And why is my brother sending me sketchy messages at eight in the morning when he struggles to get up by then on a good day."

"It's really not my place."

"Well, I tried questioning him, and now he's not around for me to do it. That means you're up. And you need to start talking."

CHAPTER TWENTY-THREE

PERRY

I ALMOST CHOKE on my tongue as I look over at Luther filling the hall. From the corner of my eyes, I catch Arlie slipping the gun into the holster under her jacket as Everett shifts back a step.

Somehow, Luther looks bigger from out behind the bar, all short brown hair and beard, basically the same length, so it's impossible to tell where his head ends and his jawline begins.

A trickle of fear slips into my stomach.

I force a smile and pretend to glance behind me. "Perry? Who's Perry?"

From beside me, Arlie groans. I don't look, just back up a bit further.

"You know what? If I see this Perry fellow, I'll let you know."

Luther's lips twitch. "Get in my office."

"See, I would, but I get the feeling that if I go in there, I won't be coming out again, and I sort of like it out here. Fresh air, nice lighting, ruthless thugs who probably want me dead ... what's not to love?"

"I'm not playing," Luther tells me.

"Not in the mood? Too bad. I'll come back later, then—" I go to turn and run face-first into a brick wall. Well, a *person* who feels like a brick wall. And I mean, I'm not a short guy, so the fact I can motorboat this behemoth's chest gives me pause. In a race, I could probably have him if I wasn't wearing jeans and my thighs weren't torn up beyond reason, but in a fight? The only short odds I have is dying.

I pat behemoth's terrifyingly wide man titties. "Are you, umm, in the mood to play?"

At his grunt, I shrink back from him.

"I'll take that as a no."

"Office, Perry."

I nod so fast my head is in danger of coming off. "Ohhh, you said *Perry*. I thought you meant the *other* Perry. Of course I'll go into your windowless dungeon room with you and not at all fear for my life." My throat is closing around my words, but there's no way out now, and on a scale of dumb to probably *should* have made a plan, I'm on one side, and Lars is laughing at me from the other.

"Both of you too," Luther adds, stare shooting lasers Arlie and Everett's way. Unlike me, the two of them come without arguing, and I guess the whole stoic thing was what I was missing in my aborted career. As it is, I'm holding back from begging for my life, and I'm mostly only able to do that because my voice has failed me.

They don't need to know that though. I'll let them assume I'm channeling their super-serious vibes.

I'm first into Luther's office. It's big enough for his desk, a chair, and four different computers lining the back wall on top of old-school metal filing cabinets. I have no idea about any of his shady business stuff, but none of that looks like a normal, average bar owner's setup.

I take the small chair in front of his desk and realize that was a mistake a moment later when Arlie and Everett hover, standing behind me, and Luther remains standing on the other side of his desk.

I'm a literal sitting fucking duck right now. Good to know.

Instead of shrinking down, I wipe my palms off on my jeans and rock onto the chair's back legs.

"This is a cute little group huddle. Are we going to wash each other's backs in the shower later?"

Luther sighs and pinches the bridge of his nose. "I keep telling myself this is my fault."

"Awesome." I bring my hands together. "Agreed. Can I go now?"

He reaches into his top drawer and wordlessly sets a gun on the desk.

The heavy metal meeting wood makes a *clunk* I feel so deep in my gut fear tries to shoot out of my ass.

"Luther ..." Arlie says in a warning voice. "You really want to do that? Over *him*?"

My first instinct is to be offended that I'm not worth murder, and then I remember that I don't actually *want* to be worth that. I want them to decide I'm a worthless little gutter rat so I can go home to Sir Squeakerton and get back to disappointing Margot at every turn.

I love disappointing her, I'm good at it, and if I'm allowed to go free, I'll make sure it happens every day for the rest of our lives.

I think that's how bargaining with the universe works?

Maybe I should have asked Lars to check my horoscope before I left?

Luther's rubbing his jaw, and this whole silent Bond villain thing is working for him. It makes his head-face meld slightly more sinister.

"It was an easy hit," he says. "I gave you three sitting ducks. You had to have actually wanted to botch the job to fuck this up." He cuts a look toward Arlie.

"Why would you give him this job in the first place?" she asks before he can direct anything her way.

"He knew about us. It was either bring him in, or kill him. This is what I get for trying to be nice. You said he was ready."

"No. I said he could make any shot."

"And yet ..." Luther spreads his hands out to the side. "He didn't. He let his guy go free when a toddler could have made the shot and then thought he could steal from me and take his payday anyway."

Everett's disappointed groan stings because yeah, yeah, I get it. Not my finest moment.

"About that," I say before he can list any other of my idiocies. "I have the money, and I thought I could, you know, pay it back. Call it even? Then we can pretend like this whole thing never happened."

His—I think blue? I dunno, it's dark in here—eyes bore into mine. "You have my money?"

I go to confirm that, then stop. "*M-most* of it?"

"Most of my money?" His eyebrows creep higher. "And you think giving me back most of the money you stole from me will call it even."

"No, I thought giving you back *all* of it would have us call it even. I'm happy to sign a non-compete and everything. It didn't even occur to me that taking it would be stealing from *you*, just your client, and I'm really sorry, Luther. Truly. If I'd known you were the one paying for the job—"

Arlie's jab to my shoulder is painful. "Stop talking."

He's still staring, and his lack of blinking is getting creepy.

"Well, someone needs to fill the silence," I mutter.

Luther's lips quirk. "I've always liked you."

A twinge of hope kicks in. "This is what I've been telling everyone."

"Everyone?" He perches on the side of his desk and looks me over. "Who's everyone?"

I'm about to say Lars and St. Clare when my brain throws up an alert. If Luther is the one I stole from, does that mean *he's* the one who wanted to kill St. Clare? Wow, this thing keeps on getting weirder.

If that's the case, letting him know that we're hanging out and playing house isn't a good move. See? Fuck you, Lars. I'm smarter than you think.

I wave a hand toward Arlie and Everett. "*Everyone.* All my

friends here. They've been telling me for years that you hate me, Luther, but I knew better."

"Did you also know better than to steal from me?"

Shit, we're back on that again. What is it with people and not being able to accept an apology? "In my defense, it was a lot of money, and I had a lot of bills, and I was sort of sick of Margot thinking I'm a fuckup all the time."

"So you thought pretending to kill a man and taking my money was a good way to prove to your sister that you're not a fuckup."

I sigh and scrub my hand through my hair. When he puts it like that, it sounds a little ridiculous. "It's not like I thought it all the way through."

"No, because if you did, you wouldn't have ended up here."

I clear my throat, gaze shooting to the gun and then back to Luther. "And where is … here … exactly? Are we talking physically here? Or metaphorically reaching the end of my life *here*?"

He tilts his head from one side to the next. "Well, that's up to you."

"It is?" Another twinge of hope hits me. If it's up to me to choose between whether I live or die, it's a simple decision.

"Of course. You wanted to make things even, so let's do it."

See? Doodle dad. He's a perfectly reasonable guy outside of all this life-of-crime, Walter White business. "Thank you. I know I don't have it all on me, but I thought we could work out a payment plan or—"

"No payment plan."

That derails my line of thinking. "Okay, but I don't have the money right now. But I could get it. I'm sure I could."

The more I talk, the more Luther shakes his head, and the more my heartbeat is trying to strangle me.

"I don't care about the money," he says.

"Really?" I'm waiting for the punchline. "But what about all the stealing and getting out your gun and—"

"Let's just say I have a very bad man who paid me for a job that wasn't done. That makes *me* look bad." His voice rises to a crack of a whip in the silent, tiny office. "We work with the honesty policy here for a reason. It means no evidence, the people I recruit are people who I know will follow through, and now you're making me question it all."

"If you trusted me, how do you know he's not dead?"

"I'm not new at this. New hires are monitored, and I get the confirmation they've completed the jobs they've been assigned. I've never had a problem. Until now."

"Wh-what do you want from me?"

"I. Want. Him. Dead."

And even though I know exactly who he means, my stupid mouth moves anyway. "Who?"

"St. *fucking* Clare. Bring him to me. Alive or dead, I don't fucking care. I'll shoot him myself if it means the job is done right, and I'll even let your incompetent ass keep the money if it makes this mess go away. I *told* my client it was done, and the second they find out it wasn't, every single person in this fucking bar is at risk. They won't stop to ask questions about who fucked up."

"I … I don't understand," I say, mouth moving only a fraction faster than my thoughts. I'm gripping my beaded bracelet like it'll somehow protect me. "What did St. Clare do that's made him enemy number one? Why would anyone want him killed in the first place? It's not like he's selling meth to children or drowning kittens."

"He lied to the wrong person and looked into things he shouldn't have."

"*St. Clare* did?" None of that sounds like him. Given how legitimately shocked he was about the whole being wanted thing, it's not lining up. "Are they sure they don't have the wrong guy?"

"They're sure." Luther's eyes slowly narrow. "You know where he is."

"I don't!"

"Yes. You do."

"How would I know where he is? I barely knew who he was when I tried to kill him in the first place."

"I gave you simple, fast jobs with unsuspecting targets. It

should have been an easy payday for you, and instead, you shat the bed."

"Well, that's disgusting."

"I'm giving you a second chance, and you better see that as the gift from God that it is. I'm giving you exactly one week. One week, and I want that *fuck* here. And if my client figures out that you didn't do what you were supposed to, I won't hesitate to throw you under the bus. Understand?"

That I have one week to figure out how the hell to get me and St. Clare out of this mess? "Got it. Who *is* your client?"

Luther ignores me and turns his attention to Arlie and Everett. "And if I find out either of you has helped him, you'll be next on my list."

"Got it."

They leave, behemoth glaring after them, and I'm stuck on my chair, feeling very much like Luther's cozy office is more like a coffin for people he doesn't like.

It's just lucky he likes me.

I guess.

I've never known lucky to feel quite like this though.

CHAPTER TWENTY-FOUR

ST. CLARE

THE FRONT DOOR opening makes the four of us leap to our feet, but we don't get further than that before Perry barrels down the hall. He's panting, sweaty hair plastered to his forehead, and for one wild moment, he comes to a stop and looks around at us all.

"Ah … hey?"

"Where have you *been*?" explodes from me and Margot at the same time.

He does that thing where he forces a laugh, trying to act like everything is fine. "Just, umm, out for a walk."

"A walk?" Margot echoes. "The kind of walk that could have gotten you *killed*?"

Perry's tan face pales, and he quickly looks around. "This isn't where I'm supposed to be. Who are you people? I'll just—"

"He told me everything," Margot cuts him off, pointing my way as she tattles on me. And I wish she didn't because the expression Perry sends me can only be described as complete and utter betrayal.

"E-everything?"

"That you tried to kill him, made a middle school pact to disappear, and have found yourself on the chopping block instead? Oh yeah. Everything."

Perry scowls at me. "You tattled to my *sister*?"

"What was I supposed to do?"

"*Not* tattle to my sister!"

"You're the one who sent her a ridiculous message this morning that had her busting down the front door and suspecting *us* of killing *you*."

"She what?"

"Yes. So thank you for once again putting me in a position I don't want to be in."

Perry at least looks sorry, but before he can say it, Elle cuts in.

"Sorry to break up this tense moment, but Perry plowed in here like the place was on fire, and I'd kind of like to know what that was about."

Fuck. That's a good point.

Perry straightens suddenly. "Nothing important. No fire. But I really think now would be a good time for you and Margy to leave. Thank you so much for visiting, and we'll meet up later this week for dinner or … umm, a funeral?"

Elle and Margot are both wearing matching *we're not going anywhere* expressions.

"You do know that while I'm not practicing law here yet, I do know what I'm talking about," Elle says, shocking the hell out of me. My initial impression of her was fun-loving trust bunny, so that proves I'm a terrible judge of character.

"I know, I know," Perry waves her off. "But I don't think I can legally do anything about this, so I'd really like both of you to leave. Immediately."

And Margot proves she knows her brother better than any of us because she plants her hands on her hips and glares at him. "*Why?*"

"Because it's highly possible this place isn't safe anymore, and I really, really need nothing to happen to you both so that when this is all over, you can yell at me and tell me I told you so."

Whatever else Perry was about to say is cut off when Lars shoots to his feet. "We're not safe?"

"It's a long story, but I *think* I was followed, so I took a bus downtown, then an Uber to the U District—and boy, did *that* wipe out some funds, I swear—and from there, I went to Gas Works Park, then took a bike, then *another* bus, ended up in some dingy area with a lot of naked people around, ordered a taxi, and—"

"Perry," I manage to say without laughing. "You went to a lot of effort, and we're all appreciative, but do we need to be worried *right now*?"

"No." He glances at his sister. "Maybe."

"Maybe?" Lars looks like his head is about to boil.

But a maybe I can work with. "First things first: Margot and Elle, you need to leave."

"This is my brother's place," Elle points out. "You can't make us leave."

"I'm not making you, but considering the three of us are in some shit, and I highly doubt you want your girlfriend in the same shit, you should probably get moving before the shit finds you too."

She eyes Margot. "Right. Okay. But Perry's coming with us."

"No, I'm not." He hurries to stand next to me. "As much as I'd love that, Luther kind of wants me dead, and you two being around only gives them two more heads to aim at."

"Morbid," she mutters.

"But true." I search Perry's face for any sign that he's worried about the confirmation he's on the line along with me or that he's betrayed by it being *Luther*. But there's nothing there, just his eyes begging his sister to leave. "You really should go."

Margot shakes her head. "This is all proof that I can't leave him alone. Ever."

The longer we stand here, the more Perry deflates. Sure, I can grudgingly accept that she makes a good point, but he's spent the morning trying to find a name for me before taking an expensive and long trip back in case he was followed. He's trying. At this point, there isn't anything else we can do.

"He's not alone," I remind her. "He has us. And at this point, you're more of a liability than a help, so you need to go."

"A *liability*?"

"Yes." Is she surprised? "While you're around, Perry will always be worrying about whether you're safe instead of worrying about himself. You want him to be okay? Go home. Don't answer the door. Look after yourself. Then when this whole thing is over, you can be as condescending toward him as you like."

Her jaw drops. "I'm not condescending."

"Sure. He just can't be left without your supervision."

I see the exact moment Margot's words sink in with her. I get that she doesn't mean to be mean, that she's frustrated and worried, but the things she says hit Perry harder than anyone else. Her dark eyes go misty.

"I'm *scared.*"

"I know …" Perry moves forward to reassure her. "I know. Me too. But I'll be able to be a tiny bit less worried without you here."

"How am I supposed to leave you knowing that I might never see you again?" She's frowning hard, holding back tears, and all I want is for them to go so we can find out what the fuck Perry found out today.

"You trust me."

Her bottom lip shakes, and Elle pulls her back.

"Come on, love. They have a lot they need to deal with."

"I swear to fucking god, if you die—"

Perry's laugh cuts his sister off. "I know, I know, you'll kill me yourself."

"No, you boob. My life will be over."

And with that little bomb, she and Elle finally leave.

Perry doesn't say anything, and the silence from him speaks volumes. The heavy way his shoulders slope forward makes me want to pull him closer, maybe hug him or protect him or— Lars turns on him before I can.

"Tell us everything."

"Not much to tell," Perry says. "Luther's the one who organized the hit on me, and he said I have a week to turn St. Clare over to him. Dead or alive."

Lars's gun is back out in a flash. "Just try it."

Perry glares at him. "Do you really think I would have told you that if I was planning to do it?"

"I have no idea what goes through your mind, only that, as you said this morning, you don't plan."

"Listen, I've already had one gun pointed at me today, am reevaluating all the friendships I thought I had, went on an expedition to get here, and now would really like—"

Lars holds up his hand, cutting off Perry's stream of thoughts.

At first, I think he's done listening to him, but then I catch what Lars has already noticed. Incessant car horns down on the road.

"What the …" I go to check out of the window before Lars pulls me back.

"Get down."

I get down, and after a second, Perry joins me.

Lars huffs. "What are you doing?"

It takes Perry a second to realize the question was directed his way. "Well, I don't want to have my head blown off either, thanks."

"I thought you said you were going to help me protect him?"

Perry's gaze darts between us. "Well, you know, it seems like you, umm, have this …"

Lars glowers at him before taking the long way to the window. He seals his back to the wall beside it and cranes his head to look out. "I think … it looks like a car is out the front. Blocking the road."

Considering it's a reasonably busy street, I'm not surprised that the beeping is getting loud enough to hear.

"Well, that doesn't sound good," Perry hisses.

"No fucking shit." Lars glances around the apartment. "Goddamn penthouses."

"What's your sudden problem with the penthouse?"

His face sets into a stormy mask. "We're on the top floor. If someone followed you and they're down there, we have no way out."

CHAPTER TWENTY-FIVE

PERRY

NO WAY out sounds like a quitter's attitude to me. Sure, I don't have a solution to our apparent problem, but if there's anything my lackluster life of hustle has taught me, it's that there's always a way.

"Perry, what kind of car was following you?"

"Like … a black sedan type of thing."

"Fuck."

"Let me guess, the car outside is a black sedan type of thing?"

"How did you know?" he asks dryly.

I scramble from the floor back into the bedroom I slept in last night and switch out my hoodie for the T-shirt, then shove my hoodie into my backpack, pull out my face mask, and hurry back into the kitchen, where I fill my backpack to the brim with all the food we bought.

"You're not actually thinking about your stomach right now, are you?" Lars snaps.

"Where's my gun?"

He looks like he's about to argue over giving it to me, but one of those silent conversation thingies takes place between him and St. Clare before Lars disappears into his bedroom and comes back with the damn thing. For all I know, St. Clare was telling him to throw me out the window, but if Lars heard "get Perry his gun," I'm not about to argue with their weird mind reading.

"Bullets?"

"You're asking for a whole lot of trust right now," Lars says. Then he pulls my bullet case from his pocket. I know it's mine because it has a smiley face with crosses for eyes on the top.

"Thanks." I load the gun, tuck it into my pants, and shrug my bag back on. "You guys ready?"

"To die?" St. Clare asks dryly, standing out of view of the window. "Don't think I have much choice."

"No one's dying today. Well, nothing except for my faith in Luther. He said I had a week, and now he's having me followed. Talk about a lack of trust."

"The fact you'd trust a guy like that in the first place makes me question your judgment skills," Lars says, checking the barrel of his own gun.

Meanwhile, St. Clare is distinctly gunless and looking less and less confident by the second.

"Hey." I pull his attention to me. "We've got this." Those wary blue eyes study me for a second.

"Do you know what you're doing?"

I shrug. "Not a clue."

"Maybe we should make a plan first?"

"We could, but the longer we spend here, the more time we're giving whoever it is to set up."

"What's *your* plan, then?" Lars asks.

"To leave."

"And?"

"And that's the plan."

I turn and head for the door, hoping they follow me but not wanting to fuck around and wait if they're not. My phone is on the fritz again, so I bang it with my palm a few times until the screen comes alive, and then I flip it open. But who to call?

Arlie is the smartest person I know, but she's also been expressly forbidden from helping me, so there's a slim chance she might not pick up. I have no idea *what* Everett does, but he looks pretty badass, so I'd imagine he'd be able to help, but then he's *also* been told not to help, and I get the impression he does what he's told a whole lot more than Arlie does.

Which leaves Tommy. Who I think is a thief or a pickpocket or some kind of person who swindles others out of all their money. I'm not sure how the fuck he could help in this kind of situation, but beggars can't be choosers. Maybe he'll be like my Robin Hood. Stealing knowledge from people to help the needy.

And I'm very, very needy.

Tommy answers on the first ring, and I could kiss him, I swear. "We never spoke," comes down the line instead of a hello.

"Ah … okay?"

"I'm serious," he says. "What do you want?"

"A way out."

His forcefully patient voice comes out. "What do you mean?"

"I'm currently in the penthouse of a building, and now there's a car parked suspiciously out the front in a no-parking zone and blocking the road, and I thiiink I might have been followed here, and the owner of that car is waiting to kill us."

"Huh. Yeah, you're fucked."

Well, thanks for the confidence. I huff. "Do you have a plan B for me?"

"Not my area of expertise."

"Is there anyone with you who *might* be able to help me?"

There's a long silence. "No?"

"Tommy!"

"Don't use my name, *Jesus*. Okay, fine. So one car means five people, max. And I can't see it being more than three from experience, and they've probably left the getaway driver near the car. You're in an apartment building, which means a choice between the elevator and the stairs, and considering they've parked like a total fuckwit, they're probably looking to get in and out as fast as possible."

"Literally none of that is good news."

"Just stating facts. If there's one guy, he's in the elevator. If there's two, they probably split up."

So basically blocking off either of our options to escape this thing. And if they took the elevator, they're already outside this apartment.

"Can you send me your location?" Tommy asks.

"I don't think my phone does that. I'm in the New Maple complex."

Tommy lets out a whistle. "That's some fancy shit. How the hell did you wind up staying there?"

"Long story," I mutter, and then a thought hits me. "Wait. They don't know we're here. Shit. Okay. Thanks, Tommy."

"What do you—"

I hang up before saying any more, then turn to St. Clare and Lars. "No one knows we're here."

"They're parked right outside," Lars reminds me.

I wave the logic away. "Outside, yes. Here, obviously. But *here* …" I stomp my foot and gesture either side of me. "No one in their right mind would think we're in a fucking penthouse."

"That's a good point …" St. Clare says.

"But what if the doorman told them?"

"In that case, we're fucked, but Walter didn't seem like a snitch, so we're going to have to take the chance."

The way I see it, they know I'm in the building, but to find me, they're going to have to check out every fucking room in this place to narrow down where I could be. They want to get in and out fast, and that is *not* a fast way to get through things.

Which means Walter is their key to figuring out where we are, so they're either in the lobby, scaring the hell out of that sweet old man, or they're already right outside the door.

We won't figure out which one unless we get going.

"Okay. Plan."

Lars has the audacity to look shocked, but I keep talking before he can waste more time.

"I'll go out first. If I'm shot, you know they're out there. If I'm not, we're in the clear. We'll all get in a separate elevator, go down to the first floor, find a window or an apartment that opens onto the back streets, and jump out from there."

"From a first-floor window?" St. Clare's eyes go wide.

"Of course." I cuff his shoulder. "You've got this."

I don't actually know that any of us *got this* or if I'll even be alive long enough to find out that answer, but here we fucking go. Shitty shitty, bang bang and all that.

I pull out my gun, puff out a quick exhale, and take off the safety. Once we're out of here, we can work out what's next, but I can't lie, I'm going to miss the penthouse. I didn't know beds could be so comfortable or that kissing a man could be so hot.

For one stalling second, I want to ask Lars if our horoscopes say we'll survive this, but if that answer is no, I don't want it.

I'm gonna manifest myself one more day.

"P-Perry," St. Clare starts from behind me.

I shush him, grab the handle, and yank the front door open. The hallway is deserted, just one long stretch of bare wall with fancy lights that opens to the elevator bank at the end. I can't make out anyone lurking down there, but my heart is *thadum-ping* heavy and loud as I grip the gun harder.

I give myself a second to scan the area before stepping out into clear range.

My guts don't immediately end up on the floor.

So that's a relief.

It doesn't do much to settle the rage of adrenaline overriding my system, and I jog the length of the hallway to the elevators. A moment later, St. Clare and Lars bolt after me.

"There's only one," Lars points out.

"There are more a few floors down. You two can get out there and find another one. Then we meet down there."

"Okay."

"What if there's no one actually after us?" St. Clare asks.

"There's someone after us."

"How do you know?"

"Because I'd prefer to believe it than sit around waiting for them to get a clear shot."

"Fair point," he mutters.

Lars laughs. "I think that's the first time we've agreed on something."

The elevator *dings* a second before it opens, and I have enough forethought to quickly wrench St. Clare out of the way in case someone is inside.

They aren't.

I return his amused look with an apologetic one of my own. "Just in case."

"I appreciate it."

Our nerves are all on edge, and as much as he tries to play it cool, I can tell this is the kind of situation he never would have thought he'd land in. We're twinsies like that, I guess, and the only one who willingly put themself in this position is Lars, so I'd like one hundred percent fewer complaints from him moving forward.

I jab at the number nineteen randomly, and we ride the elevator the whole way down. When it comes to a stop, Lars and I make sure the coast is clear, and then the two of them leave.

"Back alley?" Lars checks.

I quickly nod before the doors shut me out of view, and then I turn to hit the first floor. Before my finger can make contact though, I pause. I was obviously followed here. *Me.* They might suspect St. Clare is with me, but they can't know that for sure, and they definitely wouldn't know about Lars.

Then I think of sweet Walter and the pictures of his grandkids he was showing me before I left this morning, and before I can press the fancy number one, I redirect, and my finger jabs at the G button instead.

I try not to fucking cry or change my mind as I drop like a stone toward people who very likely want me dead.

At the very least, it will give St. Clare and Lars a head start and stop them from scaring Walter.

Margot would fucking kill me.

I push her from my mind as the elevator slows and pulls to a stop. Then I duck beside the bank of buttons and wait as the doors slide open.

Silence.

Creepy silence.

Very creepy silence inside that's blasted open only by the constant horns outside. I scan the portion of the lobby I can see, and when it still comes up deserted, I inch further out.

The loud *bang* echoes in my ears as a bullet flies right by my face, close enough to feel the heat before it lodges into the wall of the elevator.

I scream and duck back as someone shouts, "Wait! It's the other one."

The other one?

"We know you're there, Perry!"

Ah. Great. We're already acquainted.

The doors go to close, and I quickly reach around to wave them open again. "I think I'm changing my name," I inform whoever it is. "There's no Perry here. Just a … Brock." Brock is good. Manly. Strong. The type of guy who won't take a bullet to the head without avenging himself.

"Whatever the fuck your name is, you'll want to see this."

I'm about to ask what *this* is when the voice that comes next gives me chills.

"Don't listen to them. Get out of here."

Margot.

I choke on my next breath, brain short-circuiting.

All I can focus on is *no, no, no, no this isn't happening*, and wild theories jump out at me like maybe they have her voice recorded or some shit.

"Yeah, listen to your sister," the man says. "Get out of here. Her and her girlfriend would make pretty corpses."

The thought of that rolls my stomach. "What do you want?"

"Where's your mark? He's here, isn't he?"

"Define *here*," I try weakly. "Exactly."

"Don't fucking test me."

My eyes shutter closed for a second. I thought I was scared in Luther's office, but it's nothing on this. My vision is fucking all over the place, and when the elevator doors try to close again, I only just stop them in time.

"Oh," I say, like I've caught on, but I'm not at all selling it. "St. Clare? That guy. By my guess, he's probably a long, long way away by now."

"That's not good news for you."

I risk my fucking life by leaning out a little to see what's going on.

My eyes immediately find Margot and Elle. Elle's face is bleeding, Margot is snarling like a wild animal, and both of them have their hands pulled tight behind them. I know that feeling. One man has his gun pointed at the two of them, while the other stands behind the desk, gun on Walter.

"We're not going to shoot you," the guy behind the desk says. It takes me a second to recognize him.

"*Danvers*?" My voice breaks with betrayal. "I thought we were friends."

"We're *friendly*. Which is why I don't want to kill you or your sister. I just need to know where he is."

Maybe I'm too trusting, but I swallow thickly, grip my gun tight, and step into clear view. The doors try to close *a-fucking-gain*, but I wave my leg between them until they reopen.

The guy I don't recognize lifts his gun my way. But he doesn't shoot, so that's a positive.

"Let them both go and I'll help you," I say.

"Yeah, it doesn't work like that." Danvers leaves Walter and moves closer. His gun isn't pointing at anyone, but he's holding it in a way that makes it clear he's ready if he needs it.

These guys know what they're doing.

But I've always found knowing what you're doing to be overrated.

I don't think, just shoot. I'm not aiming for anyone or anything —just want to give them a bit of a scare—and while my first bullet skims Danvers's leg, the second hits the unknown guy's foot.

I'd be sorry about that if it wasn't the very thing that sends his bullet intended for me wide. The guy cries out and goes to shoot me again, but my third bullet makes them both duck.

Another one sent my way has me diving back behind the

elevator doors, and I'm freaking out about how to get to Margot and Elle when Danvers shouts, "Go after them!"

"I've been shot in the fucking foot!"

I send another shot back through the lobby and chance a glimpse at what's going on. Walter, Margot, and Elle have thankfully disappeared, the rando guy is sitting on the ground, and—

Fuck.

Danvers is running my way.

I jab at the close-doors button over and over and over. I'm gripping my gun tight, hoping I don't have to use it because I already feel bad enough about getting the other guy, but as Danvers draws closer and the stupid elevator refuses to listen, the awareness is setting in. I'm going to have to shoot him. Hopefully just enough to get him to stop chasing me and not enough to kill him, but how do I guarantee that? How do I—

The doors finally move.

They're sliding closed at the rate of slug flopping over a garden path, and I'm so fucking sweaty with panic I'm not sure how I haven't dropped my gun already.

Danvers isn't close enough, and he lifts his gun and gets off a shot right before the doors seal between us.

So he doesn't catch the way I *wail* in pain.

A fiery burn rips through my shoulder, and I glance down to find red quickly bleeding out across the white T-shirt.

My friends fur-ever T-shirt.

That bastard.

Before he can get the doors open again, I drag my good hand down every button and finally suck in an inhale as the elevator moves. Good luck to him guessing which floor I'm getting out on.

My shoulder is in goddamn agony, and as soon as the doors open on the first floor, I run. I tear down one corridor to the next, and as I spot a window to head for, movement on my left makes me stop.

Lars is holding open the door to the stairwell as St. Clare steps inside.

"Close that!"

Lars hurries to do it even as St. Clare's jaw drops.

"What the fuck happened to you?"

I ignore him, grab the potted plant right by the window, and throw it as hard as my injured shoulder will allow. The glass gives way easily—and it's lucky we're not on a higher level where this wouldn't have been possible.

"Out. Now."

Thankfully, neither of them questions me.

Lars goes first. Jumping from the first floor onto the cement like some fucking terminator, he then turns, and when I shove St. Clare ahead, Lars is ready to break his fall.

I'm not at all feeling woozy as I set the safety on my gun, tuck it into my jeans, and then give a quick plea to the universe that I'm not about to go splat.

Before I can do much more than that, I hear the door to the stairwell open behind me, and I jump.

There's a second of weightlessness, and then my feet slam into the pavement, and I pitch forward, just able to catch myself before I go face-first into cement.

My shoulder gives out a second later as squealing tires fill my ears, and Lars hauls me to my feet before I'm run over. There are snatches of everything happening around me—a shout, St. Clare swearing, the car horns louder out here—that when the door to the car flies open, I don't realize at first that it's *my* car and Tommy's sitting behind the wheel.

"Right on time, Perry." He grins, and I shove St. Clare into the back seat ahead of me while Lars jumps into the front.

A shot hits the back windshield of my baby, shattering the glass into pieces.

"Might be a good time to drive," I say weakly.

Tommy steps on the gas.

CHAPTER TWENTY-SIX

ST. CLARE

WHAT THE FUCK is going on?

I'm still panting as we fly downtown in a car that's half-deranged, a stranger taking us who knows where and Perry wheezing so hard he sounds like a squeak toy has been lodged in his throat.

Oh. And he's bleeding.

Wonderful.

"Who is this? Where are we going? And what the hell just happened?"

Perry loudly inhales, hair so sweaty it looks wet, as he reaches behind himself and pulls off his backpack, teeth clenched tight in pain.

"Got shot."

"I can see that." And as much as I'd love to remind him that he put me through the same, I can't. I don't like seeing Perry's face anything but happy, and right now, it's pinched with tension, and his big eyes hold a worry so deep I want a word with whoever put it there.

"We need to get you to a hospital," I say.

"No hospitals," the driver throws back.

"He's bleeding."

"It's his shoulder. It'll be fine."

"How the hell could you know what?"

The driver laughs. "You ask a lot of questions." Then he turns up the radio.

Perry tugs open the zipper on his bag and digs around inside for a second before pulling out his phone. It's an old thing. Bright, metallic pink, with a tiny screen on the part that flips open.

I snatch it from him. "Answer me."

Perry's actually shaking. "I went to the lobby to check on Walter. There were two guys there, and they were holding Margot and Elle at gunpoint. I need to make sure they got away okay."

Before I can hand the phone back, it rings. Perry's big, warm hand closes around mine as he takes the phone from me and snaps it open.

As soon as I make out Margot's voice from the tinny speaker, I relax a fraction. She's okay. I can feel it in the way Perry's whole body relaxes.

They barely say more than a few words before he hangs up. His phone is gripped loosely in the hand resting on his thigh when he sags back and closes his eyes.

"You'll get blood on the seat," I tell him.

Somehow, he manages a small smile. "Look at where you're sitting."

I shift forward to look down and ... well. *That* doesn't look pretty. "Please tell me this isn't the first time you've been shot."

"It's the first time."

"I don't want to know what those stains are, do I?"

"Couldn't tell you even if you did."

Wonderful. I give myself a second to adjust to the reality that I'm sitting on a lot of someone else's blood before I move stiffly back into place. "Nice car."

"It's reliable."

His sleepy voice draws my attention back to him. I don't like how gray his face is going or the way he's got sweat still building at his hairline.

"How are you feeling?" I stupidly ask.

"Sore."

"Yeah, but besides that."

Finally, his eyes crack open, and he looks at me through amusement. "You're loving this, aren't you?"

"Surprisingly, not even a little bit."

His eyebrows bunch together. "Really?"

"Yup. Weird, I know. You'd think I'd enjoy seeing my would-be killer turned protector turned hookup bleed out in front of my eyes. There's obviously something wrong with me."

His small smile slopes wider. "My charisma wins everyone over."

"Well, you still have work to do with me, but at least we've reached the level where I don't actively want you dead."

"Big praises." His eyes fall closed again.

We've left the city behind and are speeding our way through residential streets. Perry's filling out the whole seat and part of the middle, making an effort not to bump his shoulder as we take the corners.

My gaze drops from his wound to run over his bicep, down his hairy forearm, all the way to the ridiculous bracelet, and then onto his wide hand. I'm not sure what it is about him that I'm tuned in to, but knowing he's in pain doesn't sit right with me.

"Do you need a hospital? If you do, I'll make him take us there."

Perry's warm brown eyes peep open again, and he studies my face for a moment. "Nah, I'm good. Besides, all the guys dig battle scars, right? I won't be able to keep you off me."

I choke on, well, I don't even fucking know, but that was the last thing I expected Perry to say. "I know it's been a long day, but you definitely came on to me last night."

"I thought I might *die*," he says like that's some kind of defense.

All it does is remind me that he only went gay for the night to tick off some stupid, imaginary list. "Right." I can't keep the edge out of my voice. "Guess I need to make a move on finding a woman to hook up with, then. You know. In case I die."

There's nothing in the world that could make me do that,

considering my complete lack of attraction, but saying he kissed me because he thought he'd die is the stupidest fucking thing I've ever heard. If that's how he wants to play off his attraction to me, then fine, but I'm not going to play along.

Hopefully.

My gaze drops to his thick thighs, and a memory of sitting on them fills me, and fuck. Right. I'm going to *try* not to play along, even though I know that if he ever wanted to do it again, I'm not strong enough to say no.

Perry is way too fucking hot to ignore.

But I'm a big boy, I have no issues picking up, and there's no way I'm going to turn into a pathetic little yes man just because my body is tortuously in tune with him. I hope.

I have no idea how long we drive for, but I can't shake the unsettled energy coursing through me as the residential streets disappear and I watch vacant lots go by.

Perry's little finger nudges mine, and I hate how cute I find that.

"Yeah?" I ask, not looking at him.

"You mad?"

"Nope."

His voice is laced with amusement. "You sound mad."

I finally look up, and I hate how easily his eyes make me soften to him, so I quickly distract to stop him from guessing why I actually am kinda mad at him. "I'm annoyed no one has answered any of my questions."

"I told you what happened."

I nod up front. "Still don't know who he is."

"*He* is Tommy. He's a friend from Lethal Poison."

"What?" Lars turns completely in his seat, and his gun meets the side of Tommy's head before I even see him pull it out. "Where are you taking us?"

"Relax ..." Tommy blows a bubble of bright pink chewing gum before he lets it pop and pulls it back into his mouth. "I know a place."

"Is *Luther* at this place?"

Tommy sneers. "You really think I want Luther to know that I'm helping you guys? I don't have a death wish."

"Why are you helping, then?" I ask.

Lars slowly lowers the gun, but his attention doesn't leave Tommy.

"Perry's my friend."

"Aww ..." Perry lays a blood-smeared hand over his chest. "I knew I liked you."

"Arlie's waiting for us."

That's a name I've heard before.

Perry perks up. "She is?"

"Why do you sound so surprised?"

"Because Luther warned her and Everett not to help or they'd be in trouble."

"Do you really think she's the type to listen?"

"Probably not." And then Perry says something that sends my insides cold. "It's why I'm in love with her."

In ... love.

Ice fills my veins, and I'm totally unprepared for how fucking instantly I want to rage. We're heading for who the fuck knows where, and I'm going to be face-to-face with the woman the guy I slept with *last fucking night* is in love with.

Just when I thought that being shot at would be the worst part of my day.

The way we kissed keeps giving me this little gut tug every time I think about it, and now that memory is going to be replaced by seeing him with ... her. Arlie. The contract killer who showed Perry the ropes and then let him loose on me.

"Any chance you can drop us off at my nightclub?" I ask, lifting my voice to be heard over the music.

Tommy turns it down a fraction. "No can do. It's too easy to find you there."

"I have security."

"That won't stop anyone."

"I have Lars."

Tommy throws Lars an assessing glance. "And as impressive as he is, one guy isn't going to keep you safe."

"What about *me*?" Perry asks, having the fucking balls to sound offended.

"What about you?"

"*I* protect you as well. It's not just Lars."

"Yeah, but Lars doesn't go rogue when he sets out a plan, then get himself shot, then throw me out of a window. And when I asked to be dropped off, that plan didn't include you."

His jaw drops. "But we're a team."

I point at Tommy. "They're your team. You don't need to latch onto us for protection anymore."

He's frowning at me, and I hate the way it makes me want to apologize. If there's one ask I could throw out to the universe, it would be for Perry to not look so damn disappointed and for that disappointment to do nothing to me.

Out of the corner of my eye, I catch Lars glancing back at us both.

Perry slowly looks over at him. "But … we could all be a team. The five of us. With four of us protecting St. Clare, no one else stands a chance."

"He's got a point," Lars says, and this is the part where I wish we really could communicate telepathically because I'd tell him I want to be literally anywhere Perry and Arlie aren't.

Then he'd tell me to pull my head out of my ass and that this is more important than who my dick wants.

Which is a good point.

Even if I don't want to acknowledge it.

"Ever's there too," Tommy says. "But we're not sticking around. My job was to grab your car, drive you there, then Arlie's going to arm you up, Everett will take a look at your shoulder, and then we're out again."

Before I can take a second to be relieved that Arlie won't be someone I have to deal with constantly, Perry takes over.

"Wait a second, how *did* you get my car? I've got my keys."

Tommy snorts. "Who needs keys?"

Then he turns off the street we're driving along and onto a back road. It looks exactly like the creepy kind of place you'd bring someone to kill them. So I'm instantly filled with assurance that this is all totally fine and not another case of us having to run for our lives. Can I really hope for a third time lucky?

"Well, this looks creepy," Perry says, sitting forward to look out the front windscreen. It brings him dangerously close to me, and while the urge to lean in a little and brush his hip is strong, so is the urge to poke him in the shoulder.

Bet his precious *Arlie* would never hurt him like that.

All I can hope for at this point is that she's seventy-nine and Perry's joking around.

But a few minutes later, when we pull up in front of a dinky little cabin with moss-covered wooden walls and a sheet metal roof, I find it hard to worry about them bringing us out here to shoot us in the head because the woman who's waiting for us is a goddamn goddess.

Nothing like the constant reminder that you were only a means to getting off to help you value your own life a bit less.

I thought our kiss had been explosive.

Turns out it was only explosive to me.

CHAPTER TWENTY-SEVEN

PERRY

"YOU CAME!" I cry, jumping out of the car and attempting to throw my arms around Arlie. Except I forgot that one of them is basically out of commission, and instead of swamping her in a hug, I curl forward with an "owwww-shit-crap" instead.

Her warm chuckle makes me glance up. "I can't believe I'm risking my meal ticket for you."

"I appreciate it, if that helps."

"Not a bit." She reaches down to help me to my feet and steers me toward a camp chair next to a large fire pit. I'm not sure how they even get that thing going considering everything around here looks really fucking wet. We're hugged by trees on all sides, the grass is being strangled by dirt and stones and dead leaves, and there's a hint of decaying vegetation on the air.

I'll take the smog of city life, thanks.

Arlie plants her hands on her hips and looks down at me. "How did you get yourself shot?"

"Occupational hazard of being a hero."

"A hero?" She cocks her eyebrow, and I try to mirror her but fail miserably. "Whatever you're doing with your face is creepy, and you need to stop it."

"Jeez, you can't even show some compassion while I'm injured?"

"No."

I blink at her, waiting for her to go on. "No?"

"No is a complete sentence, dork."

The thing about Arlie is that she's intimidating without meaning to be. I love strong women; my momma was one before she died, Margot and Elle both are now, and it's part of why I admire Arlie. But where Margot is strong because she has to be, I think Arlie just fucking likes it. And that's the part that's intimidating.

Judging by the goose bumps racing over my skin, I'm cold, but I can't feel much of anything right now. My head is a bit of a woozy mess, my arm and chest are sticky with cooling blood, and I look and smell like I've just climbed out of a dumpster.

Meanwhile, St. Clare is still standing over by the car and looks like he's had a mildly busy day in his suit pants and button-up shirt. The way he's rolled up his sleeves should be sponsoring porn sites everywhere.

I'm about to tell him that I'm injured and he should put those slutty forearms away when Everett walks out of the small house, carrying ... I don't think I want to know. The small metal dish is shielding whatever's inside, and I'd like it to stay that way.

"What do we have here?" he asks, bald head so shiny it looks as damp as the vegetation surrounding us.

"Got nicked by a bullet."

"Really?"

"Yeah. Can you believe *Danvers* shot at me? We closed out the bar together for his last birthday."

Everett hums. "It's a hard lesson to learn."

"What is?"

"That money will always mean more than friendship in our circles."

"Then why are you three here?"

Everett doesn't answer me, just glances over at Tommy and Arlie.

Arlie shrugs. "Don't ask me. I'm here under duress."

"It was your idea," Tommy throws back.

"My statement stands."

I send Arlie my most grateful expression. "I always knew you loved me."

She sighs. "Hurry the hell up so we can go, Ever."

"Ah …" He pauses, checking both sides of my shoulder as he sets the tray down on a teeny fold-out table. "I don't think this will be a quick fix."

"Why not?" I ask, trying to see what he sees.

"Because it didn't skim you. It's still in there."

I guess that explains all the pain, then. "And how do we make it *not* in there anymore?"

He chuckles, pulls a small bottle of vodka from his pocket, and holds it out to me. "We start with this."

"You want me to drink that?"

"Well, it's either you or me, and I doubt you want me indulging when I'm about to dig around inside your body."

That's an excellent point. I take the nip, remove the lid, and throw the whole thing back. It tastes filthy, like a mouthful of nasty, burning bile, and it's lucky I'm at the point where throwing up over myself won't make much of a difference to how disgusting I am.

My feet dig into the mulch beneath my shoes, and somehow, I keep it all down. Considering St. Clare isn't far away and he's watching me, I'd like to look a teeny bit impressive. The last thing a guy wants is for the guy he hooked up with to regret the whole experience. Especially since I wouldn't mind it happening again.

"Shirt off," Everett says.

I drag my attention back from St. Clare. "I think I'm going to need some help with that."

"I can cut it off?"

"No." I grip the front of my T-shirt. "It's my favorite shirt."

"It's covered in blood."

"Just needs a good soak."

"Whatever you say," he mutters, helping me peel the shirt up and over my head. My good arm is easy enough to pull out, but it takes some careful maneuvering to peel it from the wound and get it off the other one. The prickling of the cool air picks up with the breeze, even with the fire right next to me, and I'm probably getting frostbite or pneumonia at this point, but at least I still can't feel it. Despite how much I'm fucking shaking.

Everett picks up what looks like a long, thin knife. "Three … two …"

I'm waiting for *one* when he stabs me with the damn thing, and a very unmanly squeal bursts from me. "I wasn't ready!"

"That was the point."

My teeth clench tight as Everett digs around in my shoulder, and now he's started, all I can hope for is that he doesn't bust up something vital that will lose the control of my arm. It's a very nice arm, and we've been through a lot together. Shooting guns, carrying my bracelet, and all those times it's helped me eat, drink, and jerk off.

"Is it actually in there?" I ask through my clenched jaw. "Or are you just enjoying stabbing me?"

"I can enjoy stabbing you *and* have it be in there, Perry."

"My mistake." If you'd asked me a few minutes ago whether this could hurt more, my answer would have been no, but look at that, Ever is managing. I glance over and finally catch St. Clare's eyes. "Have I mentioned yet how very, very sorry I am for shooting you?"

Instead of the indulgent amusement I'm so used to from him, St. Clare turns away and walks over toward where Lars is. They talk quietly between themselves, and I try and fail not to feel like the odd one out.

Tommy, Arlie, and Everett have each other. St. Clare and Lars have each other. No matter how much I try, I don't fit in with any of them.

But these guys showed up for me, so I have to be grateful about that.

"Got him," Everett exclaims, and a heavy metallic *chink* comes as the bullet falls into the metal bowl. Everett leans in for a better look. "I think that's the whole thing."

"You think?"

"At least sixty-five percent sure."

Those aren't terrible odds, I guess.

"I'll clean it up and then stitch you back together."

"You know how to do that?"

"Close enough." Everett wipes over the wound. "Just don't expect it to be pretty."

"Good thing I have my face to do the heavy lifting. Isn't that right, St. Clare?"

His stare bores into me in return, and I get that uncomfortable gut wrench that maybe I've done something wrong. When he doesn't answer, I turn to Arlie. "Isn't that right?"

"If by heavy lifting you mean scaring people away before they can even see your shoulder, then sure. But it's not your whole face. Only the stuff that comes out of your mouth."

I drop my head back toward the watery blue sky, the needle piercing my skin nothing compared to the abuse my shoulder's seen today. "I'm starting to suspect I'm unappreciated in my time."

Tommy laughs and waves a hand my way. "What part of all this are we forgetting to appreciate?"

Ah … Okay, he's got me there. I joke about being good-looking when in actual fact I'm probably nudging a seven on a good day. On a day like today, I'd probably give me a weak four. People say I'm a fun guy, yet none of those people have bothered to stick around, so I'm not sure they can be trusted. *I* think I'm a fun guy, but as Lars pointed out, apparently my judgment can't be trusted either. I'm loyal—just have no one to be loyal to. I have a big heart —and no one to share that with. And I'm sure I *could* hold down a job if this bad luck would stop following me.

I swallow roughly as Ever wipes over my newly stitched-up franken-wound. "Can we take a rain check on that answer?"

Tommy laughs again, but I'm not so sure I find it funny. I like making people happy, but just once, it might be nice to be *in* on the joke instead of *being* the joke.

It's nice to have dreams, I guess.

My gaze finds St. Clare again, standing on the other side of the lawn, closer to the house, and the second our eyes meet, he wrenches his away again. As much as I love that everyone showed up for me, I wish they'd hurry up and get moving so that I can ask him what's wrong. Moody St. Clare isn't a version of him that I'm used to.

He needs that spark of his back.

CHAPTER TWENTY-EIGHT

ST. CLARE

THE WHOLE TIME Perry's being tended to, the rest of us stand in a ring around him, watching every second. Sure, part of it is concern about him being a person, and he's a person in pain, but it's more than that. We all know he'll be okay. There's no reason to watch on.

But when it comes to Perry, he's like this gravitational force, and we're all floaty chunks of rock, stuck in his orbit.

Even me.

All I want right now is to disappear into the house and wait for everyone to leave, but my feet are planted on the ground, turned toward him, and I hate how much I'm tuned in to every grunt of pain.

So is Arlie.

If I'm not watching Perry, I'm glaring her way. There's a bond between the two of them where she pretends not to be interested, and he watches her through big, puppy dog eyes. It's sickening. No one is buying her disinterest because who the hell couldn't be interested in Perry?

It takes way too long for them to clean him up, show us where everything is in the cabin, and then get the rundown on what happened since he left Lethal Poison.

I'm not at all surprised when Perry tells us he wanted to check in on Walter, and the fact it could have gotten him killed sits heavy with me. What if that bullet got his chest instead? We've both come way too close to dying lately, and I get the feeling that luck isn't something we can keep relying on.

They leave in a car much nicer than Perry's—no number plate draws my attention—and when they disappear and the silence kicks in, I'm conscious not to look Perry's way again. Not even when Lars leaves to look around the property. I'm going to wedge distance between us whether I like it or not.

Unfortunately, he doesn't seem on board with that plan.

I turn around and almost run right into him.

"Are you okay?"

Him asking me that when he's the one who's injured is … well, it's Perry. "Fine."

"Are you sure?"

I try to walk away, and he hurries to fall into step with me. Still shirtless, way too close, energy wrapping around me in a delicious way that makes me want to give in. Already. Two seconds after I decided to give myself breathing room from him.

"Other than the whole being on the run for my life thing, sure." I abruptly change my direction to get away from him, but he grabs my wrist and pulls me back. Reluctantly, I force myself to meet his eyes, and it pulls a shadow of his goofy grin from him.

"I'm sorry," he says. "For getting us into this mess."

I frown because he sounds like he believes that. "I don't think you get to take all the blame."

"Well, if I'd never shot you—"

"Then someone else would have, and they probably would have done a better job of it." I should reassure him, but I'm not going to. No more playing into that connection I pathetically want to have with him.

"Maybe."

I go to walk away again.

"Can you … just …"

"What?"

That smile is gone, and he's chewing on his bottom lip as he looks me over. "You're mad at me."

"Why would I be mad at you?"

"I don't know. That's why I'm so confused."

The most stupid part is that he's being genuine. He *is* confused. The way he can be confused about why I might be mad over him using me and then fawning all over the love of his life right in front of my face deserves to go in a parody somewhere. I don't have to want a relationship with the guy to at least not want to see that.

I'm all for sex and quick hookups, but that doesn't mean I actively want to know I've been used.

"Don't worry about it. Soon enough, this will be over, and you won't need to think about me again."

"You mean … you don't want to be friends when this is over?"

Goddamn that wounded tone. I could kick him. He's not allowed to make me feel bad about wanting distance when he's the whole reason I want it in the first place. "No." I shrug. "But we'll probably be dead, so it's not like it will make a difference."

His face falls, gaze dropping to the dirt between us and hand finally releasing my arm. I didn't even realize he was still holding it, but now the grip is gone, my bare skin is more aware of what it lost than what it had. "I thought we were friends," he says.

The way my mouth is rebelling against me should be illegal. We are friends. I *like* Perry. I hate that I'm making him look so pathetically needy when he's one of the sweetest men I've ever met, but I need to protect myself too. Being sweet doesn't give him the right to be ignorant. Still, I can't stop myself from throwing him a bone. From guiding him to the answer that I know he'll never come to on his own.

"We were," I admit. "But for the future: being friends with a queer man doesn't give you the excuse to use him." This time, I really do walk away, and because I'm maybe even a little hurt, I can't stop from throwing back over my shoulder, "Especially when you're obviously in love with someone else."

I escape inside the cabin before Perry can respond. Yes, I'm a coward, thank you, but I'm also not in a place where I can hear him talk about Arlie and how perfect she is. Or accept an apology after pointing out why I'm not so ready to be besties with him right now.

With a huge exhale, I flop back onto the ratty sofa, knowing there's no way in hell I'd normally be this annoyed. Between having my life threatened, my brother missing, and the general comfort of my life turned on its head, I'm a teensy bit taking it out on Perry. Yes, it's a valid reason, and normally I'd make a joke to brush it off, then never see him again, but for right now, there's no escaping him, and everything else feels too raw.

I need some sleep. And a shower. Maybe after those two things, I'll be able to think more clearly. There's no way my annoyance with Perry will be able to resist his overenthusiastic energy for long. I'm doomed before I've even gotten started.

Couldn't I have been almost shot by an asshole instead?

The front door shoves open, and I glance over to see Perry standing there, hand on the door, dumbstruck look on his face.

"I'm not in love with Arlie!"

Slowly, I straighten, eying what looks like shock and maybe offense radiating from him. "*You* said it."

"Yeah, but, I mean … it's a joke. Like she's gorgeous and scary and good at what she does, obviously—"

"You're not making the point you think you're making."

He scrambles closer and drops to his knees beside the couch. "No, like, I have a lot of respect for her. I love her. She's awesome and kind of terrifying and a lot inspiring. I'd love to be as cool as her one day, but I'm not actually in love with her." He lets out a little laugh. "I'm not a complete idiot. We'd be terrible together. I'd drive her nuts, and she'd do nothing but put me down. I have a bit more self-respect than that."

I'm struggling to latch onto what he's saying, but relief is pooling in my chest. "Only a *bit* more?"

"That requires more soul-searching than I'm capable of."

My gaze travels the length of his face. "You know, sometimes I think you might be smarter than you let on."

He likes that. He doesn't try to hold back the way his eyes light up. But that light slowly dims as he reaches for my hand.

"Sorry I upset you. And for whatever it means, I didn't use you last night."

I'm trying not to let his warm hand and bare chest take over my brain. I can still do the thinking of the things, dammit. "Would you have kissed me if you didn't think you were going to die?"

He chews on his answer for a second. "No."

At least he was honest, I guess, even if it proves I was right.

But Perry isn't done. "And I would have missed out on the single best moment of my life."

My eyes snap back to his, and I'm worried for a second that I hallucinated the rest of that. But he's giving me that hopeful half grin, face so full of sincerity that I'm finding it hard to hold on to the delusion.

A laugh breaks from him. "Sorry, I'm being weird." He looks down at where he's holding my hand, thumb brushing along my knuckles. "Just saying … you're a great kisser. Our kiss was great. Even the first one that you hated."

"I didn't hate it."

"You hated it."

Considering it was barely a kiss, there's no point in arguing. "Only a little." I give in to the confidence trying to take over. "The second was better though."

"And the third?"

Thinking about those kisses has my mouth dry. "Definitely the third."

My gaze drops back to where the dark hair stretches across his pecs before trailing down his torso and into his jeans. I didn't get to see him last night, and if I had, I probably wouldn't have lasted anywhere near as long as I did.

His collarbones cut deep depressions through his skin, curving in a delicate way so completely at odds with the rest of his very indelicate self. Perry is a steam train. A whirlwind. Inertia. The kind of force that can't be stopped. Then there, hovering innocently over his chest, it feels like a calm secret just for me.

Before I even know what I'm doing, I lift my hand and run my fingertips over his collarbone.

Perry shudders, hot exhale puffing over my hair. It pulls my attention back to him and the way his eyes are boring into me.

"What about our fourth?" he whispers.

I try to think through the fog of lust, struggling to remember how many times we actually kissed. "Did we kiss four times?"

Slowly, he shakes his head. "No. But I'm sure if we did, that fourth time would be even better."

Fourth time.

His tongue swipes his parted bottom lip, and I watch the movement hungrily. My self-respect is long gone as the need bubbling in my gut takes over. I'm so frustratingly, embarrassingly attracted to him that all it takes is the offer to kiss me again in order to get my cock moving.

"I'd never use you," he whispers. "We might not know each other very well, but I promise I'd never do that."

And while we might not *know* know each other, in the small amount of time we've spent together, it's like my body has learned more than my brain ever could. Like my instincts have latched onto him as a good person, and that's fact, and everything Perry does keeps confirming it.

"I've heard fourth kisses are usually the best," I say.

Pure lust flares in his eyes, and the sight is addictive. I want to yank him close, press our mouths together, but the anticipation wrapping around us is driving my need higher, and I'm not sure I'm ready yet. Last night has played on my mind all day; a second time will take over my life.

His grip on my hand tightens, and I wish it was around my cock.

"I don't know what I'm doing," he mutters. "I just know that I really, really want to do it."

"Then do it."

I see the exact moment his resolve hardens, and my excitement spikes at the inevitable kiss.

At the way he moves closer.

How his breathing gets deeper.

The way my lips tingle, ready for him to—

"All clear."

We both jump at Lars's voice as he strides into the cabin.

The moment around us shatters.

Perry tugs his hand back.

My want screams in protest, and it takes every last scrap of willpower not to curse Lars out.

But he just walks over to the small fridge, grabs a can of Coke, and pops it open.

"So, now they're gone, what's our next move?" he asks.

Neither of us can answer that.

CHAPTER TWENTY-NINE

PERRY

MY NEXT MOVE was about to be mounting St. Clare and grinding against him until I came. And kissing him. Lots of kissing him.

But now, Lars is pacing and talking, and the intensity is high, but all I can think about is my dick and the way it's straining very specifically toward the man sitting next to me. I grab a dusty cushion and plant it over my lap.

"I'm sorry, are you asking me to plan again?" I don't mean for it to come out in a pathetic whine, but I'm not in control of a lot right now.

"Well, we need to do something because all of this sitting around is driving me mental."

I'm feeling a bit of that myself, except it has nothing to do with sitting around. "Can I suggest you take a long, *long* walk into the woods? I think an hour should do it."

Beside me, St. Clare coughs over a laugh, and I'm close to smothering *him* with the cushion. No more sounds from him, thank you. I'm horny enough as it is.

Lars pins me with a flat look. "No."

"Half an hour, then?" I'm straining not to hump the fucking cushion. All that keeps flashing through my mind is how St. Clare's tongue felt in my mouth and the way his cock was strong and needy against mine. There was something about the way he took control that made me burn from the inside out, and I don't think that burning has gone away much.

The whole fighting for my life thing kinda dulled it, but now that's over and I can think again, it's all come roaring back.

I'm really fucking attracted to St. Clare.

And I'm pretty sure it's *him* and not the fact I'm sleeping with a man for the first time. That's appealing, sure, and so obviously hot, but my cock imitating a war hammer is all him. That blond hair that waves just right. The suckable bottom lip. The way he sometimes looks at me like he's sharing a secret.

Do I know what that secret is?

No fucking clue.

But it's the thought that counts.

And right now, all my thoughts are about how to get him naked. Maybe if Lars hadn't interrupted, we could have taken care of that side of things and then freed up our brains for super-serious plotting things. Really, this is his fault. Because who can care about murder plots when your brain has relocated south?

Lars looks me over and smirks around the sip he's taken. "Might want to shower before you take those thoughts any further."

The second he says *shower*, my smell hits me, and fucking hell, how did St. Clare get so close without gagging? I'm grudgingly grateful for Lars breaking up the moment, considering my mouth doesn't taste good even to me, and kissing would have been a fast way to make sure nothing else ever happened between us again ever.

"After that, I want to go outside and practice some shots with you. If you're serious about helping me keep him safe, I need to be confident that you know what you're doing."

"I know what I'm doing."

"Maybe, but *I* need to be confident."

I glance over at St. Clare, and something inside me gives a little skip. I'm serious. There's no way I'm letting anyone hurt him. So if I need to jump through hoops for Lars, I'll do it.

Just … not right now.

"Can we rain check for tomorrow?" I ask. "I'm beat. So tired."

"We need to take shifts in staying awake."

"Good idea. You take first shift while St. Clare and I sleep, then wake me in a few hours."

Lars looks like he wants to argue but swallows it all back. "Great plan." There's something in his voice that doesn't sound so great, but I ignore it, too busy calculating how I'm supposed to get up without thrusting my hard-on into everyone's faces.

Maybe if I shimmy to the edge of the sofa, then do a full one-eighty as I turn?

"Leave your clothes out, and I'll throw them in the wash with ours," he says.

"That's actually … nice of you."

Finally, I get the smallest genuine twitch of Lars's lips. "I promise you I'm being completely selfish in not wanting to smell *that* for days on end."

"Works for me." I shrug. "I don't want to smell this either."

St. Clare extends both arms along the back of the sofa. "Guess I'm in the minority in not minding the way you smell."

Heat floods from my gut to my face. "Noted."

Lars sighs. "Maybe I should take that walk after all."

"Maybe you should." I have to choke out the words because while it's weird that he knows there's something going on between us, it'd also be weirder for him to not pick up on all this sexual tension. And if confirming it will get him out of here and St. Clare into the shower with me, even better.

"I'll come with you," St. Clare says to Lars, and my jaw almost hits my balls it drops so fast.

"Ah, what?"

"Yeah …" Lars narrows his eyes. "What?"

"It's a nice sunset, and it'll be too cold to go outside soon. A walk sounds great."

I can't believe the words coming out of his mouth. Doesn't he get what's happening here? Lars is offering to *leave* so we can hook up. They do that wordless staring thing again, and still, St. Clare doesn't get the message that Lars is putting out, which is a goddamn worry, considering I'm reading him loud and clear.

All six feet of St. Clare's lightly muscled, domineering, slutty-forearmed self stands and looks down at me. His gaze slides over me like a hot coffee slipping down my throat, and my nipples prick harder at the attention.

He knows what he's doing. He knows he's leaving me desperate. And maybe this is repayment for me stupidly declaring Arlie the love of my life, and maybe I should hate it, but the whole thing only makes my cock harder.

I'm ready to whimper like a fucking dog at his feet as St. Clare's eyes fill with that secret amusement before I'm left to watch them walk out the door.

Lars disappears first, and just as St. Clare is about to close the front door behind him, he pauses, half inside, and turns his head so I can make out his profile.

The way his lips move has me mesmerized, and it's a second before I register what he's saying.

"I dare you not to touch yourself while you shower."

The confidence in his tone has me swallowing hard.

Then something lights up behind his eyes that makes me shiver. "I might even reward you if you don't."

Thankfully, he walks right out and doesn't hear the *help* that bubbles from my lips. How the fuck am I supposed to not touch myself now? I'm half tempted to storm outside and drag him back in here to have his filthy way with me. He's not playing fair, and we both know it, but the real *fuck me* moment comes when I realize that I don't hate it.

It's torture, but I think I'm sort of enjoying it.

I cheat in the shower, just a little bit. While I'm scrubbing every filthy inch of me I can reach and keeping my fucked-up shoulder dry, I'm also angling my still-too-hard and too-needy dick right under the water flow. It's as bad as his sinful mouth, though, because it keeps me right on that edge of pleasure without giving me any of the payoff. I can't come like this, and all I'm doing is furthering St. Clare's mean, evil, downright maniacal plan.

He doesn't need to make me want him even more.

I already want him most.

I'm an instant-gratification kind of guy, and nothing about this is instantly gratifying. Even our orgasm last night left me wanting more. I hate this. Because I really, really *don't* hate this.

I'm about to give in to the urge for a little tug when I stop myself and turn off the water instead. I'm going to be a good boy. No touching. I want to know what St. Clare's reward is more than I'm interested in anything else. I might have a giant target on my head, but Margot and Elle are safe, we're currently in the middle of fucking nowhere Washington, and some things are more pressing than figuring out who wants to kill you.

I'd argue that St. Clare's mouth wins in importance against just about anything.

I towel off, realize I have literally no clothes to wear after dumping my jeans, T-shirt, and hoodie onto the small two-seater table for Lars to deal with, and then settle for wrapping my towel around my hips.

I eat, brush my teeth—thank you to Lars for remembering to buy these supplies and to me for remembering to bring them with us—then ... wait.

And hope like hell that St. Clare wasn't fucking with me.

CHAPTER THIRTY

ST. CLARE

"HOW LONG ARE you going to make him wait?" Lars asks.

Which is a good question because I'm suddenly getting cold feet over doing this again, but that doesn't distract me from how much I *want* to do this again. I'm a mess of contradictions, and I'm struggling to have anything make sense in my head.

"Forever?"

He calls my bluff. "Liar."

"No, but I'm actually starting to think this is a bad idea."

"That would have been helpful at this time yesterday." He shrugs, finally getting the first sparks of the fire going. "At what point do you say fuck it because everything looks bad and you deserve to take the small amount of good you have? If that's fooling around with the guy who tried to kill you, then so be it."

"You're on board now?"

"Oh, no, I still think it's a stupid idea." He pokes at the simmering flame. "And I fully intend for us to find a way out of this mess, but I don't blame you for wanting to have some fun in the meantime."

"What about you?"

"I have my horoscopes." Then he pumps his eyebrows at me. "And I'm hoping to get Perry on my good side so he'll introduce me properly to Arlie."

I huff. "She is inhumanly good-looking."

Lars turns his poking stick over in his hands. "I guess she is? Mostly, she looks like the type of woman who can handle herself and isn't down for putting up with shit." Then my best friend, who is the least romantic guy I've ever met, lets out a dreamy sigh. "I'd love to challenge her to target practice. I bet she'd kick my ass."

Well, fuck. I guess everyone is in love with Arlie these days. "And that's my cue to go."

"Have fun," he throws after me. "Wave your panties out the window so I know you're done."

I throw him both middle fingers.

Who would have thought having your best friend lusting after your mortal enemy would be enough to dissolve your doubts about hooking up with your almost murderer? My head echoes with an unhinged kind of laugh. What the hell have I gotten myself into?

I'm oddly nervous as I approach the cabin, and I have to remind myself for the billionth time that I'm not some fumbling virgin and this isn't a big deal. It's just sex. I've never gotten in my head over it before, and this is probably the worst time to start.

With a boost of confidence, I push through the door, expecting to find Perry waiting, but there's no one in the living room. It's not a big cabin, and other than here, the only other two places he could be are the bathroom or the bedroom. Judging by the light coming from under the bedroom door, I think I know which.

Given the day we've had, a shower wouldn't be a bad idea, but other than jumping out of a window, I haven't been through half of what Perry has, and I showered just before he got back from Lethal Poison. Unlike him, I'm not filling up the cabin with my man smell.

Which was way sexier than it had any right to be.

I push open the bedroom door to find Perry sprawled on one of the two single beds, towel wrapped around his hips and hands pressed to his face.

"Did you touch yourself?"

At my voice, he immediately jolts upward. "No." The way his voice strains confirms this was a very, very good decision. "And the stupid thing won't go down."

"I'm sure I can figure out a way to make it happen."

"Quickly? Because I'm going to need you to do it quickly."

Oof, he's adorable. I hate it because it pulls at this part of me I didn't know existed. I like a guy who can hold his own, but Perry somehow awakens a new, exciting side of me that loves the way he looks at me like he can't physically look away. It messes with my head.

He stands up, and immediately, my attention slips to the way he's tenting the front of that towel. I'm desperate to see what he's hiding under there.

The unbridled want in his eyes shutters as he echoes the same craving right back to me. Perry crosses the room, and there's no more hesitating as he cradles the back of my head and crushes our mouths together. His nerves are completely gone as he owns my mouth and roughly pushes his tongue inside, feeding me a groan of relief and need that sinks into my limbs and brings my own dick to life.

My hands find his hips as I tug him against me, bodies collid-ing, Perry kissing me like it might be the last time, and I'm scared he might be onto something. Neither of us knows what comes next, so I kiss him back just the same.

He tastes like mint and something I can't name but is completely him. It makes my head buzzy and light as I run my hands up his smooth, broad back.

"How do you do this to me?" he mutters against my mouth as he scrambles for the buttons on my shirt.

"Just returning the favor."

Perry shakes his head, slightly damp black hair jumping with the movement. "There's no way. No way I'm making you like this. It's not possible."

"Like what?"

"Like I'm reevaluating the importance of every other damn thing in my life."

The confession isn't what I was expecting, but fuck if I don't feel it too. It's hard to work out if it's the wild shift my life has taken or Perry in general bursting in and upending literally every-fucking-thing.

I bite down on his bottom lip, not able to hold back anymore. This driving need for him is deeper than I've ever felt, and I'm so caught up in it that when I grip his towel tighter and it comes loose, I revel at warm, bare skin meeting my hands instead.

"Love a man with easy access."

"Lucky for you, then, because I'm all out of underwear."

"What happened to the ones you were wearing last night?"

Perry groans and licks along the length of my mouth. "Dunno. Probably back at the apartment."

Of course they are. He's a fucking disaster, and maybe I should do some emotional soul-searching for why I find that so hot, but I don't. I just let him pull my shirt from my shoulders and then resettle my hands on his firm glutes.

He moans into my throat, kissing a line down to where the dip of my shoulder starts, and I shamelessly palm the muscles under my hands. God, I want to bury my cock between them. He's got the most fuckable ass, and the vibes I get from him give the impression he's never made use of it. Testing out my theory, I dip my finger gently down the top of his crease.

Perry trembles against me. "Nmpff. That's … different."

"Just tell me to stop."

"I'd rather tell you to get out of your fucking pants." The needy lilt to his words is addictive.

"Make me."

He's not careful about it, and he doesn't put on a show, which somehow makes his frantic, desperate tug of the button and zipper sexier than I could have imagined.

"Get … off …" Perry grunts before my pants slip down my legs and pool on the floor. Then he grips my boxer briefs and shoves them to the floor as well.

When he stands again, he's biting the knuckles on his good hand, eyes locked on my cock. With some breathing room between us, I take a moment to finally get an eyeful of the body he's kept hidden. Firm pecs, a hint of abs, then a thick, long cock pressing upward from full balls.

I've changed my mind. I need him in my mouth.

Before he can recover from seeing me naked, my mouth finds his. Perry matches my urgency, licking and nipping and gripping my hair with his good hand as I back him toward the bed. He's hairier than me and broader, but my muscles are more defined, and where my cock is a bit smaller, it's the perfect length for fucking.

Perry's legs hit the bed behind him, and we both topple over onto it. Our chests press together, surging lust through me, and it's not until Perry sucks an uncontrolled *hiss* through his teeth that I back off.

"You okay?"

He tries to tug me back to him. "Yeah, yeah … just caught my shoulder wrong … all good."

I duck away from his lips. "Not all good. You were shot."

"So were you." His lopsided smile does something to me. "You didn't complain about it."

"I did. Frequently. Loudly." I lick along one of those delicate collarbones. "I know how bad it is and how you need to be taken care of." I move down to kiss his sternum. "Can I take care of you?"

Perry nods so fast it looks like he's lost his voice, and when he finds it again, it's become a dry rasp. "Yeah. Take care of me."

Those big eyes of his do me in every time. "You're such a golden fucking retriever," I mutter, kissing along the trail of light hair between his abs. "I bet you've never had a mean thought in your life."

"I'm having a lot of mean thoughts right now."

"Oh yeah?" I grin evilly up at him, wondering what sort of mean thoughts someone like him would have. "Like what?"

"Like how badly I want to take your face and fuck it."

Heat blasts alive in my gut, and because I can't stop myself, I lean in and flick my tongue over his swollen head.

Perry chokes on a sound, dick kicking at the contact. "Again. Please do it again."

"I thought you wanted to fuck my face."

"I want literally anything that will get my cock in your mouth right now."

"Then do it."

With only the briefest hesitation, Perry reaches out to grip my hair. His teeth bury into his bottom lip as he guides my head so that the tip of his cock is resting on my lips.

"O-open," he tries to demand, but it comes out more like he's begging, and he has to know what it does for me.

I open my mouth and wrap my lips around him.

Perry's grunt is feral, and I'm expecting him to shove inside, but his eyes are locked onto the view as he very slowly fills my mouth with his cock. "Such a pretty mouth," he mutters. "I'm going to see this moment every time I close my eyes."

His dick nudges the back of my throat, and he pauses before pulling me slowly off again. In and out, he slides past my lips, and I don't know what I was expecting, but it wasn't this. Little bursts of precum spur me on, and I let him set the pace ... for now. Because while he might need this, I'm fucking hungry for it. For him to lose his tenuous grip on control and take everything he needs from me. I need to feel the way his dick swells before he feeds me every last drop of his cum.

"So good," he breathes before driving the pace faster. "You've had me so on edge. This isn't going to last long."

I know what he means. Kneeling the way I am has my cock hanging heavy and full between my legs, begging to be touched. I have half a mind to wrap my hand around it and get off, but I want to see just how much Perry wants out of this. Fucking my face is one thing; sucking off a guy is another. I'm curious how far his enthusiasm will extend.

Perry's grip on my hair is tightening as he speeds up his thrusts, and I'll bet he's getting close. But as much as I want that, I'm not ready for it to end, so before he can get himself there, I let his cock fall from my mouth.

His eyes snap open. "Almost … there."

"I know." I lean down and run my wet tongue over his tight balls. He *is* so close, and this is mean as fuck, but I don't even care.

Perry groans and parts his thighs wider. "What are you doing?"

"Making you feel good."

"I'm okay with that."

Is he though? We'll see. I suck his balls into my mouth, which pulls a curse from him, before I dip my head lower. I lick and suck just behind his balls before going lower and lower again. Then I slip my tongue between his ass cheeks.

"Oh. Oh fuck." The fingers of his good arm tangle in his hair while the other grips the sheets under us. "Did you just lick my ass?"

"I dunno." I do it again. "Did I?"

"You did. You licked my ass." His feet pull up to plant on the bed either side of me.

"Any objections?"

"Hard to say. It's weird, but I want you to do it again."

So I do. And the more I lick, the deeper Perry's breathing gets. I press my face deeper, and then Perry does something that almost makes me blow my load; he draws his knees up to his chest.

With a groan, I pull his cheeks apart and bury my face between them. I'm not going to do more than tease him, but the way he's so into this is doing things to me. The kind of things that have me slowly dragging my cock over the mattress to try and ease the way I'm aching for him.

I kiss and lick and suck all around his hole, sinking into how sexy the sounds he's making are. How he's panting. Squirming. I'm in fucking bliss as I work him up, and for the first time in days, everything else shuts out of my mind as I focus on him.

"I wanna come … I wanna come …"

Of course he does. I've been eating his hole for who knows how long now, and the fact he's only just started begging shows he has more restraint than I thought.

"You forgot to say please."

Perry pounds his fist against the mattress. "Please. Please, please, please."

I lean forward and swallow his cock. He thrusts uncontrollably as I swallow him down my throat, giving him all the room to use me that he needs. His precum is a salty tease, and every time his smooth tip passes over my tongue, I hum in pleasure. Perry is a fucking gift.

My hand slips back between his legs so I can gently stroke his hole. I play and suck, wanting to drive him out of his mind as easily as he's driving me out of mine. Miles of muscle stretch out in view, and I want to wrap myself up in them.

"Ah, *shit*."

His hips give a final buck as he floods my mouth with his cum. I swallow it all. Lap him clean. And when his dick slowly softens, I let it slip out of my mouth.

Perry's exhale makes him sink into the bed.

"You good?" I check.

"The best."

I crawl up his body, achingly hard, desperate for his mouth. I don't want to make him uncomfortable or feel forced into anything, but I am curious how deep this attraction goes for him. Now he's blown his load, will he still be into me?

"No chance you'd want to return the favor?" I ask, nuzzling against his jaw. "You can say no. Just looking at you is enough to get me off." I wasn't planning to say that last part, but for some reason, I'm scared of his response.

"You want me to suck your cock?"

"No. That sounds horrible. The worst."

He laughs and pulls back a little so those big, dark eyes can study my face. "I think I want to do it."

"Again, this is the sort of thing you need to be sure about."

Perry taps my jaw with his knuckles. "And again, I'm never sure about anything. But I want to try."

For a second, I contemplate telling him no, but his sincerity is one of those things I like most about him, and I can tell he means it. He wants to try, and if it's not for him, I'm sure he'll tell me. It's more of that knowing him without knowing him connection I can feel between us. Some things don't need to be said.

"No pressure from me," I remind him.

"You worry too much." He leans in, smiling lips against mine. "How should we do it?"

I reach down and stroke myself a few times, too excited by this to think clearly. It needs to be in a way that won't hurt his shoulder. "Umm ... maybe kneel beside the bed?"

His smile only widens as he jumps up and climbs off the bed, but before he can get on his knees, I stop him.

"Put this down first," I say, dropping a pillow onto the floor. "It'll stop it from hurting."

"Now who's being sweet?"

Perry sinks to his knees, and I position myself on the edge of the mattress. I think I'm more nervous than he is, and I'm holding my breath as he leans closer ... closer ... so close to my cock that he's able to flick his tongue experimentally over my slit. It's a stretch of torture, waiting to see his reaction.

"Wow," he says after way too long. "I think I'm going to be good at this."

Then he goes straight in for the deep throat.

The heat, the wetness, the suction—all followed by him gagging around me is a fucking dream. Perry's strong jaw is stretched wide, and even with the setback, he doesn't let it deter him. He's almost overenthusiastic about getting me off, but it's hard to tell because his eyes are closed, eyelashes fanning out over his cheeks, and he's humming around me like my cock is the greatest thing he's ever had in his mouth.

It's too fucking much.

Perry is too fucking much.

I steady my hand on his head and thrust a little while Perry sucks and licks and fucking *moans* like his entire life is dependent on sucking dick the best that he can. And if it was, he'd survive.

Not me though.

Because he's driving me out of my goddamn mind.

My head drops back toward the ceiling because I can't look at him anymore. Can't see his determination, can't see how much he's enjoying it. Everything from my balls to the head of my cock is overstimulated. I'm flushed, overheating in this cool room, wanting this to go on forever, but even as I have that thought, I flip from horny to *there*.

My dick swells with the pressure of my orgasm, and I barely manage to get out a warning of "I'm gonna come" before I do. Perry's struggling to keep my dick in his mouth as he coughs and swallows and tries to drink my cum like I did with him.

I know I shouldn't look, but I do.

His thick eyelashes are wet clumps, cheeks darker than usual, lips red and puffy with my cum dribbling out the corner of his mouth.

The high eases out of me, and Perry lets my dick go. We stare at each other, him kneeling, looking up, eyes bright and lips parted as he struggles to breathe.

"Did I do okay?"

My thumb finds the mess at the edge of his mouth, and I clean it off his skin. "Unfortunately, you did better than okay. How the hell do I ever recover from that?"

Pride lights up his face, and I'm hit with the feeling again.

How the fuck do I recover from *Perry*?

CHAPTER THIRTY-ONE

PERRY

IDEALLY, I would have spent the night wrapped in St. Clare's arms and marveling that I sucked an actual dick tonight. Instead, Lars wakes me up way too soon, jeans held out toward me with his eyes pointed at the ceiling, and announces that it's my turn to take watch.

A yawn tears apart my face, and my shoulder feels like it's been torn off and reattached badly. "Do we have any painkillers?" I grumble, throwing my legs off the tiny bed and trying to get them into the jeans. I'm half-asleep and in a lot of pain, and nothing feels like it's supposed to.

"Yeah, on the kitchen counter. Your friends left us some stuff to keep it clean too."

My muscles rebel, and I push up onto my feet. "Thanks."

He hesitates. "Need help?"

As much as I want to curl into a ball and tell him I'm ouchy, I send a smile his way instead. "Aww, Lars. Are you starting to care about me?"

"Never."

"You are."

St. Clare groans and rolls onto his side, blankets tangled around his legs, showing off his bare ass.

Lars rolls his eyes at me and presses his index finger to his lips. I make my fingers into a heart in return, then tug the blankets up over St. Clare's butt before I start getting ideas. I leave the bedroom, closing the door behind me, and find the one room of the cabin dimly lit and cozy. There's no way I'm not falling asleep out here. So instead of flopping down on the sofa that's calling me, I grab the painkillers, throw them back, then chug half the jug of water in the fridge before tearing into a loaf of bread. There's nothing to have on it, which blows, but I choke it down plain, and once my belly is full and my shoulder is no longer actively trying to kill me, I can think a bit clearer.

Yesterday was a fucking mess, and I'm not sure I learned anything useful other than Luther wants me dead. I can see how that would be my fault, but he really should have given me full disclosure when I signed on for the job. Burying things in unspoken fine print isn't a good idea for anyone.

Judge Judy is always very clear on that. If it's not agreed on, it's not an agreement, so how was I supposed to know that a little bit of money would be enough to get me killed?

Personally, it feels a bit extreme to me. Like, *killing* someone isn't exactly a victimless crime. Taking someone's life is … it's … that's it for them. Shouldn't I have a say in the type of thing that will change my life forever?

So I guess that's the first thing I need to fix. Which means handing St. Clare over to him. St. Clare. Whose dick I just sucked.

Right.

Can't do that.

Other than the fact I don't want to, there has to be something in gay code where exchanging blow jobs means you're not allowed to give the other guy up for murder.

So. Plan B.

My brain sobs at the thought.

I'm really, really not a planning guy.

This is slightly more than my standard daily situation though, so I probably should try.

St. Clare. He's wanted by … someone. Someone that Luther is maybe scared of? Someone who doesn't actually know St. Clare is still alive. So … that part sounds good? Except it means someone else is trying to kill him now.

But that also means that Luther is our shared enemy.

Do we kill Luther?

Would that make everything go away?

Considering the person really behind this is bound to find out that St. Clare is alive soon enough, I don't think so. We need Luther to tell us who it is. *Then* we kill him.

Which is definitely something I can do.

Even if Luther's my friend.

He said so himself.

If I'd known a career as a hitman was this hazardous, I never would have bothered in the first place.

I huff and drag my good hand back through my hair. Okay. *Think*, Perry. Focus. You can do this.

St. Clare is convinced these nightclub people are after him, so maybe I need to pay them a visit? Find some things out. Work out if it's them at all.

How will I do that? No clue. I assume an opportunity will present itself though.

You miss one hundred percent of opportunities if you don't try. Of course, that opens up the opportunity for someone to shoot me in the head, but we have to start somewhere, and that's one outcome of many.

They might shoot me in the chest instead.

I rub my sternum, not thrilled by that idea either, but what other choice do we have? None of us wants to be stuck here for long.

The penthouse would have been much better, and if they didn't find us there, we'd still be living in luxury. I did everything I could to throw off the people Luther had following me, and I really thought I did it. I'd been content to ride around in circles all day to get rid of them, and the only reason I went back when I did is because I'd been so, so sure we were in the clear.

So sure.

A sliver of fear tracks down my spine. Did they follow me ... or did they find me another way?

Tommy only knew where I was because I told him. I didn't have my backpack. It was just me and ... my phone.

I head over to the small table where I left it a few hours ago, and all I have waiting is a check-in message from Margot. Then another telling me I need to message her *now* so she knows I'm alive.

I quickly do exactly that, not wanting her to worry, then turn my phone over in my hands. It's very old and very secondhand. The thought of someone tracking it doesn't seem possible, considering the signal I get on the thing is spotty at best.

Just when I thought I'd be able to upgrade to something that gets internet, all this shit went and started. Still, to be on the safe side, I text Margot that I'm turning off my phone for a bit in case it's being traced and that I'll check in when I can.

That should do it.

I think.

If someone was tracking it though, we'd probably be surrounded by now.

And since Luther needed me to give him St. Clare, he obviously doesn't know where he is. Which means neither of them is being tracked either.

And again, if they were, we'd probably be dead by now.

I'm being paranoid. They clearly followed me, and I was too stupid to realize it.

Maybe St. Clare would be safer without me around.

I'm no criminal. I'm not cut out for any of this.

I cover my face and mini scream into my hand, just a bit, just enough to make me feel better about this shit. My fingers seek out my bracelet, tracing the familiar patterns and hearing an echo of Mom's laugh as she picked the brightest, silliest beads she could find.

This is all going to pass.

I let all the doubting go.

Plan or no plan.
This is all going to work out okay.

CHAPTER THIRTY-TWO

ST. CLARE

MY LIMBS ARE LOCKED up and not feeling great when I make my way out of the bedroom the next morning. Lars and Perry are who the fuck knows where, and without coffee to give me a jump start, they're both going to have to put up with me being grumpy and on edge.

A gunshot rips through the air, and I hit the deck fast. My heart is in my throat as I glance around, wait for a shout or an answering fire or *something*, but all I see are dirty hardwood floors and the dusty underside of the kitchen counter.

Then, a second later, the shot is followed by a muffled voice.

I ease myself from the ground and creep toward the window at the side of the cabin that looks out toward where Lars had a fire last night.

"I *told* you!"

That's Perry's voice. I move faster, pulling the tattered curtain aside to see him and Lars, both holding guns pointed toward the tree line. With no bad guys in sight.

I'm going to fucking kill them.

I cross the cabin and stalk outside to where Perry is loading up his gun again. Before I can reach them, he lets off another shot that hits the center of the circle they've cut into the tree bark.

"No way," Lars says. "Lucky shot."

"You said that the first time."

"And I meant it that time too."

"Should I try for third time lucky?"

"Or maybe," I cut in, startling them both, "you could try for not scaring the shit out of me when I've just woken up."

Perry covers his mouth, and of course it's with the hand holding his gun, leaving me astounded that he hasn't shot himself already. "Fuck. I didn't even think about that."

Him? Not thinking? I'm shocked.

Lars tilts his head. "I guess that explains the warnings about a miscommunication for you today."

"Sure. Because the horoscope obviously knew I'd wake up to gunfire."

Lars busies himself with checking his own gun's barrel. "It also said to watch the snapping at people."

"There's no way it said that."

"It definitely said that." He pulls out his phone and shows me the screen. *Curb your instinct to snap at people.*

"Well, now it's just trolling me."

Lars laughs, and Perry creeps closer. "What does mine say?"

"Aries, right?"

So help me, Perry lights up. "You remembered."

"Not a single thing you do lets me forget," Lars mutters as he looks up, I'm assuming, Perry's horoscope. "Okay. Aries. Everything seems like a mess right now"—Lars throws me a smug grin —"but that's only because you can't see the end result. You're in the middle of a major life upheaval. Stop doubting yourself and tap into your natural inner confidence to see this through to the end."

Perry's jaw drops. "Wow."

Lars whistles and looks back toward the tree they were shooting. "Looks to me like you have no issue with confidence."

"That's just shooting. It's not hard."

"It's very hard." Lars lifts his gun, takes aim, and then, a moment later, shoots. He clips the edge of the circle he drew. "See?"

Perry tilts his head. Other than Lars's shot, the other two are right in the middle. "Maybe you're not very good."

Instead of getting annoyed with him, Lars looks like he can't believe what he's hearing. "I'm actually very good. You're ... perfect."

"Huh."

Lars studies him. "How long did you say you've been practicing?"

"Umm ..." Perry shrugs. "Arlie took me out for a few practices like the week before I shot St. Clare."

At first, I think Lars's wide eyes are reacting to the casual mention of my aural casualty, but his words don't match my assumption. "Only a few *weeks*? Never before that?"

"Nope."

"Wow."

Oh, good. Looks like we've moved on from caring that Perry shot me and I'm now *missing an ear*. So great we can be casual about it.

"Wait." Lars presses his hand to his head like it hurts to think. "Were you always this good?"

"I mean, Arlie had to give me a few pointers initially, but yeah."

"And you missed St. Clare?"

Perry shrugs. "And the two others before him."

"And the guys who attacked you yesterday?"

"Accidentally got one of them in the foot."

"But you didn't hit the other?"

"Nope."

Lars is thinking about something hard now. He paces over toward the fire, picks up a chunk of firewood, then throws it into the air. It goes high and arches over before starting to fall again. "Shoot it."

Perry jumps to attention, his tongue poking out between his lips as he takes aim ...

And hits the damn thing right before it reaches the ground.

Lars only stares at him.

"Sorry," Perry says, shifting under Lars's gaze. "I wasn't ready."

"You got it though."

"Well, yeah. It was … I mean …"

"Have you ever shot a person?" Lars pushes, and I sigh.

"Don't bring me back into this."

Lars hurries to shake his head. "No, I mean have you ever *killed* someone?"

"No. Why would I do that?"

"Because it was your fucking job."

Getting frustrated, Perry scrubs at his hair—still with his gun hand. "I wish people would stop pointing out what a failure I was."

"You're not following." Lars steps closer. "You're a perfect shot, and the only time you've missed is when it was a person you were aiming for. I don't think you missed at all. I think you did it on purpose."

I frown at Lars. "You think he shot my ear on purpose?"

"I didn't," Perry defends. At least, I assume he's defending until he goes on. "I was aiming for his head."

"That's not actually *better*," I point out. "You know that's not better, right?"

Lars doesn't give him time to answer. "I think you thought you were aiming for his head, but subconsciously, you couldn't do it."

Great. If Lars is right, that means I have a security team of my best friend, who I don't want in harm's way, and a failed hitman who won't hit anyone. This is looking better by the minute.

"You know, that might explain some things."

Lars lets out a loud yawn that stretches his mouth wide. "Keep practicing. I didn't get much sleep, so since you're both awake, I'm going to have a quick nap. Wake me in an hour."

He stalks back toward the cabin, still looking like he has the weight of all our plans pulling at him. Out of the three of us, he's the only one with actual training for what we're going through, so I know he feels the responsibility more than anyone.

"I think Lars is right."

I turn toward Perry's muttered words. His eyebrows are knotted together, and there's something in the way he's watching me that's wary. "You didn't want to kill me?"

After a moment of considering my question, he answers. "I don't want to kill anyone."

"Seems like an incompatibility for your job description."

"I, umm …" Perry's dusty sneaker kicks at the dirt. "I got to meet you though. So it's not all bad."

A rush of nerves skitters through me, and I avoid Perry's eyes as they search for mine. What is it that we're doing? Having sex and passing time is what I *want* it to be, but there's this tether between my gut and his smile so that every time he unleashes one, I drop. A sudden fall. Like the ground disappears and Perry is the only anchor I have left.

None of it is worth focusing on right now. "Can you teach me?" I point to the gun, hoping to distract.

He blinks in surprise, then glances down at the gun like he's caught off guard to still be holding it. "Uh, yeah. You want to?"

"I figure it would probably help our situation."

"Okay." He's nodding hard. "You can practice with mine."

I cross dirt and crunchy leaves and tufty grass before I'm standing next to him. Perry hands over the gun. Heavier than I was expecting it to be and … wrong. I don't know if the fit is wrong for my hand or if I can sense the danger I'm holding, but I don't like it.

"Hold it up," Perry tells me, so I do.

I'm definitely not holding it correctly, but it feels awkward.

"Both hands."

I adjust so the gun is in front of me and not held out to the side. It feels a fraction more controllable like this, but then Perry steps up close behind me, arms wrapping over mine and mouth right by my good ear.

"So you sort of … aim. Like this. And then you need to expect the power rush when the bullet releases. I try to, like, channel it through my arms."

"Through your arms?"

"Yeah. Release the safety, and then give it a try."

His large hands rest over my wrists and the back of my hands, like he's trying to hold me all in one piece. His voice is doing the opposite though. The way his smooth tone is breaking my strength apart needs to be studied. The skin by my ear, along my neck, it's reacting to him in a big way, desperate to feel his touch. Aching for a brush of his scruffy jaw against it. To feel the scrape, the gentle press of lips …

"You okay?" he murmurs.

"Yeah. Why?"

"Your breathing went funny."

Fuck. Concentrate. I'm desperately trying not to get hard, but it's almost impossible with him pressed tightly against me, surrounding me with his warmth and his scent. Perry is too much of a temptation.

I remind myself to release the safety, then brace. One quick breath. Then squeeze.

The bang is loud and sharp, and I jump at the force of it. I definitely *do not* hit anything, and I'm not even sure which direction the bullet went in, and if Perry wasn't holding on to me, I probably would have dropped the gun too.

His laughter tickles my throat. "At least you didn't scream. I screamed the first time. And probably a few times after that."

"You screamed?"

"Yep. Try again."

This time, I know a bit more about what to expect, and I manage to shut Perry out for long enough to try. I don't hit the tree they've been aiming for, but at least I think I come close.

"Better."

I huff. "How am I supposed to concentrate at all right now?"

He chuckles, and proving he knows what he's doing to me, Perry turns his head to run his nose over the hinge of my jaw. His breath ghosts torturously over my skin. "No idea what you mean."

I groan, completely losing control of my cock that thickens at the contact. "Asshole."

"Again," he growls by my ear, hands tightening briefly over my wrists. "We're not stopping until you hit it."

CHAPTER THIRTY-THREE

PERRY

SHIT, he smells good. I think I'm torturing myself more than him at this point. Being wrapped around someone so tall and strong who smells like … I don't fucking know. Dirt and sweat and the weird plant-based bath wash they have here shouldn't be such a turn-on. But all of that smells so goddamn good on him.

I'm ninety percent confident it has nothing to do with the smell and everything to do with him. My cock is pressing flush against his ass, and I'm quickly losing the battle of not poking him with my hard-on. He has to feel it by now. Not that it matters—I'm not doing a great job of hiding how much I want him.

This time when I press my nose to his skin and inhale, a moan hums through my chest. St. Clare tenses against me, and then, so subtle I almost miss it, his head tilts to the side. My nose finds that crook behind his ear, and when I breathe him in, my eyes flutter closed.

He's intoxicating.

He takes another shot, but I'm so consumed by him I barely notice. I'm tuned out to everything but the way his body is making mine react. Every little particle bowing toward him. Straining for contact. For attention.

"I …" His one word shivers with a breakdown in his control. "I got it …"

My eyes crack back open, and while his aim was completely off, he did manage to hit the tree. Not the target, but I guess I wasn't specific about that. "You did," I agree. "Very talented."

Tension gusts out of his shoulders as he sets the safety and drops the gun on the grass before sneaking his hand between us.

Then he takes hold of my cock.

I choke on my surprise.

He rubs me through my pants as my hands relocate to his hips. "You really thought you could tease me like that?" he asks.

"If it's any consolation, it was a tease for me as well."

"It's not."

I grunt and rest my forehead on his shoulder. "Why can't I keep my hands off you?" It's more of a hypothetical, but I really am curious. I can't remember ever wanting anyone this much. It's consuming. So consuming it makes me forget the very real danger we're in the second he touches me because if I die like this, I'll be dying fulfilling my true purpose.

Being St. Clare's plaything.

His grip tightens through my pants, and breathing through my nose gets harder. I'm trying to keep it together, but he knows how to pull me apart, and every stroke has me breaking into pieces. I shudder in his hold.

"Please ..." I'm begging him. Again. So much for being all capable alpha man—if I could ever claim that—because it's just not possible around St. Clare. I turn into a flailing turtle the second he's around, and nothing I do can stop me from tipping over onto my shell and going belly up.

"Please what?" he asks, that teasing tone I love so much zapping through my bloodstream.

"Please ... anything. Touch me, St. Clare. Hand, mouth, dick ... I don't care."

His head turns sharply, nose bumping my ear, and I glance up to meet his searching eyes. "Could I fuck you?" His hand flexes around my cock, and I press deeper into his touch.

"Do you want to?"

"So fucking much." The words are a rasp. "But there's no way your virgin hole could take my cock the way I want it to right now."

The sound that echoes in my throat is one thousand percent not a whimper. "Goddammit, do *something*."

He nips my chin, then takes a step away, breaking all contact between us. My hands automatically reach for him, but he only shakes his head and points at the tree. "Go and lean against it, drop your pants, and stick your ass out." His eyes twinkle darkly. "You asked for this."

I'm still not sure what *this* is, but I tug at my jeans button while I walk, careful of my arm even though the painkillers are doing their job, and as soon as I reach the tree, my pants are loose enough to shove them to the ground.

I don't realize St. Clare has followed me until his warm hand presses against my lower back, encouraging me to arch forward more. Then, his fingertips brush over my hole.

I jolt but strangle my cry before it can leave me. "Oh, fuck."

His chuckle is sinful. "Like that?"

"Surprisingly, I think I did. Hard to tell though. Might need more."

"More?" His fingers skim my opening again, and the buzz it ignites is incredible.

"No one's ever touched me there before last night."

"I got that impression, yeah." He's smiling as he leans in and licks my neck. "It does something to me, you know. Knowing I'm the first. That I get to train your hole and show it everything it's been missing. I'm going to have it so fucking desperate to take a cock that you'll be begging me to fuck you every time you see me."

I reach out and grip the rough tree to try and stay upright. St. Clare's words have me doubting my legs to do their job. "You're going to ... train me?" My cock feels impossibly hard at the thought. Shouldn't that be something that turns me *off*? Not makes me want to risk splinters by humping the tree just to get some fucking relief.

"Do you not want me to?"

"No, no." I shake my head to exclamation point my answer. "I'm ready. Just clarifying."

He makes a line of wet kisses down to my shoulder, then pulls his hand away, and I hear him spit. "You're going to be so greedy for it."

When his fingers find my hole again, I rub back against them. Joke's on St. Clare because I'm already greedy for anything he'll give me. He doesn't need to train me on it when I come with a built-in *St. Clare simp* upgrade. Whatever he wants, I want it too. The thought of being fucked is … weird. How does it work? Will it hurt? Is there anything I need to do to prepare? Should I—

St. Clare's finger presses inside and cuts off every word I've ever thought. It's only the tip at first. A gentle stroke in and out that I get used to faster than I would have assumed I would. It feels … nice. It actually feels nice. This pleasant hum of something that I relax into.

"There you go," he encourages before sucking my on neck.

Every pass of his finger has me sinking into the feeling. My shoulder is aching, but even that doesn't register when St. Clare leans back to spit on my hole and this time presses his finger all the way inside.

The intrusion makes me feel full, and the pressure in my balls really, really likes it. If this is one finger, how much more can I take? Two? Three? His cock? That's what we're aiming for eventually, I guess, but it almost feels impossible. Like I'm already maxed out. But I want to try.

His finger presses in deep before pulling back and doing it again. And again. The more he does it, the more I like it, and surprisingly, it hasn't hurt once. My dick is so fucking hard, and for some reason, the whole idea of being half-naked and exposed is really doing it for me.

"God, I wish this was my cock," he says.

I sort of wish that too, but he was right before. I don't think I could have taken it. All I know is that this, *this* is good. Great. Exactly what I need. "Give me more."

"You sure?"

"Only one way to find out."

St. Clare huffs a laugh. "Perry—"

"I know, I know, you need me to be sure. But I need you to trust me, and when I say I think I'm good, it's because I want to try it, but I might change my mind. And I'll let you know if that happens."

"Promise?"

"Have you ever known me to keep quiet about something?"

"Good point." He leans back to spit again, and fuck me. I'm even tuned in to that too. His fingers massage my rim, softening it, preparing me, and then he sinks two of them inside.

Fuuuck me.

There's a stretch. Not painful but definitely weird. He's breaking down everything I ever knew, and as he pumps his fingers into me, I'm high on it. Buzzing. Every little nerve prickling alive and sending all very, very good messages to my brain. My cock is leaking, tiny beads of precum appearing at the tip with every pass of his fingers deep inside me. Like there's a flip switch that goes from his fingers to my balls, and he keeps pressing and prodding and reminding me that I'm helpless when it comes to him.

"How does it feel?"

"Good. Too good." I let out the groan that I've been trying to hold back and move my weight onto my non-injured arm. The bullet hole twinges as I reach down and wrap my hand around my cock. "I think you could probably make me come just from doing that," I say, stroking myself.

"Probably. We can try that out another time."

All these promises of more times together are exciting me as much as him fucking my ass with his fingers. They're slippery with spit, and I've loosened up enough that nothing is holding him back from pegging me hard.

Then he adds a third.

The stretch this time is indescribable. I'm light-headed with how amazing I feel, and I'm finding it difficult to catch hold of any one thought other than *yes, yes, fucking yes.*

This time, I don't bother to try and hold in the moan. I push back against him, almost riding his hand as I fuck into my fist, discovering for the first time that I don't think I've ever had sex properly. It's only been half the experience. My dick getting all the action while I had a hidden fun zone that I never knew anything about, and now that I do … St. Clare better be ready for how insatiable I'm about to become.

God, I need more. His cock, preferably. Being forced open around his dick, wider than I am now, fuller than I've ever been? That shouldn't make my limbs tremble the way they're trembling, but it's a good sign I'm not going to last like this much longer.

St. Clare peels himself away from me, free hand gripping my ass and spreading it apart. "Fuck, that's hot. You like me inside you?"

"Yes. Who the fuck knew it felt like this?"

"Every single person who's into ass play."

"Smart-ass."

He brings a *whack* down on my bare ass check. "You were saying?"

The sting hurts, but somehow, I want more. Fuck. What the hell is this? Is it crack? Sex crack? I grip myself tighter as I jerk off, rocking onto his fingers and wishing they were fatter. Deeper. "Give me your cock."

St. Clare makes a choking noise. "No."

"But—"

"If you were experienced, spit would be enough, but I'm not fucking you without lube."

I groan out my complaint. "I'm okay with a little pain."

"Nope."

"But—"

He chuckles, filthy and raspy and too much for my tiny brain. "I've got something to keep you going."

That gets my interest until he pulls his fingers out, leaving me empty and stretched and desperate for more.

Then I hear the zip of his pants, and before I can beg for his fingers back, something smooth, hot, and sticky with precum skims over my hole.

My head drops back as St. Clare rubs his cock over my entrance. He's leaking as much as I am, and the sounds of his labored breathing and jerking off fill my head. I'm still empty, I still want more, but the tease of him so close to where I want him to be is spurring me on.

"I want to fuck you too," he breathes. "It's so hard not to just push inside you right now."

"Do it, then. I dare you."

His raspy chuckle tugs at something deep in my gut. "Behave."

"Not possible." My hand keeps flying over my cock, tip extra sensitive and ready to come. So, so ready. "You're scrambling my brain."

The low hum is dangerous as he drags the tip of his cock back and forward over my hole. It's slippery as he rubs precum into my skin, and his lips fall right by my ear. "You're a whore for it, aren't you? You'd let me stick it in. Even if it hurt."

Somehow, my brain gets scramblier. I'm sweating and heated from the inside out. "Do it."

"God, you're even begging for it."

What else would I be doing? I'm so frustratingly empty, it feels like a waste. A waste for him not to use me and make us both feel good in the process. Holy shit, I'm clawing out of my skin here, and the tease of him right where I want him is too much.

My thighs are locked up as I fuck into my fist and keep trying to press back onto him. My body has taken on a mind of its own. I'm so horny, so desperate, and his deep grunt by my ear makes me want to draw that sound from him again and again.

The pleasure is building deep in my gut, and I'm convinced I can take him. And if I can't? Who the fuck cares. At least then, this desperate need would be filled, and I wouldn't feel like I'm going out of my goddamn mind.

My forearm is getting tight, but I don't stop touching myself. Don't stop pulling that high from where it's tingling at the base of my spine.

"Please, St. Clare …" I pant. "Please."

"Such a greedy little hole." He groans, and not even a second later, he floods my lower back with his cum. It's deliriously hot, and as he rubs the head of his cock against my ass cheeks, making me sticky with it, I finally let loose.

Rope after rope fills my palm as my blood sizzles with the satisfaction of my orgasm. I groan my way through it, not giving a fuck if I wake Lars because goddamn, the world should know how good St. Clare is at sex.

As long as he's only having it with me.

CHAPTER THIRTY-FOUR

ST. CLARE

PERRY TUGS UP HIS PANTS, then turns and slumps against the tree trunk before sliding down it to land on his ass. Before I can suggest getting him cleaned up, he pats the place beside himself.

His cheeks are flushed, and the way he looks at me makes it difficult to meet his eye.

"That was new."

"For you," I point out.

Perry gets this cute little frown that shouldn't be cute or little for a guy with a presence as chaotically large as his. "You don't need to be thinking of all those other times. This was new for us. And honestly, I'd kind of like to make a habit of it. Maybe it can be our new morning ritual."

The *us* thing throws me as well. Sure, I want to do that again. I didn't make a secret of it with how much we talked about me fucking him one day, but I don't think we're at the level of talking it out casually yet.

"What's your favorite sex position?"

Or maybe we are. "They're all good."

"I think I'd like to try riding you."

My brain checks out for a second. "You what?"

"Yeah, well, I love being ridden. Looking up at all of … that. It's hot. I'm curious about how it feels the other way around."

"You want to sit on my cock?"

"Sure."

Once again, I still don't know what to make of Perry. "You're interesting."

"*Me?*"

"No. Sweet, open guys regularly wander into a life of crime. I don't know what I was thinking."

He picks up a twig with his good hand and taps it against the ground. "I think you're interesting too."

I take a minute to think that over. Outside of the club, I don't think I do all that much. I'm not interesting. I don't have fun little "things" about me that are interesting to find out. I work a lot, I drink a lot of coffee, I'm a sucker for a guy with pretty eyes and a big smile, and I still share an apartment with my best friend. "Tell me more."

"Well, I never know what you're going to say half of the time—"

"Likewise." In fact, more with Perry because he's never on the same wavelength as the rest of us.

"But whatever you say, I dunno, it usually makes me feel good. I like when you talk."

I like when you talk shouldn't be a huge compliment, but it's a different one. And somehow, that makes it feel more genuine. "Okay."

"You always feel like you have a purpose. Nothing gets to you. Sometimes it's like life is a huge joke to you, and I want to be in on that. Sometimes the smallest things trigger me to panic and get so in my head that I'm in my own way a lot of the time."

I never would have guessed that about Perry. If either of us is a go-with-the-flow kind of guy, it's him. The panicky thing ... I wouldn't have guessed that either, but I guess it makes sense. It's what had him jump into this hitman thing without stopping and thinking it through.

"And then the other thing," he continues, throwing me a sly look. "Is your name."

I try to figure out where he's going with that and come up empty. "My name?"

"Yeah. I can't for the life of me figure out how someone that's as filthy as you are was sainted."

I stare at him, waiting for the meaning of what he's saying to sink in. I'm still lost. "What?"

"Don't get me wrong, I think it's awesome. Ah—both things. How amazing you are at sex *and* being recognized in that way."

"Recognized?"

"Yeah." He turns curious eyes on me. "How did it happen anyway? I didn't even realize saints were still a thing these days."

Saints. How did *it* happen? Does … holy shit. Is he saying …

I stare at him, waiting for him to drop the act. He doesn't. He just goes on waiting for an answer, and it slowly sinks in that *I'm* the one who has to give it to him. "Perry … do you, umm …" How the fuck do I even ask this? "Do you think my name is Clare?"

His eyebrows crumple in confusion. "Yes?"

"Clare being my whole name. And saint being the title?"

His lips twitch, but not like he's about to shout, "Got you," and more like he's worried about *my* mental well-being. "Yes. That is what you've been answering to."

"My name is *St. Clare*."

"I know."

"*Reilly* St. Clare."

The shadow of a smile evaporates, and his face scrunches up. "Reilly?"

"And my brother is Colin St. Clare."

"*Reilly*?" His tone inches louder.

"That's the part you're stuck on?"

"You don't look like a Reilly."

"That doesn't make it not my name."

He turns away, lips parted, staring at the cabin like he's waiting for aliens to jump out of it. Then, his good hand goes to his head. "What is happening right now?"

That, more than anything, makes me laugh. How the fuck is Perry so … Perry.

"You *really* thought I'd been sainted? Like … like … those old people Catholic schools are named after?"

His eyes widen a little. "Umm … no?"

Another laugh wheezes from me. "I say this with complete and utter sincerity: never change."

His embarrassment slowly melts away until he's smiling too. "I'm a mess."

"You're endearing."

When Perry slings his good arm around my shoulders, I let him. "I think I'm scared," he admits.

Perry and scared aren't two things I would have put together. "Really?"

"Well, yeah. This is serious shit, and I don't know how we fix it. Us, your brother, my sister, and Lars. I sort of feel like I'm pulling everyone into this mess, like a black hole, and no one deserves to be here."

"Yeah, but it wasn't you who did it. Instead of blaming yourself, blame Yanni, Luther, whoever. Not you."

Because I won't say it out loud, but Perry is one of those people who have the kind of soul that needs protecting. The kind that sees the best in people. The kind that doesn't know how not to protect people and look after them.

I like that part of Perry a lot.

"I'll try."

My phone starts to ring, breaking up our moment, and Perry quickly pulls his arm back from me.

"I'm going to clean up and wake Lars while you take that."

I'm about to tell him I don't want to talk to anyone, but when I pull it out of my pocket, ready to silence it, I see the name *Livy Sullivan* on the display.

It's so fucking weird to be on the run for my life and running a business at the same time.

I answer it as Perry leaves. "Hey, Livy, how are you?"

"Yeah, I'm great. Just busy." Her voice sounds distracted. "I know your staff said you're not working today, so I'm sorry to call, I just wanted to get these books balanced from before the opening of Saint Clare's so I can move on to working through the last month."

"Yeah, I'll help however I can, but I wasn't lying when I said this isn't my main department."

Her sigh is tinged in frustration. "Any idea of when your brother will be back?"

The reminder that no, I fucking don't shifts anxiety back into my gut. "Sorry, no. He's out of range for a bit."

There's a long silence, and I check if she's hung up, but the line is still showing as active.

"Livy?"

"No, I'm here, I …"

Her tone catches my interest. "Is something wrong?"

"Potentially. It might be nothing."

"Do you want to explain that?"

There's some rapid clicking on her end. "Those cash withdrawals you weren't sure about on the statements happened again."

I'm not following all of that, but judging by the worry tinging her words, I know it's not pointing to anything good. "Okay …"

"Yesterday, there were multiple cash withdrawals for the same amount. Here's the thing. Large cash withdrawals for the same amount at the same time every month raises red flags. It's either illicit substances, a loan that's trying to be hidden, or … services people don't want anyone to find out about. In my experience, it's rarely a good thing."

Okay, *that* I understand. Considering how preoccupied I was yesterday, I know for certain I didn't take that money, and there's only one other person with access to our account.

Colin.

"Can you see where the money was taken from?"

"Yeah, it's got the ATM details there."

"Okay …"

"Reilly, I know this is none of my business, but I'm going to be honest with you. This looks shady as fuck, and I need you to be honest with me about whether I should keep working on this? If I dig deeper and find anything illegal, I have to report it."

Illegal. Colin? The guy who plays by every rulebook? "To be honest right back," I say, "I have no idea what you could find."

I rack my memory, trying to figure out if I actually do know about them and forgot.

But … this has to mean Colin's alive. Doesn't it?

Unless someone has his card and PIN for that account. But to have his PIN, they'd have to have had him. The amounts matching up means this wasn't a random person stealing from us.

Shit.

"This is going to sound strange," I say, "but can you keep working on it? Send me the ATM details. I'll, umm, deal with it."

"I'm not in the business of getting myself into trouble," she says.

Neither am I, but here I am anyway. "Noted. Thank you."

Livy hangs up, and I'm left staring at my phone, not sure whether she's planning to look into things more or not.

"Are you okay?" Lars asks, following Perry out of the cabin.

I'm not fucking sure. "I think … I think I might have a lead on Colin."

CHAPTER THIRTY-FIVE

PERRY

"SO YOUR BROTHER is apparently missing but just dropped by a whole load of ATMs for a little cash hit?" I ask, trying to wrap my head around things. I'm channeling my horoscope and trying to be *confident*, but I'm clueless what I'm supposed to be confident about.

Fake it until I make it and whatever.

"Guess so," St. Clare mutters.

I want to reach over and pull his hand into mine, play with his fingers, and draw some of his stress my way. I'm not sure where the line between us is, though, because sex is one thing, and giving each other comfort is something totally different. Am I allowed to do that? Would Lars find it weird? Yeah, he knows we had sex last night, but plenty of people have sex for plenty of reasons, and when it comes to me, it's never because they want anything more than an orgasm.

It's sort of offensive the number of times I've been told I'm not the kind of guy someone wants to see again.

So I keep my hands in my hands and watch the way St. Clare's doesn't stop moving with the anxiety running through him.

"No offense, but if your brother is okay enough to take out money, he should be okay enough to message you not to worry about him."

"Unless someone else is behind this."

I drum my fingers on my knees to give them something to do. I dunno. This whole thing isn't sitting right with me. "Couldn't Colin have transferred the money?"

"What?"

"Well, I assume he can still log in. Why wouldn't he do that instead of getting out cash? Cash is a lot more effort, especially going to multiple places where he could easily be seen. He's a missing person. You can't really wander around the streets as a missing person. I assume. Cash screams shady."

St. Clare groans, scrubbing at his hair. "All I know is that there's a good chance he's alive, and there's a good chance he's done this because someone else is making him."

"Or …" I don't want to throw out this option, but we sort of need to. "What if there's no one behind this, and he's grabbing the money to keep paying his debts while he's in hiding but doesn't want anyone to know he's still alive, which is why he went with the cash option? I mean, shit, it probably wasn't even him taking the money out in case he was caught on a camera."

"Why would he do that?"

I shrug, not sure I want to say the next part, but hey. Confidence. Gotta do it. "You said the other nightclub isn't happy with you. But not just you. *Both* of you. I think he's probably in hiding to save his ass."

"He would have told me if that was the case."

"*Or* he wanted the guys after you both to focus on someone other than him."

I was right. I shouldn't have said that. St. Clare looks shocked, but Lars is glaring my way.

"You think his brother is setting him up to be killed?"

"No. I'm saying it's a possibility, and we need to think of all possibilities instead of focusing on only that nightclub."

"You're right." Lars stands up and paces to the other side of the room. "You really aren't great with planning, so you should probably stay out of that side of things."

"That's like accusing Margot," St. Clare adds. "It's ridiculous."

"Fine." I'll let it go. I've never met this Colin guy, so it's not like I can argue the point, and if someone tried to tell me that Margot was pushing me into the line of fire, I'd be fucking pissed.

"He always dealt with the accounts because I'm useless with numbers, but … why wouldn't he tell me … whatever this is?"

"He'll tell us once we find him," Lars says.

"K. Well. Larsy-babe, you're up. You do your …" I wave my fingers like I'm typing. "Techy things to see what you can find, and then I'll start looking into this nightclub since we have no other leads."

"Sounds like a plan."

"I'll be taking my car, and you won't be able to contact me because my phone is off, so if I'm not back by tonight, you can probably go ahead and assume I'm dead."

"Stop." Lars pinches that spot between his eyes that I've seen him do more times than I can count. "Why is your phone off?"

"I'm worried that it's being tracked."

"Well, *that's* news to me."

"If it helps, it's probably *not.* No one has shown up here yet, but after yesterday …"

"I know you have a lot of thoughts, constantly, all at once, but these are the ones you have to share."

"Noted."

St. Clare's watching me. "What are you going to do?"

"That sounds a lot like you're asking me what I have planned, and we're not going there again. I'm going to head over to Rev and talk to the guy."

"That's not a good idea."

He can say that all he likes, but we're kind of stuck. We need an out, and this will help us work out if it was those guys or not. I'm leaning toward not, but what the hell would I know? They're business owners, and I'm sure they're perfectly normal guys who would be fine with a chat. If they're not, well, that probably gives me my answer.

"Quick question," I say, half-joking and actually half kind of not. "Do you think any of my ideas are actual good ideas?"

His mouth flattens. "You know I do. The whole keeping me alive thing? *Great* idea."

"It was a great idea, which is why you should have listened to me. But you didn't. And now we're here."

"Sorry." St. Clare tugs at his hair. "This is all new territory for me too, and apparently, I'm not so good at it."

"Join the club." I stand up and grab my hoodie, pulling it on carefully over my very stained and kinda ruined new favorite T-shirt. But at least they're both clean, so that's an improvement over yesterday. "Why don't we all start supporting each other's wild ideas until we stumble our way out of this mess? I'll be as fast as I can."

Before I've even taken a step, St. Clare jumps up and cuts me off.

"They might kill you."

I understand why he's worried, but that feels like a leap. "Why?"

"Because they're not good guys."

"Yeah, but the only one who wants me dead is Luther. Whoever wants you dead just wants *you* dead, and they don't actually realize you're not dead yet."

"You can't know that."

"Actually, Luther was very clear about that part. He's stressing over killing you before the bad guys can figure out that you're still alive. If Yanni was who hired him and they know I killed you, I'll basically be a hero to them."

Lars is shaking his head. "If they ordered the hit, they did it through Luther so it couldn't be traced to them. You knowing it was them will make you a target with *more* people. If you're set on doing this, you need to say as little as possible."

"As little as possible. That's totally something I can do."

"You are so dead ..." he mutters.

That pulls me up short. "I'm about to do this big thing, and I could really use the support of my team behind me."

"Sorry." At least it looks like he means it. "If it helps at all, I don't actually *want* you to die."

"That does help, thank you."

St. Clare swallows and runs his thumb over my jaw. "I don't want you to die either."

"Well, that's a relief." I set a smile free and give in to the urge to give his hand a quick squeeze. "In and out, quick as I can. I've got this."

I get a flicker of his smirk. "I'll have a reward waiting for you when you're back."

I groan because the last thing I need walking into this place is a fucking hard-on. That's probably not the way I want to get their attention.

"Hold that thought." I grab my car keys and head out, not wanting to delay shit any further. The sooner I get on the road, the sooner I get back, and then the sooner St. Clare can give me my reward. Which is very clearly his dick and very, very appreciated on my end.

Fucking is a good way to pass the time between dangers.

It's not until I get to the car that I realize I've left my bag and gun inside. Props to me for realizing it before I got on the road though.

I head back for the cabin, and when I go to push the front door open, I catch the sound of my name.

"... the whole reason we kept Perry," Lars insists.

The what? I lean closer, ear to the door, wondering what the hell they're talking about.

"Do you really think Yanni will give a shit?"

"Can we really afford not to try?"

Try *what*? Yanni is the guy I'm supposed to find, so this feels like the kind of conversation that I should have been a part of.

"Come on," Lars says, lowering his voice. "I get it. I like Perry too. But in a choice between him and Colin, are you really telling me you're going to put him first?"

"Of *course* not." I've never heard St. Clare sound so irritated.

"Then I need to make the call. I'll ask Yanni if he knows anything about Colin, and if he does, he needs to give up the info.

I'll … I dunno. Tell him I've hired a hitman to take him out and that if he gives me what I want, I'll give up the hitman."

"We could have at least warned Perry first," St. Clare says, and I wholeheartedly agree.

They should have warned me.

Because I'm pretty stupid most of the time, but they're spelling it out in a way that even I can understand. They're going to trade me. For his brother.

The little nudge in my chest catches me by surprise, and I massage the pain away. This shouldn't be a shock for me; it was only yesterday that I got hit with the realization that I'm not on anyone's team. There's them. And then there's me.

This is St. Clare's *brother*, and I'm just the guy who's always in the way and made him come a few times. There's no competition there.

It really shouldn't hurt to have them confirm everything I already know.

Once there's a short break in their conversation, I push aside the hurt and shove open the door like I haven't heard a thing.

"Forgot my stuff," I explain, doing everything I can to sound as happy as ever.

I grab my bag, make sure my mask, gun, and wallet are all in there, and then I head for the door again.

Neither of them has moved, and before I walk out, I can't stop from letting that pain sneak back in a touch. It has my mouth moving before I can stop it. "This whole being on the run thing sucks, but at least I have you two. It makes things a bit less lonely."

And knowing that I don't really have them makes me feel lonelier than I ever have in my life.

CHAPTER THIRTY-SIX

ST. CLARE

I'M terrified he heard everything we were talking about, and it's not until I hear his car come alive with an admittedly dying sound that I dare talk again.

"We can't do it."

Lars groans and buries his face in his hands. "Do we have any other options? I'm worried about Colin. I'm worried about that damn disaster who just walked out the door. And I'm worried about you. None of us are equipped for any of this."

"You think I don't know that?"

He slowly looks back up at me. The whites of his eyes are streaked with red, and his curly hair is a hazardous mess. "This place has a bad feeling to it. It's getting to me."

"I wouldn't be at all surprised if we're sitting in a murder cabin right now."

"Do you think he's right though? Could Perry's phone have been tracked?"

"Have you *seen* his phone? It's basically a fossil."

"Yeah, but ..." He tucks his thumb between his teeth as he thinks. "If there's any possibility, maybe we should move on again."

Lars clearly can't grasp the concept of having nowhere to go. "We're not involving our parents in this."

"No, but I was thinking Colin's place might be an option. It's got that drain that runs between his and his neighbor's place. We could follow that, pop out one of the fence panels, and go in through the back."

"And if there's someone *in* there?"

"Then we'll probably die. Same as if we stay here and are being tracked."

My head is too full of worries to know what the right answer is. Colin and Perry take up a huge amount of them, but I have enough to spare for me and Lars as well. It's very much a fucked if I do, fucked if I don't situation, and I can't lie and say that I'm not curious about what we could find at Colin's. The first time I went there looking for him, I noticed his laptop on his office desk. It's been weeks now, and the police obviously don't give a shit.

"And if Perry comes back and finds us missing?"

Lars doesn't have an answer for that. In an ideal world, Perry will get us our answers, find out who's after me, and then we can turn them over to the police. In order for any of that to happen, he needs to be able to find us once he's done. Because I refuse to believe he could die over this.

Perry is the kind of guy who feels too big for this world. There's this permanent brightness to everything he does, and it draws me in. The idea that the brightness and life he has could suddenly be gone ruins me.

"We've been okay here so far," I say. "Would another day make much difference?"

"Imagine if you asked that question this time yesterday."

He has a good point. Yesterday made a *lot* of difference, and so did the day before that. I'm almost scared of what else could be coming for us.

I swallow and nod at his phone, grasping at straws to find a sign that will point us in the right direction. "What does your horoscope say?"

Even though I know he would have started the day by checking it, he pulls his phone out and opens the app. Then he reads out loud. "Sudden work pressures are set to test you today,

Taurus, but rest assured you're up to the challenge. You have the strength and energy to meet this head-on and will overcome setbacks quickly, but use caution. Decisions have a ripple effect that will last long beyond today."

Well, fuck. Up until that last line, it had sounded positive. "I'm so glad horoscopes are clear and decisive."

"You asked."

"I'm regretting it now."

"Look, it says to be cautious. And being cautious means not sitting around here waiting for someone to come knocking."

"Or maybe being cautious means not making random choices to up and leave."

Lars turns his phone over in his hands. "Okay, we'll stay. For now. Any sign of a car, we leave. And if Perry's not back tomorrow morning …"

He doesn't need to finish that. If he's not back, he's in trouble. And sitting around here won't help anything.

***

The day goes for entirely too long. Lars spends time exploring again, and I spend time going out of my goddamn brain.

Somehow, I get myself into the shower and changed without having a breakdown. Considering it's getting late, I probably should have left my clothes to get washed, but I've reached the point where I don't think sleep is going to happen, and I'm not so sure we won't be back on the run at a moment's notice.

Eating makes me feel sicker, and there's not a huge range anyway. Barely five minutes have passed before I give in to the need to *do* something. Anything. Purpose helps me feel only slightly less anxious, and when I step outside to tidy up the yard, the illusion of productivity helps tug Perry from my mind.

Mostly.

That deep, unhinged rattling inside me won't stop, and it's taking all my energy to keep it trapped tight. Because Perry is fine.

Colin is fine. There's no point breaking down over something that hasn't happened yet.

I send a quick mental plea to the universe as I stack firewood and throw metal tools into a pile. Chairs snap closed, and garbage is gathered, and I tug *tug tug* weeds from what's supposed to be a flower bed until my frantic hands redden and ache and dirt fills the grooves under my fingernails. I'm barely registering any of it. Barely seeing what I'm seeing, just moving, moving, moving.

The faster I move, the more my anxiety rattles out of me and the more my hands shake. My throat gets so thick I can feel the pressure right down to my chest. I'm freezing cold. My muscles seize. Pressure builds behind my eyes. But still, I grab and throw and tear through the yard like it's the only tether to my sanity. When the log I'm moving slips from my hold and *thuds* to the ground, frustration explodes from me, and I aim a solid kick at the wood.

The sudden pain that spikes through me breaks me out of it.

I'm panting, trembling so hard I feel sick.

I can't hold it in anymore.

My hands feel full of splinters as I hunch over the log, eyes prickling, willing all this to end.

All I can smell out here is wet decay, which clogs up any shreds of hope I had left. Where the fuck is my brother? The way I miss him has carved out a cavern in my chest that only goes deeper by the day. And the more time that passes without contact from Perry, the more I worry that Colin won't be the only one.

I can't have a Perry-shaped hole too. There's only so much I can deal with before I'm left empty.

And apparently, I'm shit at protecting even myself because I don't notice Lars has joined me until he grabs my shoulder and pulls me to him. I fold into his chest, hating that I can't handle all of this like a normal day. Just like he does. We might be best friends, but we can't be more different.

"I want to tell you everything will be okay, but …"

"There's a high chance it won't be?" I guess.

"We're not going to think about that right now." His solid arms squeeze me tighter, and it's not the most comfortable thing, hugging a wall of solid muscle, but it's keeping me together. It's not like being in Perry's arms.

"Have you tried calling Perry?"

"I haven't." Because I know if I call him and I end up getting the same deadline as Colin, I'm not going to be able to keep my shit together. I'm not doing a great job of it in general, but I think I've reached the point of PTSD when it comes to unanswered phone calls.

"His phone is still off."

It doesn't surprise me that Lars has tried. I rest my forehead against his shoulder. "You need to shower."

"Nope."

"You stink."

"I'd rather stink than walk out and find you dead."

Slowly, I ease away from him. "It still doesn't feel real. I'm no one important. It's like … does he really hate us *that* much? Why?"

"Money makes people do wild things." Lars drops onto the log, and I let out something that's been haunting me all day.

"I think I'm scared that Perry might be right. About Colin."

That shocks the hell out of him. "What?"

"What the hell else am I supposed to think?"

"He's your *brother*."

"I *know* he's my brother, but none of this makes any sense, and I've reached the point where nothing will surprise me anymore." The looming woods stare back at me. Intimidating me.

"Sticking your head in the sand won't change anything. And for what it's worth, that's not Colin. Everything is strange, but he's not the kind of guy to fuck you over."

"On purpose," I add.

"Yeah. That." Lars takes a deep breath, night starting to set in. "We're getting somewhere. I can feel it."

I wish I could.

Instead, I'm flailing further from answers than ever.

CHAPTER THIRTY-SEVEN

PERRY

IT TAKES A WHILE, but it's really not that hard. I follow Yanni for most of the day, watching where he goes and who he goes with, hoping to catch a moment where he ducks off to the bathroom alone or something and I can threaten him over a urinal.

But either the guy doesn't piss, or he's some kind of superparanoid Mob boss because he doesn't leave the guys he's with once. I'm assuming they're some kind of security, but if they are, they're pretty shit at their job—and that's coming from me! I've had approximately seventy chances to pop him through the head, and they're very lucky that this guy is more important to me alive than dead.

I pace across the low roof of the CVS next door to Yanni's club. Like Saint Clare's, they have a small courtyard behind their building, only this one isn't as clean, smells strongly of weed that barely overpowers the smell of dumpster, and has definitely seen a dead body or two in its day.

I pace back to the other side of the rooftop and lower into a crouch. My busy day of trailing this guy like a detective in a crime movie has eaten into my time and thoughts to the point that I've been sufficiently distracted from what I overheard earlier. But now, waiting on Yanni's reply, all the things I pushed out of my brain are pushing back in.

No matter how much I remind myself that I've only known St. Clare for a short time and that the time we've had hasn't always been great, it doesn't make my heart hurt any less. He fills me with so many good, shivery feelings, and all I want when he's around is to have his attention. I crave it. Need it. When it's me and him, this burst of warmth fills me so completely that sometimes I think I've died because nothing on Earth could feel that good.

Just like I'm not so sure I've ever felt this bad.

Because all of that warmth was blinding me to the fact that they were using me.

I mean, fair, I'd probably use me too.

It's not like my life is all that important, and arguably, Colin has done a lot more impressive things in roughly the same amount of time that I've been unimpressive, but maybe I haven't peaked yet? Maybe I'd like the chance to be impressive. Not going to get that chance if I'm handed over to a crime lord, now am I?

Plus, if I'm traded for another guy—even St. Clare's brother—I really will have to put a stop to the orgasms. A guy has to have some level of self-respect, and I think that's the limit I have for myself. No more hot sex. No more having St. Clare look at me in that indulgent way, like he's not sure if he wants to laugh or cry at my stupidity, no more getting to tug his body close and feel like it belongs.

I'd go back to being Perry. Kinda hopeless, usually useless, always a disappointment, and I bet once I finally get home again, Sir Squeakerton would have had enough of my shit and packed up and moved on too.

I bang the phone I bought earlier against the rooftop before I remember that I don't need to do that anymore. It's a trip to have a phone that turns right on by pushing a button and has access to the internet just, like, whenever I want it?

I'm still not sure if I want to keep the phone, but the neon green rubber frog case with wacky eyes is a strong selling point.

Can't get one of those for a decades-old flip phone.

I tap the social media app I installed earlier, and the account for Kandi Krisley pops up. Not that Kandi is an actual person. I created the account, added a hot photo from Google, and then added a whole list of people I went to school with before posting a bunch of nature and "your life, so live it" posts. The horoscope ones were a nod to Lars.

Not that he should have any right to my brilliant plan, but I really did like him too. My friends fur-ever shirt is feeling a whole lot less special today, that's for sure.

Once I got Kandi's account looking appealing, I tagged her at Rev last night, then sent Yanni a request. He accepted almost immediately, and I hit him with the killer punch: "hi."

He's been messaging Kandi all day, who thinks he's *so* funny, and he has the *best* club, and "noooo of COURSE premature balding is the new silver fox look. I LOVE it."

Yanni has eaten up every message, and I really worry that *this* is the criminal mastermind after St. Clare and his brother, because Yanni? He has no self-awareness.

Again, that's coming *from me*.

Another message finally comes through in response to my one from 9:55 saying that skipping the line out front feels braggy and rude to Kandi.

got a back entrance. meet me there and I'll let you in

Bingo.

I'm smiling as I type out a reply to "please hurry it's dark and scary," then make my way across from the roof of the CVS to the overhang above his back exit. If it's anyone other than Yanni who steps outside, I'll let myself in while they look for Kandi, but if it's Yanni—and I'm hoping it will be—I've got Judy ready in hand.

Maybe this guy likes his girls scared because it takes way too long for the heavy metal back door to ease open.

"Kandi?" a deep voice hisses. "You there?"

The man below steps out a bit further, and I finally catch an up-close glimpse of Yanni.

So *this* is the man who wants to hurt my St. Clare?

No matter how betrayed I feel right now, the urge to protect him has engrained itself in me, and as soon as Yanni turns his back to me, I drop down on the other side of the club door.

"Oy, Kandi? Quit messing around."

He takes another shoe-scraping step against the cement, and once he's clear of the door, I kick it closed with a shuddering *bang* and lift Judy to point right at him.

Yanni swings around, and surprise lights up his eyes. "Who the fuck are you?"

"Just call me Kandi."

The surprise gives way to anger and maybe even confusion, but it's hard to say in this dingy courtyard. "What the fuck is this? Did someone hire you? I've done nothing."

There's a lot to pick at there, so I ignore him instead. "We have a mutual friend."

He sneers, and for a man who runs drugs through his club, he's not bad-looking. He's no St. Clare, and I'm not attracted to him, but all the photos of him with pretty girls wrapped around him make sense.

"Let me guess who," he says, voice a rumble that sounds like he's forcing it. "Kandi?"

"No. St. Clare."

The surprise is back. "What the fuck do they want?"

"That's what we were hoping you'd tell us. Why do you want him dead?"

"Dead?" Yanni lets out a chest-bouncing chuckle. "Not surprised someone wants that."

"Not someone. *You.*" But he keeps on laughing, and I'm getting the feeling that maybe *maybe* I've missed the mark. "Ah … right?"

He shakes his head, not looking at all scared to have Judy in his face. "Nah, not me."

"You're lying." I say it even though my conviction has gotten shaky. The thing is, I'd been preparing for this rough and tough villain monologue, not him reaching into his pocket to pull out a joint. He pinches it between his lips before lighting it, taking a deep draw, and holding it out to me.

"Want a hit?"

"No?" Though I'm not convinced I didn't already have a hit

and am hallucinating this whole thing. "You realize I'm threatening you right now?"

"Sure." He shrugs and smokes more of the joint. "So what's the threat?"

"Excuse me?"

"Well, a threat usually has a 'do this or else.' I assume the 'or else' is killing me, but what exactly am I supposed to be doing to avoid that?"

It's only just occurring to me that instead of creating an elaborate catfishing plan and moping over the way my heart hurts, I probably should have nailed down an ironclad plan of attack when I faced him.

But I have him here, so what the hell do I want to know?

"Where's Colin?"

"Colin?" Interest finally catches him, and I can't place that look in his eyes. "Lost him, have you?"

"Not lost. He's missing."

"Aww, is he? Couldn't have happened to a nicer guy." Yanni holds the drugs out to me, and like my momma always used to say, I'm tempted. *Drugs are the devil, Perry. They tempt you, and they'll turn you into another person. You have to say no because one day, you'll be trying a harmless little bud, and the next, you'll be selling your body for crack cocaine.* I'm not totally sure this is what she meant, but when it comes to making a guy paranoid, she succeeded there. Still, Yanni looks totally fine after smoking this thing, and I could use some of the calmness he's swimming in.

"I'd say yes, but I get the feeling my mom would come back from the grave to kill me if I did."

He chuckles again. "It's a little pot."

"That's where it starts though, isn't it? A little pot, a little party favor, and then you're face down in a toilet cubicle, drowning in your own vomit."

He blinks at me slowly. "One of those puritan types, huh?"

"Not sure I know what that means, but we should go back to talking about Colin. You know, since *I'm* the one with a gun."

Yanni sets his hand on his hip, very obviously nudging back

his suit jacket and showing off the gun at his side. "Don't get too ahead of yourself, kid. Now, why don't you get that thing out of my face, and we'll talk like men?"

My gaze darts between the gun and his face a few times because Arlie didn't train me for anything like this. What if I lower my gun and he draws like some western cowboy and shoots me point-blank? Feels risky, but then it also feels rude to keep pointing this thing at him if he hasn't done anything wrong.

"To be clear, you *didn't* have anything to do with Colin disappearing?"

"Haven't seen him."

"And you don't want St. Clare dead?"

He gives me an odd look. "Why would I?"

"Because they opened a rival club?"

He lifts his hands in a shrug. "And why would I give a fuck about that? It's a free country. I might have tried to delay the opening a bit, but I've seen clubs come and go over the years that another preppy one on the block doesn't mean much to me."

That ... actually sounds like the truth, but bad guys are notoriously good liars, so this probably isn't one of those situations where I can trust my gut.

"How do I believe you?" I ask, lowering Judy a fraction.

"That's up to you. I didn't come into your workplace and hold a gun to your head."

"Fair point."

"Besides, I know exactly who's after him. He took a loan out with the wrong guy."

For some reason, that's what makes me believe him. Judy drops to my side. "Who is it?"

Yanni has another puff of his joint and takes his time letting his exhale out. "These new kids always think owning a nightclub will be easy money. Too bad for them."

"*Who* is it?"

"Carson Alexander. The kind of guy you want to stay clear of. You try with him what you tried with me, and they'll be scraping parts of you out of the brickwork."

"And you think he's got Colin?"

"Carson doesn't let a hundred K go easily. If he's got Colin, he'll be long gone."

"Then ..."

Yanni doesn't sound at all sympathetic. "You'll never know. He'll be the ghost that Carson is." Yanni chuckles. "I tried to warn Colin. He got too big for his boots."

"You tried to warn Colin?"

"Yep."

"Why? If he's gone, then this is an easy way to get rid of Saint Clare's."

Yanni sighs and scrubs the lit end of his joint against the bricks. "You're not listening, little boy. I don't give a shit about Saint Clare's. Colin wanted to play the game though, and this is what he gets."

"Because he borrowed some money?"

"You don't want to owe someone like Carson. Colin should have kept to himself."

I swallow, grip tightening on Judy, trying not to picture what the fuck Colin has gotten himself into and how much St. Clare actually knows. Is he really that blindly in the dark, or was this whole thing a lie? Did they send me here to get rid of me? Why? If Carson really is after St. Clare and Colin, then wouldn't St. Clare want *more* people on his side?

"Let me throw a hypothetical at you," I say, tucking Judy away. "If Colin made a deal with Carson that his brother didn't know about, would Carson then go after the both of them? Or only Colin?"

"From what I know about him—and I'm no expert—he focuses on the person he has a contract with. If he's having trouble finding Colin though ... maybe. Unlikely, but maybe."

Well, I now know a whole lot that I almost wish I didn't. It sounds like the first step for me would be finding out how much St. Clare really knows. Colin is still withdrawing money to pay for these debts, so if he's paying up, would Carson be after him at all? Did St. Clare just go along with all of Colin's plans, or was he actively involved in them?

"Wouldn't know where to find Carson, would you?" I ask.

Yanni eyes me. "You don't want to do that."

"Not sure I have a choice."

"You have a very good choice. Get the fuck out of this mess. You don't want it."

"Sort of hard for me to do that when I was hired to kill a guy I'm now falling for and might have lied that the job was done when it wasn't done, and so now I'm on the chopping block too."

"Sounds like your own mess."

"Little bit."

"My advice? Run. Carson's got a whole legion at his disposal. They do what he wants, when he wants it, no questions asked. You get messed up in this and you won't see next week."

"You're overestimating my self-preservation skills."

Yanni sighs. "Well, best of luck to you. Don't come round here again. The more we meet, the nastier I become."

"Noted."

He's about to step back inside when another question for him slips out.

"Before I got here … did Lars or St. Clare call you? And say … anything?"

"No."

"Not even—"

"Nothing. Even if they called me, I wouldn't answer."

This time when he heads inside, I let him go. So they didn't try to trade me. That *should* make me feel better, shouldn't it? The sense of betrayal should be leaving me. Any minute. At *any* point.

I scuff my sneakers against the dirty ground and lean back against the brick building.

I've finally gotten a lead.

Not a great lead, but it's something.

If this guy is as bad as Yanni says he is, I need to get to St. Clare ASAP. We need to find Colin and take out the murder man and get everything back to normal.

Which would be a whole lot easier if I could trust St. Clare.

What if he knows more than he's told me? What if he knew exactly what his brother was up to the whole time? He was *adamant* that Colin didn't do anything wrong, and I get wanting to protect your sibling, but … what am I talking about? I know St. Clare. Sort of. I know that he's sweet and kind and loves his club and Lars and is lost without his brother. I know he has a big heart and is scared, and those aren't easy things to fake.

But I don't know a thing about Colin.

If I was able to learn so much about St. Clare in so short of a time, Colin would have known it too. He'd know his brother is a good guy who trusts him. Why would he have disappeared willingly if he knew someone as dangerous as Carson was after him? If I were in Colin's position, I would have grabbed Margot and gotten as far from town as it's possible to get. Disappearing and leaving her to it … never.

So what it comes down to is that either St. Clare is a liar and knows exactly what Colin is up to.

Or Colin made all these plans and ditched, leaving St. Clare to take the heat.

I'm not sure which option is worse.

CHAPTER THIRTY-EIGHT

ST. CLARE

I SENT Lars off to bed since there was no way in hell I was getting to sleep. My ears are pricked for any little sound, nerves on edge as the darkness gets darker, and it's still me here, alone, waiting for someone I probably should have given up waiting for.

What if he's not here in the morning? Or lunchtime? My chest tightens, and I have to remind myself to breathe. It's Perry. He can get through anything.

I'm determined to stick to my resolution of trusting him.

It hurts though. Every second of going through this is testing me, and I don't want to be tested anymore. Thinking of Colin makes it hard to breathe, and now, being separated from Perry makes it hard to focus on literally anything else.

I have no appetite, no patience, and no desire to get my ass off this couch until he shows his damn face again. I need that face.

My knuckles are aching at how tightly I've balled my fists on my knees, and when a low hum reaches me, followed by a sweeping light over the cabin windows, I finally let go. My fingers are stiff, but it's nothing like the tension in my shoulders as I ease up from the dusty couch and approach the window. Lars would probably slap me for not waking him, but there's something about the sound of the engine—like it's desperately clinging to life—that makes me sure I'm not in danger.

It's hard to see outside with the buildup of grime on the glass and the light flooding the trees, but after a moment, the engine cuts off, the lights go out, and I can make out the distinct body of an old Nissan sedan.

The moon washes the person who climbs out with silvery shadows, but I know those broad shoulders. That messy hair. The way he bangs his forehead against the roof of the car a few times before stepping back, scrubbing his hand through his hair, and taking long, determined strides toward the front door.

This weird, heart-floating feeling of relief sweeps through me, and I hurry to meet him there. The second the door is open, I want to throw myself at him and make sure he's real, but I keep my feet planted firmly.

He jumps at the sight of me before he breaks into his grin. "You're awake."

"Yeah." *I couldn't sleep without knowing you were okay.* "I told Lars I'd take first watch."

He strides past me like I haven't spent the entire day half-convinced he's dead. "I'm starving. Didn't want to stop somewhere with cameras. Tell me we have something here?"

I'm slow to nod, then remember he can't see with his back to me. "Yeah, there's stuff in there."

Of course Perry would just walk in here with only one thing on his mind. Meanwhile, I trail after him, looking for any signs of injury other than his shoulder.

There's a rattle of pills as he pops open the container of painkillers, throws two back, and then drinks water straight from the jug. I watch as he goes from the fridge to the cupboard and then back again, collecting what I'm assuming are things for a sandwich.

He jumps again when he spins around, arms full of food, and finds me watching him. "You okay? You can go to sleep if you like. I'll probably be up for a while." He bounces on his toes. "Still running hot with adrenaline."

Is he serious? "I thought you were dead!"

Perry's jaw drops, followed by the supplies he dumps on the counter. "Why the hell would you think that?"

"You said you'd be back tonight, and last I checked, we've already reached morning."

"Oh. That." He turns back to the food. "Took a bit longer than I thought it would, but nothing to worry about. He didn't even threaten me. Well, much. I get the feeling I wouldn't be so lucky next time." He works as he talks, and I'm still stuck on how casual he's acting when the relief I feel at being in the same room as him, hearing his voice, seeing him move around making the sandwich, is making me want to fold myself into his arms.

Actually, not want. Need.

I'm craving to have him against me so that I know I'm not dreaming.

But that's a weird fucking reaction, so I shove it down instead.

"You spoke with Yanni?"

"I did," he says around his bite of sandwich as he packs everything away. "Rough guy. Bit of a dick and wasn't the least bit scared, which I'm trying not to take personally."

That note of offense in his voice calms me slightly. Like it's a reminder that I'm not dreaming because no way in hell would I imagine being offended that someone didn't find me scary. The man in front of me is all Perry. "What did he say?"

Perry walks over and collapses back against the couch before switching on a dull lamp and patting the spot beside himself. "Nothing good."

A spike of alarm hits me. "Is Colin dea—"

"What? *No.*" He shakes his head. "Well, not that I know of it. Yanni hadn't heard of anything, but he did give me a name."

"Really?" I sink into the space beside him, not sure I can stand up much longer. "Who?"

"Someone called Carson Alexander. Apparently, he's not a good dude."

I let that sink in for a second. "Someone actually was after him. It's not a misunderstanding."

The thing is, I already *knew* that, but it doesn't mean I wasn't holding on to the scraps of hope. The need for him to be okay overrode common sense. "If he's made my brother disappear, not being a good dude checks out."

"No, but …" Perry sets the sandwich down on his plate and turns to me. "He's apparently very, very not good. Yanni doesn't even want to fuck with him."

Great. That's even worse than I thought.

"Just …" His tone goes gravelly. "Are you sure you didn't know about this? Yanni said he took out a loan …"

I narrow my eyes. "What are you saying?"

"I'm scared he's the one after you too."

The fight rolls out of me. I'm suddenly very hungry and very tired. "I didn't." My voice drops. "I have no idea what the hell he's done."

"Shit." Before I know what he's doing, Perry wraps a long, warm arm around my shoulders and hugs me into his side. "We're gonna find him."

He sounds just like Lars.

I wish I could have their positivity, but this experience is draining it out of me.

He pulls back, rough fingers running over my jaw, thumb scraping the skin by my mouth. "Don't give up on me. We've got this, okay?"

That draws a hesitant laugh, and as I look at him, all positivity and endless optimism, my mouth moves before I can stop it. "I missed you."

His eyes light up. "It was only, like, a day."

A whole day of separation and worry and this edge of restlessness I couldn't shift. "I'm starting to think any day without you in it is a day wasted."

His exhale is a puff of disbelief, and I can't tell how I'm looking at him, but I'm struggling to believe the way he's looking at me. Like clouds parting over the sun. The tide drawing back on a sandy beach. A moment where everything feels exposed and too much, but even if my brain doesn't understand what's happening here, I can feel it. Deep and consuming. The kind of knowledge that makes me overly aware of my heartbeat and the way my hands are clenched back into fists.

The corner of his lips twitches. "I'm starting to think you might be right on just about anything."

"I like you having a high opinion of me."

"You don't give me a choice to think anything else."

CHAPTER THIRTY-NINE

PERRY

ST. Clare is so … so … Before I can sink into that handsome face and his pretty words, the conversation I overheard earlier comes back to me.

About Yanni.

And them swapping me for Colin.

I clear my throat and shift away a little. "So … there's something. A little thing. I have it in my head, and I need it cleared up so that I'm not worrying about it for days on end and—"

"What is it?"

I can't look at him as I draw in a breath for courage and let it out all at once. "I overheard you talking about trading me."

St. Clare is silent. So silent for so long that I take a glimpse over to make sure he's still there. Those pretty lips are parted, and the regret looking back at me is all I need to forgive him.

"I'm so sorry," he whispers. "I don't know how much you heard, but I know … I know it must have sounded bad. Horrible. And … yes. We were planning that. When you first asked to tag along with us, I was so worried about Colin, and Lars was worried you couldn't be trusted, and so it … it made sense."

"Right."

"But we couldn't do it. I know that doesn't make it much

better, but we talked about it, and the thought of calling Yanni ...
of betraying you like that ..."

I reach over and cover his hand with mine. "I know. I asked
Yanni if you called, and he said no. So, uh, thank you? For not
fucking me over?"

"I'm sorry we ever planned to."

I squeeze his hand, and he doesn't pull it away, which makes
me all hot in the gut. Warm in the cheeks.

Then his stomach growls so loudly I look down in shock. "The
fuck was that?"

St. Clare groans. "I haven't eaten all day. I've been too worried
about you."

I reach for my plate and grab a sandwich from my stack, then
hold it out to him. "Eat."

His fingers skim mine as he takes it with a grateful smile. I
want to say things with him are easy because the sex is hot and he
lets me explore that, but sitting here right now isn't easy. I'm
buzzing. Tongue feeling too big for my mouth. Trying not to stare
at him while he eats but catching glances anyway. There's something taking up space in my chest, building brick by brick and
filling all the holes that life has torn out of me.

"Thanks," he mutters.

I nudge him gently. "We're a team."

He likes that, which means I like it even more. I'm still not
convinced that I fit with them, but it's something I'd like to try. I'm
always scrambling for my place in the world, and I'd scramble
harder if my place could be here.

"Tell me something good about Colin," I say as we eat. Am I
convinced that he didn't disappear to leave St. Clare to pick up the
mess? Nope. But it does sound like he's in some serious shit, and
I'd very much like to help St. Clare get him out of it.

He's quiet for a moment. "He's always been an old soul. Our
parents split before I can really remember—our mom couldn't
handle being a mom—and when Dad met our stepmom, I was a
bit of a dickhead to her. Mostly it was that someone new was
coming into our space. Colin sat me down—he was probably ten?

Eleven?—and told me to cut it out. She didn't deserve it, and since Dad had looked after us for so long by himself, it was our turn to look after him by making sure she felt welcome in our home. Things didn't change overnight—I was a kid; I didn't really grasp it—but he kept at me, and I'm glad he did because she's great. That always stuck out as this huge divide between us. The way Colin sees the world so black-and-white. Sometimes I worry he doesn't have emotion, but then he does things like get me this watch …" St. Clare holds up his arm so I can see the one he's wearing. "And I remember we show how we love each other in different ways." St. Clare sighs. "I don't know what I'd do without him."

His sadness makes me sad. "You won't have to figure it out."

"I wish I could be like you."

That's shocking because never ever in my life has anyone ever wanted to be like me. "Why?"

"You always believe in the best. There aren't many people like that. Some people say they do, but most don't really believe it."

I tug at the bracelet on my wrist. "I wasn't always like this," I say. "My parents died when I was eighteen. It feels like so long ago, and then it also doesn't." The bright red plastic strawberry stares up at me, and it's like I can see Mom's fingers as she threaded it onto the elastic. "I sort of lost myself for a bit. Like I existed in a dream and I was waiting for the real world to blast back into focus." Grief doesn't work like that though. There's no stark moment where everything is better again. "I had to fight my way out of that funk. I don't even know how long it took, but one day, I'd wake up and have the energy, and the next, I'd be back to blurred edges and numbness."

"I can't imagine."

I chew, deep in thought for a moment. "It's hard to remember that time, but I obviously did it. I got there." I pull myself from those thoughts. "Now I figure it's easier to look ahead and see happiness when I've already been through the worst moment of my life and survived."

"The more I learn about you, the more you catch me off guard. I like it."

I settle back into the couch and smile at him. It's not very bright in here, but I swear I could find St. Clare even in the dark. When it comes to being hopeful, my main hope right now is that we can make it through this mess and that once it's over, St. Clare will give me a chance to see if there's anything more between us than scorching hot sex.

If he didn't look exhausted, I'd suggest it now. But his usually amused eyes have dulled, and his permanently quirked mouth is a flat line.

"You need to sleep," I tell him.

"Don't know if I can. It feels like we keep running into dead ends, and I'm stressed out of my brain." St. Clare rubs his eyes. "I just wish I knew whether it was Colin who made those withdrawals. Maybe if I had evidence he's still okay, it'd make everything so much easier."

How the hell do we get that evidence? Walking into a bank isn't an option. But if he used an ATM, most of those have cameras … right? "Do you know which ATMs he visited?" I ask.

St. Clare thinks for a second. "Yeah, Livy sent me the list."

"Right. So what we need is someone who can hack into surveillance systems, then."

"You say that like it's so easy."

For once, I think it might be. "It is. When you're friends with the baddie bunch."

CHAPTER FORTY

ST. CLARE

THEY COME.

After the conversation Perry had with the baddie bunch, where Arlie hung up mid-sentence, I really didn't think we'd be opening the door to her, Tommy, and Ever.

They're … an odd group. Now that I'm not obsessively jealous over Arlie, I can sort of understand what's making Lars—and, sadly, Perry—so heart-eyed over her. She's almost as tall as I am, a solid woman with a don't-fuck-with-me face who still manages to have this warmth about her.

Tommy, on the other hand, has this general vibe that he has no clue how he ended up here, but he's happy about it. Chaotic curls, short beard, eyes that look far too amused for the situation we're in.

Then Everett is … well, he looks like the scariest of the bunch. The bald head, slightly manic smile, long chain earrings, and dark eyeliner don't help the impression.

I'm not sure I can trust any of them, but they're all we've got.

"No one can know we were here" are the first words out of Arlie's mouth. The cabin is small as it is, but with the three of them here too, the room is feeling very squished. "Especially Luther. I'm not interested in him holding back work as blackmail to give you up. Because I'll do it. Instantly."

"Good to know," I mutter, but Perry doesn't seem worried.

"You'd never give me up," he counters, dropping onto the couch beside Tommy, who's opened a chunky laptop with a bunch of techy *things* connected to it. "Because then he'd kill me, and there's no way you'd want to go on living without me in the world. I'm too bright and shiny."

"Not sure those are the words I'd use to describe you."

"Fun and adorable?"

"When have I ever used the word 'adorable' in my life?"

"I'll be honest, probably never. But I'm a first for everything."

"Including the limits of my sanity." She rubs her temple and nods to Tommy. "Who are we looking for?"

I glance between them. "What exactly is the plan here?"

"Perry said you were looking for someone. We're here to find that someone."

"Carson Alexander?"

The vibes in the room go tense.

"Nah," says Everett. "I'm out."

"Wait. Why?"

"Because no one has ever seen the guy, and the ones who have don't live to talk about it."

"That sounds … villainous."

Tommy's attention is on his screen. "That *is* his whole deal."

"It's not him I want to find anyway," Perry says. "We're looking for Colin St. Clare, and we might have a lead."

"*Colin St. Clare?*" Arlie snaps. "You want help finding the guy Luther's got every person at his disposal trying to find? He's a ghost at this point."

Perry's sweet eyes find mine for a second before moving on. "W-what do you mean?" he asks.

Arlie looks as confused as I feel when she turns to Perry. "I thought you told Luther you weren't handing him over?"

"Luther wants you to hand my brother over?" I ask him, heart beating faster. "Why?"

"He doesn't!" Perry looks like he's been cornered. "He wants me to hand you over. I would never."

Arlie eyes me. "Who *are* you?"

"Reilly," I say, almost defensively. "St. Clare. Colin's brother."

"Oh." In her defense, there's a hint of apology in her tone. "Sorry you had to find out like this, I guess. Perry was hired to kill him, botched the job, sent your brother into hiding, and accepted his payday anyway. Now our boss is furious with him and is doing everything he can to find your brother."

I whirl on Perry, heart thunking along like it's lost the rhythm it's always held. "You lied? You said you had nothing to do with his disappearance."

"No!" Perry shoots to his feet. "I didn't. I've never seen your brother." His wild eyes fling back to Arlie. "I was hired to kill St. Clare."

"Yes," she says, but he's already shaking his head.

"*Reilly* St. Clare. Him." He thrusts a hand my way like I haven't just confirmed my name.

Arlie's expression morphs from its usual disinterest into pure pity. "No, honey. You weren't."

The thunking in my chest gets harder and faster. "He wasn't?"

Tommy breaks out into cackles, and Lars starts forward, but Ever raises his hands and diverts my attention.

"Hold on. Perry, are you meaning to tell me you tried to kill the *wrong* brother?"

It takes way too long for me to process what's happening here.

The *wrong* brother?

It was never me?

Perry goes pale, and I'm not sure I don't look the same. "I ... I ..."

Lars turns a glare on Arlie. "How sure are you?"

"Ah ... one thousand percent. Reilly hasn't been mentioned once."

His wide eyes meet mine. "You're *not* in danger?"

"I'm not?" I whip back to Perry's shell-shocked expression, and I'm smacked in the face with a thought. "You shot my ear off *for nothing*?"

"Well ..." He looks at the ceiling like it might help him. "Not for *nothing*, exactly. And I still maintain it's better than, you know, accidentally *killing* you for nothing, which I didn't do—"

"How do you go after someone and not be absolutely certain you have the right person?"

"I was absolutely certain! But I was also, apparently, *wrong*."

"Perry ..."

He scrambles over the coffee table to get to me. "Mistakes happen sometimes."

"This is a big mistake."

"Agreed. Obviously. But hear me out: if it didn't happen, we wouldn't have met."

"At this moment in time, I'm not convinced that wouldn't be a good thing." Except then his face falls even more, and the twist in my chest hates it. I want to reassure him. *Him.* The man who tried to kill me, turned my life upside down, has had me terrified about dying *for days*, and it was all a fucking misunderstanding.

"If it helps, I feel really bad about this," he says, voice cracking.

"I promise you that I feel worse."

"Seems unlikely."

"Which of us is missing a body part, Perry?"

He sighs. "Okay, I'll concede that you're feeling *a little* worse. Even if I feel downright shitty."

It's impossible to hold on to my anger when he reminds me of a kicked puppy. The thing is that while this is definitely the worst thing that's ever happened to me, I can one hundred percent see how Perry would have made that mistake. He doesn't exactly think things through, and that can't be one of the things I like about him if I'm also holding it against him. I sort of feel like I get a pass in *this* scenario, but the more pathetic Perry looks, the more I soften to him.

"Don't."

He steps closer. "Don't what?"

"Don't make me feel bad for you. If I get the sympathy in any situation, it's this one."

"Right. Yes. Sympathy." He cups the side of my jaw with my

ruined ear. "I just want to point out though, that everyone loves battle scars."

"Not the person with them."

"They're sexy. Interesting." He releases my jaw to touch his own bullet wound. "And now we match."

"We match. What a relief."

He misses my sarcasm. "And when we're old and married, we'll be able to tell everyone the story of how we met. Of our ... meet *shoot*."

I blink at him. "Don't try and turn this into a sweet moment."

"How I knew instantly that I couldn't kill you."

"Ah. So we're going to turn our *how we met* moment into a story of how you committed a crime and got away with it."

"*Almost* committed a crime."

"Sorry, do you somehow think shooting a man in the ear *isn't* illegal?"

"Well ... only if you're ... caught."

I give him a blank look, and the hopeful one I get back is too much. "You're making this up to me," I say, hating how easily I'm folding over something I should be holding against him for all time. "Later. For the rest of our lives, probably."

His grin springs to life. "That almost sounds like a proposal."

"Yeah, well, now we know that I'm actually okay and not at all being hunted, I guess we're fifty percent closer to that being a possibility." Because, what the actual fuck? This is ... this is so beyond the realm of fucking anything that I really don't know what else to say. All week, I've been running and hiding and stressed for my life ... for *no goddamn reason*.

"I need to sit down." I'm almost numb with relief as I sink into the nearest armchair.

"I need a drink," Lars says. "A big, strong drink."

"Hold on there, handsome," Arlie says. "This guy might be okay, but we haven't solved the Colin issue."

Shit. Colin. I'd forgotten about him for all of a few seconds, and the relief that washed over me completely disappears again. I might not currently be in danger, but Perry's still facing the threat to either turn in Colin or be offed instead, and I don't like either of those options.

"Where do we start?"

Tommy cracks his knuckles. "Give me what you know, a strong coffee, and about fifteen minutes. I've got this."

CHAPTER FORTY-ONE

PERRY

IT TAKES MORE like nineteen minutes, and he doesn't touch his coffee until he's done, but Tommy does it. He finds a guy who looks the least like St. Clare it's possible to look while still clearly being related. Unlike St. Clare, this guy's expression is permanently terrified, and maybe that's his real face, or maybe he's *actually* terrified. I'll hold out my judgment until I meet him.

Tommy tracked him from security camera to camera until we reached SODO and then … nothing. So I guess the first place we'll start looking is there.

"It's a big area to cover, so we'll organize supplies and meet back here tonight," Ever says. "It'll be easier to search when it's not busy."

"What type of supplies?" I ask, picturing night-vision goggles and flare guns.

"Comms equipment."

Huh. Well, that's still cool, even if slightly less cool than my first thoughts.

A yawn rips through St. Clare. "Tonight? I might try to get some sleep before then."

"Yeah, we didn't have any last night," I add, which makes it sound sexual but actually wasn't.

"First rule is to always be well rested," Arlie says. She's in take-charge mode, which is one of her hotter modes for sure. "You can't watch anyone's back if you're not at your best."

Lars's voice is more eager than usual. "Of course. You're so right."

You're so right?

I narrow my eyes, amused and suspicious. Does Larsy-boy have a crush? I mean, I can't blame him. Arlie is a force. And hey, if he's all schmoopy over her, then that's total confirmation that he's not going to suddenly turn around and decide he's in love with my pookie-bear. Maybe once this is over, I can play match-maker. I've never created romance on purpose, so it could be fun.

"Everyone okay for now?" Arlie checks.

"Sure am." Knowing St. Clare isn't in actual danger and that apparently I was the only one trying to kill him has given me whiplash, but I can't lie and say I'm not relieved. Guilty, yes. There's lots of that. But relief is a close second.

In this entire room, I'm the only one potentially wanted dead, and those odds are a lot better than what I initially thought they were.

"Do you two have masks?" Tommy asks, looking from St. Clare to Lars. "We'll need to go incognito in case we're not the only ones searching the area."

"I have masks," I answer because I already know St. Clare and Lars don't. "I've got spares. I'll share mine."

"Okay. Good to know." Tommy snaps his laptop closed and stuffs it and the other things he's brought back into his bag. "Should we meet back here at … nine?"

"Sounds good." But with them all leaving and everything put off until tonight, there are hours ahead of us where we'll be sleep-ing, but also … I *really* missed St. Clare. And I want to show him how much.

The others leave, and I wave them off before turning to Lars. "You should, uh, possibly do a perimeter check. Hang out any place not here."

I expect Lars to argue, but he must sense my ulterior motives because he shoves his feet into his boots and heads outside.

St. Clare studies me. "That excited to sleep, are you?"

"Super excited." I take his hand and tug him after me until we get to the bedroom. "Very, very excited." I make a show of flopping down onto the tiny bed while St. Clare stays planted in the middle of the room.

"Good to know." He keeps on standing there, hands tucked in his pockets, gaze taking a slow path down my body. Because I need him to hurry the hell up, I lift the bottom of my shirt, showing off my abs and a glimpse of nipple.

The way his hunger lights up his face makes me feel shivery. I've never been looked at the way St. Clare looks at me. The predatory gleam that hits his eyes is something that I didn't realize could be so hot directed at me. Sure, I've probably directed it at other people before because I'm obviously a total predator and—fine, that's a lie. I think the reason I like it so much is because no one has ever wanted me like he does. Period.

My cock thickens as St. Clare takes a measured step closer. "Pity we're supposed to be going to sleep right now."

"Sleep. Right. Answer me this. What's going to distract you more? Being a widdle bit tired or trying to concentrate with my ass *right there*, knowing you could have been inside it already."

St. Clare makes a choking noise, head bowing back as he grips the hard outline of his cock. "Why are you doing this?"

I curl my bottom lip over. "I've missed you."

"It's barely been twenty-four hours."

"Exactly. Do you know how much we could have made each other come in that time?"

Like he loses all sense of control, St. Clare plants his knee on the mattress beside me, then blankets my body with his. "You're insatiable."

He's not half-wrong. "Well, what's the point of training my ass if you're not going to use it?"

"You want me to use you?"

I nod, lust creeping through my system at the prospect of St. Clare fucking me. I'm not sure why the whole idea of it is such a turn-on when I've always been fine being the one doing the fucking, but I'm almost obsessive over it. "You have supplies in here?" I ask, dreading the thought of it not happening again.

"I do." He tugs my bottom lip between his teeth and bites down enough for a short spike of pain. "And a condom."

"We need a condom?"

"Yes."

"But ..."

He runs his nose up my cheek. "But what?"

"I sort of ... I just ..."

"Tell me."

"I like the thought of you making me all messy."

St. Clare groans and rolls his hips, steely hard cock grinding against mine. "Next time."

"Promise?"

He pulls back, looking me dead in the eye, and the way that bright blue pierces me is addictive. "In case you haven't gotten the message, I ... I care about you. I keep wanting more. I don't know what that means yet, but all I know is that something feels intrinsically off without you in my life. I'm not done here. I want more, for however long you want this to keep going."

Hearing St. Clare break this down and give voice to what I've been feeling makes my chest balloon with happiness. "Aww ... pookie."

He blinks. Frowns. "No."

"But that was so sweet."

"We're not pet naming. This is sex, Perry."

There's no way I'm interested in him pulling back now. I flip us, rolling on top of him so this time I'm the one pressing him into the mattress, all the long lines of his body fitting perfectly against mine. "This is more than sex, and you know it. I've done the just sex thing. I've been with people who aren't interested in anything more than what I can give them physically, but I'm so much more than that. I know I can be. Let me look after you and be sweet to you and maybe fall for you a little bit. I want the sex and the emotions and to look at you and know that I have my own person who's safe and home and all mine. I think you could be that person."

There's a war going on behind his eyes that takes a minute to settle. "You're putting a lot of faith in someone who's never had a real relationship."

I touch his ear and then my shoulder again, and slowly, like I knew it would, his lips fight the inevitable smile.

"We match," he says.

"We do."

He swallows thickly. "Yeah. I think I could be that person too."

My heart hums happily, and I push up onto my knees, strip off my shirt, then reach down and do the same to him. He's so damn sexy. Mostly smooth with a scattering of the lightest blond hair. Pecs that make me desperate to touch. Little pink nipples and then those grooves of his abs that have me concerned I've contracted rabies with how much I'm foaming at the mouth for them.

"Oh shit …" I rasp, flooded with the kind of heady want that's impossible to control. Each of my brain cells blinks out of commission as my gaze dips to where he's straining at his zipper.

My hands are shaking as I pop the button and drag open the fly. His cock springs free, pale with dark, straining veins and a deep red tip, and before St. Clare can say anything, I give in to the urge to lean forward and wrap my lips around him.

The girth stretches out my jaw as I sink down onto him, tongue flicking along the underside as I taste the lusty need he has for me. Sucking cock is so new and different, and I never want to stop.

His fingers grip my hair tight. "That's enough."

I reluctantly pull off and make sure my expression shows my exact thoughts. "But I want more."

"Well, you have the choice. I can come in your mouth or your ass. I can't do both."

"Not with that attitude," I mutter but give in.

I stand off the bed and strip out of my pants while St. Clare pushes his down far enough to kick off. His long, muscular legs are calling for me, but before I can disappear back between them, St. Clare rolls onto his side and pats the bed beside himself.

"Lie face down. I need to get you ready for me."

I throw myself onto the bed, and he laughs at my eagerness, but I don't care. The promise of his fingers in me is enough, let alone that I'm going to take more. "Hurry up."

"I'll take all the time I need."

Asshole. I grip the bedding in my fists, trying to stop from saying that word out loud. I need him on side here because I'm fully prepared to be fucked good and hard before we both crash out for the day.

When St. Clare climbs out of bed, I focus on breathing steadily through my nose, not wanting to complain or whine or start fucking begging or something. Patience has never been my strong suit, and after rutting against the bed a couple of times, I'm ready to give in.

Then he climbs back up behind me, and before I can tell him to hurry up again, something cold and wet slides down my crease.

I immediately tense, and it's only when his fingers follow the lube that I'm able to relax again.

"There you go," he says in a voice that makes my whole body light up. "Just let me do what I need to."

I bury my face in the blankets, hips tilting up to meet his touch. It shouldn't be this good. It shouldn't. But all it takes is him pushing a finger inside of me to not focus on that so much. It doesn't matter what should or shouldn't be happening because one finger is enough to make my ass sing, and I'm so ready for him that I rock back onto it. It's a lot easier with the lube than spit, but it's different. I dream of the day we can spend an entire weekend doing just this.

"You have no idea how sexy this looks," he says, voice a low rumble. "You're sucking me in. So hungry for it."

"I need it."

A second finger joins the first, stretching more than last time, but I love it. Love the fullness and want more. I'm mildly concerned that I'll never be satisfied, but I've never felt like this before. Never wanted someone more than I wanted my next breath.

He leans in, and the warm swipe of his tongue joins his fingers. His fingers fuck into me slowly as his tongue does the rest. Licking and sucking, slipping inside and stretching me open, getting me ready to take him.

That's the part that's really turning me on. Him prepping me to use. It's rearranged the chemicals in my brain to the point it's all I can focus on.

"I need your cock," slips past my lips way sooner than I thought it would. I always knew I'd end up begging, but I thought I could hold out at least a few more minutes than this. Not with St. Clare though. That man has me twisted and unfocused, my whole body a snappy live wire, waiting for him to amp up the sparks. "Please."

He laughs, pulling back, and this time when he presses his fingers inside, the stretch is deeper. I can feel him opening me, softening me, and I try to relax to make it easier on him, but I'm so fucking keyed up.

"I think you're ready."

"Thank fuck," I grunt.

He pulls his fingers out and *thwacks* my ass cheek. The sharp pain is almost too much, but a second after it hits, it goes from painful to pure fucking heat. I slip my hand beneath myself to wrap around my cock.

The friction is barely enough relief to calm me down, and I turn to look at him over my shoulder. "What are you doing?"

"Putting on the condom."

"It's taking forever."

"I'm also enjoying the view. You should see how loose and gaping you are." His groan rattles in his chest. "I've been dying to fuck you since I saw you in that coffee shop."

I stroke myself slowly, letting his words settle in deep. "Now's your chance, then."

"On your knees."

I push up onto them, still debating whether to get onto all fours, when his hands slide up my thighs to my ass. He grips me tight, spreads me open, and then licks a long wet strip from my balls to my tailbone.

My back arches involuntarily.

"Beg me," he commands.

My balls throb, and I don't bother to think, just word. "Please. I need it. I need you. I'm so fucking empty." My ass clamps down around nothing. "Please fuck me."

The head of his cock presses against me, and before he pushes inside, I'm already frustrated by the thin rubber between us. It doesn't feel the same as yesterday. Heated flesh against flesh. Feeling the sticky need of his precum marking up my opening.

Then he breaches my hole, and every frustration leaves me.

My muscles instinctively want to lock up, but I force myself to relax. To take him. To get everything I never knew I wanted.

St. Clare's cock feels way bigger than I expected, but he goes slow and seems to know exactly when to push and when to wait, and I have no clue about anything going on other than the fact I'm so deliciously, filthily stretched open.

His deep, ragged breathing fills my ears. "You feel so good."

That's the highest praise he could give me. My gut is flush with tingly sparks from my balls to my chest, and when St. Clare releases a long exhale, pressing tight against my ass, I melt. I'm jelly. Completely filled, brain offline, lust and happiness coursing through me.

When he doesn't move, I do it for him. Gentle strokes, on and off, until the burning stretch relieves and the delicious slide takes over. His cock is brushing that place in my ass that makes my balls tighten again, and I don't want it to stop.

I'd ride him all day if I could.

I plant my forearm on the bed, ignoring the pain in my shoulder as I jerk off. The faster I move, the more it signals to St. Clare what I can handle, and it's a relief when he takes over. When he plants his hands on my hips and fucks me confidently, overwhelming every little nerve in my ass to the point that I'm ready to come.

I'm an emotional guy most of the time. I love my family and

my friends. I'd do anything for anyone. But I've never wanted to tie myself emotionally to one person the way I want it with St. Clare. If it was my choice, I'd tie our hearts into little knots that he would never get undone again, and then we'd spend our days talking and goofing off and supporting each other and fucking in such a raw, uncontrollable way, I'd need days to recover from it.

I've never ever *ever* wanted this with another person and there have been plenty of other people.

Not one of them comes close to him.

He's made for me.

And I'll do everything to prove that I'm made for him.

His nails cut into my skin as he pounds ruthlessly against me. I'm vaguely aware of the bed meeting the wall, of his sweaty thighs against mine, of the way he utters my name in a disbelieving kind of way that tells me he's as fucked as I am.

His groan is this deep, physical thing that strokes along my spine and into my balls even as he abuses that thing in my ass, which is almost numb with pleasure. I'm twitchingly high, balls and thighs tightening every time he pegs me just right, and I'm not sure I can hold out much longer.

I want him to come, but I'm at the point where I want to come more.

I'm leaking all over the sheets, jacking myself hard and fast, rocking back into his thrusts and matching his need with mine. Every part of me is going to hurt after this, but it'll be so worth it to have what we have right now. To feel so good I could fucking fly.

"Ah, shit, Perry, this isn't going to last much longer."

The strangled way his words are uttered confirms it. But it's okay, I'm not long for either. He's tearing me up, turning me inside out, rearranging everything I thought I ever knew, and I'm enjoying every minute.

My cock swells in my hand as St. Clare lets out a grunt, hips stuttering as his dick twitches in my ass.

I imagine what it would be like without the condom. To be flooded with his cum and left used and sticky and open.

The sparking zaps in my spine get too much, and my eyes roll back on themselves as it finally releases.

I come hard, almost blacking out, not stopping to spare a thought for the bedding or St. Clare and how hard I'm riding back on him. My orgasm shudders through my limbs and then fades, slowly sizzling away and bringing back the ache in my shoulder before I collapse forward onto the bed.

St. Clare slips out, and what felt like heaven only seconds ago is starting to ache, and not in a good way now.

Only a bit though. Only enough to remind me what happened and confirm that I don't regret a thing.

CHAPTER FORTY-TWO

ST. CLARE

THIS COMMS FEELS weird in my ear. "Do we really need this?" I ask Tommy, who's just walked me through how to use it. "We have our phones."

"If you run into the type of people you don't want to run into, they won't wait while you whip out your phone to text us."

"But you said yourself I'm not in any danger."

"Walking around SODO at night is asking to be put into danger. Maybe they won't kill you, but being beaten up or robbed is high on the list of fuck yous that place has in store."

"Oh, good. I'm glad my brother didn't pick somewhere dangerous and ill-advised to hang out."

"Do you have any idea *why* he'd be there?"

I can feel them all looking at me, and yes, I do feel partially responsible for us all hauling ass out to the industrial district at night. It's my brother who's done a reckless thing, but I think he and Perry are currently tied for worst decisions where I'm concerned. "No. And it doesn't make sense that he didn't talk to me about any of it either."

"Does he know anyone who works or lives down that way?"

I frustratingly shake my head again. "Colin doesn't *know* anyone. He works. That's it. He doesn't do friends. He doesn't have anyone outside of me and Lars."

Perry's forehead crumples. "No friends?"

"I know it sounds sad, but Colin has always been a bit … operating on another level to the rest of us. He likes to play and tinker and work. Saint Clare's is his baby. I've always just been along for the ride."

"You did a lot too," Lars says, and I appreciate his support. "You built it together."

"Not enough together if he went running off to some asshole like Carson Alexander." It's hard not to feel bitter about him making choices and not checking with me first.

Everett shudders. They're all wearing black and brought clothes for us too, but Ever is the only one wearing a leather jacket. "I have no interest in playing with him."

"Let's hope Colin is super easy to find, then, and it doesn't come to that."

"Right," Arlie says, checking her watch. "We'll go in teams. Ever and Perry, me and Lars, Tommy and St. Clare."

I breathe a small sigh of relief that I'm not with Ever, but splitting up from Perry and Lars doesn't sit right with me either. "What if someone spots Perry? He's still on Luther's list, isn't he?"

"Yeah," Arlie confirms. "But no one's really paying attention to him when Colin's been made the priority. Plus, he's with Ever."

I force myself to look at the guy. "Can you handle it?"

He laughs in a terrifying way. "Not just handle it. I'll handle it and *enjoy* it."

"Not sure I want to know what that means, but it's mildly reassuring."

"Thank you," Perry says suddenly. "You three didn't have to come or help us, but I really appreciate that you did."

"Don't thank us yet." Arlie shifts to her other foot as Tommy stands and throws his arm around Perry's shoulders.

"We're friends. It's what friends do. We love you, man."

"Awww, I love you too."

Perry lights up, and I have to remind myself approximately thirty-five times that I'm not allowed to get jealous over their friendship. Or the way Perry lit up. Or how Tommy is still touching him. I'm not glaring at them. Not at all.

"Yeah, yeah," Arlie says with all of the patience I'm feeling. "Perry is great. Now, can we get on with it?"

I'm with Arlie. And not even only because of the jealousy thing. The sooner we go, the sooner we could maybe, potentially find Colin. "I'm ready."

None of these people should be doing this, and I want to believe it will be a quiet night of searching, but the pit in my gut says otherwise. Like this deep knowledge everything is about to go wrong.

"Let's go." Ever zips up the front of his jacket. "There's no use waiting around for anything else."

We head outside to where there are two cars waiting for us. It's hard to shake the urge to look around for people lurking in the shadows, and I can't believe that after only a few days of thinking I was in danger, it's taken such a deep hold of my mind.

I'm not sure I'll ever shake it.

Lars and Arlie are heading to the opposite side of the industrial district from where we're going, and before they can climb into the other car, we lock eyes. He gives me a sharp nod that I try to return as I remind myself that Lars has had training. Lars knows how to defend himself. Out of the six of us, I'm the biggest liability.

Arlie promised she'd keep him safe anyway, but I've run out of trust for people.

"Let's go," Tommy says, leading the way to the car we're taking.

He climbs into the driver's seat, and Ever takes shotgun while Perry and I climb in the back. I'm glad we haven't split up yet, and that feeling intensifies as his hand wraps around mine on the cushion between us.

"We're going to find him," he says with way more conviction than I feel.

"Of course we are." There's nothing else I can do but agree because what if we don't? It's not a possibility I'm interested in.

It's time that Colin came back, and I need it to happen sooner rather than later. Other than holding on to Perry's hand for dear life, we don't talk for the drive down there. The closer we get, the less traffic there is until we reach the imposing dilapidated-looking buildings. We're starting on the water side while Lars and Arlie come from the other direction, but being here, seeing the huge shadowy monsters, hits me with a feeling of complete hopelessness. If Colin's here—and that's still a big *if*—how the hell are we supposed to find him anyway?

There's just … so many places. Too many places. How the fuck are we going to search this whole area?

We pull up on a grassy stretch of dirt near where Colin was last seen, and Tommy kills the engine. Unlike me, the other three don't look at all bothered by the fact we're going out there and looking for a needle in a fucking haystack.

"Right," Tommy says, unlatching his door. "Reilly and I will head down that street. You two head that way."

"No worries," Ever replies, climbing out of the car. Tommy follows him, and I turn to Perry, not bothering to keep the worry off my face.

"You good?" I ask.

"Of course. We're going to find your brother, so that's one less thing for you to worry about."

"Right." Before I talk myself out of it, I lean in and kiss him. His lips claim mine like magnets, the natural force bringing us together where we belong.

He pulls back before I'm ready and flashes me a smile. "See you in a bit." He pops his door too, and I hurry to follow suit, not wanting to be left alone in the silence.

Tommy switches his ear comms on. "You good, Arlie?" After a second, he glances at Everett. "Masks on. Let's find this fucker."

Perry and Everett leave, and then it's me and Tommy and the eerily still silence all around us.

"We'll see what places we can get inside, but I'm not overly worried about searching locked buildings. If we can't get in, your brother can't either."

I hope he's right about that. I tug my mask up over my mouth and nose, then hurry to fall into step with him. I'm taller than Tommy, but he walks fast. "Why can't you find him on the security cameras like you did earlier?"

"Because there has to *be* security cameras." Tommy points toward the nearest building. "Not everywhere has them, and the ones that do are more concerned with keeping their buildings and goods protected rather than what's happening on the street. There are a lot of blind spots down here."

I can't wrap my head around why Colin would be here in the first place. We're not exactly rich and privileged shitheads, but we're still on the side of rich and privileged that stops us hanging out in creepy places like this.

"Do we yell out for him?" I ask, which is a stupid question when I'm asking in a whisper anyway.

"Do you want to advertise we're here?"

"Not particularly."

"Then maybe no yelling."

I concede he has a point. We make it to the end of the street with no sight of anyone, and Tommy sighs, then reaches up and turns off his comms. "Gives me a headache," he explains. "I've already got too many voices in my head to deal with all of them too. I'll check back in if we find a building we can get inside."

"You work well together. How long have you known them?"

We take a left and walk along the side of another building. The cement path is overgrown and shadowy from twiggy trees. "A while. I knew Arlie first, then Everett not long after. Perry showed up a few years ago and never left."

"But he's only new at … all this?"

"I wouldn't even call him new." Tommy's grinning, eyes bright. "I don't classify him as even starting. That man is way too pure for this world."

"I've seen a side of him that says otherwise."

He runs an amused glance over me. "No you didn't. If you did, you'd be dead."

Well, he's got me there. "Tell me about Arlie."

"Why? Do you want to sleep with her? Everyone wants to sleep with her."

"I'm gay, so no. Lars might though."

Tommy shrugs, pushing up on his toes to look through a high window. "She's single from what she's told us, so he might have a chance. Super picky, though, and a very short temper."

"I guess it's lucky Lars is infinitely patient."

Tommy's attention turns back to the street and we keep walking. It's freezing out, and I'm coiled so tight in anticipation of someone jumping out at us that my back is aching.

We're about an hour in when Tommy stops suddenly.

"What is it?"

Without a word, he reaches under his jacket and pulls out a gun. Then hands it to me. "Just in case."

That makes my fear spike. "Just so you know, I'm a terrible shot."

"Let's hope you don't need to use it, then." He points at a building across from us. It's a warehouse with large roller doors and high windows so grimy you can't see through them. "I think I saw something in there."

"Okay. Let's check it out." I'm trying to be confident, but it's not working.

We cross the street and creep closer. Tommy finds a side door and tries it, but it's locked tight. We keep circling the building until we find another one, and this time when he turns the handle, the door unlatches and swings open on creaky hinges.

His sweeping hand is an invitation. "After you, princess."

The pet name is almost enough to insist he goes first, but I'm not a fucking coward, and while this might be stressful and out of the ordinary, I'm not about to show him that I'm creeped out. So I go first, stepping into the narrow, dark hallway, and when Tommy follows and closes the door behind us, the whole room goes black.

"Got a flashlight?" I ask, ignoring my hammering heart.

He flips on a tiny one and uses his palm to dim the light. His brightly unfocused eyes meet mine. "Spooky."

"Can you focus, please?"

He cracks a smile and takes the lead. "There's nothing to be worried about. I'm used to skulking about in the dark. It's where I do my best work."

I eye his shadowy profile. "I thought it would be easier to kill someone in good lighting."

"Me? Nah, I don't kill anyone. That's Arlie and Ever's job."

"It sounds like Ever really likes it."

"You could say that. He's less of a hitman, though, and more of a ..."

"Yeah?"

"A butcher."

My stress levels spike. "What?"

"He's the guy you call in when you don't want someone dead, just mentally scarred for the rest of their lives."

Even the idea of that turns my stomach. "And he's alone with Perry?"

"Don't worry, we're all in it for the pay. Everyone who's good at their job knows not to do it for free."

Then what do they call this?

Somehow, that doesn't make me any less worried. Not even a little bit. I put slightly more distance between us. "And what do they call you?"

"If I bothered to give myself an alias, it would have been Loot."

Loot? "So you ..."

"Am a thief. Priceless goods are my specialty. I know exactly how to get what I want when people least expect it."

The momentary fake safety I feel over not being with a professional killer is hard to hang on to when he says things like that. "And what do you want?"

"Right now?" He shrugs. "To find your brother."

"But why?"

"It's the whole reason we're here."

My gut sinks as we leave the hall for a wide-open warehouse floor. "But you said ... you just said that if you're good at it, don't work for free. So why are you?"

Tommy turns to me, eyes shrewd, but before he can get a word out, his focus shifts to behind me. "Well, that's interesting."

Without warning, he releases his hold on the flashlight, and light floods the building. Which isn't a good thing.

Not when what I'm looking at is ten or so enormous men and women surrounding us.

"Shit," I mutter. "Sorry to barge in," I get out, sounding like I'm trying to swallow gravel. "We were looking for someone."

"They're not here," a woman immediately replies.

"Right. Okay." I go to walk backward but collide with Tommy, and the gun I was holding clatters to the floor.

The three people I can make out by the dim light immediately turn their attention to it and then snap back to me again. "That's umm—"

Tommy takes over. "Colin St. Clare. Know where he is?"

Unlike me, Tommy doesn't sound like he's shitting bricks. He keeps his attention on the woman who spoke while I watch the shadowy people surround us. My heart is getting sickeningly fast.

The woman narrows her eyes at Tommy. "No. Now, get out."

"Colin with a C," he pushes. "In case that helps your memory."

"It doesn't."

"Guy who's wanted by Carson Alexander."

This time, the answer takes longer to come. It's a man who steps in this time. "We said get out."

"I'd love to," Tommy continues, and I can tell he's smiling even without looking at him. "And I would, totally, of course. *If* you weren't lying to me."

My attention whips to him and then back to the crowd again. "You know where he is?"

"We told you we didn't. Now, you have ten seconds to leave, or you won't like what comes next."

"Ten …" Tommy says. "Nine … eight …"

"What the fuck are you doing?"

"They said I won't like what comes next—six!—so I can't wait to find out what that is."

"What are you—"

"Fivefourthreetwo ... *one!*"

And before I know what's happened, as he hits one, Tommy kicks the strength from my knees, and they smash into the concrete floor. The pain barely has had a chance to register when the shockingly hard barrel of his gun presses against the back of my head.

I freeze.

Spine turned to ice as the hairs prickling down my neck stand on end.

"What the fuck are you doing?" I wheeze.

He releases the safety with a too-loud metallic clink.

"You might want to tell Colin St. Clare that *he* has ten seconds to get his ass down here. Or he's not going to like what I do to his brother."

CHAPTER FORTY-THREE

PERRY

"WHAT WAS THAT?"

Ever grunts and stills, looking around the dark room.

My ears prick, and I strain to work out if I'm hearing what I think I'm hearing. It's hard to know out here. Everything feels so loud. The wind. The rodents that have made this place their home. Each scuffing footstep we take.

What sounds like muffled voices comes again.

"That? Did you hear it?"

"Nope."

Fucking weird. I could have sworn I heard something, but maybe it's the billion and one thoughts tearing up my brain. Ever knows what he's doing, and I need to trust that.

I don't like this much. It's such a new and weird feeling to be so actively worried about someone. I fumble through life. I don't think, I just do, and it's gotten me to where I am and—other than the whole wanted dead thing—I like where I am.

My life is chill and cruisey and fun. And it will be all those things and more in some distant future where St. Clare and I can put this behind us and have awesome lives together. We just need to find this annoying, pesky, troublesome brother of his so I can have a few stern words with him about leaving us hanging and then introduce myself as his possibly new future brother-in-law.

Which may or may not be getting ahead of myself, but what's the point of being in a relationship if you're not going to close your eyes and jump?

My ears prick as that sound comes again.

"I swear there's someone here."

Ever tilts his head like having one ear higher than the other will help him hear better. "I don't know what you're talking about."

I take a moment to listen again. "This way, maybe ..."

I take a sharp right. We're on the second floor of a huge warehouse, and other than packing boxes, machinery, and a room full of desks and computers, the place looks sparse.

It's weird to think that we're breaking and entering, though I maintain we haven't broken anything since the place was unlocked, when I'm such an upstanding citizen most of the time. Well, when I'm not shooting at people and taking money for hypothetical kills.

I'm glad that my two victims before St. Clare had the good sense to stay hidden. I really didn't want to have to explain to Luther that I actually botched all the jobs he's given me.

We creep around another corner, and there's still nothing. It doesn't make sense. I would have put money down that I could hear someone, but the further we look, the less I can hear.

Did I imagine it?

I'd like to confidently say no, but I'm not so sure I trust my thoughts enough for that.

"How long have you been working for Luther?" I ask Ever.

"Hmm ... maybe ... five years now?"

"Wow." I try to do the mental calculations on how many people he's killed in that time, but then I give up and just ask him. "Do you know how many people you've killed?"

He chuckles. "I do. Zero."

"Zero?" That perks me up. "Do you only pretend to kill them too?"

"No, Perry, that's all you." He throws me a look, and I can't tell if it's an amused or disgusted one. They really shouldn't be similar enough to be confused. "I've never been hired to kill someone."

"I thought you were a hitman?"

"You thought wrong. That's Arlie. She's one of the best. I'm the stage before her. Sometimes people are worth more alive than dead to whoever hires us. They just need a whole lot of persuasion and a whole lot less fingers."

I stare at the gleam on his bald head. "You take their *fingers*?" I hiss.

"How is that any worse than taking their lives?"

"It's … well …" Okay, so I can't really vocalize why it's worse; I just know that it is. "You know …"

"I don't."

I scrape my brain for the logic I'm sure is there. "Shooting them is over instantly. They don't know they're in danger. They're not in pain. It's … nothing. Torturing is something they have to live with forever."

"But at least they're alive."

I scrunch up my face, torn over the ethics of which is worse.

Then he chuckles. "How did the no-pain thing go for Reilly when you shot him?"

"Okay, but that was a onetime thing, and he *still* holds it against me. If I took his fingers on purpose, I'm confident he would have held that against me even more."

"Good thing, then, that you're not cut out for this life."

I sigh pathetically. "I'm worried that I'm not cut out for any life. I haven't found that place where I *fit*, you know?"

"Yet."

"What?"

"You haven't found where you fit *yet*. But there's a place for someone like you, and I know you'll find it."

"At least one of us believes in me."

"You've never seemed bothered about this before."

He's right. I've never seemed bothered because I've never *been* bothered, and I still don't know why it's tying me up so badly now. Is it really so unbelievable that I'd want to be more than a constant fuckup though? Maybe once, I'd like to be the capable guy who handles shit instead of bumbling along and—oh wow. I think I'm having an identity crisis.

Come to think of it, I probably should have picked up on this before now.

The signs were there.

I immediately seek out the comfort of my bracelet and try to channel my thoughts into something more productive.

"I don't think I know who I am," I say suddenly.

Ever eyes me. "Is this really the place?"

"Well, if not here, where? I don't see us talking about anything else, and if we can't search *and* talk at the same time, I really worry about your multitasking abilities."

"My multitasking abilities are just fine."

"Then help me."

If I didn't know better, I'd say that Ever looks horrified. *Horrified*. The guy who turns fingers into spare parts. "My multitasking doesn't extend to therapy sessions."

Well, fuck. You think you know a guy, and then he's not even there for you in a life-altering moment.

My head snaps to the side, and I'm successfully distracted as I pick up on a noise again. "Did you hear that?"

"I still have no clue what you're talking about."

I'm certain this time, and I pick up my steps like a greyhound on the hunt for blood. It was definitely this way, and I'm sure it was a voice. The further we walk, the louder it gets.

"Eight … seven …"

I glance back at Everett. "Someone's counting."

Both of us jog toward a bank of windows that look out over the warehouse floor, and it takes me way too long for my eyes to adjust.

There are people everywhere. A huge group surrounding two in the middle and—

St. Clare!

My gut bottoms out, and I'm about to turn and run to him when Tommy moves so fast it's hard to track him. He kicks St.

Clare, who folds to the ground, and then—Tommy pulls out his gun and presses it to my man's head.

The blood drains from my body so fast I swear I hear it leave in a *whoosh* that rings in my ears. Pure, blinding rage replaces it, and all I know is that Tommy is dead. He's *fucking dead*.

My gun's in my hand faster than I know how to move, and I lift it, line up my shot—

Before it's flung from my grip.

Ever crashes into me from the side, and at first, I think we're under attack, but then reality hits me as hard as I hit the ground.

It's just *me* under attack.

From Everett.

With strength I didn't know he had, he pulls my wounded arm high up my back. The scream I let out is all but silence as the pain shoots through my whole body, and then his hand comes down tight and immovable over my mouth.

"Don't make a fucking sound."

CHAPTER FORTY-FOUR

ST. CLARE

TOMMY'S WHISTLING A CHILLING TUNE, gun still firm on my head, and every time I shift, he plants it there harder, like he's reminding me what a fucking psycho he is.

"Why do we care if you shoot him?" one of the men around us asks.

"*You* don't. Colin will."

"How do we even know that's his brother?"

Tommy shrugs as a bead of sweat slips down my back. "Don't get him, then. But it won't take him long to identify what I leave you."

"I *am* his brother," I shout before Tommy calls their bluff and leaves me in a puddle of my own gray matter. "Tell him Reilly is here."

At first, no one moves, and then, a shadow on the left shifts. The man steps back and, after a hushed conversation with the woman in charge, leaves.

"Ahh …" Tommy says. "So you *do* know where he is?"

"We didn't say that."

"Didn't need to, pumpkin. And I bet he's not going to be happy when he walks in and sees this."

"What do you want with him?"

"I heard there's a lot of money on his head."

My skin cools, goose bumps prickling along the surface. Tommy said he wasn't a hitman. Is he working with Arlie and Ever? Is that why they said yes to this job? Have I led them to my brother and sealed his fate?

The way my stomach churns almost has me doubling over. "You can't hurt him."

"Shut up."

"We trusted you to help us!"

Tommy ruffles my hair with his gunless hand. "You asked us to find Colin. Well, I think we found him. You're welcome."

"Not to kill him!"

"That wasn't specified."

Holy shit, what have I done? What have I *done*?

All I need is to reach up and turn my comms on, without Tommy realizing it, so the others can hear what's happening. If he's in partnership with Arlie and Ever, it could end up putting Perry and Lars at risk, but I have to trust they can help themselves. That we can all get through this.

As slowly as I can, I inch my hand toward my ear. So slowly. So subtly. My arm is straining with how controlled I'm keeping it, but I don't want to risk giving myself away. I'm hardly fucking breathing.

My thumb brushes the top of my ear, and I creep lower, find the button—

"*Reilly?*"

My brother's bespectacled face is flooded by the flashlight, and I'm hit with too many emotions at once. Love, relief, frustration, happiness, and—when the gun leaves my head—terror.

I leap to my feet and turn on Tommy, throwing my arms out to the side. "Don't shoot."

Tommy stares me down, then, whistling that same chilling tune, he spins his gun over one finger and tucks it away. "Told you I know how to get what I want." Tommy winks.

He fucking winks.

"That ... was an *act*?"

"Sure was. You played your part perfectly, by the way."

I want to rage. I want to pick up my gun from the cement floor and point it at him, then demand to know how he likes it. I want to hit him, or set Perry on him, or tell the people around us to cart his ass away.

But then Colin talks again, and threats to my life aside, there's only one person I currently care about.

"What are you doing here?"

I turn back to Tommy with one last disgusted glare, then take long strides until I'm close enough to haul Colin into my arms. "I was so fucking worried! Where have you been? What have you done?"

He's stiff with his hug, and when he pulls back, worry lines his face. "You shouldn't be here."

"Neither should you!"

"No. You *really* shouldn't be here."

It takes everything not to snap at him. "I've had a stressful fucking night, after a stressful few weeks, so why don't you answer my goddamn questions before you start telling me where I should and shouldn't be."

Behind his glasses, Colin's eyes sweep the circle around us. "You weren't supposed to get involved in this."

"Yeah, well, I'm now very fucking involved, and all because you didn't bother with a phone call to let me know you were going into hiding for a bit."

Colin gets that scrunched-face, *I will not cry* look about him. "I was embarrassed."

"Well, that's a great reason to have me thinking my brother is dead. I'm so glad I saved you the embarrassment. *Phew*. And here I was thinking the answer would be stupid."

"I didn't have a choice."

"Of course you did!" Oh, look at that. The relief didn't last long before I spun right into anger. "It's *our* business. If you're going to borrow money for *our* business, you talk to me about it first."

"Our ..." Colin's frown takes over his face. "I didn't borrow money for Saint Clare's."

Well, I'm not expecting that. "Oh. Then … what the fuck else do you need a hundred K for?"

He shoots another quick look around before sighing and pushing his glasses back up his nose. "You better come with me."

I start to follow him when I hear Tommy shadow me. "What are you doing?"

"Not letting you go off with these strangers, for a start."

"You threatened to kill me."

"Technically, I didn't," he says, holding his hands up in surrender. "I only held a gun to your head and said a bunch of vague things."

"Oh, is that all?"

"You're taking this way harder than you should be."

"I'm starting to see why you and Perry get along so well." I turn my back on Tommy, half expecting him to grab me from behind, and the whole time we follow Colin, I'm tuned in to where Tommy is and what he's doing. If he makes any sudden movements, he's in for it. I'm not going to let him catch me by surprise again.

We leave the main warehouse, and Colin leads us down twists and turns before we reach the very back, where there's a metal flight of stairs leading to an upstairs area. He jogs on ahead of us, and I stick close to his heels, curious about where we're going and what he's doing here and, well, just about fucking everything.

When we reach the top, he pulls out a key and unlocks the door.

"You can't tell anyone about this," he warns me.

"Yeah, of course."

That must be enough for him because he pushes through the door and lets me in before he blocks Tommy's path. "Not you."

Tommy bops him on the nose. "If I wanted you dead, you'd be dead."

"It's not about that."

His mouth flattens, and then he shrugs. "Fine. But I'm telling the others where we are."

"I don't care," Colin says in that bland, matter-of-fact way he speaks. Then he closes the door in Tommy's face.

We're in what looks like an apartment. Cream-painted walls and office-grade gray carpet. Colin passes me to walk into the living area that has a kitchenette on one side and a small couch and TV on the other.

And when I register the person sitting fretfully on the couch, I'm more confused than ever.

"Onyx?"

They manage a not-happy smile. "Reilly, in the nicest way possible: how the hell did you find us?"

I glance at Colin. "Security footage. You took money from the account, and Tommy was able to follow you."

Onyx lets out a heavy sigh. "I told you to let me make those withdrawals for you."

"For me?" Colin echoes. "I would have had to give you my PIN. That's illegal."

"It's not illegal," I add. "Just against the bank's rules."

It's like I've forgotten how black-and-white Colin is. "Our accounts wouldn't have been secure. I had to do it myself."

"Yes, but now if these guys have found you, it won't be hard for Carson Alexander to do the same," Onyx points out.

I latch onto their words. "So it was Carson that you borrowed money from?"

Colin's eyes work madly behind his glasses, like he's trying to figure out how much to tell me. "Well, it's not as though I can apply for a bank loan to hire a private investigator, now can I?"

"You hired a private investigator?"

"I didn't have a choice."

"But … why?"

Colin paces to one side of the room and back again. "Yanni. He was a problem, and I needed that problem to go away."

I'm still so fucking confused. "Start from the top. It's been a long few weeks, and I'm struggling to work out how the fuck you're hanging out here okay."

Onyx pats the spot on the couch to their left. "Might as well sit down. I'm going to bake some cookies in the hope you won't hate me after you hear this."

"Hate … you?"

"Just listen. I'll be back once he's done."

Onyx leaves, and Colin takes the place left behind.

"Where are we?" I ask.

"Onyx's place." Colin twists his hands in his lap. "They've been hiding me here. I didn't know where else to go."

"What kind of shit have you gotten yourself into?"

He clears his throat with the dry snap of a twig and leans back. "Yanni and his people from Rev cost us too much money and stress with their threats and holdups. I needed a way to make him back off, and since it's not like I could borrow money against Saint Clare's, I asked around. Found Carson. He was shockingly really nice, set out the contract clearly, no gimmicks—it's clear he's been doing this for a long time. Anyway, we signed off on the loan, cash payments only, a year timeline, which I knew wouldn't be an issue once we started selling out."

I almost choke. "You assumed a hundred grand in a year was no big deal?"

"I've already run the numbers."

"And what if they're wrong?" My voice is getting steadily higher.

"Numbers don't lie, Reilly." If his tone weren't so flat, I'd have sworn it held an edge of *duh* to it.

"And you used that money to hire a PI?" I ask, moving on.

"Yes. He was great. Got me exactly what I needed. Yanni is very good at keeping his books updated with every transaction. Showed a lot of drug trade … that linked him with Carson Alexander."

"Oh, fuck."

"No wonder he warned me off dealing with Carson." He nods sadly. "I sent a picture to Yanni, telling him to back off or I'd go to the cops."

"I thought he was after you because you didn't pay him back."

"Nope. He found out I knew too much, and next thing I know,

Onyx showed up at my place, all but kidnapped me, and brought me here."

"What the fuck? Why?"

"You know how Onyx is ex-MMA? Well, they train with a whole group of people—you saw some of them downstairs. Some are pro, some are semi-pro, and some make more money fighting illegally than professionally. One of Onyx's contacts heard my name come up. They called Onyx because they knew Onyx works for us, and now ..." Colin puffs out a quick exhale. "Sorry we haven't been in contact. We've been madly working to try and convince Carson to let this go and I'd never speak about it again."

"And you couldn't have let me know? Not even a quick *hey, I'm alive?*"

He shakes his head. "It was supposed to be over quickly. I didn't think it would take this long, and I didn't want to drag you into this mess. Onyx had everyone on high alert to make sure that your name didn't come up too."

I don't even know what to make of this. I hunch forward over my knees, fingers buried in my hair.

"I just wanted them to leave us alone," Colin whispers.

Me too, but now, thanks to him, I don't think that's something we can count on. "You should have asked for help," I point out to him, but when his face falls, I can't hold on to the annoyance for long. Look at me. Between him and Perry, I'm a total pushover. "You have us too now. And we're going to figure this thing out."

He takes my hand, and at first, I think it's in support, but then he speaks. "Are you aware you're missing an ear?"

Even though he's being totally serious, I laugh. "Yeah. That's a really long story. And it starts and ends with a guy named Perry ..."

CHAPTER FORTY-FIVE

PERRY

THE SECOND we get to Tommy, lurking at the bottom of a set of metal stairs, I draw back my fist and swing. It hits his face with a satisfying *whack* and a very unsatisfying sting that shoots through my hand.

"*Ouch!*"

"I'll say!" Tommy stands, hand covering his cheek. "What the hell, Perry?"

I give him my most menacing stare, ignoring the way I'm cradling my hand in front of my chest like a kicked puppy. "Don't ever pull that shit with my boyfriend again."

"Your boyfriend?"

"Well … not … officially, but it's going to happen. So consider yourself warned."

Instead of looking scared, I'm pretty sure he's going to laugh at me. "Okay, okay, I'm warned."

I don't appreciate the way he's blowing me off. I've never had fear like I did in that second. I'd thought he was serious, that he was actually going to kill one of the two most important people in my life, and if Ever hadn't taken over and explained to me what Tommy was doing, he probably wouldn't be standing here.

"I almost killed you."

"I'd believe that if you'd ever killed anyone."

"That's how angry I was. If Ever didn't tackle me, you'd be dead right now."

Some of the humor dims. "Got it."

Lars and Arlie take that moment to join us, escorted by two men with the type of muscle you don't want to test.

"Where's Reilly?" Lars asks.

I'm about to tell him I don't know when Tommy points up the stars. "With his brother."

"You found Colin?"

"Sure did." Tommy drops into a bow. "You're welcome."

I consider telling Lars what Tommy did, sure he'll give my friend a matching bruise on the other cheek, but I hold off. We still need the baddie bunch.

The door at the top of the stairs opens, and St. Clare walks out, followed by his brother. I'm stupidly relieved to see St. Clare is okay, and my eyes follow every step he takes down the stairs as I hold back from pushing past the others to get to him. His blond hair is a floppy mess, but *damn*, it looks good on him. That, and this all-black getup we're wearing, makes him look like even more of a badass than his suits do.

"We need to find Carson" are the first words out of St. Clare's mouth. "This is all on him."

Ever grunts. "Even if I wanted to be involved with that, no one knows his location."

"Luther would." Everyone turns and looks at me. "He works with him a lot. You can't tell me he doesn't keep tabs on these kinds of things."

"He's not just going to tell us though," Arlie says. But while she says that, I can tell things are working madly in her brain.

"Another option is Yanni," Colin adds, and it throws me how different his voice is to his brother's. St. Clare's is full of life, Colin's is … like a robot. I'd been expecting them to be similar versions of the same guy. "They work together. Don't know how we'd get it out of him, but if that's our only option …"

Before they can follow that train of thought, I jump in too. "I don't think he's an option. Yanni was clear that if he had to see me again, it wouldn't be pretty, and he was borderline scared of Carson Alexander too. Next?"

"Luther wants you," Arlie says, attention on Colin. "Either you or Perry. That was the deal."

"Not loving where this is going," I admit.

St. Clare's eyes meet mine for a worried second. "Neither am I."

"Then we give up on finding Carson, and the rest of you are on your own." She shrugs. "It really doesn't bother me either way because I'm not the one who's wanted, and Luther has no idea we're working with you. I'm only saying ... we could use that to our advantage."

"Advantage?" My ears perk up at that. "What advantage?"

"If the three of us call and say that we have you both and we'll hand you over in exchange for Carson's location, there's no way he won't go for it."

"You want to ... trade me?" All the talk from St. Clare and Lars about doing exactly that comes back to me, and once again, I'm left feeling like the odd man out who no one wants. It's hard to shake the feeling, but the more I try, the more I can admit that Arlie has a point. Colin and I are the only ones who can do this, and I'd rather be the bargaining chip over the brother St. Clare just got back. The brother who, quite frankly, doesn't look like he'd survive a trade negotiation.

"Why do you look like you're thinking about this?" St. Clare asks.

"Because I am. You and Lars had the same idea at one point, and I figure I can either be offended that everyone wants to pass me around like a hot piece of ass, or I can go with it. And I think I want to go with it."

Saying it out loud confirms how I'm feeling. I want to be the guy who takes charge. I *want* to be the hero. And what's more heroic than self-sacrifice?

"I say we do it." My good-though-still-sore-from-punching-Tommy hand shoots into the air. "Who else votes yes?"

Arlie raises her hand, and Tommy takes a second to scrutinize me before he does too. Colin's hand joins mine, and then it's just Lars, Ever, and St. Clare to convince.

"You're outnumbered," I point out. "And if Colin and I are both on board, you don't get to tell us not to do this."

"I can ask you though." St. Clare moves closer. "Don't make me worry about you again."

"Unfortunately, I'm going to be worried about me continuously until this guy is out of our lives, so I don't see another option."

The way his eyes dull kills me, but we really don't have any other choice here.

"Everett." Arlie's voice diverts my attention. They're staring at each other hard. "This is our chance."

"Your chance at what?" I ask immediately.

"Nothing that concerns you."

That's not at all reassuring. "This whole thing concerns me."

"What we're talking about doesn't. It's been on the cards for a long time and isn't something you need to worry about."

I choke on indignation and thrust my hand at Tommy. "He pretended like he was going to kill St. Clare! So I almost killed him! This is where not talking gets us."

Instead of shock, she laughs. "Good move," she tells Tommy.

"Arlie!"

"Did we successfully find the brother? Yes? Good. Now, move on."

"I'm in," Ever says reluctantly, and if these three think we're not going to revisit this conversation at a later time, they're mistaken. I'm starting to understand why St. Clare held a grudge for so long.

Lars shifts his weight, throat tight when he says, "I don't want any of you getting hurt."

"Well, it's too late for that," Colin replies. "I'd like to not be in hiding for the rest of my life, so please put your hand up."

With a sigh, he half raises his hand.

"Just you now," I point out to St. Clare.

He looks around the circle like he's deeply, deeply betrayed.

"We're going to do it anyway, so at this point, you're deciding whether you'll join us."

The air gushes from his lungs. "I'm in this to the end, but this is a big ask."

"I know. I'm agreeing to someone playing tradesies with me."

"We could always run away. Far, far away."

"What about Saint Clare's? And Margot and Elle?" That stumps him. "This will be over soon. Just say you're gonna help."

"Fine." It doesn't sound at all fine. "I'll help."

"We will too."

I glance up at the person who's joined Colin. Fiery dyed-red hair, as muscular as the people around us, and a sunshiny smile that's at odds with how they make me want to cower behind St. Clare.

"If he thinks he's getting to Colin, he has to go through me."

CHAPTER FORTY-SIX

ST. CLARE

WE HEAD BACK UP to Onyx's apartment, all of us cramming into the tiny space, and while the relief in my soul over finding Colin is immense, I only have eyes for one man.

I'm sick at the thought of what they're planning.

"So …" I confirm, to make sure I'm following as Onyx sets out some freshly baked cookies. "Arlie will take Perry to Lethal Poison and tell Luther that he'll get Colin once she gets the address?"

"Not quite," Tommy says, licking crumbs off his fingers. "She's going to show him footage of Colin—maybe we'll set up downstairs—all tied up and gagged with Ever waiting with him. Once he hands over the address, I'll intercept the feed and create a deepfake of Ever shooting Colin. In other words, it'll look real but won't actually be real. Then Luther will think Colin's dead, Arlie will leave, and …"

"And the rest is up to me," Perry finishes.

That's the part I'm most worried about. Arlie has to leave without him so that Luther doesn't know they're working together, but to do that, she has to leave Perry completely unprotected. With a man who wants him dead. And my beautiful, amazing, precious soul of a human refuses to come up with a plan to get himself out.

"I still think we need a contingency plan," I push. "What if something goes wrong and Perry can't get out? We can't just leave him."

"We won't." Onyx is firm about that. "My friends and I will start hell in the bar the second we see Arlie leave."

I mean, that's … something.

Perry is so determined to do this, though, that there isn't really anything else I can do. It just feels as though my heart is being shredded, and I hate, hate, hate uncertainty. It isn't something I knew about myself before now because I've never really been tested. Uncertain times in my life were whether Saint Clare's would go well—and I had a full, controlled plan to ensure it would—and beyond that, it was college and following my parents' rules and … well, apparently, I've been far too sheltered to be thrown into whatever the fuck we're currently in.

They go back to discussing logistics, which I'm not really a part of, and when Perry glances up and catches my eye, his expression goes from hopeful to concerned. He leaves the others, and I step out into the small hallway. He follows me, bringing the smell of bath wash and the sight of his sweet eyes with him.

"What's that look?" he asks.

"Not sure what you mean? It's definitely not blind terror or existential dread."

He cracks a smile at that. "It'll be fine."

"As fine as the last time you saw Luther?"

"Exactly."

It's always impossible to know whether Perry is joking or not, but in this instance, I'm certain he isn't. "What part of being threatened to give up my brother or die was successful to you?"

"The part where I didn't die."

For him, maybe it is that simple. "You really think you'll be lucky a second time?"

"I'm counting on it."

"You put way too much faith in the universe."

"My horoscope confirmed it though. Ask Lars."

"Well, if your horoscope says it, it must be true …"

"Between that and my bracelet, I've got this." His eyes soften, and he steps forward, pulling me into his arms. God, it feels good to be here. So good that I refuse to remind myself of how limited our time like this might be. "You're sexy when you worry about me," Perry says.

"I'm even sexier when my nerves aren't on edge."

His lips brush the side of my neck. "I'm sure I'll find that out one day."

"Soon, hopefully."

"That's why I'm doing this, you know." The brown of his eyes is so earnest and warm I want to wrap myself in it. Those gorgeous eyelashes fan out, and it's so hard to think of Perry as anything but this innocent, precious man who triggers my urge to protect him.

I cup his chin, and we stand there, looking at each other, my heart trying to beat its way to him.

He clears his throat and says in a voice two notches deeper than usual, "Your shoulder is the perfect spot for my face."

"My shoulder?"

He nods. "And when I get worried about pulling this next part off, I just need to look at you because I know you'll be looking at me, and when you do … it's like you think I can do anything. No one's ever looked at me like that before."

"You can." I hate admitting that. I hate going against my worry and encouraging this, but it's true. If anyone can pull this off, it's him. It's the *if* part that worries me though, and what if *no one* can pull this off? There's no way I can lose him, and all I know is that there are so many things I want to say to him that I'll always regret if I never get the chance.

So I break down those thoughts.

Ignore the way it makes me feel sick to be vulnerable.

And I channel Perry and the way he can do anything.

"I want us to be more," I say. "Once this is over, I want us to be dating. Properly. No games. We've had enough of that. I don't think I've ever had someone I want in my life the way I want you, and I think we can do it. After all this, I really think we can get through anything."

My heartbeat is so insistent it's making me feel sick, but with every word I get out, Perry's smile grows.

"Why wait?" he asks. Then he leans in, lips pressing to mine, and he kisses me in a way that gives me hope. That makes me really believe we can get through this. "You're already mine, pookie," he mutters against my mouth.

I sigh at the worst pet name I've ever heard, but he gets this one. That can be a hill I die on at a later date. "Promise you'll come back."

"I don't need to promise. I just will."

I try to channel his confidence. "You will."

"And then we'll tell everyone that we're boyfriends, and you'll introduce me to your parents, and I can take you on a date and—"

I kiss him again, more terrified than ever.

Perry is the sweetest man I've ever met, and there's no way that's going to waste. Not when I've only just found him.

I trust his process.

No plans.

Just vibes.

He can do this.

CHAPTER FORTY-SEVEN

PERRY

I'M STARTING to suspect there's a very high probability that I cannot do this.

The fake handcuffs I'm wearing fakely feel a hell of a lot like real ones. I know they're not. I've practiced with them, but after the Tommy betrayal, I'm not sure I trust Arlie's word anymore. It's lucky I met St. Clare because there's no way I could marry her under these circumstances.

"You good?" Arlie asks, hauling me out of Tommy's car.

It's not like I can answer her around my gag, so I make a noise that hopefully translates as "yeah, great, just hoping you don't double-cross me, but so long as you don't, I'm fine." Whatever she gets from the sounds that I'm making must satisfy her because she takes hold of my upper arm and marches us into Lethal Poison.

I flinch instinctively the second we hear those tiny bells announcing us, expecting any one of the people here to shoot me in the head. It doesn't happen, which feels like a win, but I'm tense the whole time we cross the bar area until we reach the hallway to Luther's office.

Then I'm even tenser.

Lethal Poison smells like it always smells, looks like it always looks, sounds, and feels like the warmth I always expect it to. Bad things don't happen to the sound of "Miles on It," even though I absolutely know that bad things start their happening here every day.

Arlie gives my arm another firm squeeze, and I'm torn between whether it's supposed to be supportive or a warning. Either way, I'm both supported and warned as we head up the hall and reach Luther's office. The heavy door is closed, and if he meant to intimidate me more, he's succeeded.

Arlie casts a quick glance over me before she knocks.

I know how this is going to go down; we've been over it a million times in the last twenty-four hours, and everything up until my actual part in it is planned perfectly. It's what they do. There's nothing for me to worry about unless Luther suddenly decides that I'll look better dead, which I wouldn't completely put past him. I just have to hope that he's still as fond of me as he's always been.

"Come in!"

Suddenly not feeling the fondness. My gut clenches as Arlie inches open the door and pulls me through after her.

Luther is the only one here, gun on his desk, relaxed back in his chair as he watches us enter and take the seats across from him. There's something curious in his stare as his eyes roam from Arlie to me and back again.

We wait him out. Arlie, because she has the patience of a saint, and me, because she had the good sense to gag me and make sure I can't give anything away.

"Where's Colin?" he finally asks after the silence has gone stale between us.

"Contained."

"Yeah, I'm gonna need more proof than that."

Like it's some huge imposition and not at all planned, Arlie logs into the security footage they set up and turns it so Luther can see. Even without a view of the screen, I know what it shows. Colin, bound and gagged like me, sitting in a chair in the middle of the warehouse we just left, with Ever standing over him, gun in his hand.

Arlie manages a smirk, which isn't something she does lightly. "Ever isn't happy that he doesn't get to play with him."

Luther goes on studying the screen. "After all the headaches this man has caused me, I want him dead already. No more fucking around."

"Cool. Give me the address, and I'll make the call."

Luther freezes for a second before leaning back in his chair. "The deal was that you'd exchange them both."

"Yeah, but I'm smarter than that. I brought this one"—she nods my way—"in good faith. Once I have the address, you can either choose for Everett to bring the job here or get rid of him immediately."

Luther looks me over. "You're okay with turning your friend over like this?"

Arlie shrugs, and if I doubted she was the right person for the job before, I don't now. She's perfected the complete level of disconnect needed to sell her answer. "Perry's not my friend. He's a mildly annoying cling-on that refuses to leave us alone at our table no matter how many times I ask him to."

Luther huffs a laugh, and I remind myself that we planned for her to say that, and it's not at all true. "He's not that bad," Luther defends, and I can't stop myself making an *ank oo* through the material stuffed in my mouth.

Arlie throws me a shut-the-fuck-up look, and I don't know if it's real or if she's still in character. "He botched a relatively simple job. He's exactly that bad."

"Okay, then." Luther reaches into his desk and pulls out a business card. "This is all I have to go on. Carson Alexander is a middle-aged white man."

"They're my favorite," Arlie says, taking the card. She glances over it. "You know I won't be happy if this isn't legit."

"It's legit. But if anyone asks, you didn't get it from me."

"No one is going to ask."

"Good." Luther points at her phone. "Make the call. I want this over with. Now."

Arlie closes the footage, brings up Everett's number, and then hits Call.

"Put him on speaker," Luther demands. "And put the footage back on."

A spike of worry hits me because that wasn't part of the plan, but Arlie doesn't react. She hits speaker, then flicks back over to the footage.

With the way she's holding her phone, I have a perfect view of the screen, where Everett takes a step away from Colin to pick up his phone.

"Yeah?" he barks.

"It's me. You're on speaker," Arlie says.

"Don't care. Is it done?"

"It's done. Take him out."

There's barely a heartbeat of time between the final word passing her lips and—

Bang.

I jump as the gunshot echoes from the speaker, and Colin's head …

I bow forward over my knees, gagging. The thick stretch of material over my tongue doesn't do much to stop it, and my throat triggers again and again at what I saw. Even reminding myself it was fake and this is all part of our plan doesn't help at all because … *was it?*

That looked way too fucking real.

My forehead is prickling with sweat by the time I finally get myself back under control. I try to tell them I didn't need to see that, but it comes out as a stream of mangled vowels.

Arlie tucks her phone back away. "What are you going to do with him?"

"Undecided."

"Cool." She's still gripping the business card tight. "You two have fun, then."

She makes it all the way to the door before Luther speaks again.

"Wait."

Arlie's hand tightens on the door handle, but when she glances back over her shoulder, there's no surprise in her expression. Mine though? Lots of surprise. It's supposed to be the part where she walks out, and now she's not walking out.

See? This is why I don't like planning things.

"Yeah?" she asks.

Luther gestures at me. "You shoot him."

My shock all but flies off my face.

"What?"

I echo her. "*Air ut?*"

"I'll match what was paid for Colin St. Clare. I'm over this whole ordeal. End it."

She holds up the business card between two fingers. "I've actually got plans."

"I promise it'll only take a second." There's a warning in those simple words. "I won't even make you clean up your mess."

Arlie's hesitation lasts too long, but what the hell else is she supposed to do? Shoot me? Not an option I'm comfortable with.

"Unless you're more friendly with Perry than you made out?"

Arlie rolls her eyes, pulls out the gun, and stalks toward me instead.

It happens so fast I don't have time to think beyond *fuck, she's throwing a Tommy.* Whether Arlie actually would do it or not is way too uncertain grounds for me to rely on, so instead of waiting to see what she has in mind, I let my instincts take over.

With Luther's attention on Arlie, he doesn't see me coming. I push from my chair, set my heavy boot on the edge of Luther's table, and flip that fucker onto him. It hits Luther somewhere in the midsection before his chair flips, and he goes down under it.

There's a huge crash as everything slides off onto him, and before Arlie can react, I snap the fake cuffs and tackle her into the ground.

"Perry, what are you—"

With one hand, I yank down the gag and hiss into her ear, "Pretend to be knocked out."

Her eyes immediately close.

I'd bet anything Luther has security cameras in here, and it's still better for us that he doesn't know we're in cahoots and are secretly the ones after Carson. Without a second thought, I fish the business card from her pocket and climb to my feet.

There's a grunt and heavy shifting, but before I can leave, the office door flies open.

The man who'd tried to intimidate me last time barrels through the door, gun out, ready to take me down. I yelp at the sight of him, but my brain is still offline, and before he can turn in my direction, I bulldoze him.

He's strong. Way too strong. I think I only get him down because I caught him by surprise, but as we wrestle and shove and scratch—well, *I* scratch—he's quickly getting the upper hand. The problem is I've never been in a tussle like this in my life, and now that we're tussling, it's not as easy as the movies would have you believe. I can barely see. Barely have time to process I've been punched before the next one flies at my face.

None of it hurts, so my adrenaline must be running deliciously high. I stop shielding my face, and before the guy on me knows what's happening, I grab a fistful of hair and pull like I've never pulled in my life. Strands snap loose, and the more I pull and he pulls back, I *feel* the way it's trying to tear from his fucking head.

Bile rises up at the feeling, but I don't let go, not even when he aims a bruiser right at my cheekbone. I gag some more, but finally, his head jolts back in my hold, and I get enough space between us that I can bring my knee up hard and fast between his legs.

"*Fuck!*" he roars. The split-second distraction is enough to throw him off me and scramble back to my feet.

I don't stop, don't look around, don't know where Luther or Arlie are or what they're doing, but as I yank the door open, hands latch around my wrist.

Luther's thrown himself across the room to get to me, and he snarls up through bloody teeth. "Where the fuck do you think you're going?"

I try to shake him off, but his grip gets painfully tight. I've already had to fight more than I have in my life, and as my ragged breathing gets my head all spinny, I'm acutely aware that this is my last chance to get free, and I gotta use it.

I twist and shake and yank in his hold, sure I'm destroying my shoulder more even though I can't feel it … and then I remember my gun.

Motherfucker.

My hand closes over Judy, tucked in my waistband, and I bring her out and into contact with his forehead.

"Let me go!"

Luther laughs, eyes unnervingly locked on my face. "You've never shot anyone."

You know what? I'm getting sick of being known for that.

With a flicker of *something*, I lose my goddamn cool.

Judy redirects to Luther's arm, and I pull the fucking trigger. The gun is still shockingly loud, and I can't stop my flinch as the bullet sinks into his arm and splatters me with blood.

Luther's smothered scream sounds like it's dying in his chest. His nails cut into my arm as he folds over in pain, and it takes herculean strength to yank myself from his grip.

I had to do it. I had to do it.

My brain is stuck on that as I back up, almost tripping over my feet, seeing the way his skin tore open again and again.

I won't throw up. Won't do it.

My back slams into the wall in the hallway, and it's the momentum from the sudden collision that redirects me and gets my feet moving.

I fly down the hallway, lungs burning, and stagger into the bar area. Unfortunately, my very obvious *I'm fucked* demeanor, along with the cuffs dangling from my wrist, catch attention—probably the sound of my gunshot didn't help things—and Danvers jumps up from the nearest table.

"Going somewhere, Perry?"

"Ah …" My eyes dart around. "I'm trying to."

"Well, why don't you—" Danvers doesn't finish what he was going to say before he's shoved from behind. One of Onyx's friends—I want to say Viktor—lands on top of him and sends a barrage of punches down on Danvers's head.

It's like a spark in a gun barrel.

Viktor's friends immediately jump into the fray, and familiar faces from Lethal Poison join them. There are chairs thrown, glass smashed, tables upended, and I watch for too much longer than someone who *should* be running should watch.

It's not until there's noise from behind me that I jump forward and run.

Dodging fists, shaking off hands that cling to my ankles, trying not to slip over debris, I'm wheezing and sweating and worried about chafing all over again as the bar I love so very, very much descends into chaos around me.

A guy I swear I've done shots with before throws himself at me, and I flinch back in time for him to sail past and hit the ground. Fuck me. Do these guys see a fight and immediately lose their minds?

My hands close over the nearest bar table, and I fling it backward, then break into a sprint.

The door is close.

Closer.

Closer still.

I get my hand on the handle and tug, setting off the golden bells and a screeching "*Perry!*" behind me.

Then I'm out, running so hard down the street I swear I'm about to go ass over.

St. Clare is in the waiting car, and as soon as I throw myself into the back seat, he banks it into traffic.

Away from Lethal Poison.

And hopefully toward somewhere I can catch my breath.

CHAPTER FORTY-EIGHT

ST. CLARE

THE SOUNDS PERRY is making have me on high alert. He's lying squashed across the back seat, wheezing through half a groan and half a weird, dramatic war cry as he sucks in his breaths over and over. My eyes keep pinging between the rearview mirror and the road as I get us away from Lethal Poison as fast as I can.

Then I glimpse something that makes my pulse rate spike.

"Holy fuck, is that *blood*? Are you hurt?"

"Not mine." Perry flings both arms over his face and moans. "Aww … I just shot a guy."

"You what?"

"Didn't kill him. But it might have. Luther could be bleeding out on the floor right now for all I know. He isn't going to be happy with me."

I study his reflection, making sure he's not lying, and only once I'm convinced that I don't see any injuries do I calm down again.

I think someone broke my boyfriend.

"Where's Arlie?"

"Don't … know." He inhales noisily before huffing it all out again. "Left her so Luther wouldn't know we're together. She's smart though. She'll get away. Luther was chasing me, so he … didn't give a fuck about her."

I'll have to take his word for it. "Did you get the address?"

He holds a business card up above him. "Swiped it from Arlie."

"How wonderful." I hit the Call button on the steering wheel and find Lars's number. He answers on the second ring.

"How did it go?"

"Perry's with me." The relief coursing through me at that is making it hard to drive. "Arlie isn't."

"Shit. Is she okay?"

"Perry seems to think so, but we don't know yet." Even after what happened with Tommy, I do hope she got out of there. It's hard to trust them, but I get the feeling that whatever they're planning is currently aligned with what we're trying to accomplish.

Perry hits the back of my seat. "Ask him … ask him if Colin's … if he's alive."

I send an alarmed look back at him. "Is Colin okay?" I bark so loud I sound like an old person who's discovered speakerphone.

"Yeah," Lars says. "He's right here."

Perry's strangled cry comes from the back seat. "I saw his head shot off," he gasps dramatically. "I saw chunks fly everywhere."

Yeah, glad I missed that.

"Could have done without that description," Lars says.

Then Tommy's voice follows. "It *was* some of my best work."

And thank goodness for that. If Luther suspected it was faked, there's no way Perry would be with me now.

"What's the address?" Tommy asks.

Perry blindly nudges the card at my neck, and I swipe it from him, then read it out as I navigate traffic. My *boyfriend*—still so weird to think that—is still wheezing and moaning and being a complete nuisance.

Lars says something, and I completely miss it.

"Perry, my sweet, incredible man. I love that you're alive, but I'm struggling to hear the others when you sound like you're in labor."

"Tell them I'm going to need some painkillers. I think the adrenaline's wearing off, and now I'm not so sure I'm not dying."

I jerk the steering wheel too suddenly as I look back at him and only barely manage to keep us in the lane. "You're *dying*?"

"Shit. No." He forces himself to sit up, and his face is half obscured in bruising and swelling. "Still fine. Just *feels* like it. I'm hurting. All over. Maybe later, you can kiss it better for me."

"Still on the phone, Perry," Lars points out as Tommy laughs in the background.

"Scare me like that again and I'll kill you myself," I grumble.

He rests his head against the side of my headrest, opposite hand reaching around to run his fingers over my neck. Like that, he's instantly forgiven.

If that's how our relationship is always going to go, I think I better come to terms with losing every argument now.

"Found you," Tommy sings.

"Who?"

"The address. I … huh. It's a super-basic warehouse. Near the docks."

"How do we know it's the right place?" Perry asks.

"I … Give me a second."

There's the frantic tapping of keys and then more … and more …

Tommy hums. "Yeah, this doesn't make sense."

"Why?"

"Because I've got footage of the place and over the last week, I'm not seeing anyone who I'd think is Carson Alexander."

"I thought you didn't know what he looks like," Perry says.

"I don't, but I recognize most of the people here, and the few I don't, I'm running image searches on. Obviously, it could be an alias for one of them, but … how do we know who?"

"Wait. Colin." His name hits me. "He's seen Carson before. Colin can point him out."

"I'll get him," Lars says.

He must leave because the tapping goes on for a couple of minutes before he's back.

"Tommy's got some footage," he explains. "It would be a huge help if you could look and point him out. Only if you're up to it."

"I am." Colin doesn't even hesitate. "Show me."

Tommy clicks on something. "Okay, I know all these guys, so I'll just skip to—"

"Him."

There's dead silence from the other end, and I take a right, keeping an eye out behind us to make sure we're not being followed.

"Him?" Tommy repeats. "Nah, there's no way."

"That's him. That one. I know it is."

"How …" Tommy clears his throat. "How sure are you?"

"One hundred percent. He's the one who signed the contracts with me. Introduced himself when we met."

My frown feels heavy, and I almost don't want to ask. Luckily, Perry gets there first.

"Who is it?"

Tommy lets out this disbelieving little *heh*. "It's … fuck me. It's Luther."

CHAPTER FORTY-NINE

PERRY

MY PAL, my buddy, my old friend *Luther*. He's the man out here threatening everyone and footing bills for things he shouldn't foot bills for.

Now I'm really thinking about it, it makes sense. Owning a labradoodle was obviously his cover.

I just did *not* see that coming. Fuck me.

Thankfully, Tommy and Everett are as shocked as I am, so I don't feel like as much of a moron as I could. But then I remember that I had the chance to shoot him in the face and didn't.

This could be over already.

We could have nothing else to worry about.

I mentally sob again over how close I got to putting this shit behind us without realizing it, and I fucking didn't. So, *so* close.

The comms crackles in my ear.

"Still nothing," Lars says. He's set up on a rooftop across from Lethal Poison. Without Arlie, he's our best shot who will actually shoot, and between him, Everett, and me, we're keeping an eye on the place. If I'd known Luther was this dangerous, there's no way I wouldn't have gotten Arlie out too, but I really, really thought she could handle herself.

I turn the music up that I'm listening to in my other ear. Thankfully, no one saw me slip the earbud in, or I'm sure there would have been words about professionalism or whatever, but it comes right down to this:

I'm not a professional.

I've made a lot of mistakes.

And today, I'm cleaning up the biggest one of my life.

Then I'm putting it all behind me and starting my life with St. Clare. I'll probably *still* make mistakes, but none of them will be like this, and I have to trust that he'll handle anything I throw at him.

I'm nodding along to the indie pop, watching the front of Lethal Poison, filled with this sense of wistfulness and longing. Other than my actual home that never felt particularly homey, this place was always mine. My safety. My refuge.

All along, Luther had us do his bidding. Did he even have "clients," or was it all bullshit?

Maybe I can ask him all these questions before he's left alone with Everett for a while.

My nose wrinkles at that.

I don't think it matters how bad Luther is or how many deaths he's responsible for. I'm struggling. Vigilante justice is one thing, but Everett being excited over dismantling him is … unsettling. Does he deserve that? Probably, but I can't bring myself to give it a definite yes.

People aren't cars. We can't be taken apart and put back together. As soon as we're apart, we're dead, and there's no coming back from that.

And I thought I could be a hitman.

"For the love of Judge Judy, Perry Nikov. You *are* a dumbass."

"Ah … what?" Lars's voice in my ear asks.

Shit. I forgot about the whole comms thing. "Nothing. I'm good."

He chuckles, and it's the warm kind of laugh I've heard him give St. Clare. "Don't forget that luck is on your side today, Aries. You don't need intelligence."

"Well, thank fuck for that because I'm usually in short supply."

That same laugh comes again, and it makes my chest all puffy. I'm slowly breaking him down.

"Anything on your end, Tommy?" Everett asks through the earpiece.

"Still quiet."

"And we're sure he's in there?" I check for the twentieth time.

"Yes. I watched people leave after the mass brawl you set in motion to see if Arlie got out. No sight of her or Luther, just two guys entering and the bar being locked up tight."

Yep. Not feeling any better about leaving Arlie.

I don't know what exactly they're waiting for, and I'm starting to get itchy feet. It's okay for the others. Tommy and St. Clare are holed up watching surveillance, and Lars and Ever are on rooftops, whereas I'm *right* here. Lethal Poison is *right* there.

And Arlie has who the fuck knows what going on, and our so-called plans might be the very thing that has her wind up dead.

I'd also selfishly prefer for the last time I saw her to *not* be as I was tackling her to the ground and telling her to play dead. Besides, she has plenty more scathing remarks to send my way. Lethal Poison doesn't exist without Arlie and her endearing forced disdain for me.

The longer I'm expected to wait, the harder it is to stay still. They're so close and Arlie's in trouble and Luther's injured, and I have no clue who the hell these other guys are, but I like my chances. I'm nervous as fuck, but I still like my chances.

I grab my wrist, the usual need for comfort taking over as I seek out my bracelet. The beads are as familiar as breathing by this point, and having that smooth plastic under my fingertips always helps settle me.

Or at least it would.

If it was there.

I glance down, pulse spiking as I check under my sleeve and stupidly even check the other arm despite the fact it has never left the wrist I put it on. I stumble backward, searching the ground, convinced I dropped the very tight bracelet somewhere close, easy to see. Because it has to be here. It has to.

The more I search—out of blind desperation at this point—the more sickly my heart pounds. It was from Mom. All I had left. It has to be here. Losing my bracelet would be like losing her all over again.

Where.

The fuck.

Is it?

I'm flying off into panic mode as I pat down my front and my ass and scramble around in my pockets. There's nothing. It's not here.

Maybe I left it in the car or the warehouse or—

I glimpse the deep scratch marks on my wrist where my bracelet should be. Remember Luther's tight hold before I yanked myself out of his bruising grip.

Luther did this. My stomach turns over itself so violently, I stagger into the wall.

The ringing in my ears drowns out whatever the fuck is coming through the comms as my entire world funnels into this pressurized moment of existence. My bare wrist. The one tether I had to being loved and wanted in this world. The only lasting reminder of my mom.

Gone.

And he took it from me.

My rage explodes.

Hot and fire and the ringing in my ears keeps ringing.

There's a high chance I'm about to die.

But Luther is going to die first.

I break into a run.

I'm thirsting for the type of revenge that will have my chest burst open. I want to take everything Luther has ever loved and extinguish it all at once. He knows what it's like, he's done that before, and this time, just this time, he's done it to the wrong fucking person.

My name being shouted in my ear is trying to take over the constant roar of fire, and instead of letting it, I reach up and fling the comms away. It's lucky I can't think or speak or reason with myself because I save my energy for when I reach the door to Lethal Poison, and then I kick that fucker open.

It bangs into the wall, testing the hinges, rattling the windows, and then flings back in my direction again. I'm ready for it. My foot almost goes right through the wood as I send it back where it came from.

The bar is in complete disarray, and I have to shove tables and chairs out of my way as I tear across the space. I'm not being quiet or sneaky. Not stopping to worry or plan. All I know is that the second I get to Luther, this whole fucking thing is over.

"Luther!" I roar, sending a chair into the wall. "Get the fuck out here!"

He doesn't get the fuck out here, and that only makes me madder.

How dare he? How dare he cower away in his office, hiding behind bodies and aliases and his friendly barman persona.

How dare he make me like him and then treat me as disposable as everyone else has.

And how very fucking dare he take away that one symbol of strength I had left.

I make it to the hall, but before I can start down there, his office door cracks open, and a shot is sent my way. I throw myself into the wall, but it's wide anyway, not that it makes a difference. I feel super-fucking-nova, and a bullet could go right through me, and I doubt I'd feel it.

I send a shot back, then—fuck it.

I throw myself into the hallway and run as fast as I can.

Another shot.

This time close enough I think for a second it hit me, but the pain doesn't come.

The only sounds to break up my heavy breathing are the thump of my sneakers and my heartbeat drumming in my ears.

The hand with the gun reappears, and before they can get a shot away, I take aim and give Judy a loving squeeze.

A scream—not mine—quickly follows my shot, and the gun

drops to the floor. I snatch it up, kick the door open, then send a hard kick to Danvers's face for good measure.

"You motherfucker!" Danvers screams, holding his hand, but my attention has already left him, and I throw both guns up Luther's way. His arm is bandaged; there's a man with a med kit cowering at his side and Arlie—the most beautiful sight I've ever seen—unharmed and free, standing at Luther's side.

"You're okay!" I yelp.

Arlie and Luther exchange a look. "Why wouldn't I be?"

"Because you ... he ..." I use the guns to gesture toward Luther. "He's the bad guy. He's Carson Alexander."

Arlie lifts her gun.

And points it at *me*. "I really wish you didn't say that, Perry."

My jaw drops. "W-what? Are you ... working with him?"

"Did you really think he'd give me his business card if I wasn't? You were never supposed to see it."

My heart is hammering even madder than it was before. None of this is adding up in a way that I like.

"Who else knows?" Luther asks.

Well, that question sounds like a fast way to throw the others under the bus. "No one. Just me. I worked it out, and I came straight here." I tighten my grip on the gun, trying not to let my hand tremble.

"You're lying." Luther tilts his head toward Arlie. "Don't you think?"

"One hundred percent." Arlie steps closer. "We both know you won't shoot either of us, so why don't you put that gun down before you hurt yourself?"

I'm tempted to aim for her instead, but I hold steady, equal parts not wanting to startle her and give her a reason to shoot me and wanting to keep my aim on Luther in case she *does* shoot me and I can take him down with me.

"Why don't we all put our weapons down," I suggest, taking a step back. "Talk it out like grown-ups. I'm sure we can make some kind of deal."

"Or you can tell us who else knows my identity, and there's a slight chance we won't kill you." Luther sounds totally reasonable, except for the fact we both know he'll definitely kill me.

Stress sweat slips down between my shoulder blades and rolls along my spine. My body has reached fight or flight, and I want to say fight is winning out, but it's a mission to keep every roaring cell in place.

I swallow thickly and force a smile. "Or you could stop targeting me and all my friends, and no one has to die."

"Not possible. Your *friend* got involved in my business. He asked for this."

"Yikes, victim blaming in this day and age."

Luther huffs and waves Arlie forward. "Either give us the names, or we'll assume it's all of them. Colin St. Clare's gone, but who's to say he didn't tell his brother? Their little play soldier. Tommy—"

Arlie glances back at Luther. "I told you: Tommy and Everett are with us."

"Then where are they?"

"Keeping everyone in check."

A corner of Luther's lips curls wickedly. "I'll believe it when I see it."

He stands suddenly and stalks closer, pausing halfway between me and Arlie. "Give me the names!"

I'm about to tell him he can go and quite literally fuck himself when there's a loud bang from the bar. The three of us jump, but while they're on high alert, I have nothing to lose at this point.

I let off a shot that—shockingly—totally misses, so, in quite possibly the dumbest move I've ever made, I throw myself at armed people.

I launch at Luther, and the both of us tackle Arlie to the ground.

Danvers is still cursing up a storm, Arlie is trying to shove Luther off her, but I scramble higher on top of them both and throw my weight into them. I have no idea where her gun has gone or where mine landed, but I grab Luther's bandaged arm and squeeze the ever-loving shit out of it.

He howls, the sort of sound I'm sure I'll hear when I'm falling asleep at night, but I only grab harder and use his distraction to ram my elbow into his throat.

Arlie's stopped fighting us, and I wonder if we've smothered her, but I'm all out of fucks to give at this point. My pulse rate is going so fast I've got tunnel vision, and all I know, all I can focus on is Luther.

Carson Alexander.

And ending this for good.

By any means possible.

"Perry!"

At first, my name means nothing, but then the trickling awareness of familiarity seeps in over the sound of Luther's choking.

I swing toward the voice, and my heart drops.

St. Clare. Panting hard, hair in disarray, cheeks so red they looked slapped.

"Get out!" I scream at him, but the idiot runs toward me instead.

My distraction costs me.

Luther throws me off, and as I go flying, two things hit me at once.

First, Arlie has her gun, and it's pointed at me.

Second, Danvers has mine and …

It's pointed at St. Clare.

My whole world fucking stops.

The only thought in my mind is *not him!* as I jump up and shove St. Clare out of the line of fire. He flings backward as a gunshot goes off, so loud I think it might have deafened me, and so suddenly it makes my whole body seize up. Two more quickly follow, but those sound far away. Muffled.

My heartbeat is in my ears.

I'm breathing so hard it feels useless. Like all the air is going to my head and not my lungs.

"Fuck! Perry!"

St. Clare's voice is coming from somewhere, but through the

fog, something else is registering. Something burning hot and immediate.

I glance down, blinking hard, as my feet threaten to go out from under me, and the more I blink, the more I can't figure out what I'm seeing.

Since when is the T-shirt Lars bought me red?

Someone grabs me, and my legs buckle. Confusion clouds any rational thought that I had as I fling my gaze around wildly, trying to find Luther, Danvers, Arlie … Are we even safe here? Are we about to be killed?

Danvers's face swims into view, blank, staring eyes, blood pooling from his neck, and when I twist to where Luther last was, I'm not sure if I'm imagining the hole in his head or not.

St. Clare is saying something, and those shots must have been *really* loud because I can't make out the words. Just the tears rolling over his face.

I flinch as Arlie joins him and try to get away.

"B-bad."

Shit. I'm burning up and freezing at the same time. Where's the climate control in here?

"S-s-stop," I say, trying to wipe at St. Clare's tears. He's slowly coming into focus, but I can't reach him. Did the gunshot fuck my aim up to? "A-am I shaking? D-do I l-look sh-shaky to you?"

"Why didn't you stick to the plan?"

He screams it so loud I pick up on it this time.

"M-my bracel-let," I try to explain. Try and fail by the way he's panicking. Pressure comes from somewhere and almost makes me want to scream, but the sudden pain gets swept up in all the jumble and blurry and swampiness.

I just want to make him smile again. Want him to stop worrying and remember all of that forever we still have to look forward to.

"R-Reilly?" The word hurts, but I only need a few more. To tell him how I feel, to have someone I belong with.

I don't remember much after that.

CHAPTER FIFTY

ST. CLARE

MY LEGS ARE BOUNCING out a rhythm as I sit in the hospital chair, waiting for any kind of news and wanting to be literally anywhere else. Lars's hand closes over my knee again, and he murmurs, "He'll be okay," for only the millionth time since we got here.

Margot was allowed to go through when she tore in here in an oversized jacket, polka dot pants, and odd shoes, and after that flurry of activity, it's been dead out here.

I internally cringe at my choice of words.

It's been *still*. Silent. The waiting is digging into my nervous system and sending it haywire.

I don't know what Everett and Arlie told the ambulance about the shooting, and they took way too long to even call one for my liking, so if he's not okay … if he … if he …

The automatic door beside the waiting area swings open, and Margot bursts out of it. "Blood loss, lots of pain meds, but should be okay."

Every last scrap of oxygen and tension whistles out of me. I hunch over my knees, feeling even more sick than I was a second ago, while Lars rubs my back.

"So he's fine."

"They'll know more once he's conscious, but no vital organs

were hit." And like she's been holding herself up by sheer will, she drops suddenly into a crouch, arms wrapped tight around her knees. "He got so fucking lucky."

I'm nodding because I don't have the words. Relief isn't strong enough for what I'm feeling now.

Elle leaves her seat and sits beside Margot, pulling her into her arms. "We've always known Perry was something special, love. This just proves it."

"I'd like him to never, ever prove it again," she says, and then she bursts into tears. Huge, body-shaking sobs, the kind that has my own eyes prickling. I echo that same sentiment all the way down to my bones, and I'm somehow going to look after him completely during his recovery while making sure he knows how absolutely furious I am that I need to look after him in the first place.

We're a fucking team, and putting himself in danger like that isn't something he's going to do ever, ever again. Even with Margot assuring us that he's going to be okay, I'm not sure I believe her. I've been in this frozen state of horror for hours now, and while it's thawing, the process is slow, and I'm still waiting for everything to go drastically wrong again.

"When can Reilly see him?" Lars asks on my behalf, and thankfully, he does because it didn't even occur to me that it would be a possibility.

Margot scrubs at her puffy eyes. "He's sedated, but you can go through."

Thank fucking god. I forget to even thank her as I head for the automatic doors and barely stop myself from running down the hall to his room. Everything is so white and busy back here, but as soon as I see his room number, I screech to a halt.

My knees lock up, and I almost go flying right past, but nothing is going to stop me from seeing him. I inch inside, nudging the hospital-grade blue curtain out of the way, and the second he comes into view, I want to cry too.

He's hooked up to machines, hair a matted mess, and his skin that isn't bruised and swollen is far paler than it usually is. My heart squeezes at the sight.

I've always felt that Perry was mine to protect, and the feeling has heightened every day that I've known him. Seeing him like this? I feel helpless. Like my one purpose has been snatched away from me, and I'm scrambling to work out what to do next.

I take the chair beside his bed and reach out for his hand. It's not the usual, enthusiastic warmth I'm used to, but I kiss it anyway, watching his face, hoping for any sign that he knows I'm here too.

There's nothing.

No twitch.

No flicker of a smile.

No eyelid flutter.

Just sleep.

Which is good. Sleep is good. He's going to need a lot of it.

My hold on his hand tightens. Perry's the sole reason to keep my heart beating. The one who makes me want to be better than I've ever been before.

I hate seeing him like this.

***

Leaving Perry at the hospital is almost impossible, but while he's sedated, there's nothing I can do for him. Right now, I need to make sure everything is okay with my brother and that we don't need to worry anymore.

He texts me to meet him at Lethal Poison, and I'm apprehensive about stepping foot into the place where I thought my boyfriend was dying, but if this is what it takes to find answers, I'll do it. All I want is for everything to go back to normal again.

I miss Saint Clare's so much.

I miss the chaos and the fun, and I miss the way I got to enjoy myself there and not have to constantly look over my shoulder. Hell, maybe Perry will even come and work for us since I'm assuming his cafe job won't be waiting.

I make my way over the demolition site and toward the back, where I can make out voices. I'm trying not to focus on how Perry felt here, on which emotions were running wild through him, and just remind myself that he's going to be okay.

He will be.

"Hey," Colin says as I walk into the office. He's sitting on the floor with Onyx, books open around them, while Arlie is typing away at a computer on the desk, and Tommy and Everett lounge in the corner. Ever's flipping through something while Tommy has his feet kicked up, whistling that same tune he whistled with his gun pointed at my head.

"That's very unsettling," I tell him, and he grins back but keeps whistling. I look away from him and take in the room instead. "I thought there'd be a whole lot more blood than this."

And by *more*, I mean any.

"Our team is efficient," Arlie says. "The police have already been by to see where Perry"—she makes bunny ears with her fingers—"shot himself."

I don't want to be reminded of that moment ever again. The whole run here, I'd been terrified I'd walk in and find him dead, and fighting Luther on the floor was only a step up from that.

I still can't believe he took a bullet for me. He probably would have taken a lot more than one if Arlie wasn't so fast and took out both Luther and the guy who shot Perry before they could react.

"What are you all doing?"

She pushes back from the desk and stands, stretching her arms out high. "Taking over. I've wanted Lethal Poison for the last year or two. Luther wasn't running it right, too focused on his side hustle, and I'd learned enough to know that he'd moved into illegal substances."

"Drugs?"

"He imports, passes on to a colleague, and then shares a cut. Or … he did." She gets this wicked smirk. "Lethal Poison wasn't part of the drug trade when I started here, or I wouldn't have taken this job. It killed both my parents and was a firm line for me, so when I told Luther I wanted out, he blackmailed me. Told me Carson Alexander was too invested in my hits."

"We should have guessed," Everett grumbles. "All those rumors we heard about him ... all started here."

"This way was for the best." Arlie leans against the desk. "If I'd known before, I wouldn't have been able to keep him convinced I was loyal. Now, we can tell everyone that Carson Alexander wanted him dead, and who are they to question it? It's not like Carson can come back from the dead and deny it."

"That's why you helped us?"

"If you're good at something, don't do it for free. This was our payoff. I didn't know it would go down exactly like this—I actually thought Perry would be the one to kill him, which would have made things just as easy."

My foot nudges the books Colin and Onyx are poring over. "What's all this?"

"Creditors," Colin answers. "It's a mirror of the accounts my PI found with Yanni, only Carson's side of things. I've been trying to get hold of Ryan Wing all day though, and he's not answering ..."

"Who?" Arlie asks, narrowing her eyes.

"He's the man I hired to look into Yanni. Really good at his job, but then he just stopped taking my calls."

Arlie grabs her phone and types something, then turns it to show a tattooed man with long hair. "Him?"

"Yeah, how did you—"

"He's dead."

Colin's mouth drops. "What? How?"

"I killed him. It was the first hit I took Perry on."

"How do you remember that?"

"Haven't you learned your lesson about other people's business yet?"

Onyx sets their hand over Colin's and shakes their head. "Let it go. For now, we have what we need."

It takes my brother a moment, and I can tell he's struggling with the unanswered question, and knowing that Ryan's fate could have just as easily been his if it wasn't for Onyx.

"What do we do with all this?" Colin asks, looking back at the paperwork. "It's not like we can go to the police with it now that Luther's been killed. They'll ask questions and want to know how we got our hands on the evidence."

"We don't need to go to the police," I say, still bitter over them not being the ones to find Colin. "We only need to go to Yanni. Carson's gone now. He can't hide behind him anymore."

"Then … everything goes back to normal?" he asks.

Back to normal. That's … impossible to think about.

"Guess so," I tell him, and it's like all the stress leaves my brother. "Do you want me to do it?"

He's fast to shake his head as he takes another photo of the page in front of him. "I will. Well, me and Onyx. We need to face him, and you need to stay out of this mess."

For once, I'm more than fucking happy to agree.

Then Arlie cuts in. "No. We'll do it. You two need to get back to your vanilla lives and goddamn stay there. There's nothing I enjoy more than dealing with drug dealers."

"What happens to this place?" I ask, gesturing at the room.

Arlie returns to the desk chair. "We wait for Luther to miss paying all his bills, then I swoop in with the money to take over. Most of the guys here aren't loyal to him, only their next paycheck, and that's something I can offer them."

"So you're going to continue. With your … job."

"Yes." She looks me down like she's daring me to disagree with her. "There are always bad people who need to die, and I sleep really fucking well knowing that I'm taking them off the streets. That was the whole point of this place when I started here, and I want to get it back to that."

Considering how good of a shot she is, it's not like I'm about to argue with her. Especially not with deconstructive Ever sitting so close.

"Best of luck to you," I say, because what else do you tell a contract killer who's planning to extend her operations?

"Thank you." She turns toward the computer and pauses

again. "I'm glad Perry will be okay. Tell him to come and see us when he's better, got it?"

"Ah … got it."

"Good. He's family now. We protect our own."

While I don't know how to feel about that creepily sweet sentiment, I know exactly how Perry will react.

With excitement. Like a dog who's been adopted and can't stop doing zoomies.

Which means that I'm stuck with them too.

Love that for me.

"Thank you."

With that organized, I turn to leave, wanting to get back to Perry so I can look after him when he wakes. Margot is going to fight me for custody of the injured monster, but I'm not going to let her win. Not this time. She's looked after him for their whole lives, so it's my turn now.

I get all the way to the door before something bright red catches my attention, half caught between the door and the wall.

Curious, I crouch down and dig it out, a little zing of surprise shooting through me.

It's a strawberry.

And I know exactly where I've seen it before.

CHAPTER FIFTY-ONE

PERRY

HOSPITALS ARE BORING.

I'm drugged up, hooked to machines, and accumulating debt faster than a rat on an exercise wheel.

It doesn't help that I'm still groggy and, well, not disorientated, but definitely not tethered to reality. Plus, I get yelled at every time I move, so that's fun.

I groan long and loud, wanting to at least be able to get off this bed to piss.

A passing nurse must hear me because she pops her head into the room, barely repressed smile fighting her before she says, "Is it actual pain this time or still self-pity?"

"Self-pity," I admit, trying not to pout. "If you help me up for a second, I won't tell anyone, I swear."

"What did I tell you last time?"

"Honestly, Janice, bleeding out on the floor feels like a risk I'm willing to take."

"You're fun, Perry. But as much as I like you, I like my job more."

She walks out again, and I'm left with my too-slow-moving thoughts and maybe more self-pity than I had before she stopped in.

No Margot, no St. Clare, no friends, and I keep reaching for a bracelet that doesn't goddamn exist anymore. This sucks.

I'm aware that I'm supposed to be focused on the whole being-alive thing, but my legs keep going numb, and weeding through sluggish thoughts is frustrating as hell.

There's a knock at the door, and I close my eyes, letting out a long groan again. "Quick, Janice, help me up. I'm dying."

No fake-sympathetic response. Instead, there's a pause, and then, "Is this going to be another situation where I signal for an emergency and waste everyone's time?"

My eyes crack open, and there's the familiar sympathetic and indulgent look St. Clare's been so good at giving me lately. "We're in a fight," I announce.

"Is that so?" He walks into the room and pulls up the chair by my bed. "That didn't take us long."

"You've been gone forever. I'm spiraling out of my brain."

"Considering you're talking at half speed and I was gone an hour, I think we'll get past this relationship hurdle."

I reach for him, but my hand isn't working properly. "Touch me. But angrily."

"Angrily?"

"We're not in a fight if we're not angry, and I can't get angry right now, so you're going to have to do it for me."

His hand wraps around mine, and then he kisses my knuckles. "I'll do my best."

"You're already failing."

"I'm strangely okay with that." His free hand reaches up to brush the hair from my forehead, and my eyes close automatically as I nudge him for more. His fingers in my hair are so damn relaxing, and if it was up to me, he'd never leave. Ever. He'd stay here and be as constantly bored as I am. "You're a lot more alert today."

I nod, blinking my eyes back open, and as he takes his hand from my hair, I pull the other closer, hugging it to my chest. "Yeah. Feel good. One hundred percent. I think they can discharge me now."

"Nice try."

"Was it?"

"Not even a little bit." Some of the sweetness he's radiating dims as he swipes his tongue over his lips, doubt slowly creeping in. "I, ah … I'm sorry about your bracelet."

My bitterness about it tries to take over. "Yeah. Guess I was probably getting too old for it or something. Luther did me a favor."

"Did he?"

"Some people would say so."

"Are you some people?"

Of course he calls my bluff, and of course I can't lie to him. "I should be."

His lips twitch, and then he reaches down into his pocket. When he lifts his hand where I can see it again, he's holding his fist out to me.

I frown as I glance from it to him and back again. "You want a fist bump?"

"No." He laughs. "This is … well, you're not Perry without a happy charm."

A happy charm?

The monitor beeping beside me gets louder as St. Clare turns over his hand and peels his fingers back. There, resting in his palm is … I shake my head, sure I must be hallucinating.

He's not smiling anymore. He pulls my arm toward him, and then, like he's slipping the final piece into a puzzle, he stretches the bracelet over my hand and settles it on my wrist.

"That's … that's …" Shit, am I even breathing?

"Yours," he finishes, thumb running over the small plastic beads. "I found all the pieces I could, and some of them are busted up a little, and the smiley face had to be glued back together, but there were two that were too broken to save." He swallows loudly. "Sorry. But it was small on you anyway, so I thought … I thought that maybe it was time to … to add some more happy charms to your life."

I lift my wrist, slowly turning the bracelet. The strawberry is scratched but mostly okay, and it's a similar story in varying shades for all the old beads. Then I get to the other side.

My thumb runs over the bull head, then the colorful neon swirl, the lime wedge, and finally, a little gun with a heart shooting out of it.

I go back to the first one, noting the design. "T-taurus?" I whisper, moving on to the neon. "And …"

"It reminded me of Elle's apartment."

He's right. "What about the lime?"

His eyes shine as he looks at it, but I can only look at him. "Arlie, Ever, and Tommy tell me that's your usual at Lethal Poison."

"You do know Arlie is working with Luther, right?"

St. Clare shakes his head. "It was all a ploy. After Danvers shot you, she didn't hesitate to take him and Luther out before dealing with your injury."

The speckled bits of memory I have from the event rearrange themselves and make a whole lot more sense that way. I glance back at the final charm. "And the gun?"

But I already know the answer. Even as he swallows hard and I watch the way his throat bobs with it. "That one's for me."

In the history of ever, I have no words.

"Margot put it together this time. If it's covered in snot and tears, blame her. She couldn't stop crying."

But my bottom lip is shaking, and my eyes are all misty, and I have no idea if it's covered in any of that because it doesn't matter. I'm about to get snot and tears all over everything myself. "I guess we have that in common," I manage, voice all squeaky as I try to suppress the building emotion in my chest.

St. Clare stands up, lips meeting mine in the sweetest, gentlest kiss he's ever given me. I'm not sure if I'm crying or laughing, but it doesn't matter because I can blame this moment on the painkillers later.

If I was given the chance to go back to the day I walked into

Lethal Poison looking for a job and do it differently, I wouldn't. I'd make the same shitty choices again and again and again.

Because everything in between was worth it.

Just to know St. Clare.

CHAPTER FIFTY-TWO

ST. CLARE

I NEEDED to get away from Perry.

He's been on strict "no sex" orders for *weeks* now, and that man is tempting me. Every time I touch him or he touches me, there's a deep fire between us that won't go out. I've jerked myself almost to blisters, not that it helps. I need *him*.

It also doesn't help that during his recovery, he's been clingy as hell. Normally I'd love the way he always has to be touching me, but when a light breeze is enough to get me horny, waking up to his ass cradling my morning wood is too much.

With him almost recovered, I'm angrier than ever that he went and got himself shot.

The knock on my office door sets my teeth on edge.

"Come in."

Where I'm expecting Lars to appear, Perry's handsome face pokes inside instead.

"What are you doing here?" I'm not trying to sound accusatory, but he's supposed to be resting.

He looks smug as he steps inside and closes the door behind himself. "Guess who made a call this morning?"

"Gee, that's a hard one."

"It was me," he says like that wasn't already implied. Or obvious since he's been calling his doctor every day this week.

"Dr. Olick had a cancellation, so my appointment was bumped up two days."

Now he's got my attention. "And? How is everything?"

"All recovered." His grin stretches across his face. "Basically said I was superhuman. Fastest he'd ever seen. They might conduct scientific studies on me one day."

I stare at him and his stalling, waiting for him to confirm what I think he's confirming.

His smile morphs into a smirk as he turns the lock on my door. "So ... where do you want to fuck me?"

Holy shit. I switch off my computer, stand up, and shove everything across my desk. A tray clatters to the carpeted floor, but I can deal with that later. I point at the clear spot, dick already growing.

"Bend over."

Perry groans and strips out of his shirt as he crosses the room toward me. The nasty scars are a reminder of everything we've been through together. "I love when you get bossy with me."

"Uh-huh." I grab the back of his neck once he's close enough and push him until he's where I want him. Face down, ass up, and —most importantly—supported under his torso on the off chance he can reinjure himself.

Perry grips the other side of my desk and actually wriggles his ass at me. "Come on, get in there."

"Fuck me. I need this."

"Then what are you *waiting* for?"

I run both hands over his denim-clad ass. "Did you bring lube?"

He snorts. "Of course. In my pocket."

Thank fuck. Maybe we should wait until we're home tonight and can make this into something special or whatever, but I don't see the point. While Perry was in the hospital, he had a full health screening, and since we couldn't have sex for way too fucking long anyway, I went and got checked as well.

I pull out the lube, laughing at the four packets he's shoved in there, and then I reach around and pop the button on his jeans.

He's going commando, and it's only too easy to push his jeans down until they're locked around his ankles.

"Shit, you're sexy." I run my hand down his spine, all the way to his ass, where I draw it back and spank him hard. Perry howls, and damn, I hope Lars isn't waiting outside because if he is, he definitely would have heard that.

With all the whining I've been doing about sex though, surely he'd know better.

"I showered for you," he says, and he's not subtle.

I lean in and spread his cheeks apart. That little pink hole makes my cock throb with want as I run my tongue over it. "I really should have jerked off this morning," I murmur. In my defense, I thought it would be days more until we got to do this, so I'm already on edge and ready to blow, and I'm not even inside him yet.

I use my tongue to play with his hole, to soften and relax him before I'm able to slip inside. Perry's moan is also too loud for my office, but I give exactly zero fucks as I rail him with my tongue and he presses back into my face.

"Finally," he pants. "I've missed this."

I pull my tongue free and press two fingers into him instead. "What about this?"

"So much. So, so much."

Hearing him flustered and desperate is my favorite thing in the world. "You've got such a good little hole," I tell him, squeezing lube out onto it as I thrust my fingers in harder. I make sure to avoid his prostate, wanting to really drive him out of his goddamn mind before I finally fuck him. "Should I let it have my cock?"

"You should. You definitely should. I've been so patient." He's rocking back onto my fingers, trying to take them deeper, so before he can get too into it, I add another. I know he's getting frustrated as I focus on stretching and opening him up instead of giving him the hard pounding he wants.

"Want me to put a condom on?" I tease, already knowing the answer to that question.

Perry shakes his head hard. "Don't you dare. I want to feel filthy by the time we're done."

That I can do.

I pull my fingers out and get the expected grunt of annoyance from him, but I need both hands to undo my fly. I don't bother to undress, don't bother to draw it out any longer than needed. I just open my pants, pull my cock out of my underwear, and then coat it with the remaining lube.

Pressing against his opening, with nothing between us, is enough to make my blood heat. He's stretched, hungry for it, and I'm only too happy to fill him up as I push slowly inside. His body opens for me, slowly at first, and then easier the deeper I go, and it's a challenge to not give in to the way his body is sucking me in and slam home.

This is only Perry's second time at this, but with all the practice I imagine we'll be having, I'll be able to do that soon enough.

By the time I bottom out, my breathing has already deepened.

"This feels so fucking good."

"I'll say." He lets go of my desk with one hand and reaches for his cock. The scar on his shoulder is still pronounced and moves over his skin as he jerks himself off. The way he gets so turned on by me being inside him has me powerless against my want for him, and I pull back a little before pushing in again.

Slowly, I build up my thrusts, adding lube when I need to until his ass stops resisting me and I'm able to move easier. Every thrust has his back arching, has my balls knocking against his, is pushing him further up the table like it's too much, but then he's pushing back onto me like it's not enough.

Perry is so deliciously vocal, a never-ending plea that consists of my name and some really filthy words and not much else. Everything is so much better with him.

My suit jacket is stifling, and sweat slips down my back as I clamp hold of his hips and pound into him. It hasn't even only been the sex that I missed, it's this … this connection. The way that I feel when I'm deep inside him and he's spread open for me, giving, taking, begging for me. We just work. We fit. And that gnawing lust deep in my gut gets more feral every time we're together. It's not stopping. It's not ending.

This is everything.

"I'm about to come all over your desk," he rasps.

"Do it." Whenever I look at that spot, I'll be reminded of this moment.

His body locks up, and he grunts out his release, clamping tighter around my dick. I'm racing toward the finishing line, skin feeling too tight, too restrictive, when all I want is to unload. To fill him up and know he's mine.

My balls tighten, and with one last thrust, they release. I empty deep into Perry, hoping he can feel it, hoping he's loving this moment as much as I am.

I fold forward over his body, struggling to catch my breath and put out the fire in my veins.

I gently kiss the place between his shoulder blades. "You okay?"

"Perfect." He's jelly against my desk.

With the last of the energy I have left, I pull out and flop back into my chair.

He doesn't move at first, but I stop him as he's about to.

"Wait."

"Why?"

I reach across my desk for the whiskey and pour out a dash into a glass. Then I lean right back, eyes on his ass, and watch. "You want to feel filthy ..." I kick his legs as wide as his pants will let him go, and then ... after a few seconds, the first of my cum runs down his thigh.

"There we go."

I wait for it all. For every little bit of it to spill out and coat him in my release, and only then do I gather it up and push it back inside.

Perry shivers from his neck all the way down to his toes. "Do it again."

So I do, enjoying making him as messy as I possibly can. "Next time, I'll have a butt plug ready for you."

His balls twitch. "Oh yeah?"

"Yeah. Fill you up, plug you, then you'll be ready to use again when I need you."

"Oh my god." His head *thunks* against my desk. "I think I'm getting hard again."

As much as I'd love to go again right away, I also have a shit-load of work to do, so I reach down, pull up his jeans, and rebutton them. Then I pull him back into my lap. We're testing the strength of my chair as I whisper in his ear, "Maybe I can tie you up again."

"Yes, please."

"And we can have some fun with your mask?"

"Yes. Yes. The answer is always yes."

I chuckle and press my lips to his temple. "You're so perfect for me."

He wriggles against me. "You too, pookie. You and your cum."

CHAPTER FIFTY-THREE

PERRY

I'M full of mixed feelings as we walk into Lethal Poison. On the one hand, I love the place; on the other, this is where I got shot and thought I was going to die.

Very, very polar ends of the spectrum and enough to make any guy confused.

Colin has been working with the baddie bunch to keep Lethal Poison up and running. Between Tommy "easily" hacking all of Luther's accounts and making it look like he took his money and ran, the missing person's case is coming along as well as Colin's did.

The police are too busy, Luther convincingly bailed on all his responsibilities, and now the baddie bunch are going through the process of taking over the lease on the building since he's completely MIA. Part of me is worried that his body will turn up, and suddenly, we'll all be under investigation, but my pals have been doing this for a long time, and unlike me, they're actually good at what they do.

The bar has been cleaned up from the mayhem it was the last time I was here, and the baddie bunch are sitting in a corner, laptops huddled on the table in front of them while they work on whatever they're working on. They didn't even look up when the tinkling bell let them know I was here.

"Hello, people much smarter than me," I say, grabbing their attention.

"You're late" is all Arlie answers. I'd be offended if she hadn't visited me a thousand times while I was recovering, all under the guise of making sure I "stayed quiet" about what happened while she reacted to every little grunt or cringe I made.

I might have even put it on a little bit. Felt nice to see her care.

But her presence also meant that poor Lars was in a constant state of the stutters.

"Maybe you didn't hear," I reply, hands up in surrender. "I was shot, very bad. Might never be the same again. I can't overdo it."

Arlie rolls her eyes. "I swear to fucking god, if you're late for a shift, I'm going to add your name to my own list."

I look from Tommy to her again, lost. "Ah, what?"

"My list. You'll be dead."

I wave away the threat. "I got that part. What do you mean shift? I don't know if you heard, but I'm a terrible hitman. You don't want to hire me, and I'm pretty sure I'm going to take that part out of my resume. Probably."

Tommy cackles. "You weren't a *terrible* hitman, Perry."

At first, I think he's being sweet.

"You weren't a hitman—period. You couldn't even kill the bad guy."

"I was gonna." And I'm seventy-three percent sure that's the truth. "But Arlie got there first."

"You were already close to dead when I took him out."

Everett grunts. "Thanks for that. The *one* thing I had to look forward to."

"There will be a lot more bad guys out there for you to play with," she says, patting him on the shoulder like she's comforting a child. Then she turns her attention suddenly on me. "You start Monday."

Did I hallucinate half of this conversation? I point at my face. "Not a hitman. Remember?"

"On the *bar*," she finally clarifies. "You know, the job Luther *should* have given you in the first place."

My mouth drops. "You want me to work for you?"

"Don't get too excited. It's impossible to staff the bar for a place like this."

"Wait, you want me to be *manager*?"

"I don't think I said that."

"If it's impossible to staff, then apparently, a guy like me is in short supply. This is called negotiating."

Everett leans back in his chair, lips pulling upward. "You've got balls negotiating with us."

"Gotta shoot my shot." I mime firing pistols with my fingers. "Get it?"

"What have I done?" Arlie mutters, burying her face back in her computer.

"I like your spunk," Tommy says. "I bet there's a course you can take to become bar manager. Arlie?"

She actually gives in. "Fine. But only because Tommy wants it. Not me." Aww … she's basically proposing to me. She keeps talking. "And tell Lars I'll be there at ten."

There's a record scratch in my brain. "Wait, what?"

"Ten. Tonight. He needs to be ready."

"Ready for what?" Ever and Tommy look as confused as I do.

"Wait …" Tommy leans forward. "Are you going on a date?"

Arlie's gun is in her hand and against his chin before I even work out where she pulled it from. "Say another word."

He doesn't, but it's less from the threat and more because he bursts into wheezing laughter.

Lars and Arlie, huh? Guess the big man finally won her over.

"Damn it," I say, suddenly remembering something. "We were supposed to finish our show tonight. I bought popcorn."

She turns her gun on me instead.

"The last time you did that, I got shot," I remind her. "Somehow, I got through this thing without PTSD, and I'd kinda like to keep it that way."

She huffs and tucks her gun away.

"But I'll remind Lars to be ready for your *date*," I say before bolting.

Because sometimes I'm smart enough to learn from other people's mistakes.

St. Clare looks up the second I step back outside.

"You good? Everything okay?" He wasn't sure about me being here in the first place, but he's slowly trusting the baddie bunch again since Colin has been doing so much work with them.

"Sure am." I hold my arms out to the side. "You're looking at the new manager of Lethal Poison."

He blinks in confusion. "The what?"

"Well, *bar* manager, but I don't think it really makes a difference."

"They offered you a job?"

I puff out my chest. "One that comes with a qualification." I'm going to hold them to that part.

"I … fuck. Congratulations."

I accept his congratulatory kiss, wishing we weren't standing on a street in broad daylight so that he could *really* congratulate me.

"Careful," I tell him. "I'm going to know more about running a bar than you soon."

"It wouldn't be hard, if we're honest."

"Hey! Maybe we could go into business together one day."

"Or maybe we focus on getting your medical bills paid down before we start getting ahead of ourselves."

Elle had offered to pay them off for me, but if she did, when does it end? I've always been bailed out my whole life; now, it's time for me to fix things myself.

With a *little bit* of help from St. Clare.

After all, I took a bullet for him. As far as I'm concerned, this injury was equal parts both our fault and would have happened whether I mistakenly shot off his ear or not.

Which he's been gracious enough not to bring up for at least a week now.

All in all, I'd say watch out, there's a new power couple in town.

"We'll franchise," I tell him. "Saint Nikov's. Peilly's. Niclare's. We'll workshop it."

"Perry ..."

"I suppose Colin can be involved too."

"You suppose?"

"Well, he does know the most about the boring stuff."

"Mkay."

"And I can make us a signature drink."

"Of course. In this far distant future where you're a skilled mixologist and we have the financial freedom to do anything we want."

Despite his words, I can see it. Not only the future, but he's giving me that look. The one that tells me even if I don't believe in myself, he thinks I can do anything.

And I can.

So long as we do it together.

CHAPTER 54

ST. CLARE

SIX MONTHS LATER

"I don't know about this," I say, determined to sound confident and not at all like I'm bracing from going ass-over.

"What's to know?" Perry asks, as relaxed putting on roller skates as he is about anything else he attempts. He tugs the laces of his skate as tight as they'll pull then does them up in a triple knot. We're both wearing padding and gloves and helmets, while kids half our size whizz past completely unprotected.

For the love of Judge Judy—yes, it's rubbed off on me—that kid is skating *backward*. If he can do that, surely I can manage to stay upright.

"Let's do this!" Perry's excitement is contagious; at least it is, until he pushes to his feet and almost as soon as he's vertical, his skates go out from under him and with a quick *meep* Perry hits the floor, ass-first.

"Shit!" I scoot along the bench and reach for him. "Are you okay?"

Surprisingly, a laugh wheezes from him. "Damn, that hurt. But it's not like I was shot, so I'll be fine."

I groan and tug him back up onto the bench beside me. "One day you'll take something seriously and I'll die from shock."

"Even more incentive to never, ever be serious. Ever."

I can't argue with him there. He's perfect the way he is.

That sickening little rush of nerves floods through me at the thought and I flick a look at him from the corner of my eye. Every day with Perry has been an amazing experience, and for something I was half-convinced would fizzle out once all the action and excitement was over, we're still going strong.

Very strong.

So strong that I keep having multiple thoughts a day like the one I just had. Thoughts about *loving* him.

And there are those nerves again.

I want to say it already. Just put out there that I'm in love with him, but every time I think about bringing it up, he either gets distracted by something shiny, or I end up in my head, convincing myself it's both too soon and too late for the word.

I've just convinced myself that now would be a perfect time to say something, when Perry shoves suddenly back to his feet. The skates lurch dangerously and it takes about ten solid seconds of Perry teetering and slipping across the floor to reach the half wall dividing us from the people roller skating.

When he makes it, he looks back over his shoulder, bright smile taking over his face.

"I did it!"

"You did something." But despite my words, I'm wearing a matching smile because his enthusiasm is contagious.

"Your turn."

Well, fuck. I should have realized that's what comes next, but even though this was my stupid, random bucket list item, I don't actually want to try it. Perry went down as gracelessly as I'd expect from him, and I'm convinced that if I fall, it will be even worse than that.

All flailing limbs and possibly a cracked skull for my efforts.

I huff out an exhale and remind myself of my helmet. Like Perry said, it's not a gunshot. If we can get through that, a little thing like roller skating shouldn't be able to stop us.

Knowing just how easy it is to fall, I white knuckle the bench as I slowly, incrementally, put my weight on the skates and straighten. I'm practically holding my breath as I try to keep my balance against the wheels that are one deep inhale away from shooting out from under me.

It takes to the count of three to get the courage to let go of the bench and, arms extended awkwardly to the sides, I have no clue what to do next. Presumably, I need to move, but that feels ill-advised right now.

"Come on, Reilly," Colin calls as he goes speeding past us with Onyx on his other side. Onyx was a natural at this—or was as a kid, I don't know—and as soon as they were off, they grabbed both of Colin's hands and took him with them.

It's hard not to glare at the showoffs as they disappear with the small crowd of people.

"Here." Perry grips the half wall with one hand and reaches the other toward me. It barely extends halfway and there's still a lot of ground to cover for someone determined not to move. "Just sort of … shuffle your feet."

Given I saw what shuffling his feet did for him, I'll skip that advice.

Right. Move.

I nudge one foot forward but it goes too fast and when I correct with my other, they threaten to go in opposite directions and it takes a moment of wobbling to get myself figured out.

This is the dumbest thing I've ever done and that includes knowingly running into danger to protect the guy I kinda liked.

I remind myself that turned out for the best and this will too.

As soon as I've slid/rolled/wobbled/shuffled close enough, my hand closes over Perry's. He grips tight and yanks me toward him. For one terrifying moment I go too fast, sure I'm about to fall, when Perry's arms are there. He wraps me up in them and like every time he holds me, I'm in the greatest place on Earth.

"You did it!" He's so happy his eyes are crinkled as he looks down at me, and I'm compelled to add, "I did something."

Perry laughs and presses a long, sweet kiss to my lips. "So proud of you."

"That was barely roller skating."

"You're wearing roller skates and you moved on them. How much closer can you get?"

He's got me there. I've always said I don't actually want to *go* roller skating, I just want to know that I can do. And I did it. Terribly.

Like that, I'm satisfied that I got what I came for, and the feeling ballooning in my chest gets to be too much. "Perry?"

"Yeah?"

My throat is tight as I swallow. "I love you."

Surprise lights up his expression. "Oh, thank fuck! I was worried I was the only one."

"What?"

"I've been hinting but you never seemed to pick up on any of them."

For what's supposed to be a romantic moment, he's lost me, which means he's right on track. "What do you mean?"

"For months now I've been like, "oh, I love that shirt on you, love love love *it*" or "I love the way you pass me the sauce" or "love that for you, *love*.""

"I thought you were copying how Elle calls everyone love."

Perry cackles, forehead resting on my shoulder as we keep our arms around each other in an attempt to stay standing. "Only you." He pulls back to look at me again. "I love you so much that at one point I went for a heart checkup because I was sure there was something wrong with it."

"You … what?"

He shrugs. "When you've been shot you never can be too careful."

"Except you weren't shot in the chest."

That doesn't deter him. "Hey, does this mean I'm cupid? I mean, I shot you and now you're in love with me, so—"

"You're not cupid."

"Are you sure? I think there's an argument there."

I give in and humor him, because how can I not? He's single-handedly the most ridiculous person I've ever met, and it's my favorite thing about him. "It was love at first shot."

His jaw drops. "Now look who's being cute with the puns," he says, sounding awestruck.

"Seemed like your love language."

"You know me well, pookie."

I huff like the name is such an embarrassment. It's not. "That's stuck now, hasn't it?"

"I'm sure I could think of something worse if you really hate it."

I shut him up with a kiss. It's how I win all our arguments and how I plan to win all future ones. Perry is easily distracted and kissing is his weakness.

He sighs against my mouth. "You really are perfect."

"That's because we match."

He's uncharacteristically quiet for a moment and I give us a little distance to read his face. Before I can ask, he whispers, "I'm going to marry you one day."

Those body fluttering nerves fill me again. "Oh, yeah? You sound confident."

"I am." He looks me straight in the eyes. "Because you're giving me that look."

And I'll give it to him forever. If he wants to marry me one day, that's exactly what we'll do.

Perry Nikov is himbo husband material. And he's all mine.

EPILOGUE

PERRY

FIVE YEARS LATER

Everything turned out perfectly.

If you leave perfect up to interpretation.

So, I did need to take Elle's money, but I haven't missed a single week of repaying her, and I think, maybe five years later, my sister is starting to see me as a whole grown-ass adult.

Which is just in time, too, because St. Clare marrying me would have been a tad creepy otherwise. Well, that's if he says yes. I'm proposing tonight, in front of all of our family and friends, because everyone knows that public proposals are impossible to say no to.

Peer pressure and all that. I'm not too proud to stack the deck if it gets him tied to me for life.

I'm almost confident he'll say yes though. Mostly. At least … sixty-seven percent chance.

I lean over and press a kiss to Margot's bulging tummy. "Sure you're not in labor?"

"Nope. Now, stop shitting yourself and get the ring—I can't goddamn reach anymore."

"I could really use a baby to snuggle while I do this."

She blinks at me, that perfect storm of a heavily pregnant woman past her due date and her annoying brother nudging her along. "Sure," she snaps. "That's why I'm having this kid. For you."

I grab both her shoulders. "You really are the best sister ever."

"I can't wait to be back to my usual self so people—*you*—will take me seriously when I threaten to kick your ass."

She can too. Well, not pregnant, she can. I'm going to have to remember how not to test her daily once I no longer have that safety net.

I reach up into the top of the closet and grab the ring box. It's been forever since I bought this, and when I crack it open, I get all these little flutters in my gut. "Damn, I'm romantic."

"You sure he's not going to be disappointed about that piece of junk?"

I gasp and snap the box closed. "You're mean when forty weeks pregnant, heavily swollen, tired, constipated, and low on iron."

Margot hangs her head back on a groan. "Do you and Elle have to share *everything*?"

"Yes. And you really should get that lump checked out," I say seriously.

"It's the milk!"

"Wouldn't hurt to confirm," Elle says, appearing behind me. "I'm very fond of those breasts."

"Perry's proposing," Margot says. "Let's all go back to focusing on that and not on my tits."

Elle's hands fly up to cover her mouth, eyes wide, and at first, I do a rapid remembering to confirm that yes, yes, she definitely already knows this, so why the hell is she so shocked?

The answer comes from behind me a second later.

In a voice I know to my very soul.

"Ah … Perry's what?"

I think I squeak as Margot's mouth drops.

"Gotta go do that thing that I have to do," Elle manages in a strangled voice before she ditches us all.

I lean into Margot's face and hiss, "*I haaaate you,*" and then, because I'm paranoid the baby heard, I duck down to her belly again. "But not you. If you heard that, I don't hate you. Uncy Perry loves you very, very much."

Margot makes her escape, turning to me as she passes St. Clare and mouthing, *I'm so sorry!*

She ditches us faster than a pregnant lady should reasonably be able to move.

Only then do I realize we're alone.

Alone.

No, no, no, this isn't how it was supposed to happen. There's supposed to be a crowd and staring and lots and lots of pressure.

"Perry?" St. Clare asks, still sounding a little shocked.

And this, I remind myself, *is why plans fucking suck.*

So instead of the music and confetti streamers and *future Mr. St. Clare Nikov* banners—we're workshopping that—it's just him and me.

I drop onto one knee because that's how they do it in the movies, and if I can't give St. Clare all of the pizzazz, I can at least give him that.

I hold out my hand, and thankfully, his slips into mine.

"Hey." I grin.

"Skip that part," he says, still sounding like his lungs aren't working. "What's happening?"

"Technically, this is your fault," I say. "It was supposed to be a lot more stressful than this."

"Noted."

Before I say more than I probably should, I remind myself that it's not the most romantic thing to be making fake accusations during a proposal. "Ah, sorry. Scratch that. Start again at the part where I say your name."

"Okay ..."

"Reilly St. Clare, before I say anything else, I want to say that I don't remember much of what life was like before you, but I remember that I thought I was happy."

He nods, a tiny, confused line pulling between his eyebrows.

"But I wasn't. Or … maybe I was, but it wasn't *happy* happy. It wasn't this kind of happy where I'll be going about my day and then think of you and smile. Or where I'll open a bottle of Jack Daniel's and remember the time you got so drunk you tried pole dancing in your own nightclub. Or when you leave for work earlier than me and always spray a little bit of your cologne by my pillow so you're the first thing I smell when I wake up."

The confused line smooths, and I swear my steady boyfriend's eyes get all shiny.

"I have this light in my chest that's always there, and it's completely thanks to you. And while we might have started out on a shitty accident, I don't think it was an accident at all. We were meant to be. We were supposed to find each other. And now, here, I want to do this. I want to be each other's person. I want to be the Nikov St. Clares—still workshopping—and I really fucking hope you want that too. Even without all our family here to pressure you into doing it."

Then I crack open the ring box, and St. Clare goes from misty-eyed to full-blown laughing through his tears.

He picks up the gunshot-heart golden charm I had made and put onto a necklace for him. At first, he says nothing, just a whole long stretch of nothing where I sweat through my shirt and silently beg him to *say words, any words.*

Then he touches his fingertips to the necklace before setting them over the bracelet on my wrist. "We match."

"Still waiting for a yes here, pookie."

He's nodding before he answers. "Yes. A thousand yeses. And you don't need anyone to pressure me into it. Not with you."

I push to my feet and kiss him, loving the taste of him and how passionately he kisses me back.

"You know," I mutter against his lips. "We could skip tonight and hang out in this room. For old time's sake."

"You want to miss the opening of our own club?"

"Seems reasonable."

Proving he has a thousand times more restraint than me, St. Clare pulls back and hands me the necklace. "Put this on me."

I'm only too excited to. I clasp it around his neck, and it shines brightly on the brightest man I've ever met.

His hand cups my face, eyes still watery, and these days he doesn't try to hold back from showing me how much he loves me.

"Come on," he says. "You need to check everyone working knows how to make our drink."

In honor of my pookie, I *did* complete my certificate in business management, and I *did* train in how to make cocktails. The whole drinks menu at our new nightclub was thought up by me.

And for our opening night, the *Love at First Shot* is five dollars until closing.

I loved being a barista because of the customers, and working a bar is like that but *better*. People don't just tell me about their day; I get their entire life story.

This, right here, is what perfection looks like.

Family, friends, his mom and dad, who are my mom and dad. Our head of security and bestie fur-ever, Lars. And the baddie bunch, who set me up on this path and pushed me to get to where I was supposed to be and where I finally belong.

With St. Clare.

With my pookie.

A complete matching set.

Thank you for reading Himbo Hitman!

Want to know about my next series? Welcome to Wilde's End.
Population: Zero.
Preorder it on Amazon or through my web store!

For anyone who doesn't want to wait, get first access to the chapters for my next releases, see character art, and indulge in all the bonus content don't forget to join my Patreon!

ACKNOWLEDGEMENTS

As with any book, this one took a hell of a lot of people to make happen.

The cover was created by the talented Rebecca at Story Styling Cover Designs with a gorgeous image by Wander Aguiar, and edits were done by Sandra Dee at One Love Editing, with Lori Parks proofreading the bejeebus out of it.

Thanks to Tal Lewin @caravaggia13 on IG for creating the amazing artwork for my website editions.

Charity VanHuss you're the most amazing PA I could have ever dreamed up. Without you I'd be even more of a chaotic disaster and there isn't enough space to list the many hats you wear for me. Paige and Lara Janz, you round out my team in the most incredible way and I'm always excited to see what fun ideas you both have next.

Eden Finley, thank you for being there for all the doubt spirals and hand-holding. Whether you wanted to be or not.

My incredible author friends who beta read this book: you've made this so much better than I could have on my own.

Adam Gyllenhaal , you're a gem with his hilarious and thoughtful comments for both of the guys, and Kate Kauri your unhinged feral romance sensitivity reading helped get this plot into something worth reading.

Dawn Sullivan: thank you for lending the name Livy to this one and for being an amazing supporter of my Obsessed Patreon tier.

And of course, thanks to my fam bam. To my husband who constantly frees up time for me to write, and to my kids whose neediness reminds me the real word exists.

OTHER BOOKS BY SAXON JAMES

ACCIDENTAL LOVE SERIES:

The Husband Hoax

Not Dating Material

The Revenge Agenda

Just Romantically Invested

Not Catching Love

FRAT WARS SERIES:

Frat Wars: King of Thieves

Frat Wars: Master of Mayhem

Frat Wars: Presidential Chaos

Royal Scoundrel

DIVORCED MEN'S CLUB SERIES:

Roommate Arrangement

Platonic Rulebook

Budding Attraction

Employing Patience

System Overload

Forgotten Romance

NEVER JUST FRIENDS SERIES:

Just Friends

Fake Friends

Getting Friendly

Friendly Fire

Bonus Short: Friends with Benefits

RECKLESS LOVE SERIES:

Denial

Risky

Tempting

CU HOCKEY SERIES WITH EDEN FINLEY:

Power Plays & Straight A's

Face Offs & Cheap Shots

Goal Lines & First Times

Line Mates & Study Dates

Puck Drills & Quick Thrills

PUCKBOYS SERIES WITH EDEN FINLEY:

Egotistical Puckboy

Irresponsible Puckboy

Shameless Puckboy

Foolish Puckboy

Clueless Puckboy

Bromantic Puckboy

Forbidden Puckboy

Possessive Puckboy

Stubborn Puckboy

STAND ALONES WITH EDEN FINLEY:

Up in Flames

The Bastard and The Heir

FRANKLIN U SERIES (VARIOUS AUTHORS):

The Dating Disaster

A Stealthy Situation

And if you're after something a little sweeter, don't forget my YA
pen name

S. M. James.

These books are chock full of adorable, flawed characters with big hearts.

https://geni.us/smjames

WANT MORE FROM ME?

Follow Saxon James on any of the platforms below.
www.saxonjamesauthor.com
www.facebook.com/thesaxonjames/
www.amazon.com/Saxon-James/e/B082TP7BR7
www.bookbub.com/profile/saxon-james
www.instagram.com/saxonjameswrites/

www.ingramcontent.com/pod-product-compliance
Lightning Source LLC
Chambersburg PA
CBHW050603170726
48283CB00001B/84